Keep This
PROMISE

ROSE CANYON

Help Me Remember

Give Me Love

Keep This Promise

Keep This PROMISE

- Special Edition

NEW YORK TIMES BESTSELLING AUTHOR
CORINNE MICHAELS

Keep This Promise - Special Edition

ISBN print: 978-1-957309-12-5

Cover Design: Sommer Stein, Perfect Pear Creative
Editing: Ashley Williams, AW Editing
Proofreading: Julia Griffis & ReGina Kaye

Dedication

Dear Reader,

It is always my goal to write a beautiful love story that will capture your heart and leave a lasting impression. However, I want all readers to be comfortable. Therefore, if you want to be aware of any possible CW please click the link below to take you to the book page where there is a link that will dropdown. If you do not need this, please go forth and I hope you love this book filled with all the pieces of my heart.

https://corinnemichaels.com/books/keep-this-promise/

CHAPTER

One

SOPHIE

"No, no, please, Theo, fight," I beg my husband, clutching his hand. "Please don't give up."

He squeezes it back, his blue-tinged lips attempting to lift. "You be brave, Sophie. You have to be."

I can't be. I don't know how to survive in a world without him. Theodore Pearson has been my best friend since we were nine years old and my husband for the last three and a half years. He stepped in and saved me then, and I can't do it for him now. His heart is failing, and there's no chance of a transplant anymore.

"How do I live without you?"

"You—" He gasps, closing his eyes before forcing them back open to stare at me. "You are stronger than you believe. Find someone to love you the way I never could, Sophie. You have to take Eden and go."

I shake my head. He keeps repeating this, but I will not leave him. Not now. Not at the end when he's literally dying. "You can't make me leave you, Theo."

I have been by his side, praying for a miracle that I knew would never come. Theo was born with a congenital heart disease. When he was seven, he had his first open-heart surgery. When he was eleven, he had his second. The last one was a year ago, and that was when he went on the transplant list, but we've been waiting and hoping, but there is no match.

Time has run out, and he wants me to leave him to die alone.

I can't.

"If you . . . love me . . . you have to . . ." Theo coughs several times and then inhales deeply. "Go."

None of this makes sense, but three days ago, he started demanding I pack without any explanation. He said it was life and death. So, I did as he asked because it settled him once I agreed. But this is crazy. I am not going to leave him on his death bed.

I push back, confused as to why he keeps saying these strange things. "Why? How can you want me to leave you now?"

A tear falls down his cheek. "Because he'll come for you."

"Who? Who is coming? None of this makes any sense."

Theo reaches for my hand, entwining our fingers. "You are my best friend, Sophie. When you got pregnant, I married you, took care of you, and did everything I could to protect you. Now I'm asking you to do this for me. Take Eden and follow the directions."

My jaw trembles as I try to push back the tears. "Yes, you did that, but it was your idea! I didn't ask you to do those things. You are my best friend, Theo. You did all that, and now you want me to let you die alone?"

"Yes. I need to die alone."

"You can't be serious? I can't leave you now. I refuse to . . . you can't ask this of me."

"I won't be alone."

"You will."

His parents will never come. They walked away from Theo six years ago when he refused to work for his father. They hated the choices he made, so we haven't heard from them since. I called them a week ago, left a frantic message explaining his situation, and his mother's assistant called to tell me that they were out of the country and that they sent flowers. They are horrid people.

"I have not asked you for much, Fee." He uses my childhood nick-name, and a tear falls down my cheek. "You owe me for forcing me to marry you."

I let out a laugh, but it sounds more like a sob. "You have always wanted to be with me."

He rolls his eyes. "We were never like that, love."

No, we weren't, but when I came home from Vegas pregnant, Theo didn't hesitate. He offered to marry me and raise Eden as if she were his own. Ours is a marriage in name only and never once have we crossed that line. Mostly because I am not the woman he loves, the one he can never have because she married someone else.

And . . . he is like a brother to me, nothing more.

"You couldn't handle me in bed."

Theo chuckles. "I think you have that backward."

I lie beside him, my arm draped over his chest, careful of all the wires. My chin trembles, and the tears fall freely. "I love you."

"I love you too. It's because of that love that I can die in peace, so you have to let me go, and you have to leave before I take my last breath."

I shake my head in rebellion. I don't want to leave him. I don't want him to die in this room with no one. Eden and I love him and should be with him in his last moments. He's been a wonderful father to her and means the world to me. "You're asking me to do the impossible."

"Look at me, Fee." I lift my watery gaze to his. "Nothing is impossible when it comes from love. You . . . have to go. Not because you want to, but because I need to protect you and Eden the only way I can. Follow every direction."

"What direction?"

"The ones you'll find along the way."

"You're being so bloody cryptic."

Theo inhales deeply, the gasp causing his chest to lift as he uses his strength. It's growing closer to the end. "Go."

A sob rises in my throat, but I keep it down. "What are you so afraid of? Who are you protecting me from?"

His eyes close, and he struggles to breathe. "We're running out of time. Please."

The way his voice cracks at the end sends my resolve crumbling. I want to fight him, to deny this and stay beside him where I promised I would be, but how can I? Theo is asking me to go. He's begging me to listen to him, and it's clear something is wrong.

"You're that afraid?"

"Yes. Of *him*."

"If I go, you have to promise me that you'll forgive me. That you know I didn't want to go. That I would fight anything for you. You gave up your life for me when I was pregnant with Eden, and I owe you everything."

"You owe me nothing. You gave me a child to love when I never could have one any other way."

Theo's heart condition is genetic, and he's known from a young age that he would never risk having a child and passing on the illness. Eden was a blessing he never expected, and he was the savior I never knew I needed.

"I don't want to say goodbye."

He brushes my cheek. "It's never goodbye with us. Best . . . friends." Theo gasps and then smiles at me. "Never end."

I rest my forehead to his, my heart rioting against what he's asked me to do. "I keep waiting for the doctor to come in and tell us there's a heart."

"There's no heart for us, Fee."

I know this. Still, I wish it.

"You could have mine."

"If only we could share."

Another round of tears falls down my face, splashing against his chest. "Where am I going?" I ask.

"Where it's safe. To someone who will protect you where I failed to."

Theo is richer than anyone I've ever met, how he can't afford to hire someone to keep me safe in England is insane. Also, he hasn't explained *anything*. I don't understand this danger we are in or why Eden and I need to leave because of it. He's telling me nothing, and we're running out of time. For crying out loud, I can't even start a fight with him about it and demand answers as he's gasping for breath.

A part of me wonders if it's even real, even though he tells me it is. "I don't want to spend this time together fighting. You're asking me to trust that I'm in danger, and I believe you, but none of it makes sense. I will do as you ask because you have always loved me more than I deserved and have never lied to me." Although, it's quite clear he hasn't been honest about something since this is the first I'm hearing of danger in our lives.

"Look at me." I lift my head. "You deserve more than I could give. You deserved more than the love of a brother or friend. Find someone who makes you light up. Who will love Eden like a daughter. Promise me."

I don't want to promise him that, but he's dying, and I don't want to deny him anything. "I promise."

He takes my hands in his, holding them tight. "Keep this promise, Sophie. Now go. Go and follow every direction. Every single one. Exactly as it says."

I lean down, pressing my lips to his. We may not have ever been sexually attracted to each other, but we have always been affectionate. "You are my best friend."

"And you're mine."

"I will tell Eden all about her father. I will never let you go from our lives."

His eyes close, and his lips tremble. "I will watch over you both."

I sniff as the tears fall faster, and my hands tremble. God, I can't do this. I can't.

"Be safe because I can't die knowing you are still in danger. Please, grant me this."

My chest heaves as breathing becomes harder. Theo has never hurt me. Not ever. As kids, he was my protector. When my mum was at her worst, Theo was there, holding me together. The two of us have always sacrificed for one another, and I have to give him this. Even if it kills me.

I pull myself together, feeling as though I may shatter at any second, force myself to stand, and tuck him in. I can pretend we'll see each other again. I must in order to do this.

"I love you." I choke the words out.

"I love you, and I love Eden. I am sorry, Fee. I am sorry for the man I never was. I am sorry I am leaving you with this mess, but I have done all I can to keep you safe, and you must do everything exactly the way I say."

I wipe my eyes and nod. "Okay."

Gathering my belongings feels like agony, but if Theo is this worried, then maybe I need to be as well. Eden is my world, and I can't allow any harm to come to her.

As I move to the door it's as though my shoes have anchors as soles, and I pause to look at him once more. He gives me a crooked smile, his lips cracked and face sallow. I will not remember him this way. I'll remember the boy who handed me his backpack after mine tore. Or the young man who filled in as my prom date after my boyfriend broke up with me the night before. And then the man who married me and raised my child after a drunk night in Vegas with a man I didn't know. And then, I will see this man, who on his deathbed put us first to protect us from whatever mess he's found himself in, even if I don't understand any of it.

"It's okay," Theo says.

It's not, but I force a smile before lifting my hands to my lips and blowing him a kiss. "I would've given you the heart from my chest."

He grins. "Your heart is black and cynical. It wouldn't have survived in my hopeful soul."

The laughter falls from my lips, as do the tears from my eyes. "Rest now, Theo, it'll be okay."

I turn and run down the corridor, knowing if I stop, I'll return to him. I don't see anyone as I leave the hospital, but Martin, our driver, is waiting to open the door of the black car for me. He gives me a knowing look, his brown eyes filled with sadness.

When he gets in the driver's seat, I look at him through the rearview mirror. "He's gone. I need to go home."

And find out where I'm going next.

CHAPTER

Two

SOPHIE

"I don't understand," I say to Martin, looking down at the plane tickets he just handed me. "Why would I go to New York?"

"I don't know, Mrs. Pearson, these are the instructions I was given."

I want to scream because these instructions make no sense. I don't know anyone in New York. I don't have family or friends in the States. I have nothing there, and I have lost so much. Two hours ago, I got the call from the hospital letting me know Theo is dead. He's gone and a part of my heart has gone with him. She then told me that his last words were: "Go, Sophie."

I'm here, at the airport, and am about to leave my life behind for a new one, all the while not having a clue as to where the danger might come from.

Eden is asleep in my arms, and I'm doing my best to hold it together for her. "What do you mean that's all the instructions you were given? Nothing else? Where do I go now? I was told to follow directions, but no one has given me any!" I release my breath, working hard to stay calm because it isn't Martin's fault. He's merely giving me what he knows. "I'm sorry. I am . . ."

"I understand. All I was told was to give you the tickets."

Which is a direction, I suppose. "All right. Please help me inside then."

He looks uncomfortable at that request.

I lift my head to meet his eyes. "Is there something wrong, Martin?"

"I cannot follow you inside."

"What?"

"I was terminated at the moment you exited the car."

My jaw drops. "By whom?"

"Mr. Pearson. If I don't follow the instructions I was given, I will not receive the very . . . generous severance package I am set to receive."

My God. He is serious. I want to ask him how anyone would know, but then Eden lifts her head. "Mummy, where are we?"

I rub her back, rocking slightly, just in case she'll fall back asleep. "We're at the airport. We're going on holiday, isn't that going to be fun?"

She shakes her head. No, I don't think so either, but here we are.

"Daddy?"

One word manages to make me feel like crumbling to the ground. "Just us, love. Just us."

Because your daddy is gone, and you will never see him again.

I can't tell her that. Not only because I can't speak the words but also because I won't hurt her that way.

Not when I'm ripping her out of her comfortable life.

I turn back to Martin. "Then it's best you go and follow your directions."

"Thank you, ma'am."

He places the bags on the sidewalk, and I could laugh because there's not a chance I can manage all of this and Eden by myself. Yet, this is my reality.

"Could you get me a trolley? I don't want to leave our bags unattended . . ."

Martin gives me a sad smile and then lifts his hand. Someone comes over, and he hands him a large tip to bring a trolley over.

"I must go now. I am sorry, Mrs. Pearson. I . . . I'm sorry."

"Theo loved you," I tell him. "He trusted you, and that mattered to him."

He lowers his gaze. "It is why I must go. He was very clear about his wishes and that it was of grave importance I do as it says."

"Yes, he seemed to have the same grave warning messages for me as well."

The man walks over and helps load my bags for me. I thank him, and then Martin comes forward, pulling me into an unusual embrace. "Be safe, Sophie." When he kisses the top of Eden's head, there is moisture building in his eyes.

Martin has been our personal driver for almost four years. He is who drove me to the hospital when I was in labor, ensured Eden's first car ride was safe, and will be possibly the last familiar face I will see for a long time. I am going to miss him.

I force a smile and say goodbye to yet another person today.

"Be well."

Once he's closed back in the confines of the car, I place Eden on her feet and take her hand. It's time to be brave and start this new life that Theo planned without telling me because we might die.

I sigh because that's about all I can do and walk inside.

We get to the start of the line, and I look at my tickets so I can check our luggage, but the seat placement doesn't make sense and the date is wrong.

Great, I'm going to have to go to the counter and get this fixed. Thankfully, the line isn't very long, and within a handful of minutes, I'm stepping up to the counter.

"Hello, miss, how can I help you?" asks a beautiful woman with long brown hair.

"Hello, my daughter and I have a flight to New York, but the date is wrong on one of the tickets, and we are sitting apart. As you can see, she's a toddler."

I place the tickets on the counter.

She looks at them. "Yes, I see that, do you have your booking confirmation?"

"No, I'm sorry, I don't. My husband made our arrangements." I slide our passports to her. "Here are our names as well."

"I see. Let me look into this."

Suzanna, as her name tag says, types something into the computer and then blinks. "Oh, I see the issue. These flights were changed about two hours ago."

"What?"

"Yes, it seems you're not going to New York. I apologize that you had the old tickets. Instead, your tickets were cancelled, and they purchased a new flight this morning."

I have no idea what that means, but I smile and nod. I don't care where we're going so long as I'm on the same flight as Eden.

"Let me just print your new boarding passes and get you checked in." Suzanna goes back to typing and then hands me the new tickets. "Here you are."

I look at my new boarding passes—plural because we have a layover in Atlanta before we board a flight to . . . Las Vegas.

Is he fucking with me? He must be if he is actually making me go back to Las Vegas. For what? The last time I was there, I ended up pregnant.

Every part of me that wants to fight back and take my chances staying here changes when I turn around and recognize someone. His face is nondescript, just an average man, but I remember him being at our home about a year ago. There was something in his eyes, something that bothered me.

More than that, I remember how Theo was after the man left. He was shaken, and when I asked, he said to forget I ever saw anything.

I thought it strange, but Theo never discussed it again, so it faded into the background and was forgotten.

That gnawing feeling in my stomach grows, and I turn back to the agent. "Thank you, if anyone asks, please state that we are going to New York." I glance over my shoulder, and when I return to Suzanna, she nods.

A moment of unspoken connection between the two of us forms. "We're all running from something, honey."

Yes, I guess we are, only I have no idea what I'm running from or where I'm heading to.

Eden and I head toward the security lines, I don't see the man, and I start to consider that maybe I am losing my grip on reality when someone bumps into me from the side, causing my carry-on to topple over.

"I'm so sorry."

"It's fine—" The pit in my stomach grows when I see it's him, the same man I saw before.

He smiles at me and then fixes my bag. "Sophie, right?"

My heart is racing, but I hide my anxiety and nod. "Yes, have we met before?"

"I thought it was you. Yes, we met several months ago, I'm a friend of Theo's. Is he here?"

He doesn't know he's dead. "No, he's not coming on this trip with us."

I note that he still hasn't reminded me of his name. I can't recall it, but he keeps moving closer, and I need to stand my ground and not keep stepping back. "That's too bad, I tried to call him the other day."

"Oh? What was your name again? I can call him and let him know you're trying to reach him."

"Joe."

"Okay, Joe . . . do you have a last name?" I keep my voice light and laugh a little at the end to hide my nervousness.

"Webb."

Joe doesn't seem to be doing or saying anything out of the ordinary, it's just . . . I can't explain it. I'm uncomfortable, and I've had a really fucking hard day.

"I'll let him know, if you can excuse me." I try to move around him, but again, he shifts.

"I meant to ask you, how was the charity dinner last night?"

Eden tries to let go of my hand, and I use that moment to look away from him. When I glance over her head, I see someone approaching who I've also seen at my house. It was about two months ago, and he came to bring Theo a package.

Something is wrong.

This is not a coincidence. For the first time since Theo told me about the danger, I believe it.

Without taking my hand from my bag, I lift Eden into my arms. "I have to go. I'm sorry, but we're going to miss our flight."

I move in the opposite direction of the second man approaching me, when I see a third man heading our way. His eyes find mine, and then he jerks his head away as though he doesn't want me to see his face. They're closing in, and I have to go . . . now.

As I move in the center of the corridor, I pray I can get out of this.

Theo, God, someone up there must be watching out for me because a policeman walks by. I call out, and he stops. "Yes, miss, can I help?"

I force my breathing to remain steady as relief floods me. "Could you help me? My daughter is ill, and I need to get over to security. I would really appreciate if you could just stay with me in case there's an issue."

He stares at me as though I'm bonkers, which I probably am right now, but he reluctantly agrees. When I look over my shoulder, the three men are watching me, and I am grateful I'm leaving.

"Hello, Mrs. Pearson." A man walks toward me and Eden, and I clutch her to my chest. No one should know we're in Las Vegas. After the scare in London, I've been losing my mind, and it's been four very long, very exhausting days of travel.

I shake my head. "I'm sorry, you have the wrong person." My American accent needs work, but it was my best attempt. It was somewhere between *The Sopranos* and a pirate.

He smiles. "I'm Jackson Cole. Your husband, Theo Pearson, hired me." He shows me some sort of identification, but for all I know, he's one of the dangerous people who were tracking me in London, and this is just a ruse. I shake my head and start to move away, but he speaks before I'm too far away. "He told me to use the phrase . . . 'goat taco.'"

My racing heart slows a bit. "Excuse me? What did you say?"

"Goat taco." Jackson shrugs. "I don't ask why, but he said you'd know what it means."

I force my trembling jaw to ease. "I do know, and if he told you, then . . . well, it's something."

It means that he is trusted. When Theo was in the hospital as a boy, we used to make up games or jokes that were just between us. The hospital was serving tacos for lunch, and Theo and I were being silly, which led to a joke about whether they were serving goat. It then became a running joke anytime one of us was upset. We'd say it, and the other would laugh.

"I am the owner of one of the elite private security companies in America. He hired me three years ago on a retainer in the event this was necessary."

"What was necessary?"

"Your protection and answers."

Finally, someone is going to give me those. "What answers do you have, Mr. Cole?"

"When we get to the car, I'll provide you with what I can. May I help you with your bags first?" he asks.

I appreciate the offer more than he knows. I had to manage them when we arrived in Atlanta and went through customs. Then I found out we weren't going to Las Vegas, and instead, we were taking a train to Charlotte, where we were actually supposed to catch our flight to Vegas. When we got to the gate, they informed us our flight was cancelled and that we had to go to the service counter for additional information. I hadn't expected Carol, who was Theo's work friend in Atlanta, to be waiting there to give us new directions and show us to a car. We were driven to yet another airport where a private jet was waiting to fly us to Las Vegas. It has been a nightmare, and Eden and I have each had at least two meltdowns. We are worn out, and the idea of doing more of this is just too much.

While I would much prefer the answers first, this is a kindness I need. "That would be lovely. Thank you."

Jackson lifts the bags as I walk with Eden through the airport to the black SUV with tinted windows. My steps slow because I don't know this man, and I have no idea where we're going. What if he's the bad guy?

He opens the boot and loads our bags while I stand here, unsure if I should turn and run.

"What assurances do you need?" Jackson asks.

"What?"

"You look worried, and I understand that. You're in a new country, unsure of what's going on, your husband died, and you don't know me. If you weren't hesitant, I would be concerned. I don't want to force you into the vehicle, Sophie. I want you to trust that I will protect you and your daughter as I was hired to do."

I worry my lower lip and then find the words I was searching for. "You have to tell me where we're going and what exactly my husband was involved in."

"We're going to drive to Idaho, where we will meet up with a new member of my team. He will provide you and Eden with new identities, and then he will escort you to where Theo wanted you to stay."

"Why can't you go?"

Jackson smiles sadly. "I can't. The place he settled on is somewhere that I need to avoid for a bit."

"Did you do something illegal there?" I ask.

"No, but I have friends there who would question the timing of my showing up at the same time as you, and that would leave you and Eden vulnerable. I won't do that. It would require an elaborate lie, which isn't possible. Lies always have a way of exposing themselves. It's better to stay as close to the truth as we can and avoid complications wherever possible."

I laugh. "I don't even know what the truth is."

"Maybe that's the best thing. Your ignorance can be your salvation. If you're questioned and know nothing, isn't that for the better?"

I look away, the frustration building and threatening to release as tears. "How would you feel if this were your life, Mr. Cole? Your best friend dies, and you can't even hold his hand. Then you are told to leave your life behind—with no context or money. You get on a plane, going somewhere other than where someone might have known, and arrive in a place you don't have fond memories of, only to be told you're leaving again. It's as though . . ."

Jackson leans against the back of the vehicle. "As though?"

I huff. "As though we are trying to evade everything I am."

"That's exactly what we're doing. From the moment you landed, someone could have tracked you. The steps you're taking are to ensure that, if someone is watching, which Theo believed they would be, they would have lost you by now. So, us driving, changing your identities, and then moving again allows us to muddy your trail even more so you don't have to continue to run."

Eden lifts her head as I shift her. "I'm hungry, Mummy."

"I know, darling. We'll get food, I promise."

She looks to Jackson. "Hello."

He smiles. "Hello, Eden. My name is Jackson."

She buries her head in my neck, and I smile. "She takes a bit to warm up."

"I understand. I have two daughters."

For some reason, that small fact comforts me. "And if your daughter were in my shoes, what would you do?"

Jackson cracks his knuckles. "The sad thing is, my wife and children are aware that, at any point, their worlds can come crashing down. The job I do has risks, and we prepare for that, which is what Theo did. The mistake he made was that he didn't share the risks with you and Eden until moments before he died, much to my disagreement. If you were my wife or daughter, I would tell you to trust your gut. If you think I'm lying or a threat, then don't get in this car, but if you trust me and that phrase I said from the beginning is enough, then we need to leave."

My gut. God, I don't even know what to think, but he knows about goat tacos. That has to mean something, right?

I take a step toward him, and he opens the back door where there's a car seat for Eden. I buckle her in and then move to the other side of the SUV to slide in beside her. "I'm trusting you, Mr. Cole, please don't make me regret it."

CHAPTER

Three

HOLDEN

"Another one?" I ask the charge nurse who enters as I am gathering my things to leave for the day. We're moving Blakely, Emmett's wife, into her new office on Main Street, and like always, I'm late.

She shrugs as she extends something toward me. "It would seem someone loves you."

No one loves me. I'm a divorced workaholic who refuses to accept love or take a break. At least, that's what Mama James, the world's best aunt, says whenever she brings it up, which is daily.

"Did you save the box?" I ask, taking it from her.

She gives me a look that would wither a flower. "Do I look like I work in the receiving department?"

I sigh. "You have a lot of spunk."

"Dr. James, I am the charge nurse on one of the most active floors in this hospital. I manage the staff, the doctors, patients, and their families. My responsibilities are legion, and my pay . . . is not. Not to mention most of the doctors here treat my staff like the shit on their shoes. The spunk coming out of me is years' worth of pent-up hostility toward people around here thinking I have ample time to run errands. However, what you're getting now is my refusal to worry about the packaging a gift came in."

I try not to find this tongue lashing comical because most of what she's saying is right. She's shit on at every turn. I am one of those doctors who respects and admires the nurses. They work harder than most and don't receive the credit. Still, I'm new here, and I need to make sure people don't shit on me.

"I understand, it was a simple question. I do not treat you or your staff like anything on my shoes. I value the nursing staff, and I'd appreciate the same in return. I don't devalue your job. I know what each one of you do for me and the other doctors."

Her shoulders drop a touch. "Thank you for saying that."

"I mean it, Trina, you are what keep this hospital running and make the doctors look good."

She smiles a little. "I'll inquire about the box."

I lift my hand. "No need. I'm sure it won't tell us anything, and you have . . ." I try to recall what she said and then grin when it comes back. "Legions of responsibility. This is not one to add to your list."

Trina's eyes mist over, but it must be a trick of the light because all anyone talks about is how she has one emotion . . . annoyed. She shakes her head, and it's gone. "You're the smartest man I know, Dr. James."

"Can you repeat that in about thirty seconds?" I ask as I rummage through my desk.

"What? Why?"

"I need to find my voice recorder so I can just play that anytime someone says otherwise."

She laughs, and I smile at her. Mama James's advice about attracting flies with honey has never left me. I treat everyone with respect and hope it comes back. I also learned as an intern that the nurses are your best ally. They hear everything, remember everyone, and can save your ass when you need it. I have needed it.

I have never won over a charge nurse this easy, though. They're tough nuts to crack, but . . . hey, I'll take this victory.

"I should get back," she says, glancing at the door.

"Thanks for bringing this to me."

"You're welcome."

Trina leaves, and I sit at my desk, reading the postcard again. Since moving back to Rose Canyon, my life has been . . . strange. First, my best friend was murdered, his sister lost her memory, got it back, and then married my other best friend, Spencer. That was a shock to all of us, as no one even knew they had been dating. A few weeks later, I found out my other best friend, Emmett, was also keeping secrets when his freaking wife showed up.

If all that weren't strange enough, I started getting these weird packages.

The first was the Eiffel Tower figurine and a postcard of the Grand Canyon. The second gift, which showed up after the fiasco where Emmett was shot, was a Las Vegas postcard and a small statue of an Egyptian pyramid with the exact same wording from the first postcard. This one. This one is not the same. It's a trinket of Big Ben, which has nothing in common with the other two trinkets aside from the fact that none of them make any sense at all, and a postcard that reads:

Your package is arriving, and you need to pick it up.
8675300183

What fucking package? I groan and toss the postcard onto the desk.

"Everything okay?" a feminine voice asks from the entryway.

"Hey, Kate. Yeah, I'm fine."

Dr. Kate Dehring is the new head of the mental health department. I tried to get my friend Dr. Mike Girardo, the doctor who helped Brielle after her memory loss, to stay, but the hospital could never meet his salary requirements. Thankfully, Kate came in, and she's made a ton of changes, all for the better.

The hospital isn't bad, just underfunded.

"A penny for your thoughts?"

I laugh, and she enters the room. "They're not even worth that much. What brings you down here?"

Kate taps on the other side of the desk and sighs heavily. "I need your advice."

"That must be a change for you. It's usually you hearing that."

She smiles, pulling her long brown hair to the side. "This is true, but you are the expert in this field."

"Take a seat. What can I help with?"

"I want to create a program for children at the youth center where your friend works. It would be to help with coping with life's struggles and also grief. Kids are so often forgotten about, and I know the town was lacking in counseling options when your friend died. I like the idea of just focusing on all aspects for children."

I lean back in my chair. "The high school did a great job bringing in counselors for its students."

"Yes, and that's why we would be able to handle many areas of family conflict, grief, exposure to drugs and violence . . . you know, life stuff."

"I could talk to Brielle about it," I offer.

"That would be great. I started a similar program in Texas, and a lot of families appreciated having somewhere to turn to for help and guidance."

"You're right. I'll see what I can do."

Kate gets to her feet. "Thanks, Holden. I appreciate it."

"No problem. I'm heading over to meet my friends now, so I'll be sure to bring it up to Brielle."

I grab my coat and leave the hospital before my mysterious package arrives. I don't like games, and I've had enough of them to last a lifetime. On my ride over to Blakely's new office, I do my best to push all of that from my mind and focus on helping my friends.

When I get there, I am immediately put to work. On what? Desk assembly.

What is it about furniture directions? Are they purposely vague and impossible to understand? They give a screw that's a half millimeter a letter that isn't on the package, and somehow, we're all supposed to know where it goes. The worst part is that it's from the one store that everyone knows and loves, so they still shop there, regardless of the impossible instructions.

"What's the hold up on building the desk?" Blakely, Emmett's infuriating wife, asks.

I put the half-assembled drawer, which is assembled backward, down. "Nothing."

"Do you need instructions to put the thing together?"

Yes, ones in English, but I don't say that. I have to keep my false bravado up so I don't listen to everyone rib me about it for the next month. "I'm a fucking surgeon. I can put a desk together."

Blakely, however, doesn't buy it. She smirks, seeing the drawer is clearly not together right. "Then do it already. Sheesh."

I'll give her sheesh.

I start to say something back, but my other asshole best friend's wife looks at the floor and then to me. "Do you need the directions?"

What I need is new friends who marry non-irritating women.

That's not in my cards. I throw the screwdriver, which doesn't even work since this brand doesn't use normal tools, and get to my feet. "Hey, peanut gallery, if you two could do it faster, why don't you try?"

Brie lifts her hands in surrender. "I didn't say anything. You're moody."

"Yes, yes, I am." Because, once again, no one thinks my freaking stalker is an issue. All I get is crap for wanting answers. Well, fine, I don't need the actual police department when I have Blakely. She's a private investigator, and I am here as free labor, so it's only fair. "Hey, Blake, are you open to doing any kind of investigating on the side?"

Emmett shakes his head. "You're so dramatic. Seriously."

"I'm dramatic? Mr. Fake-My-Own-Death-And-Make-Everyone-Lie." I look at him, waiting for an answer to that, but he shuts up. "Even better, how about when Blakely went with the psycho, and you came unglued."

"I'd love to see how you would've handled it," Emmett replies.

"My point is that you don't get to give me shit, buddy."

Spencer enters the fray. "What are we arguing about?"

Blake chimes in. "Holden asked me for help on investigating something, and Emmett is butthurt he didn't ask him."

"I did ask him!" I yell while glaring at her husband. "I went to him about it the first time, then the second, and now, I'm asking Blakely since he's unwilling to help."

"What was this one?" Spencer asks.

I hand him the card, and he reads it before giving it to Blake.

"'Your package is arriving, and you need to pick it up.' What do you think it means?"

"Maybe it's a bomb," Brie unhelpfully suggests.

Emmett chuckles. "Or maybe it's his mail-order bride."

Oh, he's in trouble now. His wife is shooting daggers at him. "Not funny, considering where we're standing."

They continue to bicker, and then Spencer jumps in. He has the most analytical mind out of all of us. He solves puzzles in a way that I wish I could. Send me a bleeding person, I'll fix them. Send me someone with some weird rash, I got it, but when it comes to this shit . . . nope.

That's all him.

"All three came with postcards from the Vegas area," he says.

"We know you boys and your love of Vegas." Brie scoffs.

"No one loves Vegas. We survived Vegas," Emmett says.

Ain't that the damn truth.

After the hell we raised in Vegas, I was shocked Addison didn't call off her engagement to Isaac.

I fucking miss him.

He was the best man I knew. Always willing to help someone out and never wanted anything in return. His bachelor party was the most epic send-off and landed us in a lot of hot water, but it was worth it in the end.

"Did anyone ever think that we took the fall for some of the shit Isaac did?" Emmett asks Brielle.

"No, but from what I heard, *you* were the worst of them."

Spencer grins. "You were. Admit it."

"I don't remember shit."

Emmett's full of it. He remembers. I'm the one with giant holes of time missing and stories I'm not sure are even true.

"Focus, fuckers. I'm the one who doesn't remember anything about Vegas. I blacked out."

Emmett laughs. "Yeah, we found you with your dick out in that bathroom."

Spencer nods. "The *women's* bathroom."

There are some things I will never live down. We drank too much. We didn't eat. We fucked up, and apparently, I fucked some girl in a bathroom at a club.

Blakely walks over to Emmett. "I can't wait to hear your part in this."

"What happens in Vegas stays in Vegas."

They start making kissy faces at each other, and I can't take it. All of these guys went from being single to these lovesick puppies in what seems like overnight. I'm happy for them, I really am, but dear God, stop already.

"You two need to go on a real honeymoon," I say, feeling queasy as they start to tap each other's noses.

"Or you need to find a girl willing to marry your ass and finally be happy."

"Yeah, that's not going to happen. I have no desire for a woman or kids. I'm perfectly happy living a single and stress-free life."

Not to mention, I've already been married, and I know how fun divorce is not. I would prefer to keep things simple, and if I avoid the marriage and kid thing, I won't have that issue.

Before we can argue further, there's a woman knocking on the door. She's short, has long blonde hair, and looks as if she's been through hell, but God, she's stunning. Her big blue eyes are taking in the room as she holds tight to a little girl's hand.

God, these poor women trying to escape. I wish I could do more for them.

"Excuse me? I . . . I was hoping someone could help?" she says in a British accent.

Blakely quickly moves to her. "Hi, I'm Blakely, the director of Run to Me. That's my husband, Sheriff Maxwell, and this is Brielle, Spencer, and that's Holden, he's a doctor if you need help. What's your name?"

Immediately, her eyes find mine. There's a mix of relief and fear. "Holden?"

I walk over, moving slowly as not to scare her. "Yes, my name is Holden James. I'm a surgeon, and I can help if you're hurt."

She shakes her head. "No, I'm not hurt. Not . . . physically at least."

Her blue eyes don't leave my gaze, and she's studying me as though she knows me.

Blakely's voice is soft as she asks, "Is this your daughter?"

The woman glances at the child. "Yes, this is Eden."

"Hello, Eden, my name is Blakely. Would you like something to eat?"

Eden's eyes go to her mother and then back to Blakely before she smiles a little. Blake takes that as a yes, walks over to the cabinet, and grabs a granola bar. When she returns, the little girl twists her body and grabs her mother's leg.

I stand here, watching them. There's something about this woman, but I can't put my finger on it. Maybe she was a patient of mine before?

My eyes drop to her daughter, whose eyes are large and brown with little traces of hazel in them. Then her nose, it looks like my sister's. In fact, she looks just like Kira did at that age.

The woman speaks again. "Sorry, she's normally rather chatty, but it's been a very hard few days, and when I got into town, I was told to come here to find Holden James."

"You were looking for me? Do I know you?"

She tucks her blonde hair behind her ear. "My name is Sophie Pearson. We met a few years ago, my name then would've been—well, it doesn't matter, we didn't exchange our full names that night."

"Were you a patient of mine?"

It's right there. I just can't place it.

"No." She shakes her head before hoisting her daughter in her arms. "But we have met before, and while I hadn't been sure why I was sent here, now it's a bit clearer."

"And when did we meet exactly?" I ask.

"It would be a little over three years ago."

Three years.

I glance down at Eden, doing some math because this little girl has the James nose. And the way she's looking at me, it's . . .

Dear God.

"Where?" I ask quickly. "Where did we meet?"

"Las Vegas."

CHAPTER
Four
SOPHIE

We walk into a back room, my legs feeling like jelly, and I already screwed up. As soon as I spoke my name, I mentally slapped myself. I can't be Sophie Pearson any longer. Eden and I both have new names and passports. Our old lives are no longer, and we are now Sophie and Eden Peterson, which I will do my best to remember from here on out.

When Zach Barrett, an employee of Cole Security, drove us out here, he explained it was imperative I be cautious of who I trust and always use my new name. However, who could blame me for this one slipup? I am gobsmacked at this entire situation.

Oh, Theo, what have you done?

He sent me to a tiny town to find Eden's father, and I have more questions than anyone can ever answer.

Holden and I stare at each other. He is very handsome, and I chide myself for even thinking that. But his hair is dark, tousled, and the scruff on his cheeks is very appealing. I barely remember him from that night, but something familiar is in his eyes. The ones that look like Eden's.

"I have a lot of things I want to know but no idea where to start," Holden says, pushing his dark brown hair back. He sighs and then looks to me. "First, I need to ask, are you all right?"

"That's a rather hard question to answer at the moment." I spin my wedding rings and pace a little. "No. I'm not. It's been . . . well, everything is confusing, and I feel as though I should tell you, in case you haven't figured it out by now, after our night in Vegas, I became pregnant."

Holden swallows and nods. "I surmised as much."

"Right. Being a doctor and all, you've probably already done the math. Still, she is yours."

"And after all this time you decided to find me?"

I didn't. "I had no idea that I was coming here to find you. My husband arranged all of this."

"You're married?" he asks.

This definitely is not going well. I am mucking this up left and right. "I feel as though I should start at the beginning because I'm cocking this up."

"Mummy?" Eden calls from the little table, where she's been colouring in a book someone had given her. "I want Daddy."

Of all the things she could say. I move to her, crouching and placing my hand atop hers. "I know, darling. I want him too, but that's not possible." I push her blonde hair back. "I need to talk to our new friend, can you colour for a bit while I get things sorted?"

Asking a three-year-old to colour for more than a minute is a losing game, but I need as much as she will give me.

"Okay, Mummy."

"That's a good girl."

She runs off, and I turn back to a man I never thought I'd see again. "I can't say much until we're alone, but I'll give the abbreviated version." I rise to my feet and prepare to say three years' worth of backstory as quickly as possible. This should go over well. "I wasn't married when you and I met, but two months after . . . Vegas, I found out I was pregnant. My father had just died, and my mum wasn't kind during her grief. Well, she wasn't kind before that either. She demanded I get rid of the baby to ensure that my future husband, who she and my dad had chosen, would still go through with it. I refused. She threw me out. Theo and I were childhood friends, and he had a very serious genetic heart condition that we knew he would die from. He offered to marry me, raise her as his own, and give us a life he could never share with another. I was young and had been raised to believe a child out of wedlock was a death sentence in our circle. Theo saved me from all of it."

"Wow, that's a great friend, and I'm not sure what to say."

I latch on to the first part of his statement. "He was. He was the best, and while we never had a marriage in truth, we were the best part of a marriage." A tear forms, and I turn away. I don't know how to go on in this world without Theo.

"I am going to assume he passed away from that heart condition," Holden says before placing his hand on my shoulder.

I turn to look at him, my blurry vision masking his attractive face. "Four days ago, and . . . that's when I came here on his request."

"Four days?" Holden's eyes widen.

"Yes, there's more to this story, clearly, but I was told to follow every instruction along the way, and it led me here."

"So, he knew who I was?"

I laugh without humor. "It appears so."

"Wow." He scratches the back of his head. "I don't know what to say."

"I don't either. I am still not sure what exactly is happening."

Four days ago, I was married and living in Kensington. I had a beautiful home, friends, and most of all, I was safe.

Now that's all gone. Every part of my existence has died, and I am lost.

Holden nods. "How are you doing so far?"

"Not very well. I mean, it was just the holidays, and now we're . . . here. So, no, I'm not doing very well."

He smiles. "I didn't think so. So, what exactly are you supposed to do now?"

All I was told was to come here and find him, so I was hoping he was the plan or knew what was next. "You tell me."

"Umm, I don't know. I didn't even know you were coming or that you existed. Well, I knew you existed since we"—he glances over at Eden—"we've met, but I didn't know your name, and honestly, we were both pretty drunk. Half the time, I have thought I hallucinated our . . . encounter."

I was definitely not at my best that night. I came to Las Vegas on holiday with my flat mate. It was meant to be a trip to remember. We had fun, and I was enjoying myself, but on our final day there, Mum called and picked a fight because I left London without permission, as if I weren't a twenty-three-year-old adult. She ranted about it being irresponsible for me to take a week to enjoy my life. I graduated top of my class at university and deserved a bit of fun, but that didn't seem to matter to her. It had put me in a sour mood, but it was our last night in the States, so I agreed to go to Garden of Eden with Joanne and have a good time.

I got that and a whole lot more—a baby after a one-night stand in a toilet.

"Do you have a letter or instructions?"

Holden shakes his head. "I don't know what you mean."

"Theo provided everyone we met along the way with some kind of plan. I assumed you had one."

"I'm sorry to say that I have no plan."

Great. As if this could be a bigger mess . . .

"I don't know anything about you other than you're a doctor. Are you married? Do you have other children?"

He shakes his head. "Nope to either of those."

That, at least, is something. I start to ask if he's dating since I can't imagine an attractive doctor is single, but before I can, Eden gets up and walks over to us. "Who are you?"

My heart begins to race, and I look at him. "This is our friend, Holden. Can you say hello?"

She leans against me but waves. "Hello."

He drops down to her eye level. "Hey, there. Did you color that page?"

She shows him. "It's for my daddy. He's sick."

"It's very beautiful," Holden notes. "Do you like to color?"

Eden bobs her head vigorously.

"My sister did when she was little too." He leans in as though he's imparting great knowledge. "I am not very good at it, but maybe you could teach me?"

"Mummy is the best."

"Girls are much better than boys at pretty much everything."

"Am I going to see you again soon?"

His eyes meet mine for a second, but that one look is a whole conversation without a word spoken. He already cares for Eden. He may not have a plan, but it is clear he'll take care of us.

That look breaks me.

"Yes, I think we're going to see a lot of each other," Holden answers.

And I let out a sob as the overwhelming emotions crush me.

CHAPTER

Five

HOLDEN

Uhhh.

Now what?

She's crying these deep, long sobs that are wracking her whole body. Eden is standing beside her, looking confused and a little scared, and I am . . . lost. I have a kid.

A kid, and . . . she's staring at me.

So, I do the only thing I know to do in this situation and call for reinforcement.

"Brielle! Blakely! Help please."

I pull Sophie into my arms, holding her close as she continues to cry, and give Eden an awkward smile, which is probably more creepy than reassuring, but I'm doing my best here.

A few seconds later, the girls burst through the door.

"What did you do?" Brielle asks incredulously.

"I have no clue, but could you maybe take Eden out and let me talk to Sophie?" I ask with the same forced smile.

Blakely glares at me, which I return with an eye roll and then tilt my head, indicating they should go.

Sophie's hands grip my shirt, holding on for dear life. As soon as they take Eden out of the room, I pull back a little to make eye contact. "Sophie, why are you crying?" I sort of feel like an idiot asking since, why wouldn't she be crying?

Her husband died. She left her home and is exhausted after traveling for four days, which I'll unpack later because, why did it take four days?

She looks up at me, her tears falling. "I'm scared. I'm scared because you don't have any directions, and I came here because I had to run. He told me to let him die alone because we could be harmed."

"Harmed by who?"

"I don't know!" She chokes out the words, and I can hear the agony in them.

I pull her tight against me, offering her whatever protection my arms can give. I feel awful, and the mother of my child shouldn't have to feel scared and alone. "Sophie, you're safe."

She shakes her head. "I'm not."

"Why do you think you're in danger here?"

"Because you didn't even know I was coming or why I am here."

I am not following. "You're also sick. Is that why he sent you to me?"

She wipes her face with the back of her hand and blinks a few times. "Who is sick?"

"You."

Her lips part, and I wonder if I shouldn't have said anything, but the first two postcards said a patient was coming, and I have to assume that, since her husband sent her to me, she is that patient. Does she not know something is wrong?

Sophie sits back on her legs, working to stop the tears. "I'm not sick. I haven't had so much as a cold since Eden was born."

Maybe he meant care in another way. Still, I've spent months thinking I was getting someone sick who needed my medical help.

"So, neither you nor Eden are sick?"

"Why would you think I was?"

I explain to her the series of gifts and letters I got, and she asks a few questions about details, which I do my best to answer.

"You believe Theo was sending you messages to prepare you?" she asks.

"I do. I think the warnings were to let me know that, when you finally got to me, I would take care of you, and I will do that, Sophie. If I knew about Eden . . ." I run my fingers through my hair. "I would've been there."

She looks away for a second. "I didn't know where to start to find you. I didn't even know your full name, and it was Vegas." Then she lets out a laugh. Not one that makes me think she's gone insane, but one that's more as though she can't believe it. "I think you're right about the warnings. I'm just fucking livid. For months he knew about you! He knew that we were in trouble, and we would need to leave and come here. He lied to me for God only knows how long." Sophie turns to face me. "Theo never told me anything about what kind of trouble he was in. He waited until he was on his death bed to inform me that Eden and I were in danger and needed to leave immediately. Then it was this rush to get out of London. We went through a weird switching of planes. We flew into Atlanta, then I thought we were going straight to Las Vegas, but I was diverted to a train to Charlotte and *then* a flight to Las Vegas. From there, I went to Idaho before coming here. It's been four days of following misleading directions and being lost. I'm not sick. I'm exhausted, and I don't know where we go next."

She's not going anywhere. No way am I going to allow her to run around America if she is in danger. The best place for her is here. I know that sounds crazy since we met one time, fucked, and now have a kid, but I have a kid.

I have a daughter.

If she is really in danger, I am not going to just let her run off.

"You have no reason to trust me, but I promise I am not going to let anyone hurt you or Eden. I think the plan was for you to get to me, but just . . . I don't know, without being tracked. You're here now, and I would like to help you both."

Not just because Sophie is clearly in trouble or Eden is my daughter, but because this girl needs someone. I've been that person before. When my sister died when I was fifteen, and my parents lost their fucking minds, I was the one who suffered the most. I was lost, alone, terrified, and had to lie about how things were. It was Mama James who came to me, took me out of that house, and made sure I was safe after they failed me in every way.

Safety shouldn't be a commodity in life, it should be a given, but too often it's not.

I would never be okay with letting this situation go unresolved.

"Eden doesn't know that Theo is not her father," she whispers.

"I understand."

Her blue eyes fill with tears. "I didn't want to lie, but . . ."

I stop her there, lifting my hand. "You did what you had to do. I'm not judging you or asking you to upheave her world more than it already has been, but I can give you a place to stay, and . . . well, I can be your friend if you'll let me."

The tears finally fall, but she nods her agreement.

"What the hell are you going to do?" Spencer asks once he and Emmett can finally get me alone.

"What do you think I'm going to do? That's my kid and the mother of my child."

Emmett clears his throat, glancing away.

"What?" I ask, already knowing what he's thinking.

"I'm not saying a word."

"You don't have to speak it to know you're actually saying something."

We know each other much better than that. He's thinking what they're both thinking and were probably talking about when I was in the back with Sophie and Eden.

Spencer exhales loudly. "Just that it would be a good idea to have a paternity test done, which"—he holds up a hand to stop what I'm about to say—"I am sure you already have thought about."

"Of course I have."

I really haven't. I don't know why I didn't since I'm a damn doctor, but I just know. That's my daughter.

"Good," Emmett replies. "I don't want to see you get hosed."

"You think she's lying?"

Spencer watches her as she sits in the other room eating a sandwich from the diner. "I don't. I think she's here and has no idea what's going on, but you don't know her. You have no idea if she's a murderer or her husband really did send her here to find her daughter's father."

"She's in trouble. Or, at least, she thinks she's in trouble," I tell them. There's no point in keeping any of this from them. Not just because Emmett is law enforcement and both of them are trained to kill someone in seconds, but because they know me and will figure it out. I'd rather get it in the open now.

"What kind of trouble?"

"I'm not sure, and she doesn't seem to either. All I know is that she said her husband sent them here before he died to protect them. I don't know, maybe he just wanted to make sure Eden knew her father."

"So, you're going to take her in?"

I look at him, wondering who the fuck he is. "Of course I am. What the hell would you do?"

"Take her in," he answers without pause. "I didn't think you'd do anything different even if she weren't your kid, which you don't know for sure." Again, he feels the need to reiterate this.

"I'm not going to leave her on the street to freeze to death."

Emmett clears his throat. "Just a reminder here, she wouldn't be on a street. Blakely has safe houses for the runaways. I know for a fact she'd offer one to Sophie and Eden."

A part of me wonders if that's not the best idea, but then the other part of me doesn't want that. I have missed every minute of that little girl's life, and I really don't want to miss more. It's crazy since I have had zero desire for a family. In fact, I did everything I could to fuck up any chances of that, but now it's here, in my face, and I don't want to push her away.

Plus, if she is in danger, I don't want her alone.

"Sophie and I have a lot of things we need to work out, and maybe spending time together is what we need, but I will keep that in the back of my mind."

A laugh falls from Spencer's mouth. "You're a freaking idiot."

"So are you."

He shrugs. "Maybe, but you and I know that forcing a woman to spend time with you isn't going to win her over."

"She just lost her husband, and I am not trying to win her over. I'm trying to build some kind of a friendship so I can help her." And all of that is true. Sure, Sophie is stunning, and I'm attracted to her, but I'm not stupid. There is no way in hell I am walking into the mess she's in.

"Sure you're not. I saw the way you were staring at her."

Fucking Spencer. "Like the woman who raised my child that I didn't know existed?"

"Yeah, we'll call it that."

Before I can reply, Sophie walks in and gives me a weary smile. "Blakely offered us a place to stay, so if you'd rather, we can do that. I could maybe find a hotel, if there's one close?"

The fucking hell that's going to happen. "No, you'll stay with me.

You don't know the area, the hotel is a shithole, and I would prefer you and Eden be safe with me," I reply, keeping my voice even.

She nods. "I'd prefer that. I'm bloody tired and probably wouldn't sleep if we were in a strange place alone."

This woman has been through hell, and I know only a fraction of what's happened. I want the opportunity to learn as much as I can from her. If we know who we're dealing with, it'll make matters easier.

"Good, let's head there and get you settled."

My house isn't anything to write home about, but it has three bedrooms and is on the outskirts of town where it's quiet and no one will bother us.

I help them into the car, borrowing a car seat from Run to Me. Blakely has a lot of supplies for anyone who shows up in need of sanctuary. The ride takes no more than fifteen minutes, and we are both silent through it. Sophie's head is turned toward the window, and I have no idea if she's sleeping, but I don't want to disturb her.

When we pull up the drive and park, her eyes meet mine, and they're filled with—resignation and sadness.

"I'm not sure what to say," I confess.

"I'm not either." She turns to look at Eden, who is asleep in the back seat, bundled up in a blanket and winter coat. "I feel as though I lost everything in one moment, and I know for you, it must be a different set of emotions."

Her loss is my gain, and even though I don't want to feel that way, I do. I have a daughter, who I never knew existed, and now she's here.

I'm not happy that Sophie has had to go through any of this, and I wish it could've come around differently, but I can't stop thinking about the fact that there's a little girl who I get to know because of it.

"I think we're both overwhelmed and need a little time to figure things out."

She laughs once. "I don't know that time will change anything, Holden. We have a child together, I am homeless, without much money, and I'm questioning everything I thought I knew about myself."

"What does that mean?"

Sophie turns away, wiping her cheek. "I don't know who I am anymore. The life I'd built, the woman I was, is all gone in one moment. I am no longer married, and I was instructed that I can never return to anywhere I've been before. Not back to England or even France, where I spent only a few months after university. I cannot see family or friends. My life must be erased, or we could be killed. And why? I don't know. Theo was a good man. He didn't do anything but help people invest their money and get rich. So, why must my whole life change? Who am I if I can't be that girl? How is it that our lives are in danger because of his choices?"

I let all of that sink in before offering, "Your husband must've known something about someone powerful."

"I'm sure he did, but I don't. The only thing he ever asked of me was to attend parties and galas with him. That was the most I was involved. I had my own career, which is gone now as well."

"What did you do?"

She shakes her head. "I was a painter."

"Why can't you paint now?"

"I will always paint. I will never be able to ignore the lure of a brush, but I can never sell it again—not as myself, at least."

"Because?"

Sophie's gaze turns to the maple tree on the right. "Because that girl has disappeared."

CHAPTER
Six

SOPHIE

Holden's home is small but clean. It's nothing like my flat in London. It was open and airy with white walls and modern appliances. Everything was maintained by our butler and house-keeper. The nanny came each morning to help with Eden while I went into my posh studio.

I loved our home. I loved that Theo ensured our every need was met, and I hate that it's all gone.

It isn't as if I believe I should have it all, I just never thought much of a life without it. Holden hauls our last suitcase into the spare bedroom, and I follow him in.

The room is adorable. It's painted a lovely shade of light blue, and white curtains frame the windows. On the wall to the left is a queen-size bed, there is a dresser on the wall to the right of it, and the small planks of oak covering the floor look as if they're the original hardwood.

It's pretty, but not my home.

He scratches his neck and sighs. "I'll get the back bedroom cleaned out in the next day or so. You can both stay here, or if you want to take my room, I'll sleep on the couch."

"There's no need for that. Eden and I can stay here together. Thank you," I say, truly appreciative for his kindness.

It's quite unnerving to have a child with someone and not know them. If I were to pass him on the street, I might look twice because he's attractive, but then I'd go on my way.

That thought makes me stop. I find him attractive.

After all the years of thinking that part of me had been erased, being near Holden has awoken it a little.

Well, I am not going to think about that because, as of now, we are staying in the same house together because my husband willed it so.

"I'm sorry it's not bigger or ready, but I didn't anticipate company."

"It's fine. Truly. I just appreciate you letting us stay here."

"Of course I want you both here. What can I get you?" he asks.

"A week's worth of sleep."

I wish I were joking.

"I could get you medication if you need help sleeping."

I shake my head. "It's quite all right. It's more that I've not had much sleep than my being unable to do so."

He nods slowly before saying, "The bathroom is through that door there." He points to the one on the far left. "The one beside it is a closet, and there should be towels in there. I honestly don't come into this room much, but when I moved in, Brielle and Mama James set it up."

"Mama James?"

His smile is affectionate. "My aunt. She's more of a mother to me than my own is. She takes in all things broken and lost before fixing them up and letting them go."

"Well, it seems she has her work cut out with me then," I say, trying to sound light and funny, but I can hear the pain in my voice. "Not even she will be able to repair what's wrong with me."

"I don't believe any person is broken beyond repair, Sophie. We may be a little worse for wear, but all we need is a little time, and we heal. I've seen people come back from unspeakable pain stronger than they ever could have imagined."

Maybe in a medical sense he has, but how could someone possibly survive losing almost everything essential to who they are?

"And what if the broken parts can't be seen?"

"I don't think we have to see it to heal it."

"I hope you're right, Holden."

"I do, too, because while you may feel broken or lost, I see a strong woman who is neither of those. You crossed the ocean alone with a child, not knowing where you were going and having just lost the man you love. I see a woman who fought when so many may have given in. Don't forget that." Holden's words seep into my soul, and I cling to them.

I nod once. "I will do my best to remember."

"Good. I'm right down the hall if you need anything. I have a lot of patient notes to catch up on, so I'll be awake for a while . . ."

"Okay."

Then he leaves, closing the door behind him, and I let my eyes drift to where Eden sleeps, tucked tightly into the blankets. My need for things to be in order rises, but I don't have the wherewithal to do anything. I can't even be bothered to write in my diary. I'm not quite sure I want to remember what I am feeling right now, anyway. So, I climb into the bed, wrap my arms around my daughter, and cry myself to sleep.

The smell of bacon fills my nose as my eyes flutter open. I blink, unsure of where I am. My hand moves over the cool sheets, finding them cool and vacant. Where is Eden? I sit up, looking around, and then I'm on my feet, throwing my cardigan around my shoulders and rushing out the door.

As soon as I turn the corner into the eat-in area, I breathe for the first time.

She's safe.

She's sitting at the table with Holden, a plate of eggs and bacon in front of her. Her brown eyes are staring up at him with her warm smile.

I must exhale loudly because both of them turn to me.

"Mummy!" Eden exclaims as she climbs down off the chair and runs to me.

Holden also stands. "I thought you might want the sleep, so I made Eden breakfast. Would you like some?"

"That would be lovely, thank you."

We all take a seat, and he dishes me a plate of food. Eden goes back to hers, chopping on another slice of bacon. I haven't eaten in what feels like days. Nothing has seemed appetizing, and I was too stressed to handle much more than a piece of fruit or a muffin.

However, I could devour everything on the table.

"I ate two pieces, and I had fruit and two eggs," Eden says around a smile.

"Two eggs?" I say with my brows rising. "You must've been quite hungry."

Her little head bobs up and down. "I like the bacon here, Mummy."

There were things I loved eating when I came on holiday. The one thing I remember most was the difference in bacon. I can't wait to eat it again and see if it lives up to the memory.

I take a slice and bite in, moaning softly as I do. Well, this is exactly as I remember it.

"Good?" Holden asks with a knowing grin.

My hand covers my mouth, and I laugh. "That obvious?"

"The moan gave it away."

"Well, it is heavenly. Our bacon doesn't quite taste this good in London."

"Glad the US has at least that."

I lower my hand and smile at him. "At least there's that."

"Mummy, can I watch the telly?"

"Sure, go grab your tablet and sit nice on the sofa."

Eden's hands clap together and then she's off, leaving Holden and me alone at the table.

I try not to stare at him and remind myself of my self-made rules, but he's so handsome. His hair is a mess of chestnut brown, but it's perfect for him. There is a five o'clock shadow dusting his cheeks and contouring his strong jawline. He has a face I could paint.

Holden clears his throat. "I have to head into the hospital today for a few minutes. I explained that I had family come in unexpectedly, and I needed to be here. Another doctor offered to cover my shift, but I need to grab some things from my office to finish up here."

It's nuts to me that this man, who was wasted at the club, is a doctor. I know that sounds a bit judgy, but the two versions of him are so contradictory. So many things about that night are a blur, but us meeting has always been something I can recall in perfect detail.

"That's fine. We can stay here while you run out."

"Or you guys can come with me. This is a very small town, and if we hide you away, people will think there's a reason. It's best we decide what we're willing to tell people and stick to that."

"I don't understand," I confess. "What does the town have to do with anything?"

"Our town is amazing, filled with caring and wonderful people who thrive on gossip. It's just the way it is, and from what I've learned, it's better to just go out there and be the one who sets the tone of the story."

"You want me to meet people here and tell them my story?"

He shakes his head. "Not like that. We'll come up with something that's close to the truth, and it'll make things easier, trust me."

"What is close to the truth?"

He glances into the living area, where Eden is contently watching a show. "It took me less than a minute to realize that Eden is my daughter. While I don't have a DNA test to prove it, she's identical to my sister at that age. It's not going to take Mama James or any of the people in this town very long to see the resemblance. If we deny it, I think it'll cause more drama."

I wring my hands, nerves hitting me at this next thing. "Do you . . . want a DNA test?"

"I don't need one."

At that, I'm shocked. "What?"

"I don't need one. I believe you, and . . ." His gaze settles on Eden again.

I look over, concerned at whatever she might have done, and I could cry because she's doing it again. She's lying down, head hanging off the seat, legs up on the back, watching television with the tablet beside her.

"Does she always sit that way?" he asks, forgetting the statement he was in the middle of.

I sigh, embarrassed at her pose. "Eden, we've talked about this, darling. You can't sit like that."

"It's comfortable," she protests.

"It can't be," I argue.

Holden quietly laughs. The heat fills my cheeks. No matter how many times Theo and I would reprimand her about it, we'd find her in the same position moments later. The worst was the day she did it in church at a wedding. I wanted to crawl under the pew and wait for the Lord to call me home.

"Mummy, I like this way."

My shoulders fall and that feeling is just as intense. I turn to Holden and say, "I'm sorry, I can make her sit right, but she won't last long."

He shakes his head. "Don't. I sat like that until I was fifteen when I watched TV or played on my Gameboy."

"You did?"

"I was always getting shit from my parents and sister. It was comfortable."

My eyes move back to Eden, and I smile. "I always thought it was odd, as no one in my family ever did that."

"Well, let's hope that's all she inherited from me."

"Holden? I know that Eden is your child, but how could you not want proof?"

He leans back, and after a moment, he finally answers, "Have you ever just known something? Without it being confirmed?"

"Of course."

"Well, that was how I felt. I looked at her and knew. If you had come to me after that night, or if we had known each other before, I wouldn't ask for a paternity test. Just because you're here now doesn't change that. I appreciate you offering the option, and maybe if we ever need it, we do it then. However, I believe you and don't need a test to tell me what I already know."

My hand moves to my mouth. I can't believe he said that. It's too much to believe this man is real. "I wish so many things went differently that night. We'd be having a very different conversation if they had."

"What do you mean?"

Maybe we would've dated. Maybe we could've raised her together. So many things could've been different if we'd known each other . . . I don't know. If any of that had happened, then I never would've married Theo, and I wouldn't have given him the one thing he wanted—a family. While he wanted a wife and children, he never wanted a child to inherit his condition.

Still, Holden and I missed an opportunity.

"Just that . . . we should've talked. Exchanged phone numbers or at least last names before we . . . you know."

Holden chuckles. "I'm honestly shocked I was able to perform with how much I drank."

Even in his drunken state, he was still good. The best I'd ever had, which isn't exactly saying much as I don't have an extensive history. I'd dated a narcissist prior to meeting Holden, and he never once cared about me at all. It was his needs, and mine weren't relevant. So, maybe he wasn't good? I don't know anymore. It's been so long since anyone has touched me.

Holden's deep sigh reminds me of his previous statement. "Sorry. You were . . . well, you were able to."

"Was I good?" he asks with a joking hint in his voice.

I laugh, unwilling to admit my thoughts. "You passed out immediately following."

"That's not what I asked."

I grab a piece of bacon and shrug. "You weren't bad."

Holden drops his head to his hand. "I'm not sure whether to laugh or cry. I wasn't *bad*? That's not a glowing endorsement."

"I was not exactly sober either." And while I remember most of it, I don't want to admit how many times I've replayed it. "I honestly don't remember all that much of the act, but you were wonderful during the lead up to it."

"Good to know that I had game that night."

I roll my eyes and let out a giggle. God, I haven't giggled in a very long time. It feels nice, even if it's just a moment. I trace patterns on the wood grains and stare at my finger as it moves. "You were kind. I remember that. There was a guy who was being aggressive, and you stepped in, pulling me to you and shielding me."

"As much as I'd like to take credit for doing it out of chivalry, I was black-out drunk. For all I know, I could've been falling and thought you were a pillar, which was why I grabbed you."

"Let's pretend it's the other," I say, shaking my head. "Anyway, you may have been drunk, but you were still nice and told me I was beautiful."

"I remember that. I thought you were so gorgeous. By far the most beautiful woman I'd ever seen."

"Thank you."

"You still are." He raises his hand. "Not that I'm hitting on you, I'm just saying that you're still beautiful. It wasn't past tense, that's all."

I feel the heat rise to my face. *Jesus, Sophie, get a damn grip. He is not hitting on you as he said. He is being sweet.*

"Well, you're better-looking than I remember as well." I offer the same compliment back.

Holden's chest pops slightly. "How much better?"

"Slightly," I say teasingly.

"Slightly because I'm like a fine wine that gets better with age, or slightly because you couldn't see much in the club?"

More like you're incredibly attractive and the last man who made me feel desirable.

"You're trouble, aren't you?"

"You have no idea . . . or, maybe you do, actually." Our gazes move to Eden. "You named her Eden because of the club?"

I nod. "I didn't know your full name or how to find you, but I wanted her to have a part of you in some way. It's silly and a little ridiculous, but I liked the name, and she was heavenly to me. She is perfect, and I honestly can't imagine a world without her. Theo agreed it was fitting as well."

"Can you tell me more about him or what happened?"

There's a lot to tell, and I am honestly not sure what to say. Jackson made it very clear I was to keep everything about Theo's past to myself. I am to trust only a man named Holden, and I was to be very careful not to give anything more than superficial information. If my whereabouts are discovered, it could be dangerous for me and Eden. Jackson never did tell me what exactly I was running from or who the threat to me was, but if it was bad enough to send me halfway across the globe, it was bad enough for me to take seriously.

Still, it would be nice to know more than that. If someone does come for me or my daughter, I should have a way out of it. He also gave me two phone numbers of people who work for his security company and are keeping an eye out for us. One is Zach Barrett, who drove us to Rose Canyon and would be around for a few days before he had to return to Michigan. The other is Miles Kent, who Jackson said would be staying around longer than Zach.

All of this is a bit much for me.

"To be honest, I am not quite sure what happened."

"I can understand that, but what about Theo? You mentioned you were childhood friends. Did you always have feelings for each other?"

I laugh and then look away. I don't want to admit any of this, but I feel as though lying to Holden isn't fair. The shaky breath escapes my lungs. "Theo and I were never . . . well, I loved him with my whole heart, but we were never intimate."

"You were never . . . together?"

"Not in that way. We were best friends, but not lovers. I was never attracted to him either."

I can see the confusion in Holden's eyes, but I won't say more than that. In all our years together, I just never wanted more.

"But you were married for a while, and you never . . ."

"Never. We tried to kiss once. It was quite funny because we broke apart and started laughing. Then, maybe after Eden's first birthday, one of my university friends made a comment about how Theo and I should at least try to sleep together since we were married and all. We set a time and place, all very professional feeling, and when he came to my room, we ended up watching a movie and decided never to listen to anyone again. You are the last man I slept with," I admit.

That rocks him back. His brown eyes widen and jaw falls a little slack. "You're kidding me?"

"I'm not. I couldn't cheat on my husband even if we weren't married in the biblical way. Discretion was very important to Theo and me. My family were influential, and if they hadn't believed we were truly married, they could've made things difficult. My mother passed away about eight months ago, which meant I probably could've stopped worrying about that, but it seemed wrong. Theo had no one, and I felt it was the least I could do as well."

That wasn't the complete reason. It was also that I didn't ever want to be hurt again. Being with Theo was a safe choice. It meant there was no risk of loving and losing. It meant no chance of another pregnancy and no more explanations. There'd been safety in my marriage, and I'd clung to it, losing the other part of myself that longed for love.

Holden leans forward, his hand resting on mine. "I'm sure he loved you very much to be able to do what he did. To marry you to protect you from whatever wrath your family would bring and raise Eden as his own."

At that, I let out a bark of laughter because it's utter rubbish. "If he loved me, he would've given me an idea of what I was dealing with. Instead, I had to walk away as he was dying because whatever he was into risked our lives."

I am trying very hard to forgive Theo because I can't imagine he wanted this outcome, but there were more than enough opportunities for him to talk to me. I could've helped or at least been able to form my own plan.

Then there's the fact that he knew who Eden's father was. How long had he known? Was it days, weeks, years? I spoke to him about this so many times when she was a baby. Theo knew how I longed to know who her biological father was so I could give him the chance to be a part of her life. He knew what it was like to have her in his life, and he took that from Holden . . . and from me.

"You know he sent me letters. Well, I'm assuming it was him anyway."

"You mentioned it, but I'm not sure I quite processed that information yesterday."

Holden rises and walks over to a cabinet and places down three postcards and trinkets of random things. "These are what came before you did."

"May I?"

"Of course." He pushes them toward me.

My heart sinks. "This is his handwriting." The thick script I'd know anywhere. When he was too sick to be around people, we'd pass notes, and I knew his handwriting as well as my own. "What is this on the bottom?"

"That's my medical license number, but I never understood why it would be there. It's why I thought I was getting a medical patient, not a daughter."

I laugh once. "The trinkets confuse me. They're rather sporadic. Nothing connects or is a theme."

Holden arranges them in a row. "This is the order they came."

"Always with a Vegas . . . oh my God! The Eiffel Tower is where the Garden of Eden Club is, and the pyramid is because I stayed in the Luxor . . . in Vegas. Big Ben is because I'm British."

He chuckles. "It all makes sense then."

"It does, but why the cloak and dagger mystery? Why not just call you and explain instead of sending some bloody mini statues?"

"We do some crazy things for the people we love, but it doesn't mean they are the right choices. I can't imagine him making you walk away when he was dying was easy."

Unwanted emotions fill me, and I turn my head. "I know . . . but I wish I knew why and now what."

His hand tightens. "Now you're here, and I'll do everything I can to protect you and Eden."

I turn to him and smile softly. "Thank you."

He nods. "Let's get ready and get our story straight so I can keep that promise."

CHAPTER
Seven

SOPHIE

"Are you sure you want to go into town already?" I ask from the doorway as Holden grabs the paperwork he needs.

"It's better we get out in front of it. At least with Mama James," he assures me.

"Okay."

I hate the idea of having to answer questions about Eden or being judged by those who don't know me. All too often, the woman wears the mark of shame. I was young, drunk, and slept with a man in a club without even knowing his whole name. I'm a whore, a slut, or a harlot who just wanted to trap a man with money, whereas Holden is a stud who "got lucky." I have never understood why a woman is shamed for the same act a man is congratulated for, but this is my lot, and I've endured, as we all do.

Still, I don't know these people, and while I made a mistake, a miracle came from it. Eden has enriched my life beyond measure, and I don't regret my decision or the consequences from it.

I say that now with three years distance. That day, I regretted every second.

Holden smiles warmly. "I promise, it won't be bad."

"Holden? Is that you?" calls a tall woman with dark brown hair. She's wearing a white coat and holding a tablet as she approaches. I can't think of any other word to describe her other than striking. She's slim, but not too skinny, and she walks proudly. It's clear she's confident and someone with an air of authority.

"Hey, Kate. I'm not really here," he replies. "I just came to grab a few things from my office and bring my friend Sophie and Eden in to see where I work."

She blinks and then looks at us both. "Hi!" Her eyes are soft and kind. "I'm Kate Dehring, I don't think we've met before."

I extend my hand. "I'm Sophie, an old friend of Holden's who just came into town."

Kate looks down at Eden and then to Holden. "Oh. How nice."

Holden places his hand on my back. "We have a lunch date and are running behind, did you need me for something?"

Kate shakes her head. "It can wait. I just wanted you to consult on a patient, but I can ask Dr. Trumble."

"I know how much you love him."

Kate snorts. "Yeah, he's a peach."

"If it can wait, I'll be back in a day or so. I'm taking some time off to spend with these two."

"Of course. It's nothing urgent. We can spend time talking about everything another day, but if something changes, I'll call or text you. Have a great time at lunch." She waves as she walks down the hall. "Nice to meet you, Sophie. I'm sure we'll see each other a lot since you'll be around Holden."

"Nice meeting you too."

Holden walks us down the hall and out to the car. The entire time my mind is racing. Something about that encounter leaves me uncomfortable. She's very pretty, I wonder if . . . God, I never even considered that he might be dating someone. He must be, considering how handsome and successful he is.

Oh, Sophie, will you ever learn not to be attracted to a man you can't have or that doesn't want you?

This unnerves me to my core. I just lost my husband, and here I am, thinking of another man. True, Theo and I weren't really married, but still, I'm being ridiculous. I can't be truly attracted to Holden, can I?

He's kind, smart, incredibly good-looking, I know he's . . . well-endowed, and he's Eden's father. It's also been a very, very long time since I've looked at another man with any possibility. This is a daft idea. I'm clearly not thinking straight and not dealing well with the new status of my life—known as the hot mess.

Still, when we get to his car, I turn to him. "Are you dating her?" I ask, instantly hating myself for blurting it out.

"Who? Kate?" he asks, seeming confused.

"It just seemed like you wanted to get us away from her or . . . I don't know. I was just curious if you're dating?" I wish I could disappear like the puffs of air from the heat of our breaths.

"Absolutely not. First, I don't date doctors or nurses. Anyone in this hospital is off limits. I learned that lesson in Los Angeles. Second, she's dating George, who is a deputy here. I like George, and he is literally the doofiest guy I've ever met, so it's entertaining to watch them together. I don't go after attached people—oh, and I'm not attracted to her anyway."

"It's none of my business. I don't know what came over me just now. I'm truly sorry. I didn't mean to . . ."

"You didn't do anything wrong. I'm just telling you that you don't have to worry about being the baby mama in some strange love triangle. There's no one who will try to run you off, not that I would let them anyway, considering who you and Eden are to me."

I don't know why that comforts me, but it does. It also stirs a new layer of questions as to where I stand with him.

When he said it, I wanted to sink into him.

I force a smile. "I appreciate your honesty and kindness."

"I'll always be honest with you. I don't like secrets and lies. I've watched two of my friends almost lose their lives because of them."

"What do you mean?"

Holden looks away, and then back to me before speaking. "The last six months in this town have been hard. You met Spencer and Emmett, but you didn't meet Isaac. He was the best friend any of us ever had, and one of the best guys in general."

I find that hard to believe since Holden took Eden and me in without a single hesitation. He has been nothing but nice to a girl he barely knows and his daughter he didn't know he had.

He continues. "He was killed, which has triggered a lot of pain and sadness. Brielle was injured in the same incident, and she suffered memory loss, and . . . well, that's a story all on its own. But then Emmett almost lost his life, and Blakely was put in protective custody. It's been . . . a lot."

"And here I thought my life was fucked up."

"You are now my drama, it seems. A gorgeous girl rolls into town, three-year-old kid in tow, and . . . poof, I have a kid."

I look away, hating that for him.

"Hey," Holden says, tilting my chin back to him. "I'm not upset about it. I was honestly feeling a little left out."

At that, I roll my eyes. "I don't think this is something anyone wishes for, Holden. We don't come without baggage."

"We all have baggage. I have a past, which includes you."

"Yeah, well, you don't seem to have any flaws that I can see. You're practically perfect." Once I'm done with my rambling speech, I clasp my hand over my mouth. I am a bloody idiot. I just blurted that out in the car park where people are walking. Damn it.

"I'm far from perfect. I am a doctor who has made the wrong choices at times, and sometimes it cost a patient their life. While it was never negligent, it weighs on me. I knocked a girl up in Vegas and then passed out—that's you, by the way." I laugh. "I was married, failed at that. Jenna is a great woman, but I wasn't the man she needed. We all have flaws, Sophie, and what I'm doing now isn't heroic, it's what any man should do."

Not any man. I dated a horrible man who I ended a relationship with a few days before I went on holiday to Vegas. He never would've opened his home to me like Holden did.

"I don't agree, but I do appreciate it."

Eden bangs on the window, and then he says, "I think that's our cue. Plus, it's freezing out here."

When we get into the car, there is an awkward silence around us. I am not sure what to say at this point. My entire life feels out of control, and I am grasping for something to hang onto.

Holden drives, tapping his thumbs on the steering wheel, clearly not as much of a headcase as I am. I clear my throat. "I apologize for being a bit of a mess."

"You're not a mess, and you have nothing to apologize for. If the roles were reversed, I am pretty sure I'd be losing my mind."

"I'm quite certain I am."

"Well, if you aren't, you will be after today. We're going to Mama James now, and you're going to love her. She took care of me after my parents took off and is the only real family I have. I'll warn you, though, there will be a lot of questions, but I'll do my best to field them."

Nerves hit me. "Is she going to be cross?"

"About what?"

"Not telling you about Eden."

Holden shakes his head. "Not at all. Mama James doesn't really get mad about anything. She's truly a saint. I don't know how she came from the same family as my father and is the way she is. There's no one more kind than her. Sure, she'll have questions, but then you'll be a part of her family."

I don't know anyone like that. I grew up in a home with parents who used love as a weapon. Family wasn't a word that held any value to them. It's why I work so hard to make sure Eden knows she's loved unconditionally.

Maybe now she can have more, maybe she can have the type of family I never thought possible.

CHAPTER
Eight
HOLDEN

I'd be lying if I said I wasn't about to shit my pants bringing Sophie and Eden to my aunt's house, but lying is what I'm going to do.

The truth is, the quicker I get this over with, the better it is for all of us. Mama James will bear the gossip so Sophie and I don't have to. While the idea of using my aunt as a human shield doesn't make me feel all that masculine, I'm man enough to at least admit it . . . to myself.

We pull up, and Sophie sighs.

"It'll be fine," I tell her because I really am confident my aunt will not make Sophie the villain. It'll be me. Rightfully so.

"I feel like the story we said has disappeared. I can't remember what I'm supposed to say."

"That we met in Vegas, you were living in England, we're going to need a location that isn't London," I tell her.

"We can say Manchester. My best mate lived there, so I know the area fairly well."

I nod. "Manchester it is. You and I didn't know each other the night we . . . hooked up and had no way to reach each other." All of this is the truth so far, which is really the best angle we can play.

"And how do we explain my sudden reappearance?"

"You came back here for a work event and saw my name in a news article."

Sophie laughs a little. "That's a bit farfetched."

"More than your dying husband sent you here to find me so that I could protect you from whoever may want to harm you?" I ask with a brow raised. "Not to mention, I *was* in the paper, and Mama James has it on her fridge."

"Point taken. Okay, so I came here for work, but I'm an artist, which isn't actually a job most travel for."

"You work for a painter, aren't there curators or something?"

"Yes, that could work." Sophie nods and then starts to chew on her thumbnail. It's something I noticed she does whenever she's deep in thought.

Even a small lie feels hard when it comes to Mama James, but Sophie and Eden's safety matters more. I'll need to make sure my friends are telling the same story as well. That way, Emmett won't say something contradictory and get Mama James upset.

"Look, if it gets to be too much, just let me talk so that you don't have to lie when it comes to that part."

Before we can exit the car, there's a knock on Sophie's window.

I look over, immediately ready to fight, and see my aunt standing there with her lips turned up and head tilted to the side.

I know that look. The one that says she is aware I am up to something, and it won't fly.

"Hi, Mama James," I say, plastering on my signature smile that sometimes works. "You should be inside where it's warm, my favorite person in the world."

"Not today, Holden."

And sometimes my charm doesn't.

I glance at Sophie. "Let me explain it all, okay?"

She nods.

I get out of the car and walk over to my aunt and kiss her cheek. Before I can open Sophie or Eden's doors, Mama James starts in.

"Who is that woman and that baby who could be your sister's clone?"

"Will you let me get them out of the car so I can introduce you?" I ask.

"Yes, yes, of course," she says, stepping back and pulling her coat tight around her.

I open Sophie's door first, helping her out. When she starts to shrink into herself, I pull her beside me, placing my hand on her back. "Mama James, this is Sophie Pearson."

"Peterson," Sophie corrects.

"Sorry, Peterson. I'm a little nervous," I try to explain the slipup that I know wasn't one as I pull open the back door. "And that little girl is Eden." She's passed out in the back seat, which is probably better for everyone while I explain this.

I have the story all in my head, but one look in my aunt's hazel eyes, and I can't do it. I can't lie to her. She has been my rock through most of my life, and I have done everything to be the man she helped raise.

"Almost four years ago, I met Sophie at a club in Las Vegas. I was drunk and took advantage of her, not even bothering to get her full name or number. She went back to England, found out I'd gotten her pregnant, and we just reconnected. I'm assuming the tears in your eyes when you look at Eden mean that you know as well."

Mama James covers her mouth with her hand and then looks in the back seat. "She's your daughter."

I nod. "She is."

Then her gaze moves to Sophie, and she moves forward, pulling her into her arms. "My sweet girl, you are an angel for taking care of that baby without help. You are an amazing woman."

Yeah, she is, both of them are.

Being worried about how we were going to explain everything turned out to be pointless. What I should've been concerned about was Mama James trying to embarrass me. That is what her freaking mission is. She's shown baby pictures, brought out my report cards, notes from girls in high school, and now the insane woman is busting out my wedding album.

That's where I draw the line.

"No more," I demand evenly to Mama James. "Please, you're ruining my image."

"You don't have an image other than the one of your pants being around your ankles as you pass out," Mama James scolds.

Yeah, Sophie shared that little tidbit.

"It wasn't my ankles," I mutter. It was my knees, but whatever.

Eden comes running in, holding Pickles, the cat that will never go away and hates me. "Mummy, can we keep Pickles?"

Sophie smiles. "No, darling, that's Mama James's pet."

She clings to him, the cat purring in her arms. "I love him. Can Santa bring me a cat?"

"He looks like he loves you too," Mama James says with a grin. "You should bring him to . . ." She looks to me, confusion glinting in her eyes. I know she wants to say my name but probably doesn't know what Eden calls me.

"Holden," I finish for her. I turn to Eden. "And, no, you shouldn't bring him to me, he doesn't like boys or anyone with a soul."

Mama James scoffs. "That's not true. He loves Eden, me, Sophie, Spencer, and Emmett just fine. And I should take a spoon to you for that comment."

"Well, then he doesn't like smart men who have a soul."

That cat has been the bane of my existence since he showed up. He stalks me, coming close then backing away, toying with me and trying to keep me on my toes. Then, just as I drop my guard and assume he is going to leave me alone, he attacks. I have had more scratches from this stupid cat than I care to admit.

Afterward, he's docile and lies in Mama James's arms with a smile. I swear, the cat smiles only once he's drawn blood.

"I don't know what you did to Pickles, Holden, because he is the sweetest cat to everyone *but* you."

"Sure, I must've done something."

Sophie walks over, petting Pickles as he rests in Eden's hold. "He seems quite calm."

"He really is the most wonderful cat."

"Oh, yeah, totally sweet and wonderful . . . for a demon," I muse.

Mama James rolls her eyes. "Maybe if you were nicer."

"Maybe if he didn't try to claw my eyes out . . ."

She waves her hand at me. "Oh, stop it. He was trying to climb on you, not claw your eyes out."

Yeah, sure, we'll go with that. He waits until her back is turned before he begins his attack. Of course, his stupid angelic face gets him out of trouble.

Eden kisses the top of his head. "He's the sweetest kitty."

"He sure is . . . not."

Mama James sighs heavily. "Eden, any time you want to come cuddle Pickles, you can come here. My house is always open."

"Oh, I'm sure you're all too happy to give her a reason to visit."

She smiles. "I miss having a houseful of children."

I know she does. She was always feeding us and making sure we had cookies. Coming here was the best part of our day. After school, my friends were always trying to convince me to let them share my loot.

Mama James turns to Sophie. "How long are you planning to stay in Rose Canyon?"

"I'm not sure." Sophie's voice shakes a little.

"She can stay as long as she likes, but there's a lot we're working out."

"In order to stay, I need to get a job, but . . ."

"Well, if you need help with Eden, I am home all day, and there's nothing I'd love more than to spend some time with her."

Oh Lord. "No way are you taking her to your old-lady meetings," I jump in so Sophie doesn't have to answer.

"What is wrong with my meetings, and who are you calling old?"

"Your lot. Six old ladies meeting up to gossip under the guise of charity for children, what could go wrong?"

Mama James drops her jaw. "Holden Xavier James, you will not disparage those women. Each one is like a grandmother to you and has always supported you."

She's lost her damn mind. "Who? Barbara, who tried to get me to marry her granddaughter who is fifteen years older than I am so I could"—I make air quotes—"fix her? Or maybe Alta, who filmed me rolling through a stop sign, called the cops on me, and played it in church! And then there's Tina. She is always making lewd comments to me and pinching my butt when I pass by her too closely." That draws a giggle from Sophie. "All your friends have a few screws loose."

I don't bother to mention Marylou, who I suspect put ex-lax in her husband's milkshakes for years and then complained about his constant stomach issues, or Desiree, who slept with her husband's brother for years, and I'm not one hundred percent sure her daughter is her husband's. Yeah, they're totally the best role models for my daughter.

Mama James stares at me. "Did you run that stop sign, Holden?"

I give up. "Not the point."

"I think it is. Did Alta need to show it to the church group? No, but she runs the projector and said she put the wrong video clip on the playlist, and I happen to believe her. It's not her fault you were embarrassed by your own actions. As for Barbara, well, can you blame her? Lizzy isn't getting any younger, and you're such a good boy. You could've helped her. Tina . . . that woman is just a horn ball, and I can't speak for that." Mama James reaches for her knitting basket. "However, I am practically your mother. I would never harm that child, and you know she'd be well loved with me."

"I know that."

"So, your objections aren't valid, are they?"

Only she can scold me like this. "No, ma'am."

She nods and turns to Sophie. "I know you don't know me very well, dear. I am sort of family to you both now, and I would love if you'd come visit during the day. If you need me to watch her while you look for a position, I would be happy to help. We have a youth center in town where Brielle, who you may not have met but is a wonderful girl, works."

"She's met Brie," I explain and instantly wish I hadn't.

The fire flashes in my aunt's eyes. "She met her? She met your friends first?"

Sophie steps in. "I was looking for Holden when I arrived in town, and he happened to be with them."

That seems to mollify her. "Oh. Well, then you know Brielle is very sweet, and she could probably help you find something."

"Don't push, Mama," I warn. "If Sophie is staying in town and wants a job, then she'll reach out."

I have no idea what she's going to do. She may leave in the middle of the night, so I want to temper any expectations of her living here long term.

"Of course, I'm just offering."

"I appreciate it," Sophie says. "Eden would enjoy getting to play with Pickles, I'm sure."

Pickles looks over at me, his eyes narrowing. Yeah, joy is all he and the demon that inhabits him brings.

"All right, I need to get back to the house and get some work done," I say, ready to wrap this up before Pickles decides to attack me.

Mama James gets to her feet and helps herd us all to the door. "I expect to see you very soon, Holden. My leg hasn't been feeling too good lately. When you looked at it last, things improved, but only when you come by."

Over the last year, I've watched the vibrant woman start to deteriorate. About ten months ago, she fell and broke her leg. Thankfully, it happened when she was at one of her knitting meetings, and they were able to get her help immediately, but I worried about what would have happened had she been hurt while home alone. How long would it have been before someone noticed? I had a medical bracelet made for her as well as a monitoring system that she could use to get help. When I came back a few months ago, I noticed she wasn't going to the doctor, the limp was bad, and she had forgotten to take her heart medication for almost a week.

She's the only family I have left.

"Have you gone to physical therapy?" I ask.

"Yes, every week."

"Is it helping?"

She shrugs. "I like going. The girls there are wonderful. I just think it's better after you visit."

I smile. "I miss you too."

"Then come by, and be sure you bring Eden and Sophie as well. I have a feeling this leg will be healed in no time."

"You are a master at guilt," I tell her and then kiss her cheek.

She leans down a little. "It was very nice meeting you, Eden."

Eden twists side to side. "I like Pickles."

"Anytime you want to visit him, you can come."

"Tomorrow?" Eden asks, looking up at Sophie.

Sophie laughs. "We'll see." She turns to Mama James. "It was lovely spending time with you. Thank you for being so kind, despite what you may have thought at first."

Mama James lifts her hand to Sophie's cheek. "I thought you were wonderful, that's all. Please come by, and I meant what I said about if you need help."

Sophie meets my eyes. "I think we'll be here for a while, so I may need that help."

God, I hope so because I don't want them to leave.

CHAPTER
Nine

SOPHIE

"Let loose, Sophie. You're so uptight! You're finally done with Edward . . . you need to live a little," my flat mate, Joanne, says as she hands me a drink.

"I'm not like you, Jo!" I yell over the music.

"I know. So, try it. It's fun."

"I don't even know what to do," I admit.

"See that guy?" She points to a tall man with dark hair and broad shoulders. "Go kiss him."

That's not going to happen. "Jo!"

"What? It's what I would do."

I huff. "You know that won't happen."

She smiles and sways her hips. "Fine, then chug your drink."

That's a much better option than kissing some random man in a club. I lift my glass in a sign of cheers and then let the liquid flow down my throat.

Jo screams and then laughs. "Who is going to buy my mate a drink?"

A few guys raise their hand, and one dashes off to the bar. Jo seems to relish in the attention while everyone laughs and has a good time, but I stand back a bit. I always do. Theo always gives me shit for it, claiming that I'm a wallflower and if this were the Regency era, I would die a spinster. Thankfully, it's not a hundred years ago, and I am able to be shy without it destroying my life.

Still, I envy Jo. She doesn't care what people think. She lives out loud and is unafraid of what her parents or society think. I would give anything to let my walls down, just once, and be bold. To do something reckless and be completely free, but I never will. It's just not who I am. Although after the discussion with my mother before we came here, it's rather appealing to break some rules for once.

"Here you go, gorgeous," the tall man who went to the bar says, handing me my drink.

"Oh, thank you."

I don't really want to drink this since I didn't see the bartender make it. Theo was adamant that I at least be smart. I smile, place the drink to my lips, and pretend to taste it.

Jo, who has been watching the whole exchange, reaches for the drink. "You don't drink that." She takes it from me, and it sloshes all over. "Fuck!" Her laughter grows as she's wiping it off her arm. "I'm a sloppy drunk. And I just wasted your time. I'm sorry about that."

"No worries," he replies, but the tight set of his jaw says he's annoyed that he just spent way too much money on a drink that ended up all over the floor.

Jo wraps her arm around me, her lips against my ear. "No way were you drinking that. I don't trust any of these men."

I smile, loving that my friend protected me in a very *her* way. "I don't want to get wasted."

She scoffs. "Too bad, darling." Jo grabs the man beside her and says, "You get to buy me and my friend here a shot. If you're very nice about it, I might just dance with you."

He goes along with her flirty demand and buys us both two shots. We quickly take them, and the alcohol from earlier mixes with it, causing my head to spin. I'm not drunk, but I am feeling a little loose.

Jo kisses my cheek. "I'll be back. I'm going to dance with him."

I nod, order myself another drink, and then stand with my back to the bar. I slowly sip the vodka and coke before walking toward the dance floor, watching her dance without a care in the world. The music is loud, the bass pumping in a sexy rhythm that has me moving my hips a bit.

A warm body presses against me from behind. The cologne is musky and strong, burning my nose a little. "Do you want to dance?"

I turn and come face-to-face with the man who bought me the

drink that Jo spilled. He towers over me, and I can't quite explain it, but I don't feel right. My gut is screaming at me to get away from him.

"You scared me." Forcing a smile, I step back, but he tugs me against him, causing my free hand to fly to his chest.

"You okay there?" he asks, as though I were falling or something. "Did you trip?"

I push against his chest a little. "Yes, I'm fine. Thank you for catching me."

Instead of releasing me, he pushes more. "I thought you wanted to dance?"

"I'd rather not, thank you, though."

"Come on, it's the least you can do."

I keep myself calm, knowing my options are limited, and I need to think. If I can get him onto the dance floor, I can get to Jo. "One dance?" I ask, wanting confirmation.

"For one drink." His attempt at being cute isn't working.

"All right."

We walk out to the area where I last saw Jo, but I don't see her as I start to dance. We move to the music, his hand never leaving my back as he moves us back and forth. I keep glancing around, trying to see her. Then he turns me slowly, moving our bodies so his leg is between mine. I shift away a bit because my skirt is short, and I really don't need it pushing up.

Once again, he moves his leg into the same spot, this time putting his other hand on my thigh, sliding it up toward my ass.

I shove him back, pulling my skirt down and moving away. "Please don't do that."

He moves closer, a sly smile on his lips as I retreat, only to trip back into someone dancing behind me. I fully anticipate ending up sprawled out on the drink-slick floor, but then there are arms around me, and I'm back on my feet, staring into the most stunning brown eyes I've ever seen.

"Hello," I say and then want to mentally slap myself.

The man glances toward the prat I was dancing with and then back to me. "Are you okay?"

I shake my head. "He won't leave me alone."

He nods and then grins, wrapping his arm around me. "Hey, thanks for dancing with my girlfriend. I was running late."

"Excuse me?" the guy asks, his eyes going to me and then to my savior.

I place my hand on his chest and head on his shoulder. "This is my boyfriend."

"I bought you a drink." The vein in his forehead starts to bulge.

My fake boyfriend reaches into his pocket and pulls out a twenty. "I appreciate that. Here, no hard feelings."

The guy takes the twenty, scoffs, and leaves. For the first time, I exhale without fear building in my chest.

"Thank you," I say, stepping back.

"Of course. What's your name?"

"Sophie," I say with a smile.

"Nice to meet you, Sophie. He was being a creep?"

I nod. "Very much."

"Well, I am happy I saw some of it and stepped in."

I lean in so I don't have to yell as much. "Me too. We should dance," I say, shocking myself.

He grins. "For appearance's sake?"

"And because I owe you that much."

The man extends his hand toward the middle of the dance floor. I take it, wrapping our fingers together and pretending like a rush of warmth doesn't flood my body.

I can't remember the last time I felt this. I don't know that I ever have.

When we get to an open space, he smiles. "I'm Holden, by the way."

"It's nice to meet you."

"Let's turn your night around, Sophie, and make it one you never forget."

I wake up, feeling a bit flustered after the dream. It's been so long since I thought of that night. So long since I remembered the way Holden made me feel. I went from being so afraid of someone to feeling safer than I ever had, which is a testament to how nutty I am.

Eden is beside me, her face relaxed in blissful slumber. The clock reads two in the morning, and while I should try to go back to sleep, I'm wide awake and a bit confused.

I rummage through my bag on the side of the bed and grab my diary. It always helps me assemble my thoughts, and heaven knows I need to do that. Once I find it, I walk over to the chair in the corner and turn the lamp on.

With my pen poised above the paper, I start to write.

Dear Diary,

It's been over a week since I've had the time, or maybe more the desire, to do this, but I need to get out my feelings more than ever.

I have lost Theo. He died, and not only did I lose him but also everything else. My home, my friends (not that I had many), my country, my name, and job. I miss him. I want to walk into his study and tell him about Eden hanging upside down again and have him help me come up with ideas to stop her. I want to hug him, explain my grief over everything happening, and I can't.

Instead, I am here at two in the morning, writing to you.

My only friend in this world.

Although, that's not quite true. In losing Theo, I have gained Holden.

Theo forced me to go because Eden and I are in danger. From what? I don't know, but I'm in Rose Canyon to start new. I am angry because of this. He should've told me when he discovered Holden's identity. He owed me that much. Instead, he kept it and revealed it when I cannot seek answers as to how or why he lied. None of it makes sense. My heart is literally torn in pieces. How can I love Theo, trust him, know him as well as I know myself and, yet, not know him at all? I am so angry at him for lying and dying and leaving.

I am also confused about Holden. He is the last man to have ever touched me. He and I share a child, and while we don't know each other, I feel safe with him.

I'm starting to question my sanity. That's really the heart of it.

It makes no sense to trust him. We met one night in passing that resulted in our child.

I can't even think about the fact that I am attracted to him because it feels wrong. I shouldn't feel this way, right? I know my marriage wasn't sexual, but I loved Theo.

None of this makes sense, but I dreamt of the night we met and remembered his touch, so maybe it's the loneliness. Maybe it's the fact that I never thought I would want a man again—or, at least, if I wanted one, I wouldn't have the option to have him. But now I might want someone, but I'm a widow and shouldn't want to be with anyone. There is no reason that I can't be with someone, aside from the danger I know nothing of but could be hunting me nonetheless.

CHAPTER

Ten

SOPHIE

"Mummy, can we see Daddy?" Eden asks as I am getting her dressed.

I don't know how to tell her this. I have been struggling so much over what to tell her about Theo's death or how to do it. She loved him so much, and there was no one in the world he loved more than her. She never got to say goodbye. She never will have some of the rituals that help with grief.

But it's time.

I won't lie to her any longer.

I take both her wrists in my hands, getting low so we're eye level. "Eden, do you remember how Daddy and I told you that he was sick?"

She nods. "He's at the hospital."

"He was. He was very sick, darling. His heart was weak and tired."

"Is he sleeping?" she asks innocently.

"Not quite, Daddy has gone to Heaven to be with Granny," I tell her. Eden wasn't old enough to understand my mother passing away, but we spoke of her being in Heaven often enough.

"Will he come back?"

I move my hands to hers. "No, he can't, but we can talk to him at night or in our prayers."

Her long lashes open and close as she ponders this. "Can I give him a hug?"

Pushing back my tears, I force a smile. "You can always send a hug to anyone you miss, do you know how?"

She shakes her head rapidly.

"You place your arms like this." Holding her wrists, I wrap her arms around her chest. "Close your eyes." She does. "And you think really hard about who you wish was here and squeeze as tight as you can."

Eden hugs herself, and I close my eyes, doing the same, wishing it were Theo hugging me back. He gave the best hugs. The way his warmth wrapped around me made me think that nothing could harm me as long as he was near.

"Mummy, do you think he felt it?"

I open my eyes, looking into my daughter's brown ones, wide and full of hope. "Yes, my sweet girl, I think he felt it."

She wraps her arms around my neck, holding me tight, and I let a tear fall as I hold on to what's left of my world.

There's a knock, and I turn to see Holden leaning against the frame. "I didn't want to interrupt."

I wipe my cheek. "You aren't . . ."

"Holden!"

"Hi, bug."

"My daddy is in Heaven with my gran."

He squats down. "I bet he's met my sister Kira too."

Her eyes widen. "You have a sister in Heaven?"

"I do."

"Do you give her hugs?" Eden asks innocently.

Holden wraps his arms around his chest the way I just did, closes his eyes, and squeezes. "I just did, and I asked her to go find your dad to check on him."

Eden lunges forward, hugging him around the neck. Holden chuckles, catching her, and tightens his arms around her.

She squirms after a second and turns to me. "Can I play with my toys?"

"Sure."

Before we can say another word, she darts off into the living room, which has become Eden's wonderland.

I sit on the edge of the bed. "She likes you."

"I'm glad."

I laugh once. "Yes, but I mean she truly likes you. The two of you have already bonded, and it's lovely to see."

"She is easy to bond with."

I look up at him. "Yes, she is."

"Are you okay?" he asks with concern laced in his voice.

"No, but it was time to tell her the truth."

He gives a sad smile and sits beside me on the bed. "I don't know that there's ever a right time to tell a kid their father is gone."

No, there's not, and I have a feeling Eden's questions won't end after telling her this once. "There are many hard conversations ahead of us, aren't there?"

Like when I talk to her about Holden's place in her life.

He reaches his hand out, covering mine. "I'm in no rush, Sophie. Whatever is best for Eden is what's best for all of us. Do I want her to know that I'm her father? Of course. Do I think now is the right time? No. She had a dad, and she lost him. That's hard enough. I think we take this one day at a time and go from there. Besides, it'll happen over time. We don't have to even address it."

Holden James is a wonderful man. He makes me feel as though everything just might be okay.

"And if it's weeks or months? How do we explain this to people?"

"We don't owe anyone an explanation. I think you'll be amazed at how Mama James works. She's one of the wonders in this world with gossip. She'll put the rumors to bed, and we'll go on telling our story the way we want."

"Your aunt is honestly a lovely woman."

"She is. She's why I moved back to Rose Canyon this year."

"You mean you weren't always here?" I ask.

"No, I was a big shot doctor in L.A. and loved it there. Really fucking loved it there. The weather is a million times better than this, but it doesn't have Mama James. I came home for a visit maybe once a year until Emmett called and said she fell and broke her leg. I rushed up here, got her settled, and the last visit, when Isaac died, I noticed some things that concerned me."

"Like what?"

He sighs. "She wasn't going to the doctor, and I worried it was her memory, but she remembers every damn thing. It's her heart, though. She had issues when she was younger, which she had a successful surgery on, but the walls are weakened and her cardiologist said her blood pressure needs to come down. It was enough for me to come back and be close to keep an eye on her."

"Are you truly this perfect?" I ask. "I have heard of men like you, but they always seemed like a myth."

"I am not perfect." Holden gets to his feet and moves around the room. "She's my only family, and she deserves not to be alone. I do what I think is right."

That right there solidifies what I thought. How does he not see it? It's rare that anyone would give up their career for anything, let alone come care for an elderly relative, yet he did.

Without thinking, I get to my feet and stand in front of him. "I spent the last four years wondering about the man who I made a child with. I'd fantasized about you, dreamt of the kind of person I hoped you were. Now I know, and I can't quite believe you're real."

Holden's lip pulls up. "You're making me sound heroic when I'm not."

"To her you are. I believe that heroes are selfless. They risk for others, regardless of the cost to themselves. Is that not what you did when you gave up your life in California?"

When you welcomed Eden and me into your home without hesitation?

He shifts his weight, and it's clear this is making him uncomfortable. While I don't know all the sordid details of his past, I don't need to in order to see the good in him. The way he's given Eden and me whatever we needed and not even thought twice about it is all I need. That's the mark of a hero.

That's the mark of a man that I've prayed for.

"Let's not talk about this. I came in because I have a surprise for you."

"For me?" I ask, feeling a little uncomfortable.

"Come on." He extends his hand, and I place mine there. We walk toward the back of the house, and he pushes a door open.

The room that was his office is now completely redone. It has a large bed with a nightstand beside it. There is a lovely chest of drawers and sheer curtains on both sets of windows.

"This is lovely," I tell him.

"You both need your own space, and we can redo the room Eden's sleeping in to be a little more appropriate for her now that you have this room."

I walk around the space, feeling so much gratitude that it is overwhelming. "You really didn't have to do this."

"I did. I want this to be your home, Sophie. Both of you should feel comfortable here."

"We are, and . . . thank you." Without thinking, I wrap my arms around his neck and hug him.

He hugs me back, and I feel his lips at my temple. "This makes it all worth it. Welcome home, Sophie."

Dear Diary,

Today is the first day I haven't cried. The first time I didn't lay in bed, hating my husband, wishing he were alive so I could kill him myself. Today is hard because of that. Hard because I feel so much, but not all of it is anger and grief. Holden cleared out the back room for me, set up a proper bedroom, and called it my home. I was so overwhelmed and happy.

Happy that I found somewhere, someone who is selfless and willing to give without hesitation. He doesn't ask anything from me, and he gives in acts of kindness as well as truths that I didn't have before.

I'm grappling with my emotions.

How can I feel even a little happy about the fact that, even though Theo is gone, I have Holden in my life?

It's crazy. It's wrong. All of it makes me feel an immense amount of guilt. I should not be happy. Full stop. I should be miserable at all times. I shouldn't be happy when Holden smiles at me. I shouldn't feel flutters in my belly when I catch him looking at me. His handsomeness definitely shouldn't be on my mind.

Yet, it is.

I know that, in a way, it's understandable, right? I am a woman with needs. I have neglected them by telling myself there are more important things for me to focus on. I was fine with what I had. Friendship is acceptable to many women, and more than my parents ever had.

And just because I look at Holden this way, doesn't mean I'm doing anything wrong.

At least, that's what I have to tell myself because it doesn't feel understandable. It feels like betrayal to Theo.

Which I can't reconcile.

Each time I say how wrong it is, I follow it up in my head with how Theo really wasn't my husband. We never made love. We never had that intimacy of sharing a bed. We were a fucking Regency romance novel with separate bedrooms. No, we weren't even that because, at least in the novels, he would visit my bedroom. My door never opened.

Not unless it was Eden coming to wake me.

Still, I feel loyal to him. I have no idea if he ever was with another woman, which maybe I should've asked, but it didn't matter to me. So, why do I feel it matters to him?

I tap my pen on the paper, pondering my maelstrom of emotions around this.

Then, as I start to write, there's a loud knock on the door.

I freeze, looking up without lifting my head. Holden is at work, and it's our first day being here completely alone. Eden is napping, and since I've been here, no one has just stopped by.

I'm not sure what to do. Do I open it? What if it's the person I'm supposed to be running from, and they've found me? Nerves start to build, and I consider my options of escape.

I could go out the back, but if there are multiple people, that might not be the best idea.

Then, I hear another knock, which is followed by a voice. "Goat tacos."

Jackson.

I rush to the door, feeling relief that it's not someone looking to harm me. I still peek through the hole to make sure it's him before I open the door.

He smiles. "Good to see you, Sophie."

"I'm glad it's you."

"Don't worry, I've been watching, and like I said, we have people here keeping an eye on things."

Yes, but it's not that simple not to worry.

"I haven't seen anyone."

"You're not supposed to."

"Is Zach still around?"

"No, he went back, you have one new guy and Miles is still here, they're both completely capable."

Still, it would've been good to get some kind of signal so I knew he was around.

"What are you doing here?" I ask, remembering how he said he couldn't visit because he knew people here.

"I was able to use my friends in town as a way to come check in. How are you doing?"

"I don't really have an answer for that. I'm assuming you know why I am at this home and that I was meant to find Holden?"

He nods. "Theo informed me of Holden's connection to Eden. It's part of why he wanted you here more than anywhere else. What better place to send someone than to a man who has every reason to protect her? It's what I would've done in his shoes."

"Yes, instead of being honest and allowing me the opportunity to do it on my own, how very noble."

Jackson snorts. "I didn't say nobility had a role in this."

"So, you came to check on me?"

"Partially. I came to see Spencer and Emmett to discuss the trial they're testifying in, and then I also have something for you."

"What could you have for me?" I ask.

He extracts a letter from his breast pocket and then hands it to me. "This is from Theo."

I am getting rather annoyed with all of this. If Theo had so much to say, he could've bloody well said it when he was alive. Now he's dead, and I'm getting a message from him? I put it down on the table and huff.

"Not happy about the letter?"

"Would you be? He knew the identity of Eden's father. He was involved in something that required me to move quite literally around the world and take a new name. I don't have any connection to my friends or the people we knew for years. I am living in someone's house I don't even know without a single idea as to what I'm supposed to be doing now. Do I live and get a job as this new version of Sophie Pearson?"

"That's the thing, you're Sophie Peterson. You get to decide that."

"Well, I liked being Sophie Pearson. I liked my life, my home, my work. I liked it all, so Theo can take his letters to the grave he buried us all in."

After the words are spoken, I hate myself for them. I am just so angry at it all. If he had talked to me before, I could've made plans with him. So much of this wouldn't be as confusing as it is. We could've gone beforehand, together, and I could've been at his side.

Jackson looks at the letter. "You knew Theo better than anyone, Sophie. He wasn't cruel, was he?"

"No, not cruel."

"Then read the letter. Your and Eden's safety was all he cared about. It was never meant to hurt you, and I think this may be what he felt was the only way to protect you."

As angry as I am, I could never ignore it, and I bet Theo knew that too. "Why did I get this now? Why not the day he died?"

Jackson grins. "I was told to get this to you exactly seven days after his death. I didn't trust anyone but myself to ensure it was delivered."

He turns to leave, but I call his name. "Will I see you again?"

"Yes. And remember that you're safe here. You can choose what you want to do, whether it's to stay and build a life here or leave. Theo didn't give instructions beyond that we were to protect you and give you information as you might need it. If you want to leave Rose Canyon and go anywhere else in America, we'll facilitate it."

"But not London?"

"No, Sophie, you can never return there."

So, I am somehow safe in America? I had to come to Rose Canyon, but I don't have to stay? If he were still alive, I'd throttle him.

"I don't understand any of this. You know that, right?"

Jackson chuckles. "It's clear as mud."

The door opens behind me, and I turn to see Eden waking from her nap. She will never keep a secret if she sees Jackson. She took to him immediately, and I go to block her view, but before I can take two steps, I hear a *click* and turn to say something, but he's gone.

Disappeared into thin air.

That's a brilliant trick.

"Mummy!" Eden yells and comes toward me, arms wide.

"Hello, my love."

I scoop her up and kiss her cheeks. "Did you have a good nap?"

"I got to ride a pony in my dream."

"That's wonderful."

"Is Holden here?"

Another man that seems to have made an impression on her. She wakes up before me each day, careful to get out of the room without stirring me, and has breakfast with him. This morning, they had pancakes and bacon. Bacon is always included.

I gave her a bit more time before I came out, wanting her to have a chance to know her father.

"He's not home yet, but he should be back any minute now."

"Can I colour?"

"Of course."

She's gone within a moment, off to the area in the living room where Holden put a few colouring books he purchased and a few dolls. Each day, there ends up being another thing for her in the home.

When I hear a car door slam, I walk to the window, and sure enough, Holden is walking up the steps.

He smiles when he sees me, and I wave a little, a flutter stirring in my chest.

I wish the man weren't so damn handsome.

That smile is what I remember most. When we danced, his eyes never left mine, and throughout that night, he was always happy. It didn't matter how little I remembered the next day, I could never get that grin out of my mind.

I grab the note that is sitting on the table, shove it in my back pocket, and stand there, waiting. When he walks in, the energy in the room shifts. "Hey," he says, dropping a backpack but keeping his hold on a shopping bag.

"How was your shift?"

"Exhausting, but . . . I'll be fine. How was your day?"

"It was . . . good. I feel like I'm settling in well."

Holden's face brightens. "Do you think you'll settle a little more?"

Do I want to stay here and make friends? At this moment, I have nowhere else to go, but I do have Holden, who has missed three years of Eden's life. It wouldn't be fair for me to take her away now that he just found her.

It wouldn't be fair to Eden either, who has lost so much.

I give Holden a soft smile. "We probably should since we'll be staying in town for a while."

When his eyes brighten, I know I'm making the right choice.

CHAPTER
Eleven

SOPHIE

I am so nervous. I know it's just lunch, but it feels incredibly strange. I am going out on my own today for the first time since I arrived in town. But . . . baby steps. When Brielle and Blakely asked me to go to lunch with them, Holden was insistent that he and Eden would have a grand time at Mama James's and that I should accept the invitation.

I get to the door, exhale deeply, and enter.

Brie spots me right away and waves. I smile and head to her and Blakely. "Hello."

"Hey! I'm so glad you could meet us. I had the day off, and I like to pry Blakely out of the office once a week to eat a meal instead of trying to solve the world's issues on an empty stomach. We've been doing our lunches for a few months now."

I take a seat and laugh softly. "I'm sure she appreciates your care."

"I don't," Blakely says without pause.

"She's kidding. She does. She's just frustrated because she has a meeting with the attorney after lunch. Ignore her."

"Oh? Is everything all right?" I ask.

Blakely sighs heavily. "It will be. I was involved in a stupid case a few months ago, and the trial begins in like three or four months. The prosecutor just wants to meet with me again to go over my story and make sure everything is accurate, and I'm prepared to testify."

My interest is piqued. "What is the trial about?"

Blake and Brie share a look before Brielle begins. "It's a long story, but a few months ago, my brother was killed. I was the only eye witness, but I suffered a head injury that left me with partial memory loss. It was horrible, and . . . we ended up hiring a private security team to help us because my husband is friends with the owner. In the midst of uncovering everything, I stumbled into some crazy stuff. Spencer and I worked to uncover my memories, which led to me finding out I had been engaged to Spencer and no one knew. Blah, blah, long story there. Anyway, after we thought we had figured out who killed Isaac and it was all behind us, Blakely came to Rose Canyon and unveiled a whole other underground trafficking ring that had ties to people here."

"Emmett was almost killed, I was kidnapped, and we caught the asshole," Blakely finishes. "Now it's time to make sure he can never harm another girl."

My eyes must be saucers as I try to absorb that information. Theo sent me here to be safe, and now I'm finding out about this? Jesus Christ, how the hell is this better than being in London? Still, I find the only words I'm capable of speaking. "That's . . . terrible. I don't even know what to say, quite honestly. I'm a little terrified to be here now."

"I promise you, this town is incredibly boring, and I'm not really sure how the hell we ended up with any of this happening, but it's fine because he'll be in jail the rest of his life," Brie says. "Anyway, I grew up in this town, and the most exciting thing that happened was when we won the regional championship. It's truly that lame here."

Clearly not. "I'm not sure a trafficking ring and a murder are lame."

Blakely's hand moves to cover mine. "It's really all Brielle's fault. If we can get rid of her, the trouble might disappear."

Brie slaps her arm playfully. "Bitch. I am not the drama. Am I? Oh, God, am I?"

"You're absolutely the drama."

"Really? Because I feel like you're way more dramatic than I am." Brie smirks and then turns to me. "She's totally more dramatic."

I smile. "I feel as though I am the drama now."

"You totally are," Blake says with a wink. "But we apparently thrive on it, so welcome."

"Thank you."

The waitress takes our order, and then a portly man walks over.

He's short and has a mustache that loops a bit at the end. "Hello, girls."

"Hello, Mayor Stengel," Brie says first. "I didn't see you when we came in."

He rests his hands on the back of both their chairs. "I just got here. It's lovely to see you both, and who is this?"

"This is our friend Sophie. She's a friend of Holden's," Blake explains.

"Ahh, I've heard wonderful things about you from my wife. It seems Mrs. James is quite fond of you as well. Welcome to Rose Canyon, I'm Mayor Stengel."

I nod. "It's nice to meet you as well."

"And you're from England?"

"Yes, I am."

"Wonderful. You'll have to bring some culture to this town. A few years ago, we tried to do a festival of cuisine from around the world, but it ended up being a barbeque with the same food as always," he explains.

"I don't know what culture I could bring, but I will endeavor to do what I can."

"I like you already." He chuckles. "Have a nice lunch, ladies."

I wave as he walks off, heading to another group, who all greet him enthusiastically. Blakely sighs heavily. "I know I have zero reasons to dislike him, and yet, here I am, plotting his demise . . ."

Brielle shakes her head. "Blakely and the mayor had a rough start, but he is a nice man who loves this town more than anyone I know."

"Then why don't you like him?" I ask Blake.

"When I got into town, I was so sure he was involved in the case I was working. Every instinct I had was telling me it was him, and then I found out it wasn't. His son is sketchy too." She glances toward the mayor and then back to me. "I think part of it is my own need to be right, so I keep searching for something that makes me not feel completely inept."

Theo was that way. He needed to be right more than anything else, and it drove me mad when we fought. He couldn't just admit he was wrong, and he'd somehow invent something to prove his point, even though we all knew he was reaching.

I think of the letter sitting in my bag that I can't bring myself to read yet.

It's equal parts fear that it says something I need to know that I'd rather not, or it's filled with rubbish.

My world feels as though it's gone topsy-turvy, and I can't find my bearings. If he adds more to it, I will never be all right again. And I really need to be all right.

Brielle rests her hand on my wrist. "Are you okay?" I must've spaced out. "Sorry about that. I was daydreaming, it seems."

"About anything in particular?"

I shrug. "Not really."

"Did you have any more thoughts on what your plans are?" Blake asks.

"I'd like to stay here for a while. Eden adores Holden already, and I would love for them to have a relationship."

Brie gives me a warm smile. "I'm glad you feel that way. We'd love to be Eden's aunties and your friend too."

It's crazy to me that by losing the only family I had left I gained a completely new one.

"I would love that."

"Good." Blake smiles. "So, if you're staying here, what are your plans?"

"I'd really like to find a way to work with painting that's flexible. Brielle"—I turn my attention to her—"do you think the place you work would hire me? I can teach all kinds of different techniques from basic skills to more advanced. I have a degree in art history as well as education. I would love to put it to use."

"Absolutely! We don't pay very well, but it's rewarding in other ways."

Money is something I absolutely need to worry about, but I'm sure I can make do with what little I was given and whatever I can make from working.

"I understand, and anything is better than where I am currently."

"Good! I'll talk to my boss tomorrow, and I'll call you or Holden to let you know what she says."

A plan is good. A plan to stay in Rose Canyon is definitely not what I thought, but for the first time since Theo's death, I am excited at the possibilities of where my life may go.

CHAPTER
Twelve
HOLDEN

Today has been a horrible fucking day. The only bright spot is coming home to Eden and Sophie.

Already I'm thinking of the house and them being my home.

I'll unpack that shit at a later date.

When I park the car, I sigh heavily, my head falling against the headrest. I lost a twenty-one-year-old patient, she coded, and no matter what I tried, I couldn't get her back. She just . . . died, and I'll have to wait for an autopsy to find out more. After I dealt with that situation, I got a call from Seattle that has screwed with my head even more.

I thought we were done with this. It's been weeks of silence regarding missing girls or Jane Does showing up, and I . . . should've known better than to forget this world is a shithole. This time it's not Portland, but close enough that I got the call.

So, tonight, on what should've been a fun poker night with the guys while the girls nagged us, I have to discuss this new tidbit of information.

No point wallowing out here, though. I grab my bag and head inside where Sophie and Eden are curled up on the sofa, reading a book.

All the frustration, anger, and stress of the day disappears.

Eden's head turns. "Holden!"

She climbs out of her mother's arms and comes rushing toward me. I scoop her up, clutching her to me. One day, she'll do that yelling Daddy. I don't know when, but I can't wait for it. I love this kid with my whole heart. In one instant, my entire life changed. No longer is it about work and the other bullshit in my life—it's about her.

This little girl who owns me.

And her mother who, God help me, I want as well.

Sophie stands, a smile on her perfect lips. "Hey, how was work?"

"Horrible, but it's over." I grin as I tuck Eden more securely in my arms. "And what did you do today?"

"We went and played with Pickles, and Mummy went to run an errand."

"You saw that mean cat?" I ask, also wondering where Sophie went.

"He's sweet!"

"He's not."

Eden giggles, resting her head on my shoulder. "I love him."

"Well, someone has to love rotten things."

Sophie shakes her head. "I went to the youth center to meet with Jenna, who . . ."

Fuck. "Is my ex-wife."

"Yes, that was very interesting." Sophie lifts one brow.

When I mentioned I had an ex-wife, I probably should've elaborated that she lives in town and is the director of the youth center.

"Was she nice to you?"

Jenna isn't mean. That's one of the things I hate about her. Whenever we "fought," which was really more like bickering, she was always so level-headed. Not that I wanted to be slapped or anything quite so dramatic, but she never *fought*. For anything. Including us.

"She was, actually. I was gobsmacked when she told me who she was, but she welcomed me to town and wanted to hear about my painting and what I could do for the youth center if I were to work there."

"Good. So, did you get the job?"

Sophie beams. "I think so. I explained our situation and that I needed to ensure Eden was cared for. She offered to let me bring her to stay in the nursery as well."

All of it sounds great, and from the way Sophie looks, it's clear she's happy. "See, it's all working out."

"I miss painting," she says softly. "I miss it, and the idea of touching a brush to canvas has my heart lifting."

The happier she is here, the more likely it'll be that she stays. "Then I can't wait for you to do it again."

Sophie takes a step back, biting her lower lip. "Holden, I'd like to talk to you about something."

It's clear she's nervous, and now I am as well, but I tamp it down and focus on letting her tell me what it is before I jump to conclusions.

"Sure."

"You know I want to stay here, not just because I think you're wonderful, but also because you deserve to be with Eden . . ."

"I'm going to go back to part two, but you think I'm wonderful?"

She laughs. "Maybe I exaggerated that part a bit."

"We'll go with wonderful, but go on, what's on your mind?"

"As you know, I don't have any access to my funds, and I was told not to touch it even if I could. I'm assuming whoever Theo has me hiding from is watching our accounts, so I was hoping we could stay with you. Just until I get a job and make enough that we could move out. All I have is a bit of cash, and I don't know how long it'll tide me over."

I take her hand like I've wanted to since I saw her. "You don't have to move out. If you want to work and save your money so you're not trapped, do that, but don't leave. Stay with me. My house is paid for, there aren't any bills I can't manage, and . . . I like you both being here."

Big risk to say all that, but here it is. Coming home from the hospital and them being here is truly amazing. I have never felt so at ease. Plus, I want to soak up as much time as I can with Eden.

"You're sure?"

"Positive."

"Thank you!" Her smile is wide, and she leans over and kisses my cheek. "It won't be a lot of money, but it's a step, and it's not too much time away from Eden."

"I think it's great. Now, I have a favor to ask you . . ."

"Yes. Whatever it is, I'll do it."

I raise a brow and smirk. "Anything?"

"You would not be asking for those favors."

She's right. I would never. Still, it's fun to tease her. "No, but tonight is poker night, and I would like you and Eden to come with me."

"I'd love to go!"

"Good. I'll go shower, and we'll head over."

"Sophie! You came!" Blakely says, pushing right past me and going to her. She loops her arm in Sophie's and guides her inside without even acknowledging me. "Come in, it's freezing out."

"Nice to see you too, Blake."

"I see you all the time, Holden, and most days I'd rather not."

Emmett comes around the corner and grins. "Seems you're not the favorite anymore."

"I'm not sure I ever was."

He chuckles. "You were never mine."

I flip him off. "I hope you have something stronger than beer for tonight. We're going to need it."

"Are we waiting for Spencer, or are you going to clue me in why we have to talk? Is it about Sophie or Eden? Like, maybe you took a DNA test—"

I lift my hand, cutting him off. "Eden is mine without a test."

"Holden . . ."

"No, listen. I don't need a test to tell me what I already know. Mama James said the same thing when she saw her. She knew, just like I did. As I said to Sophie, had she come to me right after, I wouldn't have questioned it. While I absolutely hate how it all happened and that I've missed three years of her life, a DNA test doesn't change what I see when I look at Eden. I'm done talking about this, and I'll take it as an insult if you say otherwise."

"All right. I won't bring it up again," Emmett assures me. "So, if it's not about the girls, is it about the dead husband?"

I wish I knew something about that, but I don't. No matter how hard I try to figure out if there is something about them that I'm not seeing, the only thing that stands out is my medical license number. It is almost as if the person who sent them wanted to remind me that I am, in fact, a doctor. So, I requested Theo's medical records.

Now I just wait to get it and see how many hoops I'll have to jump through in order to obtain it.

"No, but I got a call from a doctor in the Seattle area. He wanted to discuss a patient he has—a young girl with a lot of similarities to Keeley and the other girls. Apparently, he was in Portland when Keeley showed up in the morgue and is friends with the ME there. She was admitted to the hospital two weeks ago, and she's alive, but barely. He thinks it's tied to the Wilkinson case based on the similarities. He was aware of my involvement and reached out."

Emmett's jaw tightens. "That's not possible. Ryan Wilkinson is in jail awaiting trial."

"And you think his organization folded because one person was arrested?" I challenge.

It's been quiet since Ryan was arrested, and while I hoped it would stay that way, we all knew it wouldn't. He threatened that there would be more, if not girls, then trouble with someone who is pissed. He'd made it clear that he wasn't working alone, so until the police figure out who else is involved, there will be more.

"Of course not, and we have the FBI involved and looking into it. Blake was in contact with someone from her old team, and they told her they found a connection to someone in Texas."

"That's good, and we haven't gotten anything from Wilkinson on the girls who were already in Portland?"

Emmett rolls the scotch in his glass, sighing heavily. "Nothing."

Before I can say anything else, Spencer walks out. "Look at this sad bunch of idiots."

"And look who completes the picture," I toss back.

"True. Very true." Spencer pours himself a drink then takes a seat next to us. "Why does it look like one of you is going to wreck my evening?"

"Another doctor I've worked with called me about a girl who might be linked to the case. Young, pretty, injected with all kinds of drugs, and found without any identifying information. She's in a coma, so we can't get answers from her yet."

Spencer's head falls back. "You know, the three of us don't have to save the world. We can let the police there handle it."

Emmett laughs. "My wife sure thinks we do, and if there's a connection, I am the police and can help."

"Your wife also thinks you are a catch."

I raise my glass and smirk. "We all know the truth on that one."

Emmett ignores us. "So, you want to just ignore it, Spencer?"

"Of course not. I just would like to enjoy our lives for once. I'd like to have time to actually heal from the hell we've endured. Brielle may look like she's normal again, but she's struggling. She jumps at loud noises and still has trouble sleeping. Anytime I say Isaac's name, it's as if the air deflates from her."

"It hasn't been that long," I remind him. "From a medical standpoint, she's still in the trauma of what happened. That first year isn't easy."

Spencer glances at his wife and then to me. "I know, and she's seeing Kate now, which is part of what has me not losing my damn mind over it all. She goes weekly, and it's starting to help a little."

I nod. "Kate's a great doctor. Incredibly smart and in tune with her patients."

Emmett shakes his head. "She's also dating George."

Ahh, George, our deputy who truly baffles all of us. He's a nice guy, which is probably what Kate sees in him, but he's awkward and often finds himself in the strangest situations. The two of them are truly the most unlikely pair.

"Mama James loves George," I remind them. She thinks he is perfect.

"Mama James loves all things that are in need of fixing. It's why she loves you so damn much," Spencer jokes.

"And you."

"Touché. But she really loves Emmett, so let's focus on that."

"Or we can focus on what has Holden all tied up in knots," Emmett suggests.

"I'm not tied up in anything."

"Oh?" Emmett asks. "We've kept our mouths shut since Sophie got here, but time's up. You can't tell me that having the one-night stand you had in Vegas show up with a kid in tow doesn't have you fucked in the head."

No, I'm not. I'm . . . well, I don't know. I actually try really hard not to think about it or wonder if I'm going to wake up and they'll be gone. So much of it doesn't make sense, and it irritates me that Sophie's husband knew who and where I was and still robbed me of being a part of Eden's life. I would've been there, loved her, been . . . well, everything a father should be.

"I'm more worried about Sophie than anything."

Spencer's smug grin appears over the rim of his glass. "Worried about the fact that you have feelings for her or her safety?"

"Her safety."

"So, you do have feelings for her?" he counters.

I walked into that one. "I obviously care about her. She's the mother of my child."

"And she's beautiful," Emmett adds in.

That instantly pisses me off. "You're married, aren't you?"

"Doesn't mean I don't have eyes, asshole. Sophie's gorgeous and seems really nice. Blakely likes her . . ."

Spencer nods. "Brie too. She said lunch with the girls was great, and she is really happy about her working at the youth center. Mama James also stopped me yesterday to talk about how much she loves Eden and how Brielle should get Sophie a job."

I swear, my aunt is the most meddling human I know. "That woman is determined to keep her here."

Emmett laughs. "Did you expect anything different?"

I glance through the sliding glass door and see Sophie laughing with the girls. Eden is at the table, eating something I'm sure she shouldn't, but Sophie looks so natural and at ease. As though these girls have been her friends for a lifetime instead of a handful of weeks.

"Things don't add up with the messages and what she's said. I can't protect her if I don't know the truth."

"What makes you think she's lying?" Emmett asks.

That question rolls around inside my head. "It's just the timing of it all. The letters, the packages, then she shows up, completely unaware of whatever her husband is hiding her from. When Jenna and I were married, she couldn't fart without me knowing it."

Spencer snorts. "Holden, you were married when you were twenty. You and Jenna didn't have secrets, and you didn't have a life. You have no idea what their home was like."

I fill them in on what little I do know about her life back in London, including how Sophie and Theo may have been married, but they were never intimate.

"Wait, so the last time that poor girl had sex was in a club with a guy who can't remember?" Spencer asks with a smirk.

"She said it wasn't bad."

"Glowing endorsement." Emmett lifts his glass, clanking it against Spencer's. I really hate my freaking friends.

"My point is that they were friends. Look at us, we have the same type of friendship she had with him, and we tell each other everything," I remind them.

The two of them share a conspiratorial look.

And then I remember my two best friends are lying dickheads.

"Right. Well, what I should've said was that I tell you fuckers everything, and you're both assholes who lie."

Spencer reaches out, gripping my shoulder. "I wanted to tell you about Brielle, but she and I didn't want to put anyone in a weird position with Isaac."

"I didn't ever plan to say shit to either of you, so . . . there's that," Emmett says unapologetically.

One lied about being engaged and the other about being married. Now I understand why they chose to keep their relationships a secret, but when I found out, I was pissed. We've been friends since grade school, and it really felt like a slap in the face.

If Isaac were alive, he'd have kicked both their asses, and I would've helped.

"You both are shitty friends."

Spencer shakes his head. "No, we're all just trying to figure our shit out. People keep secrets for a reason, and I think Sophie is the same."

"Do you think her story has holes in it?"

"Oh, I definitely think there are holes. I think she has secrets, and I don't think they're small either. However, she doesn't know you or trust you—yet."

Emmett speaks before I can say anything. "The other option is that she is telling you the truth and her husband lied to her. In that case, she's dealing with coming to terms with that too."

"If her husband really didn't tell her about you, there was a reason, and maybe she really doesn't know what it is," Spencer finishes. "We can debate this for days, but Sophie seems to be staying, which will give her some time to open up to you. In the meantime, we can see about Jackson's company looking into Sophie's husband and what he might have been involved in."

I hadn't even thought about that. As much as I hate the prying into her life, it would really help if we knew what her husband had gotten mixed up with. "Tell him to be discreet, not that he wouldn't, but we don't need anyone asking questions and alerting them to where

Sophie might be. I just need to know what he was involved in that would cause his wife to have to flee."

"She might be involved and is playing games with you."

"I don't think she is. We've talked about her life back in England, and she seemed to be happy."

Spencer rubs his chin. "None of this adds up. If he was good with money and knew there was a possibility this was going to happen, why not set her up with a really good exit strategy? Why not make sure she had money, a place to live, and her own security? It's what I would do if it were Brielle."

"Unfortunately for us, he's dead, so we can't get those answers." As much as I'd like to because Spencer is right. If my wife had to disappear, I would make sure she wasn't left to the mercy of others.

Unless that was the point. That she must rely on my kindness and stay here.

Emmett lets out a long sigh. "Well, Jackson was here not long ago, and I have to call him this week anyway. I can mention it and see if he'll help us out."

"Why was he in town?" I ask, wondering if it has anything to do with the girl who turned up in the Pacific Northwest.

"To, once again, try to persuade me to come consult with them."

My eyes widen at that. "What?"

"Yeah, he's considering opening a branch up here and asked if I'd be interested in working for him. I don't know."

"You'd be perfect for it," Spencer says. "You ran a military unit, you have the combat experience, you know the area, and I'm pretty sure you'd make a fuckton more money than you are now. Plus, if what Holden thinks is true and that girl in Seattle has something to do with Portland, it would give you a lot of tools at your disposal."

Emmett runs his hand through his hair. "I need to think it all through. In the meantime, I'll see if Jackson will look into that girl in Seattle."

My eyes find her again, blonde hair up high on her head, blue eyes sparkling as she smiles at Brie and Blakely. I want this. I want her to come to dinners and raise our daughter here. I want what my two best friends have—a family. I will protect them, but in order to do that, we have to know the truth about what she's hiding from.

"And see what he can find out about Theo," I add on, not taking my eyes from her. "I need to know what I'm up against."

CHAPTER
Thirteen

SOPHIE

"Mummy, I had an accident," Eden says with tears in her eyes.

This is the third time this week that she's had an accident, and it breaks my heart to see her so upset. I worry that she's struggling to adjust to all the sudden changes in her life, but bedwetting has always been something Eden struggled with. Plus, she's been drinking a lot of water, so that probably isn't helping. "It's okay, darling, let's go clean it up."

She wipes at her cheeks, and we head into the bathroom. I clean her up as best I can and change her clothes. "Eden, did you wait too long?"

"No, Mummy, I didn't even feel it."

"All right." I'm not sure what to say to that.

"Can I have a drink? I'm thirsty."

I smile and nod. "Of course, just a little since it's close to bedtime."

Grabbing the bag of soiled clothes, I walk out, holding her hand. Blakely is outside the door. "Is she okay?"

"Yes, just a little accident."

She smiles down at Eden. "You know, I have some ice cream in the back where all the boys are. Would you like to go get some?"

Eden's eyes brighten instantly. "Can we?"

Blakely extends her hand to her. "Come on. Let's go annoy the men."

My daughter doesn't even look back as she runs off with Blake. All her life, she's been in a very small circle—me, Theo, Martin, and a few friends. She had some friends at school, but we never had them over, and she never went to their houses either.

We just never quite fit in, which never bothered me since I didn't like half the people I knew anyway. They were so dodgy and boring. I didn't want to go shopping for nonsense or drink at noon and complain about my husband. I loved Theo.

Seeing her circle widen makes me hope for a different life now.

One sort of like what I see here. Friends having dinner on a random Thursday and telling funny stories.

"Hey, everything okay?" Holden asks as he enters the kitchen.

"Everything is great."

He glances over at Eden. "Did she spill something? I see she changed."

I blink, surprised he noticed. "She had an accident. It's been happening more often since we got here, so I had a change of clothes with me."

"Has she always done it?"

"Just a few times she wet the bed at night, but nothing more than normal kid stuff."

Holden smiles softly. "I'm sure this is an adjustment period for her. The time change, new people, the loss of her father . . ."

"We'll get through it, right?"

He takes my hand and squeezes it. "We will."

Before I can even open my mouth, he releases me, but I swear I can still feel his warmth against my skin.

Holden clears his throat. "You ready to head home?"

Home, what a novel word.

"Ready when you are."

"Perfect, let's head back home, I have a long day at the hospital tomorrow."

We find Eden on the back porch, eating ice cream with Blake and Emmett. Spencer and Brielle are curled up on the couch, holding hands and having a conversation without words. It's so intimate that I have to look away.

Once Eden finishes her treat, we return to the house. I give Eden a bath, get her tucked in, and walk quietly to my room. It's then that I sit on the edge of my bed, staring at the letter Jackson dropped off weeks ago.

I want to read it, but I am afraid of whatever is inside.

There's a knock at my door, and I shove the letter under my pillow before I softly call out, "Yes?"

Holden opens the door. "Did she get to sleep okay?"

I nod. "She was tired after tonight."

"My friends adore her."

"They are really wonderful with her. Everyone has been."

"Good. Are you heading to the youth center in the morning?"

"Yes," I say, feeling a bit nervous. "I haven't had a job in a long time. I'm excited to get to paint again, though."

Holden walks toward the bed, stopping at the end and looking a bit hesitant. "Sophie, what was your last name when we met?"

The question stuns me a little. I'm not sure what to say. "I don't know if I can tell you."

"I believe you changed your name when you came here, you slipped up once," he tells me honestly.

"I did."

"I just wonder, if I'd asked you your last name the night we met, what would it have been?"

Had I told him my whole name back in Vegas when we'd met, he'd know what it was anyway, so I don't see the harm in telling him now.

"Sophie Armstrong. That was my maiden name."

"Thank you for telling me."

"Honestly, there's not much you don't know at this point."

"And anything you do tell me, I would never share."

I believe him. Holden has every reason in the world to keep our secrets—Eden.

Holden walks over to me, crouching low. "I care about you both, and . . . as much as I hate how it happened, I'm happy you're here."

Cupping his face in my hand, I smile. "I feel the same. I wish it had been different, but at the same time, I don't. Finding you and getting to spend this time together has meant a lot to me. You've been a wonderful friend and have allowed Eden and me to settle in quite nicely here."

His lip quirks up into a grin. "Good." He pauses before saying, "I should go."

I nod, yet neither of us moves. There's a shift in the air that's filled with longing and tension. Him being in my room with my hand still cupping his cheek has suddenly become very intimate.

I wish I were braver and could kiss him. I wish I were the woman he met in Las Vegas who took what she wanted, but I am not that girl.

I look into his brown eyes, wishing I could read his thoughts and praying he can't see mine.

Holden clears his throat and rises, my hand falling away. "Good night, Sophie."

I watch him retreat to the door. "Good night, Holden."

He doesn't stop, and when I hear the door click, I lie back on my pillow, hearing the crunch of the letter. Pulling it out, I stare at my name written in Theo's familiar scrawl. I may not be brave enough to kiss Holden, but I am definitely able to read this. I sit up and move my finger under the seal, trying to imagine when Theo wrote it and wishing he had just talked to me instead.

I carefully open it, pulling out the linen paper with the flourished P printed up top. I had this paper made for him when he closed his first deal. I smile at the memory because he had been so proud that he'd gotten his company off the ground without his father's help.

His messy script fills the page, and I take two deep breaths and start to read.

My Dearest Sophie,

Goat Tacos are served daily in Heaven, just in case you didn't know.

Forgiveness is also in abundance here—at least, that's my hope because I know I need a lot of it. More than anything, I need it from you.

If you have this letter, then you've met the team of people who will do what I cannot since I am dead—protect you and Eden. I am going to assume that you followed the directions and are where I hoped you'd be. If you didn't, then you wouldn't have this letter, and I would be speaking to no one.

Since we are working on assumptions, then it's most likely that you've cried, told me to fuck off, and spent no short amount of time angry, but I hope you will allow me this explanation and not destroy this letter before you've finished. I have reasons, and they are:

I am a selfish ass.

A prick.

A fucking bastard.

And a coward.

I am selfish because I didn't tell you and waited until I was dying before putting this plan into motion. Selfish because I wanted just a little more time with you and Eden.

I'm a prick for those same reasons above.

A bastard because I tried a million times to be honest and failed every time.

And a coward for not having the strength to talk to you about this. I was afraid if I told you any of this before that you'd leave, and I wouldn't have the only thing in this world I truly needed, you and Eden. I was also afraid if I told you, you'd be in worse danger than you are now, my love.

As you have likely already assumed, I was an idiot and trusted the wrong people. I allowed my desire to be rich and better than my father overshadow what was right.

Of course, I didn't know that until it was far too late to get out. My only options were to continue and not let them know what I discovered as I made plans to protect you both once I was dead, or go to them and quite possibly be killed. I chose the first option. The one thing that is keeping you safe is that you know nothing. So, I will not tell you what or who or why. All I will tell you is that you can trust no one from our past. No one without the password, Sophie.

I invested in the wrong people, and it is a choice I will regret long passed my last breath.

You must start over in America because, as long as you are there, you're safe. You must never return to England, and you must do whatever you can to move on.

I'm not even gone, and I miss you, Fee. I hope you can forgive me and know that everything I have done was to protect you.

Love,

Theo

Oh, Theo . . . what in the world did you get into?

CHAPTER
Fourteen
HOLDEN

Sophie is working late at the youth center tonight, and instead of going to hang out with Emmett or Spencer like I normally would've done, I'm getting my nails painted as snow falls outside.

"You're sure this color looks good on me?" I ask Eden, eyeing the polish that's smeared up to my knuckle.

"Uh-huh. It's very pretty."

I smile. "It's something."

"Next I have to put it on your lips!"

"Nail polish on the lips?" I may not have a very extensive knowledge of makeup, but I know that is definitely not how it works.

"It will be so pretty," she assures me.

I don't think it will be, but I'm not going to be the guy to break her heart. "How about I paint your nails after," I suggest.

How hard could it be? I am a doctor, I've operated on people with precision cuts, I can handle some paint.

Oh, how wrong I am.

As soon as I start, Eden starts to tell me a story, which requires her hands, and she doesn't care if her polish is wet or if I'm in the middle of painting a nail.

"And then I went on the airplane, and I was so tired, but Mummy was sad. She was crying." She grabs my face with her polish-covered fingers. "Holden! Do you cry?"

"Everyone cries sometimes," I tell her.

She sighs heavily. "I don't like to cry."

"Why not?"

"Because my nose runs."

Solid logic. I look out the window, finding that the snow is coming down harder now. I grab my phone and call Sophie.

"Are you on your way home?"

"Yes, Dad, we're on our way," Brielle answers instead of Sophie. I roll my eyes. "No one asked you."

"I'm driving Sophie home since you didn't offer to come get her." I'm going to kill her. "I did offer, and she told me no."

"Your chivalry is dead."

"You're going to be if you keep giving me crap."

"Enough, children," Sophie chides. "I'll be home soon. Is Eden okay?"

"She's great. She painted my nails, face, and parts of the floor."

The two of them laugh. "Perfect. I'll see you soon."

"Drive careful, Brie."

"I will." She huffs and then disconnects.

I do my best not to act like a nervous idiot, but I can't help it. I clean up the polish the best I can, which requires a lot of scrubbing because I have no idea if we have remover anywhere. I really didn't think this through when I said it was fine to do it.

Thirty minutes later, Sophie comes through the door, shivering and brushing snow from her jacket.

"It's getting quite treacherous out there. I am worried about Brielle, but she refused to stay."

That girl has no sense of self-preservation. "Is she still out there?"

"No, she left before you could come bully her."

I sigh and grab my phone to call Spencer. "Hey, your wife is an idiot. She is driving home from my house now."

"What the hell was she doing at your house?"

"Driving Sophie home, and before you start, she drove off before I could tell her to stay the night."

"All right. Thanks for letting me know, I'll spank her when she gets home."

I gag. "Dude, she's still little Brielle to me."

"And that's what makes it even more fun."

I hang up, not wanting to hear anything more, and Sophie is grinning at me. "You have nail polish on your neck."

"I won't be surprised if I find it in my nose."

She chuckles, and Eden comes running out of her room. "Mummy! Did you see the snow?"

"I did. Once it stops, maybe we can play in it for a bit. I brought home gloves and a snow suit from the youth center."

This snow storm came without much warning, and I didn't have time to go get snow gear, so I'm glad she was able to find some.

"Yay! I want to build a big snowman," Eden says with bright eyes. "Can we?"

Sophie nods. "Absolutely, darling."

"Bug, why don't you let your mum in the house so she can warm up?"

"Okay! I get more makeup!"

Anything but that. I watch her as she runs into her room and closes the door with a giggle. Sometimes, I look at her, and my heart aches. I don't know how I lived in a world without her, and I pray I never know anything but this.

Over the last few months, we've settled into a comfortable rhythm. We work, Sophie stays late two nights a week, and I get one-on-one time with Eden. During the day, Mama James watches her, falling deeper and deeper in love with her as well.

And my feelings for Sophie keep changing too. We are friends, but there's this underlying sexual tension that I am slowly losing my ability to ignore.

"Would you like tea?" I ask her, clearing my throat and the thoughts of how I'd like to warm her snow-kissed lips with mine.

"That would be lovely. I'm going to change and check on Eden."

She heads into Eden's room first, but then comes out seconds later with a smile. "She's already asleep."

"Already?" I ask.

"You must've worn her down. Did you only paint nails?"

"We read a few books, watched a show, and she supervised making dinner and cleaning up. She ate everything and had some juice. Overall, it was a normal night together."

Sophie shrugs. "Whatever it was, it wore her out."

"Mission accomplished then. I'll be in the living room if you want to watch a movie still."

"Give me about ten minutes."

She heads off, and I go in the living room, searching through the list of possible movies to watch. There's the typical girly crap, but I haven't had to endure one of those since my ex-wife. We could go superhero or thriller, but I have no idea if she likes those.

I'm saved when she emerges in a pair of cotton shorts and a sweater that hangs off her shoulder. Her blonde hair is piled up on top of her head, and she's wearing her glasses. The sexy-girl-next-door look is in full effect.

"Did you find something to watch?"

Yes, your incredible legs. "I was waiting for you."

She smiles, pushing her glasses up the bridge of her nose and grabbing her tea. "I like just about anything."

I like you. I like your legs. I'd like to kiss you until you can't fucking breathe.

Dear God. How the hell am I going to get through this without embarrassing myself?

"How about a mystery then? There are a few new ones that are kind of suspenseful," I suggest.

Shoving down the ever-growing desire, I smile and pray she takes the other couch.

However, nothing seems to be going my way, and she sits next to me, tucking her legs underneath. "Wonderful. I love suspense."

I get up, needing to stop myself from staring at her bare legs, flip the fireplace on, and grab the blanket off the back of the chair for her.

Covered. She needs to be covered.

I drape the blanket over her, and she looks at me with confusion.

"I figured you might get cold. The temps keep dropping."

As do my brain cells because my blood is in another part of my anatomy.

"Thank you."

This is different for us. Usually, we go into our respective rooms after Eden goes to bed. Our days are busy with my shifts being insane and her hours always changing, so we're both worn out by the time dinner is cleaned up. However, we both have off the next few days, and since we'll be snowed in, I thought maybe this would be a good idea.

I was wrong.

I'm a goddamn idiot.

After searching for anything that will involve guns and chaos, I find one and press play. Sophie settles deeper into the couch, and I probably look ridiculous because I'm keeping way more distance between us than would be normal. If I stay away from her, I won't want to touch her.

"Have you seen this before?" she asks after a jump scare startles her.

"No, you?"

She shakes her head. "You just don't seem fazed."

It's because I'm not focusing on the movie. I couldn't tell you a damn thing that's going on. But I can tell you how her breathing has been or how she's moved her legs thirteen times under that blanket. I can tell you how many times she's taken a sip of her tea, licked her lips, and shivered.

"I guess I just expect what's coming," I lie.

She laughs softly. "I wish I could. Are you cold?"

The question surprises me. "Cold?"

She lifts the blanket and then scoots toward me. "You keep shivering a bit. Here, I can share."

What the hell do I say to that? I'm not cold, in fact, I'm over-fuck-ing-heating. Between the fireplace and my blood simmering for her, I'm shocked I'm not openly sweating, and I don't know what I can do to calm down. I am debating running outside and tossing myself in a snow drift.

Sophie tucks us both under the blanket, and I open my arm to allow her to snuggle against my side. Honestly, it would have been ridiculous if I hadn't.

Without pause, she moves next to me, resting her head on my chest. "Thank you."

"For what?"

She doesn't say anything for a moment and then speaks. "All of it. The only reason I've made it through these last few months is because of you."

"I haven't done much."

She sits up, hand on my chest. "Not done much? Are you mad? You've done everything. Not only given us a place to live but also made it a home. Eden adores you, and you're wonderful with her. All of this could've gone differently, but you've given us everything. Most of all, you've given us safety."

Jesus, I want to kiss her. That's the only thing I keep hearing in my head—the goading chant, urging me to do something dumb.

Kiss her, kiss her, kiss her.

I lift my hand, brushing the soft skin of her cheek with my knuckle. "I'm not so selfless, Sophie."

Her eyes widen, and desire swims in the pools of blue. "I think you are."

"I want you both here. I want to keep you safe, but I also don't want you to leave."

She wraps her slender fingers around my wrist, but she doesn't pull my hand down. She just freezes us here.

"That's not selfish."

"What I'm thinking right now isn't selfless, I can promise you that."

Her breath hitches. "And what are you thinking?"

I am so afraid to scare her. She's been through a lot, but I am aching for her. "How beautiful you are."

"You think I'm beautiful?" she asks as though she can't quite believe it.

"You know I do."

"I think you're very handsome," Sophie confesses, and I swear I light up inside. One stupid compliment, and I can't think straight. Not that I could before, but I don't see how that's relevant. "I look at your lines, how the light moves around you, and would love to paint you one day if you'd be open."

"Nude?" I tease. Well, I'm sort of teasing.

Her cheeks turn pink. "If that's what you really want."

I chuckle, pulling her tighter. "Watch the movie, Sophie, before I do something really stupid."

Like kiss her, touch her, and warm her everywhere.

CHAPTER

Fifteen

SOPHIE

A comfortable heat surrounds me, and there are faint crackles in the background. I'm so cozy, I never want to get up.

"Sophie, love."

I twist deeper into the delicious heat. "Mmm."

A low laugh reverberates through me. "Wake up, sleepy girl."

"No," I mumble, wrapping my arm tighter around Holden.

"You missed the movie."

"Don't. Care."

His arm tightens, and my eyes snap open. Holden. I'm asleep on Holden. I sit up quickly, slightly disorientated and embarrassed. Fuck. "I fell asleep."

"You did."

"On you."

"Well, sort of."

Sort of. I was lying on his chest. I remember the beat of his heart and the way his steady breathing lulled me into a dreamy state. The glow of the fire and the warmth of his body made my eyelids grow heavy. Damn it.

"I'm sorry."

"For what?" Holden asks with his head tilted.

"For . . ." What am I sorry for? Cuddling with him? Falling asleep when we were supposed to be watching a movie? Wishing we were in a bed so I could really be comfortable with him?

All of those are things to be sorry for, but I'm not quite sure which one to go with. I know that last one definitely will not be repeated. "Not watching the movie."

Holden shrugs. "You didn't miss much. The movie was pretty fucking lame."

"Then maybe it's a good thing I fell asleep." I offer him a smile.

The truth is that I barely sleep. Every noise wakes me, making me wonder if someone is in the house. I'm always on edge, waiting for something or someone to pop out of the dark. Feeling safe for a bit allowed me to finally relax.

"Listen, anytime you need me to be your pillow, I'm here."

"I appreciate the offer." Although, it's a dangerous one to accept. I could become too comfortable and forget that this life could unravel at any point. I don't know what or who or why I had to run away. I have nothing other than a letter that tells me no information and a hope that coming here was enough to keep us safe.

But, with Holden, I want more than just a half existence, and with each day that passes, we become more of a family than anything else.

I cook some nights, then he does, and we both care for Eden. He has taken to his role of parenting quite splendidly. He adores her, and she thinks he's perfect, which I find myself agreeing with.

I stare out the window at the falling snow, blanketing the ground in an untouched sheet. While I am not a fan of the cold, I do love the snow. There is something magical about snowfall, how it repaints the earth in brightness. It's freshness that hints at a new beginning just on the horizon.

Could I have that?

I want it. I would stay here, in this warmth, with this man who has given us a new start. The past is covered and forgotten by the newness that he offers.

It's right here in front of me, but I am so afraid to grab it.

"Hey, where is your mind?" Holden asks, adjusting the blanket around me.

"In a fantasy," I admit.

"Was it a good one?"

I smile, letting out a short laugh. "It could've been if it were possible."

Holden takes my chin between his thumb and pointer, gently nudging me to look at him. "I've dreamed of things I never thought

KEEP THIS PROMISE - SPECIAL EDITION 119

were possible, and sometimes they do come true. You may think it's a fantasy, but that doesn't mean it can't become reality, Sophie. Dreaming is how we have hope for a better future."

"And if that future is still terrifying because, while I may want it, I don't know that it's right?"

He must know I'm speaking of us.

Please tell me you want the same and that we'll find a way.

No, that's daft. I don't want that. I need him to be the strong one, damn it.

"None of us really know if something is ever right, we just have to have faith."

And that's where I am struggling.

I yawn, and Holden chuckles. "Come on, you need to get some sleep."

I get to my feet, fold the blanket, and wait as he gets himself up. We walk down the hallway to our rooms. I'm not sure if I should say something or, if I did, that I could keep from kissing him.

When we get to my door, he speaks first. "I have an early shift Friday, but I was hoping after, maybe you'd let Mama James hang with Eden so we could go grab something to eat and talk?"

"Like a . . ."

God, that sounds as if he's asking me on a date, which would be crazy because it's so soon. I'm not ready for that. But maybe I'm being forward by thinking that. What if it's not a date, and he wants to talk to me about parental rights?

We would have to figure out something because I can't even dispute things. Holden's name isn't on the new birth certificate.

"Like a dinner," he finishes before my panic really sets in. "Nothing more than two friends having dinner to talk about life."

"All right." I'm sure he can hear the hesitation in my voice.

"Sophie, I promise, it's nothing. I just would like for us to hang out and get to know each other more. Eden loves going to Mama James's house, and we know she's safe there. I'll even have Emmett put a patrol car on her block if you want to have another layer of comfort."

"Do you mean that?" I ask.

"The patrol thing? Yeah. Also, I have a friend who does private security that'll be in town this weekend, I can see if he can do me a solid."

I keep my voice even so that I don't just end up telling him that there's already security keeping an eye on us and say, "That's really sweet. Are you sure?"

"I'll ask Emmett and Spencer to talk to Jackson. If he can't, I'll get it taken care of."

Jackson? Jackson is his friend? I didn't think it was Holden that he knew, but now it makes sense. He didn't want Holden to see him at his house when he brought Theo's letter and, a while back, Blakely had mentioned Emmett hiring private security. I'm so stupid. I didn't even put two and two together.

Is anything in my life really what it seems?

Then I look at Holden. Who has been open, and I like him. My past is my past, and I would rather look forward.

"Then I would love to have dinner with you."

I head in my room, smiling like a total dork, and try to force myself to sleep.

Hours later, I am still wide awake, so I grab my diary and pen.

Dear Diary,

It has been just over three months since I arrived in Rose Canyon. Three months of settling into a life I didn't know I was meant to have.

Once again, I'm faced with this feeling that I can't understand but is equal parts happiness and sadness. Not because I left England because, with that, I am at peace. I miss some things, but what kept me there was Theo, and he's gone.

When I painted today, I thought of him. I remembered him coming into my studio, making fun of whatever I had done, and the two of us laughing at his silliness. He always could make me laugh, but he has also hurt me deeply.

And my life I had is gone. I want more than that. I want . . . love and a life.

Holden makes me feel alive in a way that Theo never could. I'm a woman when I'm near him. A woman who very much wants a man.

We have friendship, but there's something simmering—more like boiling —a passion that is going to spill over. I am not sure how much longer I can resist it or if I even want to.

It's more the fear of what Theo might have done or been involved in. I will never forget the day he died and the way he sent me away. How he pleaded with me to go and leave him to keep us safe.

Safe from what?

That is something I still don't know. What if none of this is real? What if Theo created this elaborate scheme to get me here because he knew I would never have the strength to find Holden on my own? There have been no threats. No one new has suddenly appeared in town. But I didn't imagine what happened in the airport, so I worry that, if I let my guard down, that will be the moment something happens. All of these questions circle the drain in my head.

That is what I don't want to bring into Holden's life, which is irrational since I already have by just being here.

Still, I am lying in bed as the clock keeps ticking, thinking about how it was to be held by him. How I wanted so badly to wrap my arms around his neck and kiss him. To properly have a night together because he's what I dream of.

"So, you have a date?" Blakely asks as we have our weekly coffee at the shop.

"It's not a date. It's dinner with the bloke I eat dinner with every night."

It's starting to feel more like a date the closer we get to it, especially since the girls seem convinced it is one.

"Whatever you say, Sophie." Brielle smirks.

"Don't start. You both have told me your love stories, and I am not impressed by either of your decision-making processes."

They grin and sip their coffee. Blake puts her cup down first. "Listen, you can call it what you want, but don't lie and tell me that you're living with Holden, and you don't feel anything more than friendship."

Brie nudges her. "She might. She did it with Theo. Maybe it *is* just friendship."

It's not. I never longed for Theo like I do Holden.

They both watch me, and I just shrug.

"What does that mean, Sophie?" Blake asks.

"It means a lot of things. I like him more than a friend, yes, but we all know my life isn't uncomplicated. How would that be fair to him?"

"Holden is a big boy, he can handle himself," Brie says. "And he really likes you."

"And how do you know this?"

"Because I have known Holden James since I was five years old and, trust me, this is a date."

I groan. "I don't want to lose what we have."

"I've been there, sister." Blakely's voice is full of understanding. "Emmett was my best friend, I loved him, and I walked away for what I thought was his own good. It's never really that, though. If you were honest with yourself, which isn't a trait I possessed until recently, it's because you're scared. Not for them, but for you."

I am not lying to anyone about why I am afraid. I know exactly why I'm terrified to let my heart in, and it's really two-sided. "I'm not going to let my past hurt him."

Brie reaches her hand out. "Let me ask you this, what if your past never comes? Are you just going to live with this cloud over your head and never be happy?"

"I am happy. I'm working, raising Eden with her father, and have friends. What more could I need?" I counter.

Blake sighs. "You know that's not what she meant."

"No, but this week, I'd like to talk about anything other than this dinner."

Brie sits back, hands in the air. "Fair enough."

Thankfully, we end up talking about Spencer's writing and Emmett's trial, which begins in a few weeks. It's crazy how close to death he, Brielle, and Blakley came.

"I just want it over, you know?" Blake says almost absently.

"It will be soon. Then we can all move on," Brie reassures her.

She nods. "I love my work, I really do, but there are times when it's incredibly hard to see these girls. Some are broken, so high they can't see straight, or end up as Jane Does. I just want to help them the best way I can."

"And you are. Both you and Addison have done amazing work already," Brielle assures her.

"Addison, like your sister-in-law?" I have heard mention of her a few times, but they kind of dance around the topic. None of them say much, but there is a sort of collective sadness.

"Yes," Brie answers with a smile. "Well, she was more than that, really, but when Isaac was killed, she couldn't handle being here. Her family all left the area, and she's over on the East Coast now. There was so much . . . uncertainty after the murder that it was better for her to leave. I just had always hoped she'd come back."

"I'm so sorry. I imagine it's hard to have her gone."

Her shoulders rise and fall. "It's fine. She's really happy in Pennsylvania. She handles the East Coast Run to Me office, which has given her a really great sense of purpose as well as a solid excuse for her to stay in Sugarloaf. Everything else aside, her being there is helping her heal."

Blakely smiles at me. "Sort of like you are being here."

Each day being here I feel as though I'm healing and finding my place, the one where I was always meant to be.

"I never thought of it that way," I admit.

"Well, it's clear as day since you're happy—and going on a date."

We all laugh, and I don't correct them because a part of me really wants that.

CHAPTER
Sixteen

HOLDEN

I t's two in the morning, and I can't sleep. All I keep thinking about is this not-date-date we're going on and how much I want to kiss her. When we put Eden to bed tonight, there was this moment where I thought that maybe it was going to happen, but she pulled away.

So, here I am, wound up and irritated. No use laying here and driving myself crazy. Tossing my legs over the side of the bed, I get up and head out to the kitchen. Maybe a glass of milk and cookies will do the job. Those, a bag of chips, and some gummy bears might get me through the night.

I realize this makes me sound like a teenager, but I am who I am.

I tiptoe, careful not to wake Sophie or Eden, but when I turn the corner in the kitchen, I walk straight into someone.

The gasp is loud, and then cold liquid is dripping down my bare chest. On instinct, I reach out to grab Sophie before she can fall to the ground.

"I got you," I say as her hands grab my shoulders.

Once she's steady, I release her and glance at my chest and then at her.

We are both covered in juice.

"I'm so sorry." She grabs the dish rag and starts wiping my chest off. "Eden had another accident, so I cleaned her up, got her to bed, and came in here to get a drink because I couldn't sleep . . ." Her other hand rests over my heart, and her touch, that warmth from her fingers, causes other parts of me to awaken.

I grab her wrist, pulling her hand away so she stops touching me. I'm losing my mind with her hands on my skin. "Is Eden okay?"

"She's fine. She must've drunk too much before bed."

"Good, I'm sorry about the mess. I shouldn't have snuck up on you."

"I should've put a light on."

We're here, in the dark, where I can't see her, but I can sense her. All of her. I can hear her soft breaths, smell her delicate rose and sandalwood perfume, and feel the heat of her body still close to mine, and I want to kiss her.

I want to pull her close and taste her lips.

I release her wrist, afraid that if I keep that connection, I won't stop myself.

But when I do, Sophie brings her hand back up to my chest. The only sounds are the two of us breathing a little louder than before.

"Maybe it's better to stay in the dark," Sophie says softly.

"Why is that?"

"No one can see what we do."

"That's not true, gorgeous. There is nothing in the dark that can avoid the light forever. What you do there doesn't stay hidden just because you can't see it."

I feel her breath on my chin and imagine those blue eyes searching mine.

"We happened in the dark . . ."

When her fingers slide up slightly, I can't stop myself from touching her. My hand is on her back, tugging her closer. Sophie comes willingly, and as much as I want to kiss her—and I want it so fucking bad—I know that if I do, I'll somehow screw up any chance I have with her.

She has to kiss me. She has to be ready and able to trust because I don't want her to ever feel shame over us or what we did.

So, instead of doing the one thing I want, I place my other hand on her back and move slightly.

"Dance with me, Sophie."

Her forehead touches my chest, and we sway a little. "Dancing in the dark is what got us in trouble."

I chuckle against her ear. "I think it was the bathroom, love. I don't remember dancing then, but I'll always remember tonight. When you spilled juice on me and then danced with me barefoot in the puddle."

I feel her head move side to side. "Holden?"

"Yes?"

She pauses, and my heartbeat quickens as her finger moves as if she's tracing something against my skin. "I like you."

"That's good," I say with a soft laugh.

"I like you more than I feel like I should."

I like her a hell of a lot more than I should, but I don't say it. Instead, I turn us a little and rub my thumb along her spine. "I don't think there's such a thing."

Her soft sigh fills the room. "I'm not ready to like you that way."

She has been through hell, and I don't doubt that she's scared, but I would burn the world down before I hurt her. The feelings Sophie has, I share as well.

I like the way she smiles.

I love her voice and the way she gets animated when telling me a story about her life. When I'm at work, I count down the minutes until I can get back.

She gave me more in the last few months than I ever thought possible. She gave me a daughter, but even if Eden didn't exist, I would gravitate to Sophie.

Her warmth radiates off her, and I crave it.

"Then we'll dance until you're ready."

"Can you order another bag of IV fluids for the patient in room six?" I ask my head nurse, Trina.

Since that day in my office, she's been much nicer to me. "Of course, Dr. James."

I give her a wink, and she heads over to the nurses' station while I make my way to the coffee area. It wouldn't matter if this were actual sludge, I'd still drink it right about now.

I pour it into a mug, take a gulp, and choke it down because I'm pretty sure it is just that—sludge.

There is about twenty minutes left in my shift, and while it's been a pretty slow day, it always seems to pick up right before you're ready to leave. Tonight, I need that not to happen.

I have a sorta date.

"Hey, Holden, how's it going?" Kate asks, picking up the coffee carafe, flinching, and putting it back onto the warmer.

Lifting my cup, I give her a smile. "It's going."

"You're drinking that crap? I'd rather fall asleep on the floor than drink the coffee at the patient station."

"It's caffeine, and I don't have time to run to the cafeteria."

She laughs. "Well, we do what we must."

"How is that case going that had you stumped?"

Kate puts her tablet on the ledge and sighs. "You know, I struggle the most with the girls in that age range. They're always a bit funny about telling the whole story. She had a lot of bruises, which is why I was hoping you would order the full body scan."

"To check for what?"

"I think she is being abused. I'd like to see if she has any healed fractures or current damage even. She mentioned being with several other girls, and when I asked her to elaborate, she mentioned an ambulance. I don't know, it raised my red flags, and when I mentioned it to George, he told me to follow my gut, which leads me to you."

The Wilkinson case. I'm sure Emmett told George about it.

"Which one?" I ask in case I'm wrong.

"The one with the guy who killed your best friend and almost killed the other . . ."

I like Kate, but the circle on the details is really small. Until I talk to Emmett, I'm not overly comfortable sharing what I know. Although, if her boyfriend is telling her stuff, she probably knows more than I do.

"Honestly, I don't know anything, but I'm happy to order the full body scan. We can check for previous injuries. Have a full tox screen and blood workup been ordered?"

She thumbs through the tablet for a second before saying, "It looks like this is it."

I take it and scan through the results. White blood cell counts are elevated, but that could be anything. Then I look at her toxicology report, she has some traces of opioids, which according to her history, were prescribed. "I'm not seeing anything alarming here. What makes you think she's linked to a case?"

Kate lets out a long breath through her nose. "Sometimes I think it's intuition. Or maybe it's hope that it is because then I would have a starting point with her. She doesn't talk, not much, at least. Just says she's better, but there's nothing better. Her mother is trying everything she can to get her to open up, but she won't. All we know is that she was going to school, seeing friends, and everything seemed normal. Then, one day, she just . . . never came home. Everyone assumed she ran away and was gone about three months. We know she was using during that time because of the treatment plan after to help her detox."

That makes me wonder why the doctor would be prescribing painkillers.

"You don't think it's just a girl on drugs who ran away?"

"I don't know. It just doesn't seem like any of the normal things I see were there. Of course, her parents could be oblivious, but I think it's something else. I want to get to the root of the issue and help her heal from what's happened. It's just impossible to navigate trauma without the cause. I called Mike Girardo to see if he had any ideas. Of course, he said something about electrodes and sage . . . I don't know."

I laugh. "He broke through with Brielle."

"He did, and now, I . . . well, he did. He is amazing, and I have to do the same with this girl."

I'm sure she was about to say something about Brielle, but she caught herself. There's a level of confidentiality we try to maintain, but we're authorized to speak about our patients if it's related to treatment. Still, Brielle is a friend of mine, and Kate knows it, so I appreciate her not breaking confidentiality and possibly putting me in an awkward position.

"If you want, I'll take a deeper look into her file and compare it against another case that has a similar profile. I can see if there's a connection that was missed."

"That would be amazing. I really believe this girl didn't run away. I think she was held somewhere. I've dealt with my fair share of both, and she's reactive much more to a trauma than a choice."

My phone buzzes, letting me know my shift is up and it's date night. "I'll check it out. I have to go."

"Got a hot date?" she asks.

I grin. "Something like that . . ."

And I hope for something a bit more.

CHAPTER

Seventeen

SOPHIE

"Now you be a good girl for Mama James, okay?" I'm crouched down in front of Eden, attempting to say goodbye to her for the third time. There's something about going on this date that has me rattled. I wrote in my journal about it, which usually helps.

Except, apparently, when I am writing about going on the date that's causing my anxiety.

Holden, who has the patience of a saint, hasn't said a word each time I've turned to go back.

"Yes, Mummy."

"And if you feel like you have to go to the toilet, you go right away."

"Yes, Mummy."

"And no sweets. You don't want a tummy ache. Be nice to Pickles. If he doesn't want to be held, don't try to pick him up."

Holden scoffs. "Please, torment the cat. He deserves it."

Mama James tsks. "Maybe if you were nicer to him, he wouldn't hate you so much, Holden Xavier."

"Yeah, I hear demons are repelled by kindness."

"You are ridiculous," Mama James chides and then takes Eden's hand. "Don't you worry, Sophie. We will have a great time, and if there are any issues, I'll call right away."

I force myself to stand and take a step back. It is incredibly difficult to leave her here unprotected. Holden moves closer, his hand resting on my back, lip at my ear. "Emmett is on duty and will come by every hour. I promise you, Sophie, I will protect you and Eden with everything I have. Do you trust me?"

My heart races as his words create a rush of safety around me. I move my head, looking into his deep brown eyes. It blows my mind how much I trust him. It's clear that he is a great man and a good father. He didn't let my fears go unheard, he ensured that my—*our*— daughter is safe.

"I do trust you."

His smile makes my chest tighten. "Good. Let's go have dinner, and we'll call to check in whenever you need."

It seems so silly, but the fact that he even said that means the world to me. I lean down to kiss Eden's cheek and then Mama James gives me a hug. "Have fun, and we'll call if we need you."

Holden helps me into my coat and then places his hand on the small of my back. He opens my door and then closes it once I'm in. I know he said this wasn't a date, but all of this feels very date-like, and I can't stop smiling, which has me questioning my sanity.

When he gets in the driver's seat, I turn toward him. "I promise I'm not usually this neurotic."

"You're not neurotic, Sophie. You've been through a lot and have every right to be nervous leaving her for longer than normal."

"Well, and it's for a date."

"I thought we weren't going on a date," he teases. Damn it. Now I feel ridiculous, but Holden takes my hand in his. "Just relax and know that Mama James would terrify anyone who tried to come near Eden. I would never leave her otherwise."

"How can you feel this way about her already?" I ask. "You love her."

"She's my daughter."

"But . . . you only just found out."

Holden shifts to face me better. "When they placed her in your arms after you gave birth, did it take days or a moment to love that child?"

I answer instantly. "Not even a moment."

"The moment I saw her, I knew she was mine, and I felt the same way. I don't need weeks or months to love that child. She's mine . . . ours. I am her father, whether she knows it or not, and all I want is to protect her from the horrors of this world. Now I get to spend time learning who she is and loving her even more. If Theo was anything like me, he felt the same, and that's why you're here. He sent you here because he knew that only a father would trade his own life for hers."

A tear falls down my cheek, and the riot of emotions battle in my chest. There's relief because I have worried about all of this as well. There is hope because I had no idea that Eden would ever know the love of a father after Theo died. I worried that she wouldn't have someone to do all the things that daddies do. To find Holden, a kind man who already loves her the way only a parent can, soothes my broken soul. Then I feel a bit of anger toward myself and, again, Theo. On top of all the other things he kept from me, for him to have kept this from me, to have robbed me of something I could've shared with Holden, it makes me want to scream.

Holden wipes away my tear. "Why are you crying?"

I look out the window, composing myself before turning to him. "I had no idea a man like you existed, Holden James, and I am both happy and sad we are here tonight. Happy because you are a good man who I am so incredibly blessed to share a child with. Sad because, if Theo hadn't died, we wouldn't know each other. Sad because you should've seen her first smile and steps. You should've been able to hear her first laugh or word. You were robbed of all of those moments, and instead of being angry, you are . . . you."

"I'm upset I missed it all, but I've seen horrible shit in my life. I've watched kids die of cancer, abuse, neglect, and other things that haunt me at night. I could be angry, and I can wish I had what I didn't, or I can be the man that Eden and you need. I choose that."

"Me?"

He grins. "Well, you are my baby mama."

I laugh. "I am, and you're my baby daddy."

"All kidding aside, I'm here for you too."

Do men like this really exist? If so, I really did have luck in Vegas.

"Thank you, Holden."

"Let's go get dinner and then we can get back to Eden."

I like that plan, and I am starting to really like him too.

CHAPTER
Eighteen
HOLDEN

This isn't a date. I keep reminding myself of that whenever I want to reach across the table and take her hand. Or when she smiles at me, those blue eyes shining in the candlelight, and it makes my dick hard. I may not remember much about us meeting, but I remember the way she looked at me. It was the same way she's looking at me now.

"Tell me about you as a little boy," Sophie says.

That shakes me out of it. "What?"

"What were you like as a child?"

I place my fork down. "I was a normal boy, I guess. I had my fair share of scrapes and bruises. What about you?"

"I was very quiet. I grew up in a home where children weren't seen or heard," she replies. "It fostered a very deep love for reading and drawing."

"Which led to your love of painting," I finish.

She nods. "I would sit at my window and just draw the outside world how I saw it in my head. Things in my life weren't always picturesque, but on the canvas, they were. My parents split their time between London and Surrey. We owned a ridiculous home in the countryside and went on holiday there at least once a month."

"Did you like it?"

"The house? It was stunning. It had an indoor swimming pool and a cinema room, which was unheard of at that time. It was my great grandfather's mansion and passed down to my father. He loved that house more than I think he loved my mother or me." She laughs without humor. "Well, I know that's true. He didn't care much for either of us. Still, when we went there, I could live in a different world. Where little girls were swung around on the perfect lawn instead of kept off it. Where I could run to my father, and he'd smile with arms open. They weren't bad parents, just not affectionate. They put on a good show, though. Everyone believed we were a model family that had it all."

I know that all too well. My parents were absent most of the time and neglectful if they were there. I grew up not knowing much about parental love unless I was with Isaac or Emmett's family. Most of all, I try very hard not to think about Kira and how they killed her. "My family was that way. The outside didn't match the life we lived behind the walls. We had a nice house, it wasn't big, but it was better than most of my friends' places. They were also the biggest hypocrites I'd ever known. My father was the pastor of a church a few towns over, and my mother was a teacher. Here they were, telling people to care more, to love and respect what we have, but they basically ignored their own children. Mom cared about her appearance in the community, and my father, well, I can't even get into that. My sister Kira and I basically raised ourselves because our parents were always working with someone who needed them more, not seeing we were falling apart."

"It seems we had very similar childhoods. Parents who cared more about others than their kids."

She doesn't even know the half of it. My parents are why my sister is dead.

"And yet you're nothing like that with Eden," I say, not wanting to expose that part of my past yet.

Sophie's gaze drops as she shakes her head. "I think that's what I struggle most with. As a mother, how does a parent not love their child? How do they claim they do but then push them away the second their child does something they disagree with?"

"You mean about when you came home pregnant?"

"Yes. But my father was really who would've cast me out without a backward glance. He never would've entertained his perfect daughter having a child out of wedlock. He was all about appearances, and he and my mother basically arranged my marriage before my father's death. They wanted me to marry a business adversary, which would have secured the merger of their companies. I was nothing more than a business transaction, and I wanted no part of it."

"I understand that."

She nods. "Theo did too. His parents were equally wretched. They resented him for ruining their picture of idyllic life. They wanted a perfect son, and instead, they got a son with a heart defect that would cause them to miss out on life." She places her napkin down on the table and sighs. "I hated them. They were horrible people, and when he became an adult, they washed their hands of him and his medical care. Too busy trying to catch up on the life they lost having to care for him. Not that they did much of that anyway. Always sticking him with a caretaker or leaving him at the hospital."

"Sounds like all our parents could've lived in a commune together."

"The land of shit for parents?"

I smile at that. "Mine would be president."

Sophie leans back, watching me. "Worse than Theo's parents?"

I nod.

A few moments ago, I didn't want to share this part of me. I hate my parents for what they did. Neglect doesn't always follow the lines society thinks it does, and it isn't always visible until it's too late.

"How so?" Sophie asks.

"They're the reason I'm a doctor."

"That doesn't sound like it makes them monsters."

"The reason I wanted to become one does," I say. If I had been trained. If I had known anything about my sister's condition, I could've saved her. I could've done so much, but I was fifteen and knew nothing about being sick. My sister told them about what was happening, and they rolled their eyes before going back to saving the world while Kira suffered.

"You can tell me, Holden." Sophie's voice is soft. "I assure you that I have no room to judge another, and I wouldn't anyway."

There are only six people in the world who know what happened. Six people who were there and saved me after losing her.

"My sister died from a diabetic coma when I was fifteen. She was nine. Kira was never in their plans. They wanted one child, just for appearances' sake, but then my mother got pregnant with her. From the day they found out, it was utter despair. I was happy, I remember being excited about having a sister. I . . . I don't know, it all feels like it blurs together. We raised ourselves, cooked for ourselves if Mama James wasn't around. Back then, she was working full time but did her best to check on us. However, you had two kids trying to make food, it really wasn't healthy things."

"You were alone that often?" Sophie asks, concern filling her voice.

"There was one time when I didn't see or hear from our parents for six days. I was twelve, taking care of Kira. My mother went to a conference, and my father was probably sleeping with one of his parishioners."

I will never forget that time. I thought they died, but I was scared enough not to say anything because one of the kids at school had been removed from his home and separated from his siblings. The idea of not having my sister was scarier than doing what we could to survive.

"Oh, God!" She gasps. "That's terrible."

"When we were young, I hid a lot of things. So, as much as my parents are to blame, I am as well. I lied about Kira's problems, thinking the truth would make things worse. I downplayed everything."

She reaches her hand out. "You were a boy. You never could've known there was something wrong."

"I know that now, but I struggled for a really fucking long time. I blamed myself, then my parents, and now I just do whatever I can to make sure it doesn't happen to anyone else."

"I am so sorry."

I think about how hard things were then and how my parents also found a way to blame me. She died when I was a sophomore, and by senior year, my parents had deteriorated into complete assholes. I was lucky that Mama James removed me from that house. It's because of her that I'm half the man I am.

"It is what it is. I miss my sister. I wish she could've met you and Eden. I think she would've grown up to be a remarkable woman if she were given the chance."

"With you as her brother, I'm sure of it."

Sophie moves her hand away, and I miss her touch. I don't know how I am already feeling things for her. It makes no sense. She's hiding things, and here I am, wondering if it's okay to make a move since she didn't have any kind of romantic feelings for her husband.

I am going straight to hell.

But opening up to her feels . . . good. I haven't talked about Kira in so long that I'd forgotten how it felt to say her name.

My ex-wife loved her. She and I used to talk about her all the time. Jenna was my high school girlfriend and would spend days at my house when my parents would disappear. Kira thought Jenna was the most beautiful girl in the world. I agreed at the time. Looking back, it makes me think that losing Kira caused me to hold on to anything I loved even harder, which was why I proposed to Jenna our sophomore year of college, and we got married three months later.

I just couldn't lose her.

I couldn't lose anything else.

Then I realized that holding on to things that were meant to be free was worse than losing them. It was prison.

When she handed me the divorce papers before med school, I understood it. I'd trapped her and tried to get her to live in my box, and she couldn't do it. She was stronger than I was to leave, and in the end, it was the right decision for us both.

At least that was the bullshit I fed myself.

Sophie leans back in her chair, grinning at me. "Dinner was amazing. Thank you for bringing me here and just the entire evening."

"I'm glad you liked it."

"I liked the company as well," she says, her cheeks turning pink.

"I did too."

I like her, and I shouldn't. We have a shitload of baggage we need to deal with before I try for more.

But then those goddamn eyes are staring at me, making it hard to think with the correct head.

She sighs heavily. "All of this could've gone so differently, you know? I could've arrived and found out you were married with your own family. I can't imagine how I would've handled that."

"Don't you think your husband knew that wouldn't be the case?"

"Oh." Sophie blinks. "Yes, I suppose he did." She falls silent, staring at the candle for a moment before lifting her gaze to me. "He said something a few months before he passed. I didn't give it much thought because Theo and I always joked about our awful love lives. He said something about how, once he died, I'd finally be sent to the right man because I couldn't find him if he were two feet in front of me. We laughed so hard, but after that, he would make little comments about Eden and me being sent to someone who was better than him." Sophie looks away again. "I think he . . ."

I wait for her and then run my thumb along the top of her hand. "Meant me?"

Her head lifts, and she nods. "If he thought that, you must've met him."

That thought never crossed my mind. Now, I wonder if Theo had come to meet me. Did he freaking interview me for the job of taking his wife and my kid? "I've never been to London."

"He traveled a lot. Not as much the last year, but before that, he was always gone. He did financials for a lot of big companies that were based in the US. I remember when Eden was a baby, I would complain that I married him to be a single mother anyway."

"Did he ever come to California?" I just received his medical file, and I recalled something familiar about a patient I met. I can't remember details, but I'm starting to wonder if it was him.

"You know, I'm not sure. He was in Atlanta a lot, I know that. It sounds silly that I wasn't aware of all the places he went, but he traveled so often that I stopped paying attention."

I know that well. I did the same when my parents were gone. It was more of a surprise when they were home. "Do you have a picture on your phone?"

Sophie looks down at her hands. "My phone was actually taken from me. It was part of the many things I lost as I ran from whomever was chasing me, and my new one doesn't have any pictures of him on it."

"Okay . . ."

She perks up. "Oh! I can get a photo." Her hand moves against the screen as she searches and then she smiles. "Here, this is his social media account."

I take the phone and look at the photo. The two of them are standing side-by-side, and he's holding Eden in his arms. They look like the perfect family, all smiles and love. He was just a bit taller than Sophie, which means he would have been shorter than I am, and had light brown hair. I definitely don't recognize his face.

"You mentioned your phone was taken, who gave you that one?"

Her lips part, and she attempts to smile. "I bought it. I was in Las Vegas, and I . . . I got a phone so I could contact the police if I needed."

Her inability to look me in the eyes tells me that isn't the truth. My gut says to call her out on it, push for the information she's keeping, but my heart says to let her tell me when she's ready.

I decide to give her a little of both. "The less I know, the harder it is for me to protect you. You must've had help along the way, and I won't push you to give me more information than you're willing to, but I would rather you tell me that you can't or won't say it than lie to me."

The look on her face makes me want to kick my own ass. "My help came from someone at each stop who gave me a note from Theo, telling me the next step. I'm sorry if I'm not able to tell you more than that."

"Don't be . . . I just want us to be able to talk. If you can't tell me, I understand, but just tell me that instead. The fewer falsehoods we have to worry about, the easier it will be for us."

She nods. "I can't tell you who helped me along the way. It was made very clear that their identity must be kept from you and everyone else."

At least she's telling me something. "Okay. And this person is trustworthy?"

"Theo trusted them, and they've done everything they can to keep me and Eden safe."

The questions I have are insurmountable, but again, I need to walk a tight line. "Then, *when* you can tell me more, I hope you will."

"I will. I know that Theo doesn't look like he was a great guy, but he was. He was there for me when I had no one, and whatever mess he got himself in, he did what he could to keep us away from it and ensured we'd be safe when he was no longer here to protect us. It's the only reason I got on that plane and have followed all the directions. And I think it led me where I should've gone . . . to you."

CHAPTER
Nineteen

SOPHIE

Holden starts to say something, but the waiter comes to the table, halting our conversation. "Excuse me, Dr. James?"

"Yes?"

"There's a call for you at the bar. They said it's urgent."

He gets to his feet quickly, pulling out his cell phone. "Give me one second." I nod, but he's already moving toward the bar. I'm not sure what to do, so I watch him as he takes the call. After a second, he hangs up and rushes back to me. "We have to go."

"Is everything okay?"

"We need to go."

I stand, grabbing my bag, and he helps me with my coat. "Holden, you're scaring me."

"That was Emmett. Some girls just showed up at Run to Me, and they need me there as soon as possible to help."

"I'll go with you," I say quickly. "I can help if you need it."

"Sophie." He sighs. "I don't want to take you in there. Trust me, you don't want to see any of this. Especially since you're not a medical professional."

I might not be, but I've done a lot of things many would be disgusted by. "No, but I took care of Theo for years. I did a lot of things most nurses did. I can give injections and help with wound care."

He opens my door for me and then rushes around. "I can drop you off at Mama James's."

I place my hand on his forearm. "Let me help. I can at least bring you clean supplies or . . . just be there."

His lips form a tight line. "Okay, but just know that I have no idea what I'm walking into. Just that Emmett said to get there immediately."

"I understand."

We get in the car and head back to Rose Canyon. We were only a town over, but the drive feels as if it takes ages. Holden is focused on the road, and I rest my hand on his arm. "Holden, we should call Mama James, would you mind if I do so you can drive?" I ask.

"Of course. Yes, please."

I grab his phone and dial the number. She answers on the second ring. "Hi, Holden. Eden is doing great. She had a snack, and I just got her in her pajamas."

I smile. "It's Sophie, and that's wonderful. I'm glad she's doing well."

Her voice lifts as she says my name. "Sophie! Darling, she's an angel. She and Pickles have played for a bit, and now she's just doing a puzzle with me. I did want to tell you she had an accident, but it wasn't a big deal, we cleaned it up and that was that."

This is happening a lot. "Did she drink a lot?"

"She had a big glass of milk and then she got preoccupied. It was probably my fault for not telling her where the bathroom was. I apologize."

"No, no, it's not your fault. She's had a few accidents this week. I should've mentioned it."

"Don't you worry. Is everything all right, or were you just calling to check in?"

Holden makes a turn and slows as we approach the office on Main Street. "Holden has a medical emergency, so we're going to be quite later than we thought."

"I have Eden. You do whatever you need and please don't rush on my account. Okay?"

"Okay," I say before disconnecting, feeling relief at her kindness.

He pulls around to the back of the building where there are two police vehicles and three other cars parked, one I believe is Blakely's.

When we stop, Holden and I get out, and he heads to the boot, pulling out two bags.

"Can you bring this in?" he asks. Gone was the man I was just out to dinner with. This man is calm, determined, and focused.

"Yes, of course."

"I'm sorry, Sophie," he says, the mask slipping.

"For?"

"I wanted tonight to end better than with me being called to an emergency for God only knows what. Run to Me is a safe haven, and if everyone is here right now, it's something serious. I didn't want to bring you into this. I want to protect you."

He is so sweet. "You are protecting me, but I want to help people as well. I may not be a doctor or anything like that, but I can be here for you and other people who need help."

Holden steps closer to me, lifts his hand, and brushes his thumb against my cheek, making my heart race. "This wasn't supposed to be a date, but I really wished it was."

Oh, Lord. I wished it more times than I could count. I really wish he would kiss me, but it's not the right time. I should've kissed him that night in the kitchen, but I was so afraid.

"Then maybe we'll have to plan one," I say, finding courage I didn't know I had.

He grins. "Maybe we will."

"Holden?" a woman says from the back door, and we move apart.

"I'm here."

"Oh, thank God. The one girl is in bad shape. She has bruises on her face and . . ." The woman from the hospital stops talking when she sees me. Her long brown hair is pulled back, but wisps of hair are falling around her beautiful face. "Sophie. I'm sorry, I didn't know you were here." She turns her attention back to Holden. "I was over at George's house when he got the call, so I came with him."

"Sophie and I were at dinner, and we both rushed here as well."

She smiles. "We have four girls and could use all the help we can get." Kate goes back inside, but we don't follow right away.

Holden lifts the second bag and then takes my hand. "I need to explain something. Run to Me helps girls who have either run away or are victims of human trafficking or domestic violence. Blakely works with a team, which is me for medical triage, Kate for mental health, and Emmett and

George for law enforcement when they are requested. When I enter that door, I won't be the same. I know that sounds crazy, but I'll be hyper-focused and only thinking about the medicine. I won't be able to divide myself. I'm sorry if I say or do anything rude. According to Emmett, when I'm in that zone, I'm a world-class asshole to everyone but my patient."

I squeeze his hand. "You'll always be a hero to me, Holden. Let's go."

When we enter the back door, my heart drops to my stomach. There are three girls who can't be much older than fourteen. The first girl is blonde, but her hair almost appears brown from all the dirt and mud in it. She has bruises all down her arms, tattered clothing, and tear streaks down her face.

The second one looks slightly better, but there is a gash on her cheek.

The third girl is the worst, and immediately, I see what Holden warned me about. His hand releases mine, and he quickly moves to her, asking her permission before looking over the cut on her arm. He and Blakely are speaking back and forth as he crouches in front of the girl. Then they disappear into the back.

Brielle walks over to me. "Hi."

"Hi, what can I do to help?" I ask.

"Blakely asked if someone could just sit beside the girl on the end. None of them have told us their names or what happened, but Kate has already assessed her and is going to talk to the one on the couch while Holden helps the girl in the back." She motions to the other girl. "I am taking notes until Emmett tells us the next steps."

"There's another in the back?"

Brielle nods. "She's in the worst shape, so we brought her there for privacy while Holden works."

"What happened to them?"

Sadness fills her eyes. "We don't know yet, but the one in the back was stabbed and probably had every bone in her right arm shattered. There is a triage back there where Holden can deal with non-life-threatening injuries, and then once we have seen to their needs, we transport them if they need additional help."

Wow. I was in the back when I came here and didn't notice it. "Well, I'll do whatever I can. Any suggestions?"

"Just be there. She may want to talk and give us some clue as to what happened or she may not. Kate thinks she's in shock right now, so don't push her to talk if she doesn't want to."

"Okay."

"Here is the device we keep on and use to record anything said in here. It can't be used in court, but it helps us piece things together later if we need to."

I accept what looks like an ordinary pen. "Whatever you need. Do I try to talk to her?"

Brielle shrugs. "Sometimes it's best not to. I usually introduce myself and offer what I can. It's really a crap shoot if they respond. We aren't too sure if they're on something either."

There is a long, painful wail from the girl in the back room, and both of us turn to look. Brielle shifts, and I nod. "Go, I'll do what I can for her."

She hurries off, and I walk toward the girl at the end. I sit, my back against the wall, not speaking while the young girl, who is covered in dirt, rocks slightly. After a few moments, she looks over, and I smile softly. I don't know how to do this, but these girls came here afraid and lost, so the least I can do is sit with her. She looks to me, back at her knees, and back again a few times. Once her eyes meet mine for longer than a heartbeat, I speak. "My name is Sophie. Would you be able to tell me your name?" She shakes her head, rocking a little faster. "That's all right. We don't have to talk. Is it okay if I sit with you for a while?" She doesn't say it is, but she doesn't shake her head either, so I take that as permission. "If you need anything, just tell me."

For a long while, we sit like that—her slowly rocking herself and me a silent offer of support. It isn't until another scream comes from the back that her fear-filled eyes meet mine, tears starting to pool. "She's my friend."

"What is her name?" I ask just above a whisper.

"We don't have names."

I know that's not true, but I decide not to pry. "What are you called then?"

She twists her fingers together. "Two eighteen."

"And your friend in the back? Does she have a number?"

"One seventy-three."

"What about your other friends?"

She shakes her head. "Didn't give her a number yet. The other is two forty-nine."

I push down the bile in my throat at the fact that these girls have so clearly been stripped of their identities. The number part makes me wonder if they're random or in order.

The girl closes her eyes and rests her forehead on her knees. After a moment, she tilts her face just enough for her to see me. "Where's your accent from?"

"I'm from London."

"What's it like?"

I tell her a bit about my home. The history, the sights, and my favorite places. I describe what it was like to walk around Piccadilly at night and all about the little shops in Covent Garden. If I try really hard, I could pretend I'm actually there. I can see the cobblestone street and smell my favorite bakery where I would take Eden for a cookie.

The sounds of people talking as they make their way around fills my ears. My hand tightens, remembering Theo pulling me toward the tube as he dragged me to the next thing he wanted to explore.

He was always adventurous that way. I liked to have a plan, and he wanted to let the wind take him somewhere new.

"It sounds magical," she says. "I close my eyes a lot and imagine being anywhere else."

"And where do you see yourself going?"

She sighs, head back against the wall. "I'm usually with my sister in our corn field. I hated it before, but now it's warm and bright. I can feel the sun and hear the sound of her laughter as she chases me through the rows. I go there and stay for as long as I can. I miss it, and I don't want to be here anymore."

My chest aches for her. I don't know anything about the geography of the States or where she's from, but I understand the feeling of home.

Hopefully what she says will help Emmett, so I ask another question.

"Where were you escaping from?" I ask hesitantly.

Her eyes gloss over as she looks at me, but then her lids lower and a tear falls. "Hell. We've been in hell."

CHAPTER

Twenty

HOLDEN

Sophie and I are sitting in the car out back of Run to Me. Neither of us can speak. Neither of us move much either.

It's been a grueling two hours. I was able to stitch that poor girl up enough that we were able to transport her to the hospital. Kate offered to ride with her since George was escorting our private vehicle with the other three girls. No one even considered calling the paramedics, and thankfully, Sophie didn't question it. She is the only one who isn't aware of how Ryan Wilkinson used his ambulance to abduct young girls. Blakely went as far as to purchase a vehicle, transform it into a mobile hospital room, and hire fully-vetted private paramedics just to avoid ever having to use that emergency service again.

I sit here, my hands shaking slightly as the adrenaline wanes.

Then I feel her hand against mine as she laces our fingers together. I glance over to find her watching me, concern tight on her brow.

I need to say something. To apologize or thank her or something.

But I can't.

I can't say a goddamn word.

I shift, and so does Sophie at the same time. I release her hand, and she brings both to my face. The two of us breathe each other in as the air grows thick in the car. I use every damn ounce of self-control I have not to maul her right here.

"Sophie," I say softly.

Her eyelids flutter for a moment and then she looks at me. "Holden . . . I . . ."

Our mouths collide, and it's heaven and hell and everywhere in between. I press my lips to hers desperately, needing to feel her, to kiss her. Her head tilts to the side, and she opens for me. This kiss is absolutely not what I wanted it to be. It's hungry and filled with the fucking nightmare we experienced tonight.

Our tongues melt against each other's, and her hands move to the back of my head, holding me there. The soft moan that falls from her lips has my cock hard in an instant.

There's no tenderness in this. No softness. It's all passion and anger and . . . fuck. She deserves to be kissed better than this.

Damn it. She deserves more.

Not another mauling by me.

Before I can break away, she pulls back, her hand covering her mouth. "Oh, God. I . . . I'm so sorry."

"You're sorry?" I ask. "You didn't do anything wrong. It's me who is sorry."

Fuck. Twice now I've used her, and the first time I don't even remember.

"We can't do this, Holden. Not now. Not when we just . . . went through all that."

Our eyes meet in the moonlight. "I'm such an asshole."

"No! God no!" she reassures me, turning her head to look at the back door of Run to Me. "I care about you. I want to kiss you, I really do, I'm just afraid that we're going to regret doing this now—like this."

The last thing in the world I want is for her to regret a second with me. "I don't want to do that."

"I know, but there is so much we have to discuss. Things we didn't get to talk about."

"Like what?"

Sophie shakes her head. "I might have to leave suddenly, and then what? What becomes of us then?"

"And what becomes of me if you leave and take Eden?" I counter. "You're not the only one who risks being hurt. I love that little girl, and I want to be the father she needs. I want to be the father I could've been from the beginning."

"I know this. I think about it all the time. I worry that I'll have to pack a bag and run away. It's going to be hard enough if . . ."

My heart is pounding as I force myself to keep calm. "If what?"

"If I fall for you. If I have to leave and lose you as more than just what we are now. If I have to hurt you by taking Eden, that will be bad enough, but if I love you, then what?"

Maybe she's right. It was idyllic to think that maybe Sophie could be more. No matter how much I want her or how many nights I lie awake in bed, wishing I could hold her, my asking her for more is unfair to her and Eden. She could turn around tomorrow and disappear, and if the worst-case scenario she described plays out . . . I'd fucking lose my mind.

"Then we stay friends only and, what?"

Her gaze falls to her lap where she twists her fingers. "Suffer, I guess. I'm not sure how I'd keep my heart out of this, but I know it isn't something I should risk while there is still a chance I'd have to run again. Believe me, that isn't what I want."

"Then what do you want?"

"You."

That word is like a gunshot in the car. "I'm right here. I'm not afraid."

"I am! Don't you worry about the fact that, at any moment, things could change?"

"So you'd rather let fear take away your chance at happiness?" I counter. She shakes her head, looking away. "This is your choice, Sophie," I remind her. "I wasn't sorry that I kissed you. I was going to stop for a completely different reason. I don't want to make the same mistakes with you."

I might as well lay it all out on the table.

"What mistakes?"

"Where I'm out of my mind and treat you like you mean nothing."

"You have never treated me that way."

"That's good to know, gorgeous, but we had a beautiful moment the other night, then we went to dinner tonight, and it was perfect until I got that call." I sound like an idiot. As the words are coming out, I want to punch myself in the face, but Sophie needs honesty more than anything. "What I'm saying is that I *want* to kiss you. I want to kiss you so fucking much. I think about kissing you all the goddamn time, but the last time I did, I ended up passing out in the bathroom stall."

Sophie exhales. "It seems we've moved to a new location."

"I don't want that. I planned to walk you to your door, put Eden to bed, and kiss you properly."

"I would've liked that, but we both know it's not a good idea. Not when we have so much to lose."

She isn't ready, and I won't push her. "That's the thing. We're already losing without ever getting to enjoy the good parts."

And with that, I put the car in reverse and try to put the idea of more with Sophie behind me.

"Good grief, Holden. Were you in a war?" Mama James asks as she sees me.

Her hair is in the rollers she sleeps in with a long nightdress, as she called it, that zippers up the front. The slippers I bought her with the better soles on them at least are new, but this was the scene of my younger years.

Mama James in all her glory.

Her home is my favorite place in the world. It smells like cookies are always in the oven, and I knew that when I was here, the outside world couldn't touch me. I can remember when I moved in, she put my things in my room and pointed to the boxes, informing me that they weren't going to unpack themselves. I spent hours doing that, and when I was done, she had a plate of cookies and glass of milk on the table.

We sat for hours talking about all that happened and what it meant for me. It was the first time I ever felt like I was given a choice on what I wanted in life. I could've gone and lived with Isaac, his family would've taken me in without hesitating, but her house was where I needed to be.

"Is this what war looks like?" I ask her.

"It probably does. You're a mess."

I kiss her cheek. "You always know how to make me feel better about myself." She scoffs. "Our emergency was not exactly what I expected."

"I would hope not." She turns to Sophie. "You still look lovely, dear."

Sophie smiles. "Thank you for watching Eden."

"Oh, posh!" She waves her hand, dismissing the appreciation. "I miss having kids running around here. It keeps me young. She was wonderful and fell asleep watching *The Sound of Music* with me. I am assuming it's from the head rush of watching it upside down, which Holden did as a boy. I thought the music would soothe her, maybe it did. I love that movie, it's so beautiful and the songs are not like what's in movies these days."

"I hate that movie."

"You have no taste, Holden. And no one asked you. What did I teach you about injecting your opinion when no one asked for it?"

I'm instantly ten years old again. "Keep your mouth closed if you can't be kind," I repeat in the same voice I did at that age.

"That's right."

"You know I'm an adult, right?"

She shakes her head. "Yes, well, you're my nephew, and I love you, but you still need a good reminder of the rules in this home."

"Forgive me?" I ask, knowing she already has.

"Of course, you sweet boy. I could never stay mad at you."

I turn to Sophie. "I have a face women love."

Sophie laughs. "I think the saying is a face only a mother could love."

"That too." I wink, trying to inject the humor back into our night. "Now, we should get Eden home and in bed. Where is she?"

"In the living room."

We find her curled up on the couch, her thumb resting on her lips as if she's not sure if she wants to suck on it. I'm rooted to the floor for just a second, looking at her. Sometimes, I can't quite process that I have a child. A little girl who I didn't know existed and missed so many moments with. So many things in my life have changed in such a short time that none of it actually feels real.

I have a daughter.

I say this to myself daily because it's not like I had nine months to prepare for fatherhood.

"Holden?" Sophie says from over my shoulder. "Are you all right?"

I nod. "I just didn't want to wake her."

I bend down, scooping Eden into my arms. She's so small and immediately nestles against my chest. I shift her a bit and feel wetness under her legs.

"She had another accident," I tell Sophie.

"This is happening a lot."

I quietly count how many times Sophie has mentioned Eden having an accident, and the higher the number gets, the more worried I become. This doesn't seem normal. When I lift her up to feel her forehead, she lets out a deep sigh and the smell hits me. Fear like I've never known before floods through my veins.

"We have to get her to the hospital."

Sophie's eyes widen. "What? Why?"

"Sophie, has Eden been drinking more than normal? Around when the bedwetting started up again?"

"Yes, and that's why she is having accidents."

Frequent urination, increased thirst, and the smell. The smell of syrup and fruit. I remember it. I remember my sister giving me a kiss before she went to sleep that night. She never woke up again.

"We need to go. Mama James, we'll be back to get her things."

"Holden, what is it?" my aunt asks, tears filling her eyes.

"I think this is diabetes, and if I'm right . . ." I can't think it. I can't finish the sentence. "We have to go."

Her hand flies to her mouth, and a tear falls.

"Holden, what do you mean you think it's diabetes?" Sophie moves closer, her hands resting on Eden's chest.

"All the symptoms are there. The increased thirst, frequent urination to the point that she's having accidents, and there being an almost fruity smell to her breath. That's an indication of ketoacidosis. We'll take her to the hospital to get her checked out, and if it's not what I think it might be, then at least we'll know. If it is, then we can get her blood sugar stable so she's out of the danger zone. Just . . . trust me that we have to go now, okay?"

Sophie nods quickly, and I am already moving out the door. I could call the ambulance, but it would've been another ten to fifteen minutes, and I am not waiting another second to get her help.

"Is she going to be okay?" Sophie asks once Eden is buckled in and we're on the road.

I need her to be, and I didn't notice anything out of the normal until now. Hopefully, that means it hasn't gone unchecked for too long.

"I'll know more once I can check her levels, but she'll be okay. I'll do everything I can to make sure of it."

Sophie brushes Eden's hair back, and I focus on getting there, ready to do anything I need to save my daughter.

CHAPTER
Twenty-One
SOPHIE

The moment we arrive at the hospital, I feel as though I lose my mind. Holden called ahead to inform them we were coming, what his suspicions were, and what he wanted prepared once we got here. Eden has been off and on sleeping since we got her in the car. She can only last a few minutes before she dozes off again.

Once again, the man who was at Blakely's just an hour ago is back. He commands everything around us, including making sure someone is managing me.

I stand, watching them work around her, pricking her finger and yelling out numbers. He has a nurse draw blood, orders fluids, and a scan of some sort. All of it feels like it's happening in another world.

It isn't until Eden looks at me with tears in her eyes that I snap out of it. "Mummy!"

I rush over, rubbing her cheek. "It's okay, darling. It's okay. Holden and his friends are just checking you over."

"I'm scared."

I am too, but I can't admit that. "You have nothing to be scared of, my brave girl. Just let the doctors and nurses help."

Holden takes her hand and smiles at her. "We're going to give you some medicine to feel better, okay, sweetheart?"

Her little eyes are filled with fear. "I want to go home."

"I know, but here at the hospital, we make people feel better so they can. We need to put a little tiny tube in your hand. It won't hurt, and your mummy and I will be here the whole time. You can squeeze our hands as hard as you need to, okay?"

"I don't want it to hurt."

"It'll be a quick pinch and then you're going to feel so much better. It's going to give you the medicine you need."

"Dr. James?" The nurse knocks on the door.

"Come in. We're ready. This is my friend, Rhian. She's the best nurse in the whole hospital."

Rhian smiles at the compliment and then at me. "Hi, Eden."

Eden doesn't reply as her jaw quivers and she tries to climb into my arms. I hold her in the bed, kissing the top of her head. "Eden, listen to Mummy. I know you're afraid, but you don't have to be. Do you remember how scared you were when we got on the plane to come here?"

Her watery gaze finds mine. "Yes."

"It's time to be brave like that again. Rhian isn't going to hurt you, but you need to sit still so she can give you this medicine."

Eden glances over at Holden. "Can you do it?"

Holden shakes his head. "I'll be right here with you."

Rhian comes closer and explains parts of what she's going to do. As time passes, Eden relaxes a little, and the nurse distracts her by touching her hand, her arm, and her fingers as she explains what each part of her body does.

"Now, I need you to do a really important job for me," Rhian tells her. "I need you to keep this arm super still. You can't move or it might make a big mess. Can you do that for me?"

Eden nods, but it's clear she's afraid.

Rhian does as she explained, and thank heaven for nurses because she gets it with one poke and only a few tears from Eden.

Holden pushes her blonde hair back. "Good job, bug."

They start the IV, and Holden checks everything again. He asks someone to bring him a tablet.

Eden doesn't say anything as her eyes close again, and this time, my anxiety doesn't spike half as badly as it did in the car.

"I need you to tell me what's happening," I say to Holden as he walks toward the end of the bed.

He motions to the door, and after looking at Eden again, I reluctantly follow.

"It's good that she's resting here. They're pushing fluids, but her sugar levels were definitely high. We are giving her fluids for the dehydration and insulin to stabilize her blood sugar. She'll be monitored very closely, and once we know more, we can talk about what happens next."

"So, she has diabetes?" I ask, feeling broken.

"We need to do a few more sugar tests to confirm, but in my medical opinion, I believe it is."

"Oh God," I say, my hand against my throat. Could this night go any more pear-shaped? We had a lovely dinner that was cut short by an emergency. Then our daughter could've died because she has diabetes, and I didn't even know.

"I thought the bedwetting was just because of the move. How did I not know? I didn't think there was anything wrong. She was so thirsty all the time, and I just gave her water without questioning it," I explain. "I didn't know to say anything. I should've known!"

"You didn't do anything wrong. I explained it away too. It's not your fault."

I shake my head, stepping back. "I am her mother. I should have known."

"Sophie, stop. I'm a doctor, and I didn't see it before tonight either. But we caught it, and we're here. I am going to do everything I can to help her. Okay? I will take care of her. It's going to be okay."

I nod because I needed to hear those words so much. Nothing has felt like it was going to be okay. Everything has been one blow after another, and I am exhausted—so bloody tired of it all.

Before I can say anything, a doctor walks over.

He extends his hand to Holden. "Dr. James." They shake before he does the same to me. "Miss . . ."

"Peterson," I finish, remembering the correct name this time, and shake his hand as well.

"Peterson, I'm Dr. Baxter, and I'll be handling your daughter's care from here on out. I know Dr. James already started his workup, but he knows he can't do that . . ."

Holden huffs and moves forward. "Jeff, I appreciate you offering to step in, but it won't be necessary."

"Holden, you handled the emergent care, which is fine, but now you hand it over. That's protocol."

His hands clench and relax. "I don't give a shit about protocol."

"Well, I do, and since I'm the acting supervisor, that's the way it goes. Due to extenuating circumstances, I'll allow you access to Eden's chart, and you will be able to consult with the staff, but no orders coming from you will be executed."

Holden steps away, running his hands through his hair. "You've got to be kidding me."

"Holden?" I ask. "I don't understand."

A long breath leaves his chest, causing him to look slightly deflated. "I . . . I can't treat Eden."

"What? Why not? I want you to be her doctor."

"I can't, Sophie. We aren't allowed to treat immediate family."

I blink. "Oh."

Dr. Baxter interrupts. "It's protocol because, when it's family, sometimes even doctors can make rash decisions that aren't in the best interest of the patient. So, it's to protect the patient as well as the physician. As I said, he can consult, and I promise you that I will treat your daughter as if she were my own."

I want to cry. At least when Holden was in charge, I was confident that her doctor wouldn't allow anything to happen to her. I don't know Dr. Baxter, and the thought of a total stranger holding Eden's health in his hands is terrifying. I must've made a sound because Holden is moving toward me, pulling me into his arms. "It's okay. Dr. Baxter is excellent, and I'll be here the whole time."

I nod, tears falling.

"It's overwhelming, I know, but I promise, Sophie, I may not be her doctor, but I am her father, and I will *never* let anything happen to her."

I grip him tighter, holding on because I might just fall apart if he lets go.

Twenty-Two

SOPHIE

I do my best to sleep, but between Eden's machine beeping and the constant foot traffic, it is nearly impossible. I sit up, opening my eyes and finding Holden's chair is empty. He has kept vigil by her side, talking with everyone who enters and offering suggestions. I check my phone and see it's only three in the morning.

Eden is sleeping peacefully, so I walk to the doorway to see if he's in the hall.

Through all of this, he's been a rock. After he and Dr. Baxter spoke about Eden's numbers, he made me take the recliner, put blankets over me, and told me to rest.

I don't find him, but I do spot a nurse standing at the nurses' station. "Do you know where Dr. James is?" I ask.

She gives me a soft smile. "He went to his office to go over some test results. He said that, if you needed him, to call. Would you like me to do that?"

"No, no. I can go see him. I don't want to leave her, but . . ."

"Why don't you go, and I'll sit with Eden. I was just about to go on lunch and read, so I don't mind sitting beside her instead."

"Oh, are you sure? I don't want to put you out."

"You're not. I promise, no one will ever look for me there. My name's Harlow, by the way."

"It's nice to meet you, and thanks for keeping an eye on her, I appreciate it."

I'm about to try to figure out where Holden's office is, when she adds, "Ms. Peterson, I know you both came in quickly, but . . . would you be more comfortable in something else?"

I'm still wearing the dress from last night. Changing out of these clothes would be nice.

"You and I look to be about the same size. I keep a spare set of scrubs." She reaches under the counter, grabs a bag, and pulls out a bundle of light blue clothes. "His office has a changing area if you need to freshen up."

I take the offered scrubs and smile. "Thank you."

"Of course."

"Can you direct me to where his office is?"

She explains the route, which seems easy enough to follow even though I'm so tired and overly emotional. This has been such a traumatizing event. Even more so than what brought me to Rose Canyon. Eden is my everything, and I worry so much about the future now.

I arrive at the office with his name on the door and knock softly.

"Come in!" I hear him yell.

When I enter, his head is resting on his fist, and he's holding a piece of paper in the air, but he doesn't look up at me.

"Did you bring me her latest blood tests?" he asks.

"I didn't."

Holden's head lifts, and he stares at me with bloodshot eyes. His hair is a disheveled mess, and he's also still wearing the same clothes he had on last night.

He looks exhausted.

"Sophie, you're awake. Is Eden okay?"

I reassure him quickly, entering and closing his door behind me. "She's sleeping still. One of the nurses said she would stay with her for a while so I could clean up."

"That was nice of her."

"Yes, I appreciate it. Have you slept at all?"

"No. I have been going over the blood tests and wanted to see the results of the most recent one before Jeff got them. He's a good doctor, but I know him well enough to know that he'll hide things for my own good."

"Do they look better?"

The deep sigh tells me they don't. "This is from six hours ago, and they're what I expect, but not ideal. She's stable, which is the most important thing. She'll get fluids, and we'll give her more potassium, so that will help. We will do several blood sugar tests today. Some before meals, some after."

"And what about her life? Does she live normal with this? Is this something I did? Maybe in my pregnancy?"

"You did nothing. If anything, it could be me. My sister had Type I Diabetes, and it's often genetic. Jesus, I didn't even think. I just . . . fuck."

I watch as the agony rolls across his face in waves. "It's neither of our faults, Holden."

I'm not sure he believes me, but at least his gaze finds mine again. "Maybe not, but I promise, Sophie, she will have a normal life, just things we need to watch with her food. It'll seem daunting at first, but then it'll become part of our everyday life."

Our.

Even after what happened, he still puts us as a unit. It makes me want to crawl into his lap and let him wrap me in his arms. I'm trying so hard to hold on to my flimsy excuse because I am unsure of the future.

Not like anyone ever knows, but it's too hard to think about losing Holden.

I clear my throat, lifting the bundle of clothes. "The nurse said you have somewhere I could change?"

That causes him to look at himself. "Shit. I should do the same. I look like hell."

"You've had a lot happen in the last twenty-four hours."

The quirk in his lip makes my heart flutter. "You can say that."

I wonder if he's thinking about the kiss too.

No, I will not think about the kiss or him or us.

Holden points to the door. "There is a bathroom through there. I'll do the same and then head down to Eden."

Pushing my thoughts down, I return his smile. "Cheers."

"Of course."

I walk into the bathroom and flip the small lock on the doorknob. There is a stall shower in the corner, a toilet, and sink. Underneath, Holden has a set of clear plastic drawers. There are some hygiene items like a toothbrush, deodorant, a comb. I would love to brush my teeth at least, and thankfully, there is a spare.

I clean myself up before changing into the scrubs the nurse lent me. When I leave the bathroom, Holden is sitting on the sofa in his office, head in his hands, and . . . shirtless. He doesn't look up as I approach him, and then I hear the faint snore.

Poor man is so exhausted he's sleeping sitting up. I place my hand on his shoulder, careful not to startle him, and he lifts his head.

"What? Are you okay?"

"Yes, I'm fine. You fell asleep." I clear my throat and look at his naked chest. "And mid clothing change."

"I just—" He pauses. "I figured I would wait for you to get done and then try a cold shower to wake up."

"Why don't you nap?"

"I can't. Fuck, I can't, Sophie. I can't close my eyes without seeing Eden limp in my arms. She looks so much like my sister, and then to see her that way . . . I have to fix this. I have to make sure she's okay. I lost my sister because of this, and I can't let the same thing happen to Eden. I'm a doctor. It is my job to notice when something is wrong, and I didn't see it in my own child. I'm so fucking sorry."

My jaw shakes, and there is this new pain in my chest from seeing him upset like this. "I was so scared. I should've known something was wrong."

His hands move to my shoulders. "You did nothing wrong."

"You said you missed it, but so did I. Do you think I shoulder the blame?"

His eyes never leave mine. "Of course not."

"Well, then how would I blame you? I know you love Eden. You'd never let anything hurt her—or me. You've been our champion, and I can't bring myself to think of what would have happened if not for you. Why do you feel it's your fault? How long has Eden been in your life? Months. That's it. I've had her three years, and I didn't notice her symptoms were more than just her having trouble adjusting to the upheaval to our lives."

The tears fall as my guilt crushes my chest. I'm aware that he's a doctor and trained to see medical issues, but I'm her mother. The one who gave her life and knows her best. All this time, I've been explaining away issues, and it could've killed her. I never would've known to bring her to the hospital.

I bring my hands to his face. "You knew what it was, and you saved our daughter, Holden. I would've brought her home and put her to bed, and then what would've happened?"

His lids close, and I feel his jaw tighten beneath my touch. "She could've died."

"But, instead, she's resting and getting the treatment she desperately needs."

His forehead falls to mine, and I let this moment settle over me. Right here, the two of us are tucked away from the horrors of the world. The last day has been a series of highs and lows, and my feelings are a bit too close to the surface as I let my tears fall.

Holden's thumb brushes against my cheek. "Don't cry, Sophie."

"I was so afraid. I knew you would do what you could, but I was so afraid."

"I will always do what I can for you both, I promise."

The room is growing warmer as emotions threaten to overwhelm me, but then Holden's promise settles over me, soothing the storm a bit.

He moves his face a little closer, rubbing his nose against mine. I want him to kiss me again. I need him to absorb everything around me and take away the fear and pain.

So, I do what I know will do exactly that, I kiss him.

Holden responds in an instant, his hands cupping my face as his mouth moves over mine. This kiss is exactly like the one we shared in the car, only this time I won't be stopping him. I need this. I have to shut off my brain for just a little bit.

"Sophie." He sighs my name as he kisses down my cheek. "Tell me to stop."

"Don't."

His hot kisses move to the other side as he makes his way up my neck. The heat of his breath on my ear causes me to shiver. "I want to rip these clothes off you and kiss every inch of your body. I'm not in control. I want you, need you so fucking much. I can't say no, but . . ."

"But what?" My voice is shaky as need builds.

"I won't be able to be the man you need."

I push his face back, looking in his eyes. "I just need you, however you are. Please, Holden."

"This is your last chance, Sophie." He slides his nose down my cheek, his voice sending shivers down my spine. "I won't be able to hold back."

My breathing is ragged, and I don't care. I want him too much to care. "Please."

CHAPTER

Twenty-Three

HOLDEN

Her plea takes every reason I had to stop this away. I want her so much that it's an ache inside me.

Today has taken me to a dark place, and Sophie is the light. Before she came in, I was lost in anger and self-loathing for where we were. I missed every sign with Eden. I could've lost her just like I lost Kira, and it would have been my fault. I just keep going back to the moment I walked into Kira's room and found her unmoving. No matter how much I shook her, she wouldn't wake. Fear like I'd never known took hold of me, and I was alone. Those thoughts, the smells, sounds of sirens, the faces of my three best friends who ran to my house when they saw the lights . . . all of it was there. All of it haunting me.

Then she was here, offering solace just by being near, and I will selfishly take all she gives.

I move my lips back to hers, and she moans into my mouth. Her hands are against my chest, sliding down to my belt. I feel her tug on the buckle, pulling it apart.

Using the space between us, my hands go to her breasts, letting the perfect weight rest in my grasp. Our mouths break apart just long enough for me to pull her top off and toss it aside. Then I unclasp her bra, and the sight of her is almost too much.

I'm so hard as I dip to take her nipple between my lips, and a sharp gasp of pleasure escapes her.

Wanting to hear that sound again, I suck the sensitive bud hard and roll it gently between my teeth until she's arching closer, silently begging me for more.

I don't remember ever feeling this way before. Not only the desire for someone, but also a physical need for them.

Only her.

Only she will make this go away.

"It's been so long, Holden. Please don't make me wait."

"And what if that's what I want? What if I want you to beg for my cock? What if I want to hear every dirty thought you have and all the ways you want me to make you scream?"

"Is that what you want?"

I kiss her neck while pinching her nipple. "Answer my question first."

"Holden," she moans and takes a step back, only to end up pressed against the wall.

"You're trapped now, sweetheart."

I run my tongue around her nipple, and her hands fly to my hair. "Oh, don't stop."

The begging again. I can't resist.

There is a smirk on my lips as I pull back. "I like it when you beg."

"If I keep doing it, will you give me what I want?"

"Only if you're very good. Can you be good, Sophie?"

A flush paints her cheeks as I move my hand down her body, purposely not touching the places that will make her feel good.

"Holden, please." She has no idea how close I am to losing control and fucking her right against this wall.

"Please what?"

"Kiss me." She lifts up, pressing her mouth to mine. I kiss her deeply, sliding my tongue against hers, and my hips move, grinding against her heat.

God, I want to be inside her.

This time, there will be no forgetting.

"Sophie." I breathe her name as I lift her, and she wraps her legs around my waist. My mouth never leaves hers as I move us to the couch, where I can do all the filthy things I have thought of these last few weeks. "Tell me what you want." My hand moves against her silky skin, over her perfect breast, and down her stomach to where there's a slight bump from where she carried our baby. It only makes me want her more.

Her body is a temple, and I am going to say a prayer when I enter.

"I want you to touch me," she says in a broken whisper. "Please."

"I am touching you." I drop to kiss along her collarbone, hiding my smile as I move my hand a little lower.

"Yes. Keep going."

Her hips lift just enough to urge me on, and I give in.

I make my way inside her pants, feeling her wetness through her panties before I slide them to one side and sink my fingers into her heat. Thank God she wants this as much as I do. I circle her clit, moving back and forth as she rocks against my hand. "That's it, beautiful. Take what you want, show me how much you wish it was my cock."

"Oh, God," she moans. "I want you so much."

I want to hear her beg again. "Do you?"

Her eyes close as I move my fingers a little faster. "Yes."

I bring my lips to her ear, running my tongue along the shell. Sophie moans softly and traces her palms down my sides to my waist, catching the top of my pants and working them down over my ass.

When she wraps her fingers around my cock and strokes my full length, I nearly burst.

"God, Sophie, you feel so fucking good."

"So do you. Take it away, Holden. Please, let's forget everything except us."

Her wish is my command.

After pulling the bottoms of her scrubs and panties off, I rearrange us on the couch. A part of me considers what I'm doing, but I'm too far gone to stop. I rub my cock over her clit, dying to get inside her. I need her far too much to take the pause we probably should.

She takes my face in her hands. "Don't stop."

That's all the encouragement I need.

I pull my fingers from her heat and wait until her eyes find mine as I lick each finger. "You taste so good, I can't wait until I can have you come against my tongue. Where I can memorize your taste. Do you want that?"

Her eyes roll back in her head. "Yes, but not now."

"No?"

"No, right now, I want something else."

I want to hear her say the words. "What do you want?"

"You know." She pulls her lower lip between her teeth.

My finger moves back to her clit, giving her enough pressure to drive her crazy but not enough to make her come.

"Say the words, baby. Tell me what you wish was inside you other than my fingers or my tongue."

"Your cock."

"That's what I thought." I grin. Our eyes are locked, and while I want to fuck her senseless right now, I want to make her a promise of what we will have the next time. "When we do this again, we're going to do it right. I'm going to take my time, lick, suck, and kiss every inch of you, and you're going to let me."

Then I slide deep inside, letting her warmth surround me.

Sophie's soft cry tears at my chest, and I clench my jaw, trying to find one last scrap of control. I'd forgotten it's been years for her, and I'm fully seated. "Are you okay?"

"Yes, God, yes."

I smirk and then pull almost all the way out of her before slowly sinking back in, trying not to lose myself in how perfect she feels around me. I go slow, allowing her to adjust to my size, but it takes every drop of restraint I have to do so.

"You're so tight. It feels so good."

"Holden, move."

I do, thrusting steadily, drinking in every whisper of pleasure that falls from her lips. I'm lost in her. Lost in the moment, and no longer is my mind filled with sadness, it's all Sophie. The sounds of flesh against flesh fill the room, and her fingertips rake down my back as she arches against me. When she cries out, I slant my lips over hers to swallow the sounds.

She's close. I can feel her tightening even more.

"That's it, Sophie, let it go. Let me take it, baby." I slip my hand between us, shifting my hips so the angle is different and I can play with her clit. "I'll catch you when you fall," I promise.

I don't know that I've ever seen anything as beautiful as she is right now. Sophie's naked, eyes closed, bottom lip between her teeth, and tits bouncing as I fuck her is an image I wish I could capture and look at any time I wanted.

Taking her hips in my hands, I adjust the angle again, driving deeper. She gasps as her fingers wrap around my wrists. "Oh, God. Oh . . . Holden," she whispers and then falls apart.

Her eyes find mine as pleasure crashes through her. I'm so close to following her, but I want to wring out every bit of her orgasm.

When she collapses, I know I'm not going to be able to hold back any longer. "Sophie," I say as I pull out seconds before I finish, spilling over her stomach.

My heart is pounding as I work to catch my breath. I hold her because I don't know if, after this passes, I'll have the chance to be this close to her again.

For the moment, the distance she wants between us is gone, and I'm going to savor it.

Sophie kisses my neck, her fingers making tiny patterns against my scalp.

After enjoying it for a second, I meet her gaze. "Are you all right?"

She nods. "I'm great. Do you have something I can clean myself with?"

Fuck. "I didn't . . . I didn't even think about grabbing a condom when we started."

"I know," she says. "I didn't either until you were about to finish. At least you remembered and pulled out. That's something."

"Seems to be a pattern we follow, sex first, think second."

I head into the bathroom and grab her a towel to clean up with as I do the same. We get dressed in silence, though there is a lot to say, to figure out. Now isn't really the time since neither of us is in our right mind and we're exhausted, but I don't think letting it go is best either.

I walk out of the bathroom to find her leaning against the arm of the couch. Her eyes lift when I come to a stop in front of her. "So . . ."

She smiles just a little. "Buttons."

"What?"

"It's something my gran used to say. If you said so, she'd say buttons. Sew buttons."

"Clever."

"She was. I adored her very much."

"And do you adore me right now?" I ask.

"I do."

"That's something too, then."

Sophie shakes her head. "So is what just happened between us. Just a few hours ago, I had a million reasons why we couldn't kiss, but they evaporated when I found you here. All I could think about was this, us, and I just want to be honest about my fears."

"Let's both process everything, but I want you to know that your reasons don't change how I feel about you or how I think, deep down, you feel about me. I like you a lot, Sophie. I want to be a part of your life, not just as Eden's father. You can set the pace on how fast or slow we take this, but I'm here and will wait if that's what you want."

All I can do is lay my cards out on the table and hope they're enough.

CHAPTER

Twenty-Four

SOPHIE

I check on Eden, she's still fast asleep, and Harlow is sitting in a guest chair next to her bed.

"Did she wake at all?"

Harlow puts her e-reader down. "Not even a little. Do you feel better now that you got out of your clothes?"

My cheeks fill with heat, but then I realize she's talking about wearing the scrubs. "Yes, yes, thank you. It was so kind of you to offer me these."

"It's nothing. If you need me to stay longer, I can . . . I don't mind." Harlow's gaze moves to her device longingly.

"Are you at a good bit in your novel?" I ask.

"I'm at that point where I'm not sure if I want to hug or slap the author," Harlow admits.

"What are you reading?"

"Romance. It's the best genre."

"I agree, I miss reading. Once I had Eden, my time became far too scarce, and I would fall asleep with the book in my hands after one page."

I always loved to escape into another world that was filled with possibility and hope. The idea that love was strong enough to mend the broken bits in a person. There being a perfect soul who could help me become the best version of myself was a fantasy I desperately needed.

"I gave up reading a few years ago, but when my fiancé cheated on me, I found a story that was so similar in premise, I thought . . . maybe I could relate to her and figure out a path. I needed to know someone else, even if they were fictional, understood what it was like. Then I read every book by that author, which led me to an author friend of hers, and . . . here I am now, over five hundred books on my device and no end in sight."

I chuckle softly. "The heart of a bookworm shouldn't be denied, so I think I'll take you up on your offer and maybe go get some fresh air."

She grins. "I'll stay here . . . for Eden's sake."

"I appreciate it."

When I walk out of Eden's room, Holden is standing at the nurses' station, now wearing a pair of scrubs. His wide shoulders are pushed back as he talks to Dr. Baxter. I slink away, quietly moving down the corridor, hoping neither of them notice me since I look like a staff member.

It may be cowardly, but I am not ready to face him.

I begged him. Literally, begged him.

I may never meet his eyes again. I'm mortified by my behavior.

The electric doors slide open, and the cold air hits my face. I inhale through my nose, allowing my lungs to expand, and when I exhale, I do my best to let the stress go with it.

It doesn't work, of course, but it was at least worth a try.

There is a bench over to the left where a garden is probably beautiful in the spring, and an ambulance sits under the canopy, but there isn't another soul around.

There is so much rolling around my mind, questions on what to do now. Once again, our lives have been irrevocably changed. Eden will need to be monitored, our diet must change to account for her diabetes, and then there's the fact I had unprotected sex with her father—again.

"What is wrong with me?" I say aloud. "Of all the cock ups in the world . . ." I groan. "As if I didn't know what might happen and haven't already reaped the consequences of that same action. Stupid, Sophie. I'm ridiculous. Absolutely mad."

"Are you all right?" says a deep male voice to my left.

I startle, my hand moving to my chest as though I can catch my heart as it moves.

"Sorry I startled you. I just heard you talking and wanted to be sure you were okay." He moves closer with his hands raised.

The young man moves a little more in the light, and I see his uniform. "Yes, sorry. I was just berating myself."

He's wearing a paramedic shirt and blue trousers. His dark hair is pushed to the side, and there's scruff along his jaw. The man is very attractive, not nearly as good-looking as Holden, but still, he's not at all ugly.

"I do that often. I'm Stephen."

I take his extended hand. "I'm Sophie."

"Do you mind if I sit?"

"Not at all." I pull my coat tighter around me, feeling the nipping winter wind.

He flashes a smile. "Are you new here? I know most of the nurses, and I can't say I've seen you before."

Confusion hits me until I remember what I'm wearing. "Oh, I'm not. My daughter is actually a patient. I . . . just came out for a bit of a break."

And to hide from Holden.

"I'm sorry to hear about your daughter, how old is she?"

"Three."

"Is she okay?"

I shrug a little. "She is now, but it'll be a long road. She has diabetes, it seems. We rushed her here last night."

"The good thing is that you got her here and can get her treatment."

"Yes, it's a good thing."

"How long have you been in the area?" Stephen asks.

I'm not sure who this person is, so I'm going with half-truths where I can.

"A few weeks. We are visiting a friend in Rose Canyon."

Stephen chuckles. "I live there. My father is actually the mayor."

And this is the man Blakely was extremely concerned about.

"I met him not too long ago. He's lovely."

"He's something. You probably shouldn't be sitting out here in the cold alone in the middle of the night."

I blink. "Oh? Why not?"

"It's not safe. There has been some crime lately."

Right. I know all about that. Just last night I was slapped in the face with that. "You're right. I wasn't thinking when I wandered. I just needed to breathe for a bit."

Stephen chuckles. "I'm kidding. You're perfectly safe here. There's always someone around, and really, this area is where a lot of people sit at all hours of the day. It's tranquil and allows us time to reflect."

I let out a heavy sigh. "I wasn't sure if you were serious or not. It's been a very long day, and I'm not really myself."

"I'm sure it's hard when it's a child. Listen, the team here is amazing, and I'm a paramedic, so if you ever need help with your daughter, I'd be happy to come by. Diabetes is manageable if you have the right tools and help if needed."

That's really kind of him, and I'm about to tell him as much when a hand settles on my shoulder.

"There you are, Sophie, I was looking for you."

I blink because Zach Barrett is standing behind me. His tall frame blocks the moon behind him and casts a shadow around me. "You were?" I play along.

He comes around, standing between me and Stephen. "I'm Zach, and you are?"

"Stephen, I'm a paramedic and was just checking on Sophie here."

Zach nods. "Thank you. I wasn't sure where she went."

There's an edge to his deep voice that's protective and firm, and my heart begins to race. I haven't seen Zach since he dropped me off down the road from Run to Me, and Jackson mentioned that he'd gone home, so I'm not sure why he's back in town. That aside, he wouldn't have shown himself if he didn't believe I was in danger.

"Do you know this man?" Stephen asks, shifting to catch my gaze.

"Yes," I say, getting to my feet and looping my arm in Zach's. I'm not sure what role we're meant to play, but either way, this is friendly. "This is my good friend."

Zach's frame seems to grow. He's definitely not giving Stephen an inch. "As I said, I appreciate you keeping her safe."

Really, what the hell is going on? Is Stephen a threat? Surely not. He was perfectly kind and is a paramedic for heaven's sake.

"Of course. Be careful, Sophie."

I watch in silence as Stephen heads back to the ambulance. He raises a hand after he's seated, and I return the gesture. As soon as the vehicle is out of sight, I drop my hand and step back. "What is going on? Why are you here and not Miles? When did you get back?"

"I just got in two days ago, we had to pull my replacement back, and I wanted to check on you and Eden anyway."

"She's sick," I tell him.

"I know, but she has you and Holden to care for her."

Neither Holden nor I are capable of making mature decisions right now. "Why did you interrupt that conversation?" I ask him, not wanting to discuss Holden.

Zach runs his hand over his beard. "What did he say?"

"Nothing . . . why?"

"I'm just curious. There are some things about his past I don't like."

"Zach, what is going on? Is Stephen dangerous? Is that why you showed yourself?" I ask, feeling a panic building.

He takes my hand and urges me to take a seat on the bench with him. "Sit, and I'll explain."

He tells me about Blakely's suspicion and how certain things weren't lining up with Stephen and his story. She was positive that he was involved in some way with the deaths of the missing girls. Zach looked deeper into Stephen's alibi and found two dates that didn't match up.

"Well, he didn't say anything strange."

"He offered to come to your home and help with Eden. As soon as I heard that, I moved in. We have no idea if this guy was involved, but the person who was arrested is Stephen's best friend, so I'm not willing to take chances."

I don't want to defend Stephen, as I don't know him at all, but the same can be said for me. "And I was married to a man who was clearly involved in things he shouldn't have been. I knew nothing of Theo's investments or his work, so it might be a bit unfair to assume that Stephen was involved with whatever his friend was doing simply because they were friends."

"I know, and it sucks, but my job is to keep you safe."

"And I appreciate that, but am I not allowed to talk to anyone? Who do I trust? It's clear that Holden and his friends are fine, but are there others I should be wary of?" I ask, needing some guidance.

"Just be careful with Stephen, that's all."

"Be careful," I say in exasperation. "I am careful of everything, and look where I am now. In America, with no money, no family, a daughter who is sick, a man who kisses me and then I sleep with him on the sofa in his office like a fool. I have lived my entire life being careful not to upset my mother or my father or get Theo overwrought and send him into heart failure. I can't . . . fucking hell, I just said." I just said I slept with Holden on the sofa.

Dear Lord, Sophie, can you not keep anything to yourself?

Zach grins. "So that's why you were on the other wing for a while . . ."

"Don't you dare judge me," I warn.

Zach and I spent almost a full day in the car together as we made our way from Idaho to Rose Canyon. I was not in my right mind and beyond exhausted. I chattered away like a magpie for hours until I wore myself out and fell asleep, which probably was the best part of his drive—my silence.

"No judgment here. I have no room to talk. I have a failed marriage under my belt, a kid I didn't know about until he was an adult, and a girlfriend who also happens to be said son's ex-girlfriend."

I blink at that last one. "You what?"

"I'm a complicated man. Not for nothing, Holden and I have a few of those in common. No wonder I like the guy."

I roll my eyes. "What am I doing, Zach?"

"You're dealing with the hand you were dealt. It's not like you asked for this to be your life, but that's the way it goes. Holden cares about you and Eden. I guarantee you that none of this is easy for him either, but that's the way it goes, right? Believe me, nothing in my life has gone easy, but I'm happy. I'm really fucking happy with Millie. I didn't think I'd ever say this, but being happy is a choice. I know that sounds shitty, but it's true. You can keep feeling sorry for yourself, or you can live, and I think Theo sending you here, and all the measures he took to ensure your safety, means that he wanted you to choose right."

His words hit me in the chest, forcing the air to hang around before I can breathe again. My whole life I have wanted to be happy. I believed it was possible, but I didn't know how to make that happen. What if he's right? What if I have been choosing to be unhappy instead?

I turn to thank Zach for his advice, but he has disappeared as though he were never here at all.

I get up and walk back inside, no longer choosing to run away from the possibility of happiness.

Of course, my plan doesn't go the way I thought it would. Holden isn't in Eden's room because he's helping with another patient, so I'm sitting here alone, overthinking.

Before I get too far into my thoughts, a nurse enters with a cart. "Good morning. I need to draw some blood and test Eden's blood sugar again. We'll do this two more times today."

"Of course."

She walks over, pricks her finger, and Eden doesn't flinch.

"Is it normal for her to still be sleeping like this? She has barely woken."

"She's had a rough day, and her body is working hard to recover from the stress it was under. Dr. Baxter and Dr. James are keeping a very close eye on your little girl. If she's sleeping, I say let her rest."

"Thank you."

"Her levels look good. I'll put this in her chart and let the doctors know your concerns. Dr. Baxter should be in shortly to give you an update."

She leaves, and I go back to looking outside. The sun is peeking over the mountain range in the east. It is such a lovely landscape here, but with the beaches to the west, it's like two worlds that don't quite belong cohabitating in harmony.

If anyone had told me this is where I'd be, I would've laughed.

Yet, this is where I am, and as awful as I used to think leaving England would be, it hasn't been.

I've made friends, found a truly wonderful man who happens to be the father of my child, and every avenue for happiness is right in front of me.

I let out a long sigh and hear a soft voice behind me. "A penny for your thoughts?"

Holden.

I shake my head. "I don't know that they're worth a penny."

"Is that because I wouldn't want to buy them?"

"No. I think you'd probably want the last one at least."

"That's a start then."

I smile, even though he can't see it. "I was thinking about life and choices. How we make choices and then, good or bad, there are consequences we must face."

He moves so his chest is against my back. "We don't have to face what happened this morning right now."

Maybe not, but I can't go on pretending it didn't happen either.

I turn, my eyes finding his in a heartbeat. "Not all consequences are bad, are they? Can we not have something good come from the things we do?"

He looks to Eden. "You just have to see our daughter to know that good can come from what we deem a mistake."

"And because of Theo's cock ups, we found you, and she can have her father."

Holden turns his head back to me. "And can I have more, Sophie? Can I have you?"

I want to say yes. All that talk about living my life and having happiness suddenly doesn't feel so possible. However, fear is not how I want to live my life. I do not want to be afraid. If I am in danger, if someone does want to kill me, is this the way I want the end to be?

Alone.

Afraid of what good I could have.

No, it's not. I want to live and be loved. Truly loved. I want a man to come home to me, kiss me, and tell me that I am his world. I have never had that, and I deserve it.

"We have to go slow," I tell him. "Not because I don't want more with you, but because I don't know what more even looks like. We have to think about Eden as well."

His hand cups my cheek. "I can do slow."

Then his lips touch mine, and I forget all my fears.

CHAPTER
Twenty~Five
SOPHIE

"This pack stays on your hip and tells the machine in your arm when you need medicine," Holden explains as Eden stares at the clear wrap around her insulin pump on her arm.

"Do I still have to do the needles?"

He smiles. "Not nearly as many."

It's been a long five days filled with tests, explanations, and possibilities, and I am struggling to keep it all straight. We have had a lot of visitors. Mama James came nearly every day to spend time with us and give us each some time to clean up. Brielle and Spencer came yesterday, bringing Eden a bouquet of balloons and lots of toys. Emmett and Blake also have visited daily, though they spent most of the time filling Holden in on whatever is happening with the girls they helped. I haven't had the energy to focus on it, but they seem to have some ideas as to where the girls are from and have been helping them.

And yesterday, we had a visit from the mayor, which was kind.

Holden has been patient and has gone over things with me multiple times. Eden's diabetes is best managed with a self-regulated insulin pump. Every three days, we must check the medication levels and change it if needed. We can check her blood sugar on our phones throughout the day. If her levels drop, we need to give her sugar, but if they're high, the pump will dispense insulin.

"I don't like the needles," she says, her lower lip wobbling.

"And that's why we're doing this, but you have to be a good girl and help us too, okay? You must tell us when you don't feel well and eat what Mummy tells you," I explain. A lot of her diet must change, but Holden has assured me that we'll make the appropriate steps for the entire house. While that is probably the most daunting change, it's far from the only one. I'd never realized there were so many things that went into regulating a person's blood sugar.

"Okay, Mummy."

"That's my good girl."

The nurse enters the room with paperwork. "I just need you to sign these, and you'll be all set to go."

I scribble my signature, and she smiles. "You're all done. If you have any questions, please don't hesitate to call Dr. Baxter."

Holden coughs. "Or me."

The nurse grins. "Yes, or you. There is a follow-up appointment set in a few days to check the pump, but other than that, you guys have a wonderful afternoon. Bye, Eden."

Eden waves. "Bye!"

Once she's gone, Holden gets to his feet and takes Eden's hands. "You ready to go home, bug?"

"Yes! I want my dolls and my colouring books, and I want to snuggle Pickles!"

I laugh as Holden's expression sours a touch.

"Mama James said we can stop by tomorrow."

"I want to go now," she says with wide eyes.

Holden's shoulders droop. "All right. We can stop by there today."

I look at him, a smirk on my lips. "You gave in awfully quick."

"Did you see those eyes?"

"Yes, and you're going to have to resist them," I tell him.

The last thing we need is Eden getting her way all the time.

"I have a hard time resisting either of you."

My stomach flips at that. Since the night in his office, Holden has not made any advances when it comes to us. We've shared a few sweet kisses, but that's it. I am not sure if I am happy or upset by that. He's doing as I asked and taking it slow, yet I wouldn't mind just a bit faster.

"I think you've done quite well resisting," I tease, hoping he will take the bait.

"Did you want me to have *less* willpower?"

I shrug. "Maybe just a little."

"Mummy, what's willpower?" Eden asks, and we both chuckle.

"Nothing, darling."

Holden scoops her up, and we head out the door. We are halfway to the elevator when I hear my name being called.

"Sophie!" I turn to see Stephen heading toward us.

"How do you know Stephen?" Holden asks warily.

"I met him the first night we were here. I was sitting outside getting air."

Before I can elaborate, he is in front of us. "Stephen," Holden says as he shifts Eden to his other side.

"Holden, good to see you."

Holden doesn't reply. I can feel the tension building. "It's nice to see you, Stephen. Are you here for a patient?"

He nods. "Yes, Alta Day, actually. She had a knitting accident, which I didn't even know was a thing."

"Is she all right?" Holden asks and then turns to me. "She's a close friend of Mama James."

"Oh no!"

"She's fine," Stephen offers. "The ride here she chastised me for my hair being past my ears. Then it moved on to the car I drive and how loud it is going down the road and how I should find a way to make it more appealing to the ear, whatever that means. She cut her hand pretty good, but I don't think it'll require stitches."

Holden chuckles. "I'll make sure I check on her later."

"How is your daughter?" Stephen asks, looking at Eden.

"Better, thank you," I say. "We're heading home now."

Stephen looks to Holden. "Oh, are you . . ."

"Yes. I am." Holden's tone brokers no argument.

"Good. I'm glad she'll have around-the-clock care."

Holden lets out a short huff. "Yes, she will. I take care of those I care about."

"As do I."

Oh, this is going very badly, very quickly. "Stephen, I hope you understand, but we really need to get Eden home."

"Of course, I'm glad to see you guys doing well. I'm sure I'll see you around, Sophie."

He waves and then heads back inside the hospital. I think of what

Zach said, how Stephen was one of the main suspects. He seems perfectly nice, but I can't really trust appearances.

I turn back to Holden, who shifts Eden again. "Was that our friend, Mummy?"

I smile, not sure what to say. "Not everyone is our friend, love. But we are always kind to people, right?"

She nods. "Holden is our friend."

"Yes, he is."

"And Emmett?"

I nod. "Yes, and Spencer too."

"I like Emmett," she says innocently.

Holden grins at her. "Why is that?"

"He gave me ice cream."

"Solid reason, but remember that ice cream is something we only have at special times."

"Is now a special time?" Eden asks.

"No."

I laugh. "Look at you, saying no."

He winks.

"Now *is* a special time, Holden." Eden pushes his cheek so he has to look at her.

"Why is that?"

"Because I didn't have any ice cream in the hospital."

I wait to hear his response to this logic. "All of that sounds good, but we have to be really strict these next two weeks to make sure that the medicine is working like we need it to."

Eden sighs dramatically. "Can I have two cakes?"

Holden laughs and then spins her around. Eden laughs without restraint as the two of them twirl.

I shake my head with a wide smile as we head to the car.

"Mummy, are you going to have a pump in your arm?" Eden asks as I'm tucking her into her bed.

"Nope, you're the only special one."

Eden smiles and then starts to pull her covers back. "Where's Duck?"

I move her pillows and check under the blankets, but I don't see it. "Did we bring it to Mama James?" I ask.

She shakes her head. "Duck stays in bed. He likes the blankets."

This duck has been in her bed since she was born. "I remember."

I get up and search under the bed, but it isn't there either, so I walk around the room, checking to see if maybe it was thrown or . . . who knows. Eden's routine has always been to put Duck on the pillow with the blanket pulled up.

"Did you find him?"

"Not yet."

He's not on the floor or in the laundry basket, so I go through her drawers, and when I pull open the last one, he's sitting on top.

"Eden, did you put Duck in the drawer?" I ask with a smile.

"No."

"Well, he got in here somehow."

Her hands are outstretched for her beloved animal. "You ran away, you silly duck."

"You misplaced him and need to make sure you don't put him in a drawer next time."

Eden's big eyes find mine. "I didn't. He was in bed. I kissed him before I left."

I release a sigh and give her a smile.

"All right, let's get you tucked in."

She nestles down in the covers a little more. "I miss Daddy, but I like Holden."

My heart stutters for a beat because I know this is an opportunity to say something, but I'm not sure what. She is much too young to comprehend biological father and what all that means. Holden and I discussed not making it a thing and allowing everything to fall into place naturally.

"I like Holden too," I admit.

"And Holden likes you both," he says from the doorway.

"Can you tell me a story?" Eden asks.

He enters the room and settles on the other side of her. "I could, but I'm not sure you'll like it, it's about a crazy cat."

She giggles. "I like cats!"

"Yes, we're going to work on that. Emmett is going to bring his puppy over and see if we can get you cured."

"If I remember correctly," I break in, "Blakely said that Sunday is a crazy dog."

"Yes, the people in this town need help with their domestic animals, but that's for another time. Do you want to hear the crazy cat story?" Holden asks.

Eden nods enthusiastically.

"There was this cat named Mopey. She was the prettiest cat in all the world. But Mopey never told anyone her name." His eyes widen. "She was a mysterious cat with mysterious eyes. If anyone asked who she was, she wouldn't speak."

"Why not?"

Holden looks to me. "Why do you think she did that, Sophie?"

I roll my eyes. "Maybe Mopey was afraid of the people asking too many questions if she said one thing."

He shrugs and continues the story. "Sounds fair. One day, Mopey met another cat, he was very handsome with soft fur and dazzling eyes. He was quite the catch, and Mopey thought that—"

"Colon," I cut in.

"Colon?" Holden's tone is quite unhappy.

"Yes, it's where the poop collects, I hear it's quite full of it, actually."

"Full of what?" Eden asks.

"Poop," I reply.

His smirk makes my heart race. "Fine, Mopey and Colon, the best love story ever told. Anyway, Colon drank way too much . . . milk. He was really not feeling well that night. He was hanging out with all the other cool cats when he ran into Mopey. She instantly wanted to be Colon's best friend."

Eden tilts her head. "Why?"

"Because he was super nice."

"Or because Mopey was also not feeling well from the milk she drank. She was rather unlike herself," I offer.

"This is my story, Sophie. No more butting in."

I raise my hands in surrender. "I'm so sorry. I didn't mean to interrupt. However, I'd like it noted there are historical inaccuracies and timeline issues."

"It's fiction." He turns back to Eden. "Now, Mopey and Colon really liked each other. She was also very beautiful, and another cat was being mean to her, so Colon saved her."

Eden sucks in a breath. "Like a prince!"

"He was a prince, in fact."

"The Prince of Poopville," I say under my breath.

"Hey, Poopville is a very nice town filled with wonderful people. They are happy to have Colon as their leader," he teasingly scolds.

This story is just too much, and yet, I love it. The three of us curled up, telling silly bedtime stories after a harrowing five days. It feels so right, so perfect, even if the story is about two drunk idiots who have no idea what they were doing then—or now.

"This is silly, Holden."

He taps her nose. "It is, but I didn't get to the best part. After Colon saved Mopey from a horrible mean cat, they were happy. She moved to Poopville and became the princess of poop."

"Oh, that's enough," I say through laughter. "You need to get some sleep."

Eden opens her arms, and I lean down, letting her wrap her arms around me. Then she does the same to Holden.

"Good night, bug," he says, kissing her cheek.

"Good night."

I kiss her other side. "Good night, my darling girl."

"Good night, Mummy."

On our way out, we click her lights off and softly shut the door. Standing in the hall, alone, the energy shifts. The air feels heavy with anticipation. We haven't been alone since the night we had sex in his office.

I'm unsure if he'll kiss me now, if I want that, or if I will be able to keep myself from going to him.

Holden releases a heavy breath and extends his hand. "Come with me."

I place my palm against his, and his fingers close around mine. He leads me to the sofa, and I laugh.

"What?"

"The sofa?"

He blinks and then chuckles. "I swear that wasn't what I had in mind. I just wanted to hold you for a while."

I'd like him to hold me forever.

"Why?" I ask.

"Has anyone ever just done that, Sophie? Has anyone just let you feel safe for a bit without wanting anything in return?"

Theo and I used to cuddle, but in the last two years, it became rarer. He was working a lot, and his heart wasn't what it was. He needed more care than he was able to offer, and I accepted that. It was what he needed.

However, I don't think anyone has ever offered what Holden is suggesting.

"No," I say softly.

He sits and then opens his arms. "Come here."

I sit beside him, and he arranges me so I am tight against his side. Then he moves us so we are lying down, facing each other. Holden's arms are wrapped around me, and my head rests on his chest.

I feel the weight of the world start to lift a bit at a time as we lie here. I close my eyes and think . . . a girl could get used to this.

CHAPTER

Twenty-Six

SOPHIE

I awaken to feeling weightless yet moving.

I open my eyes to find Holden carrying me toward my bedroom.

"I'm sorry," I murmur.

"For what?"

"Falling asleep when you were intent on holding me."

"I wanted you to feel safe." He gently kicks my bedroom door open and then walks over to the bed.

"I can walk."

Holden grins. "I'm not ready to let you go yet."

I like this. I like the warm tingles that he stirs in my heart. It's as though the life I never thought possible is within my reach, and I just need the strength to grab it.

Carefully, he places me down on the bed, and now it's me who is not ready to let go. When he moves away, I grab his wrist. "Will you lie with me in here?"

Holden looks to the bed and then me. "You're testing my restraint."

I don't want to test him. I just want to be with him.

Then, without my having to ask again, he moves to the other side of the bed. Before he lies down, he hands me my diary.

Confusion sweeps through me. I put that in my side drawer —always.

"When you came back for clothes, did you remove this?"

Holden shakes his head. "No, I only went in the closet and grabbed what you asked for. Why?"

"I put this away in the drawer. I . . . I guess I took it out and forgot."

Maybe the nights in the hospital have left me unbalanced.

"We've had a rough few days. Mama James did come in, maybe . . . not that I think she'd go through your things."

"No, of course not. It must've slipped my mind."

There's something that doesn't sit right with me about that, but I am too tired to think through it.

"Come here." Holden settles next to me and holds his arms out. I don't wait, I curl into him, loving how I fit right in the crook of his shoulder. I drape my arm over his side and squeeze a little. "I like this."

I tilt my head to get a good look at him. "Like what?"

"Lying in bed with you."

"It's a novelty for us," I say, joking.

"A first. We've taken care of the strange places to have sex."

I shift again, this time placing my hand on his chest and resting my chin on top of it. "We seem to lack the more conventional places."

"And where would you choose? If we were going to try to adhere to normalcy?"

He wanted to let me take the lead, and right now, I want to lead us both into temptation. Pushing up, I move up so I'm nearly on top of him. "We could try a bed."

"We could, but . . . which bed?"

"We're in a perfectly lovely bed now."

He pushes my hair back, keeping a soft grip near the back of my head. "You're perfectly lovely."

I lean down, pressing my lips to his. Holden's fingers tighten a little as the kiss deepens. His mouth tastes of mint, and when he slides his tongue against mine, I moan. Kissing Holden is unlike anything I've ever known. It's sweet and sinful, and he makes me believe in happiness.

He flips me so I'm on my back, his hand running down my side to my thigh before he hooks it over his leg. "You make me lose control," he says, kissing his way down my neck. "I promised myself we wouldn't do this. That I wouldn't push you."

"You're not."

"Sophie, you drive me wild."

As though I don't feel the same. "Kiss me."

Holden's lips return to mine, and once again, I fall apart. It's as though my brain completely stops working when our lips touch. It's rather ridiculous, and yet, I don't care. I don't care that I wanted slow. I don't care that we have a million reasons not to be together. None of it matters because, in this sea of uncertainty, he's become my anchor. He's strong and steadfast, rooted where I need him most.

There's a playful nip on my lip, and then he rests his forehead on mine. "I want you so much, but we've rushed everything. You asked for slow, and even if it kills me, I want to give you that."

I could fall so deeply in love with this man.

My fingers move to his thick hair, pushing it back. I wait until his eyes find mine. "For so long, I have been alone. I've forgotten what it was like to be touched, cherished in a way beyond friendship. All of this is quite scary, but it's also lovely. You aren't pushing me, you've allowed me to lead, and I'm asking you to, slowly, give us the night we never had."

Holden moves off me, which has embarrassment crashing through me. I am a bloody fool. He doesn't want the same thing, and I just made myself look ridiculous. He gets up, removing his wallet and phone from his jeans, and then he comes around the bed, extending his hand.

"What are you doing?"

"Stand up."

I'd rather crawl under my covers and forget I ever said anything.

"Sophie, give me your hand," he orders.

Not wanting to feel any sillier, I do it. He pulls me up and into his arms. "If this were our first night together, our first time, I would've wanted to see you."

"See me?"

"Yes, love, I want to see every inch of you. I want to touch every part of your body. I want to taste you and feel you come on my tongue." He turns me so his lips are against my neck. "You want slow? I'll go so slow you're begging me to hurry. I'll make you come so hard you see stars." I shiver as his mouth glides down the crook of my neck. "Your skin is like silk." His big hand moves under my shirt, moving against my stomach. I want to shrink away, but Holden will have none of it. "Here is where you held our child. Here is where I want to kiss more than anywhere."

"More than anywhere?" I challenge.

"Well"—he chuckles—"maybe not, but I want to worship you, beautiful girl. I'll go as slow as you want."

He moves his hand up over my breast, pulling my bra down so I spill over. When his thumb brushes against my nipple, my knees buckle. I don't fall, though, not when his other arm holds me up.

"And what about what I want to do with you? Since this is our first time?" I ask, my head falling back on his shoulder.

"What would that be?"

"I want to see you too. I want to touch you, feel you on top of me and beneath me. I want to kiss you and have you inside me."

"Turn around," Holden instructs as his hand falls away.

Once I'm facing him, his fingers move to the hem of my shirt, and slowly, Holden lifts it up over my head. My blonde hair cascades down, just brushing the tops of my breasts. Without a word, he slips my straps off before unhooking the back of the bra.

My first instinct is to cover myself, but I don't. He wants to see me, and I want the same privilege with him.

"You are stunning. God, you're perfect."

I am far from that. I have a rounded belly that refused to go away no matter how hard I tried. There are stretch marks on my sides from my pregnancy, and my boobs aren't nearly as perky as they were four years ago.

My head begins to shake, but he tenderly takes my face in his hands. "Don't tell me you're not. Don't tell me you don't agree because it doesn't matter what flaws you see, sweetheart. I see beauty. I see strength. I see resilience, and I see someone who I very much want to make love to. You are perfect, Sophie Armstrong."

My heart is racing, and my thoughts are a riot. I can't make sense of what I'm feeling because it's everything at once. He says these things, and it's as though he has some kind of magic that allows him to reach into my heart and say exactly what I need to hear.

"There is no such thing as perfect," I manage to say. "There is just the truth in this moment."

"And what is the truth?" he asks.

I gaze into those soulful brown eyes, my pulse pounding in my ears. "That right here and now, we are perfect for each other. That you make me feel beautiful and wanted."

His cocky grin forms before he says, "I want you, love, make no mistake about that."

I don't doubt him, but I want to do this right and feel his skin against mine. So, I move to his shirt, tugging it off him and tossing it to the floor. Then I undo the button on his jeans and slide the zipper down. He stands like a statue, allowing me to do this at my own pace.

My pulse is going double time as excitement and nerves take turns crashing through me. When we had sex a few days ago, it was fast and hurried. There was very little time to think through the consequences, but that's not this time.

This time, we're both sure, and we're both on the same page.

I push his underwear and trousers down, and my knees tremble. How is this man real? Holden's body is glorious. He's hard and strong, and his cock juts out, long and thick. I have seen and touched it before, but it appears much larger than I remember.

"Touch me, Sophie," he says as an order, but also a plea. "I need to feel your hands."

I run my fingers across his broad shoulders and down the strong muscles along his arms. My hand wraps around his wrist, urging his hand to my hip, then I continue my exploration. I move up along the ridges of his stomach, which is hard as steel, and to his chest before resting my palm over his pounding heart.

"One organ that controls so much," I muse. "One organ that can both give and take."

His other hand moves to my chin, nudging it up to meet his gaze. "My heart is strong, Sophie."

I nod. "I have spent much of my life listening and waiting to hear that."

"Hear it now. My heart knows what it wants."

The breath in my lungs expels slowly, and my heart begins to race. "And what does it want?"

"You."

His mouth is on mine, and I wrap my arms around his neck. We play for power, each teasing the other, as Holden walks me backward toward the bed. When the back of my knees hit, he breaks the kiss and then jerks his chin.

"Lie down."

I really wish I didn't find him being bossy so damn hot, but I do.

I'm lying back on my elbows when he pulls my shorts off, leaving me completely naked. The heat in the room rises as he stares down at me. There is no mistaking the lust in his eyes as he licks his lips.

Thinking he might join me on the bed, I jerk up when he goes to his knees and then slides me to the edge of the bed.

"I thought—" I start to say something about him lying with me, but he opens my legs and places a kiss on the inside of my thigh.

"You thought what?"

My breathing is faster, and I feel incredibly self-conscious. It's been so long since I've had this done to me. My ex hated it, and the two other times Holden and I have been together, foreplay wasn't exactly in the cards.

"Nothing. I have no thoughts," I say, wishing that were the truth.

He chuckles against my skin and then blows a stream of air against my core. Oh, sweet Lord.

That is nothing compared to what comes next. His tongue slides along my seam, and I nearly jump off the bed. Holden's hands are locked on my legs, keeping me where he wants me. I fall back, unable to hold myself up as he licks and circles my clit. His tongue moves in soft, easy strokes and then quickens. I pant and moan, sweat trickling down my neck as I fight to hold back.

Not because I don't very much want to come, but because I never want this to end.

My muscles strain as the pleasure builds in a steady rhythm. Each touch like the beat of a drum, and Holden knows every time to strike. The pounding in my ears grows louder, and I bite hard on my lip, trying to keep from yelling.

Holden's finger slides into me, which is almost my undoing, and my eyes roll back. Dear God. I am going to lose my mind.

I can't hold on any longer. It's too much. Too perfect.

My hands fist in the blanket as I lose my mind in the most perfect orgasm of my life.

His name falls from my lips as he continues to wring out whatever pleasure he can, and as I start to come back to myself, he kisses his way up to my neck.

"You're even more perfect when you come."

I laugh softly at that. "I think you are perfect when I come."

He smiles down at me. "Good. I plan to be perfection a lot."

"A bit presumptuous, aren't we?" I tease.

"Hopeful."

So am I.

He moves us so I'm on top. "You're in control, sweetheart. What do you want?"

"You," I say simply.

I want him and us and the possibility of a future and family. It feels so surreal, but there it is. Holden is exactly the man I have longed for.

"Then I'm yours."

Holden grabs his wallet and removes a condom. He smiles at me before tearing it open. "Again, not presumptuous, just hopeful this would happen."

"I call it prepared." I smile and kiss him as he rolls it on.

He guides my hips, moving me right where we will fit. I want to remember everything about this night. Our eyes meet, and I refuse to blink as I sink down onto him. He fills me slowly as I adjust to the invasion, and only once my body is flush against his does he release his grip on my hips and move to cradle my face between his palms. Then the whole world seems to pause as we stare at each other—two halves becoming one.

We make love. That's the only word I can use to describe it. It's not a fuck, we've done that. It's not sex, we've done that too. This is more —it's everything. It's emotions and trust swirled into what words cannot say, so we use our bodies. I want him to be as overwhelmed as I am because it's both scary and glorious.

To be truly and properly adored like this is more than I knew was possible.

Neither of us say a word, almost as though we're afraid to break the spell we're under. There is no one else in this world but us right now. It's as though the space around us blurred and all that connects us to reality is each other.

Holden moves his hips faster, riding me from the bottom. My hands are on his chest, and once again, I am chasing an orgasm.

My breathing is labored, head swimming as I can feel a wave cresting, ready to take my feet out from under me.

"Holden." I breathe his name, unable to hold back.

"I'm close, Sophie. I'm so close, I need you."

I close my eyes, letting go of everything in my head, doing nothing but feeling the immense pleasure of making love.

Then the orgasm crashes through me. My arms give out, and I fall against his chest. Holden's hands hold me in place, and he pushes deep two more times before he follows me over.

We lie here, both panting and sticky with sweat as he trails his fingers up and down my spine. After a second, I roll to the side, staring up at the ceiling.

"That was . . ."

I turn my head to see his beautiful face and say, "Everything."

He kisses my nose. "Everything. I'm going to clean up and grab us a snack. Stay right here."

When he leaves, wearing nothing but his jeans, I do the most girly thing I've ever done and squeal to myself, kicking my feet. That was amazing, and I am so ready to do it again.

CHAPTER

Twenty-Seven

HOLDEN

I head into the kitchen, needing sustenance after that bout. Next time, I'm going for a triple-orgasm night.

I grab the cookies as well as the bag of M&M's I keep stashed in the cabinet. They have peanuts in them, so it's protein. Then, because life is about balance, I swipe a banana for Sophie.

As I'm walking through the living room, I stop dead in my tracks. Theo's medical record, which was absolutely in my bedroom, is out on the table—open.

If Sophie had seen it, she would've said something. There's no way she did this or knows about it. I look around to see if there's anything else out of place, but it doesn't look like it. Still, the hair on the back of my neck is raised.

I put down my contraband, close the folder, and put it in the file cabinet. I'll deal with telling her about that later. The last thing I want is to keep secrets from her, but I'd at least like to have some idea of what to say.

In the meantime, I walk around the house, not noticing anything else out of place. The doors are all locked and windows shut, so if someone had been in the house, I don't see how they got in. The only people with a key are Mama James, Emmett, and Spencer. I can't imagine any of them rummaging through my shit without asking, so I contemplate how the file ended up on the table as I grab the food and head to Sophie.

She's in bed with the sheets up around her, and she's writing in a book. "Are you telling your diary about the mind-blowing sex we had?"

She looks up with a sly smile. "Maybe."

I walk over to what would be my side of the bed and dump the spoils of my snack raid.

"I thought we were eating healthy?" she asks, looking at the goods.

"With Eden, we are. Plus, I brought a banana." I lift it up, and she rolls her eyes.

"That's for you then."

"Oh no. I'm not eating that while you get the good stuff."

Sophie quirks one brow. "You brought the banana, you eat it."

"And what snacks would you have chosen?"

"The banana."

"Then why the hell am I going to eat it?"

Sophie shrugs. "Because you brought it for me, and now, I want these." She snatches the bag of M&M's and pops a few into her mouth.

She's so damn beautiful, and I don't know what I did to deserve a chance to have this life, but I'll take it.

"What?" Sophie asks with wide eyes. "You're staring."

"Because I can't take my eyes off you."

She smiles softly. "You're very sweet."

I grab the bag of M&M's from her hand. "And so are these."

Sophie lies against my chest as we eat candy and split the banana. I hold her in my arms, grateful that this is where we are. Before falling asleep, I look at the app, making sure Eden's sugar levels are okay. It looks like she went a little high, but the machine gave her insulin, which is exactly what she needed.

"Everything okay?" Sophie asks.

"Yeah, her levels look good."

"Good." She breathes a sigh of relief and then yawns. "Will you stay the night with me?"

"Do you want me to?"

She smiles up at me. "I'd very much like it."

After moving all the food to her nightstand, I shift so I can hold her more comfortably. Sophie rests in the crook of my arm and then drapes her leg over mine. "Comfy?" I ask.

"Very."

"Good."

Sophie lets out a contented sigh, and I smile. "I like this."

She tilts her head up to me, and her blonde hair falls around her shoulders. "What?"

"This, us. I like holding you, making love to you, kissing you, coming home to you. I like it all."

Sophie's eyes sparkle in the light. "I do too. I didn't know I would ever feel this way again."

"What way?"

"Happy."

My fucking heart aches at that single word. "I didn't either."

"Because of your divorce?"

It's not something I talk about often, but Jenna leaving me was a huge blow. "I loved my wife. I wanted to build this life with her because it felt like it was what we should do. She was the only reason I made it through Kira's death. When I tell you I was a fucking wreck, I'm not downplaying it. Kira was my world. When she was sick, I knew something was wrong. I would listen to her talk about being sick and tired. She would drink water from an endless tap and still be thirsty. When she went to my mother—" I pause, not really wanting to discuss this part.

Sophie runs her finger down my cheek. "It's okay."

I shake my head. "I wish it were, but it's not. My mother told her to get over it."

"I'm so sorry."

I kiss her nose. "You did nothing, but I appreciate that you care."

"Of course, I care, Holden. It was wrong, and a mother is supposed to love her children. There's nothing I wouldn't do for Eden."

"I know. It's why you're here."

She smiles. "I wouldn't say Eden has anything to do with why I'm in bed with you."

I laugh. "No, that's all me."

"A little about you."

"Only a little?"

"Well, maybe more than a little," Sophie teases.

I love the fact that we're lying here after an earth-shattering night together and able to talk and just be open. It's something I haven't had in a long time, and I hadn't realized how much I missed it. Sure, I had a girlfriend here or there, but nothing serious. No one I would ever talk to about my sister. They were casual flings that never even went past a month. Nothing felt right, not until now.

She runs her finger against my lips. "Tell me about your ex. Why did you divorce?"

I sigh, hating this part of the story too. "Jenna and I got married because it was what we thought we should do. We were young, and honestly, I think we got married because we were afraid of losing each other. If we were tied together, then we could force ourselves to work. It didn't, obviously. Instead of being happy and this united couple, we resented each other. I think we were just too young and immature. She came to me about two years into our marriage, right before med school, and said she wanted to leave but wasn't sure what I thought. I told her we should probably just end things."

"You didn't see a future?"

I shake my head. "Nope. I saw . . . nothing. She said she felt the same, and a month later she filed for divorce. I signed without any fanfare. After I found out she came back to Rose Canyon, I went to med school in California and then settled there. It wasn't an ugly divorce, but I started to wonder if I wasn't just meant to be alone. I didn't love anyone else. I never yearned for a wife or kids. It was easier for me to have less complications and be alone."

She stays quiet, almost as though she has to digest that last part. It's just that it's all different now. Those feelings aren't the same anymore, I want that. I want her. I want Eden and this life.

"I see."

No, she can't. I tilt her chin to me. "How I felt then isn't how I feel now. I see a life with you. I see a future that wasn't possible before. You have changed everything for me in a way I never dared hope for. You and Eden living here has given me this . . . chance for more. Things I thought I just wasn't wired for. I'm happy with you, Sophie."

"I am too. I can't believe it, as it feels so fast, but it's right. I think that, in a way, I have been waiting for this, which sounds silly. After that night in Vegas, I would imagine you and me, especially as my pregnancy progressed. This child was growing inside me—half you and half me, yet I didn't know the other part. So, my mind would create you."

"And do I live up to the hype?" I ask.

"You've exceeded it."

I push her hair back and rub the soft skin beneath her eye. "You have no idea how much I want you."

"If it's anything like the way I want you, then I think I do."

"Stay with me, Sophie. Stay and see what we can become. Let's not fuck around with time because we both know it's not infinite. I know we said we'd go slow, but I want us to be more."

"What is more?"

"Together. I want you to be mine just as much as I'm yours. I don't know what it all means or how we navigate it, but I want to kiss you every morning when you wake up beside me."

I know there are a lot of complications to what I'm asking. We have to think about Eden and what she'll understand. She's young, but honesty is the best way. One day, we're going to encourage her to acknowledge me as her father. I don't know how much she'll remember of Theo, but at some point, it'll happen.

"And what do we tell people?" she asks.

"What people?"

"Your friends, Mama James, Eden."

"We tell them the truth. That we are together, and if they have an issue with it, they can fuck off. My friends knew this was going to happen. They've been giving me shit since the day you walked into my life. As for Mama James, she loves you and would never say anything bad about it. If anything, she'll be ecstatic. As for Eden, I don't know, what do you think?"

"I think we tell her that we're together, and maybe it'll lead to her eventually asking if you could be her daddy." Sophie yawns, and her eyes start to close.

I lean down, pressing my lips to her forehead. "Good night, beautiful."

She twists, hugging me closer. "Good night, love."

I move to the left and shut the light off . . . holding Sophie and vowing to never let go.

We wake before Eden. "Good morning, handsome," she says softly.

"It definitely is."

"What time is your shift?" She kisses my chest.

I huff. "In about three hours. I wanted to go for a run and then have breakfast."

She sits up, pulling the sheet with her. "I can make us eggs."

"And bacon," I remind her. It really should be its own food group.

"Of course. Eden would have it no other way. I'll make her toast with peanut butter too."

"Bacon!" The door flies open and in rushes Eden. "Mummy! I want bacon!"

Quickly, we both grab for the blanket and cover ourselves as she bounds toward Sophie's side of the bed. Sophie grabs her, pulling her so they are chest-to-chest, and I quickly grab my pants, pulling them on with a speed I didn't know I could move at.

"Mummy, Holden is in your bed."

Sophie makes a few noises. "Uhh, well, he, umm, Holden and I are . . . well."

Now dressed, I come around the side of the bed where Eden is and save Sophie from floundering any more. "I like your mum."

"She's very pretty."

"I agree. I like her very much, the way adults like Emmett and Blakely or Spencer and Brielle like each other."

"They kiss." She wrinkles her nose.

"They do."

"Do you kiss Mummy?"

I look to Sophie, who says, "We kiss each other because we care very much about each other. The way a mummy and daddy do."

I wait to see if Eden asks the million-dollar question. "Is Holden going to be my new daddy?"

And it comes like a fastball down the middle.

"Yes, Holden *is* your daddy, not because Mummy is dating him, but because he will always be your daddy."

Eden seems to ponder this with her head tilted up. "Always? What about my old daddy?"

"He will also be your daddy. You are the lucky girl who got to have two daddies and a mummy who loves you more than anything else in the world."

She climbs off Sophie's lap, pulling the sheet with her and allowing me the glimpse at a boob. Eden stands before me, watching me curiously.

"What do I call you?"

"You can call me Holden or whatever you want."

"Okay." She shrugs and then runs toward the door. "Can we have bacon *now*?"

The two of us laugh softly. "Sure thing, bug. We can have bacon, but first, let me check your sugar."

She skips back, blonde curls bouncing, and I grab the monitor off the nightstand. "Ready?" I ask.

"Can you sing the song?"

"Of course. Click," I say once.

"Click," Eden says.

"Click," Sophie follows.

"Click," I say again.

"Boom!" Eden gives me the all clear, and I press the button to test her blood.

"Good job, bug."

Her reading looks good, but her machine must've dosed insulin a second time last night because she was high in the hospital most mornings.

When the door shuts, Sophie lets out a long sigh. "Well, that was one way to handle it."

"I think we handled it well." I walk to her, pulling her out of bed with the sheet wrapped around her. "Get dressed, sweetheart, or I might have to remove this sheet and do something very stupid."

She grins. "You don't have time for that, darling. You have to make bacon, that little girl won't allow you more than two minutes before she returns."

"I could do it in two," I say with a laugh, and she rolls her eyes. "All right. Get clothes on and meet me out there." I snap the sheet away and shamelessly take in the view I could get very used to waking up to. Sophie squeaks and then shakes her head as she grabs a robe.

"Go before our daughter walks back in."

I wink, grab my shirt, and head into my room. Once changed into running attire, I walk toward the kitchen but stop short when I find Sophie standing at the table, looking over a file. A file I put in a drawer last night.

My blood runs cold for several reasons. One, someone was in this house, and two, Sophie just found out that I have Theo's medical record.

Her eyes snap up. "Why do you have this?"

"I'm a doctor, and I sometimes review medical records."

"I am aware of that, but why do you have *Theo's* medical record?"

"Do you remember how the postcards Theo sent had my medical license number on them?" Sophie nods. "Okay, so, it made me think that he was trying to call attention to something that was in his record. I wanted to make sure he didn't leave some clue as to what the hell is going on in there, knowing I'd pull the file and find it."

Sophie clutches it to her chest and then runs her tongue over her lips. "And is there some clue?"

"No."

"Of course, there's not because my husband was a selfish bastard! He bloody well knew what he was involved in and lied to me for who knows how long. Why didn't you tell me about this? Why did you keep a secret from me when you knew that everything for the last three months has been secrets and lies?"

I hate that she feels betrayed by me. So many times, I debated telling her, but it felt wrong to tell her until I was sure there was or wasn't anything to find. "I didn't want to give you false hope. It was a shot in the dark that I'd find something, and so far, I haven't. If I had, I would've told you."

She places the file on the table, her finger tracing the edge. "Why would you leave this out?"

Having to answer that question is far scarier than having to explain the file in the first place. "I didn't."

"Holden, it was open on the table when I came out to make food. Eden went back in her room to get dressed, so I doubt it was her."

"It was out when we got home last night too, and I didn't leave it like that. The *only* place I've ever opened it was my room, and last night, I put that file in the drawer there." I point to the cabinet. "It wasn't out when I came to bed, Sophie."

"What?"

"I need to call Emmett."

"Do you think someone was in the house?" she asks, looking around. "I do."

In fact, someone had to have been unless I have a ghost, which I know isn't the case. "Oh my God!" Sophie runs to Eden's room and throws the door open.

I follow her, and when I come to a stop in the doorway, Sophie turns to me. "We have to leave."

"No. Sophie, you're not going anywhere."

"We aren't safe here anymore. I have to pack a bag."

She releases Eden and goes for the bag in the closet. "Eden, get your toys."

"Stop. Sophie! Stop." This is getting out of control.

"Mummy? Where are we going?"

I pick Eden up, who has tears in her eyes, holding her. "Everything is okay, bug." Sophie's shoulders slump as a sob breaks from her chest. She keeps her back to us, and my heart shatters.

I promised to protect her, and she feels unsafe.

I kiss Eden's temple and put her down. "Can you go in the kitchen and have an apple?"

She pouts. "No apple!"

Of all the days. "I know you don't want one, but I need to talk to your mum."

Her dramatic sigh would be adorable at any other time, and I'm thankful when she heads to the kitchen without more protests, leaving me and Sophie alone.

"Sophie."

"My diary . . ." She sniffs. "I always put it in the nightstand, but it was on the bed last night, and someone was in this house while we slept. I put you in danger, and I have to leave."

I turn her to face me and pull her into my arms. "You are mine to protect, Sophie. I will not let anything happen to you, do you hear me? If you leave, then what? Where do you go? Do you think they won't follow? How will I live with knowing you could be hurt, and I'm not there to stop it?"

"How will I live knowing you could be hurt because of me?" She pushes out of my arms.

"I will fix this. We'll find a way to figure this out, but we can only do that if you don't leave. Promise me, Sophie. Do not run from me. Let me stand beside you and fight."

She wipes her tears and then meets my eyes. "I promise."

Relief floods me. "Thank you. Let me call Emmett, and we'll get to the bottom of this."

"Okay."

I walk back to my room, make the call, and within fifteen minutes, he's knocking on the door.

"What happened?" Emmett asks as he walks in.

I run through the story the best I can, telling him where everything was and where we'd found it, and then he asks Sophie the same thing.

"Anything else out of place?" he asks.

"Not that I can tell," I say. "Nothing was taken from what I can see, just moved or . . . I don't know."

He looks to Sophie. "When we got home, Eden's duck wasn't on her bed where she normally leaves it."

"Where was it?" I ask.

If it was just somewhere on the floor, that's not alarming, but if it was moved to a place that doesn't make sense, then that's another thing.

"In her drawer, which I thought was odd because it isn't something she's ever done before."

Emmett writes all this down and then looks at me. "And you checked all the doors and windows?"

"They were all locked last night when we went to bed."

"Okay, well, I'm going to take another look just to be safe, but it's clear someone was in the house."

"Do you think whoever Theo was worried about has found us?" Sophie asks.

"Easy," I say, taking her hands. "We don't know who it was yet, just that they were looking for something. If they wanted to hurt you or Eden, they could've done so but didn't. It seems like they just wanted to scare us."

She inhales deeply. "They accomplished that! They were here when we were sleeping."

"And they didn't ransack the place or take anything. It kind of seems as if they were looking for something and wanted us to know it."

"The file I understand, but my diary only has my personal thoughts in it. I haven't written in it much since Theo's death, but still . . . I don't have anything in there other than my clear confusion about what is going on in my life."

I take her hand in mine. "We're going to install cameras everywhere and an alarm. I'll make this place a fortress if that's what I need to do."

Emmett is looking around, taking photos, and dusting the doorknobs to see if he can find any prints that aren't ours. For now, it's all we can do.

"Okay."

"I'll ask George if he got any calls about suspicious people last night. Maybe we'll get lucky and everyone being extra vigilant because of the Wilkinson trial will work in our favor. Honestly, Sophie, right now this could have nothing to do with you. Holden has to testify in a few days, so this very well could be a message to him."

I lean in and kiss her cheek. "Either way, I'm not going to let anyone hurt you or Eden." They'll have to kill me first.

CHAPTER
Twenty-Eight
SOPHIE

Emmett and George searched the property without finding anything, but what surprises me most is that Jackson hasn't tried to contact me to find out what's going on.

Holden took yesterday off, and while he tried to get his shift covered for today too, he didn't have any luck. My job has been wonderful. They gave me the rest of the week off so I can get Eden situated. Tomorrow evening, we're going to see Mama James to go over all of Eden's care so she can be there without us worrying. Although, I don't know if anything will allow me not to worry about my daughter.

Even though Emmett and George spent hours searching the property and talking to neighbors, Eden and I are going to be alone today, and it has me unsettled. Not only because I've been jumping at my own shadow for the last twenty-four hours but also because I'm terrified something is going to go wrong with Eden's pump, and I'm not going to know what to do.

"Maybe I can come with you to work," I suggest.

"You've got this, Sophie. I'll be checking her blood sugar on the app and let you know if I see anything. We just tested it and it was right on point with what the app read, so it's good. Remember it'll fluctuate all day long. When she eats, if she plays, the weather, all of that can affect her," Holden says, squeezing my hand.

"I know you showed me all of this, but it still worries me. What if I get her carbohydrates wrong?"

I am not a doctor, and while Holden has spent time going over everything, asking me questions and answering all of mine, I worry. So many things can go amiss, and Eden is my everything. If she gets sick, I don't want to react badly.

"You are more than capable of handling this. Eden is doing great. We can both monitor her sugar levels from our phones, and if she goes low, give her some juice, two of the glucose tablets I showed you, or put honey under her tongue. If it's high, the monitor will give her the insulin she needs. Just follow the diet the hospital created and breathe, love."

"Okay," I say, not feeling all that confident, but I don't have much choice. The nutritionist gave us several daily meal plans that will help keep her regulated, so as long as I follow them, she should be okay.

"You can always call for an ambulance if you need to."

That is hopefully not going to happen.

"I don't know if I'm more worried about Eden or someone coming in the house again. You really feel comfortable with me being here alone?" I ask, needing to voice my concerns.

"Yes, because Spencer is coming over in a few minutes to stay with you."

"What is Spencer going to do? He's not a police officer, is he?"

Holden smirks. "No, he's better than that. Spencer trained with the Navy SEALs for a while, and he is just as deadly, if not more so, than the cops. I trust him, and he will protect you until I can get something else in place."

"Okay," I say before blowing out a slow breath to try to calm myself. "I just can't help feeling like the world beneath us is shifting."

"It always is, but I have to go work and then meet with the attorneys to go over my testimony. I think Emmett was right when he said this probably doesn't have anything to do with you." He cups my cheeks and brings his lips to mine. Just that brief kiss helps ease my nerves. "Either way, there are cameras, the alarm system, and Spencer. Nothing is going to hurt you."

He can't promise that, but I appreciate the effort he's made thus far. "I'm also worried about you."

When he walks out of here, if this is about him, then what? He could be run off the road or attacked at the hospital. I don't want to be paranoid, but there is so much uncertainty in our lives. If we had some answers, maybe I wouldn't be so worried. We'd have a starting point, but right now, we have nothing.

He pulls me into his arms, and I melt. "I can take care of myself. It's you I worry about. I don't want to go back to a life before you, Sophie."

"I don't either."

"Good. I'll call you when I get to the hospital, okay?"

I can't really ask for more than that. "All right."

He gives me another kiss, and then Eden runs in. "Are you leaving?"

"I am. Be good and make sure you eat whatever Mummy tells you."

She twists her torso and smiles at him. "Then can I have ice cream?"

He laughs and taps her nose. "We'll see."

Eden wraps her arms around him and squeezes. "I'll miss you, Holden-Daddy."

Holden and I just stare at her for a frozen moment, and then he clears his throat. "I'll miss you more, bug."

After he hoists his backpack over his shoulder, he winks at me and blows a kiss to Eden. "I'll see you girls later tonight. Be good!"

I watch out the window until he pulls out of the driveway and then Eden tugs on my hand. "May I watch a show, Mummy?"

"Yes, sweetheart. I need to go make a phone call, so stay in the living room."

"Okay."

I debated making this call last night, but I wasn't left alone long enough to do it. I go back in my bedroom and dial the number for emergencies only.

"Sophie, are you okay?" Jackson asks as soon as the call connects.

"I don't know. Someone was in the house."

He sighs. "I heard. It was my fault it happened. Zach had to return to Michigan, and my other guy couldn't get out there until today. It has been quiet since you got there, so I didn't think it would be an issue. Miles is still there, he sent me footage of the person who entered the property, and our technical team is running recognition, but the guy was smart and really hid himself well."

"Did Miles see him?" I ask.

"He caught him coming out of the house and chased him to a car, but he couldn't catch him. We are running all the information but haven't pulled anything up yet. I have sent a third person out to Rose Canyon, and if Holden does what I think he will, I'll be there soon as well."

That confuses me. "What will Holden do?"

Jackson chuckles. "Ask me to come out. If he or Emmett do, it'll actually make it far easier to protect you and Eden. I'd also be able to have a larger contingent of guys assigned to you."

"Is that not going to draw more attention to us?"

"Yes, but at this point, I think it's more of a risk not to have a security team presence. Even though there has been nothing before now that would indicate any trouble for you, we can always allow everyone to believe we're there for Holden's security. Now, tell me what you know from last night."

I tell Jackson the same thing Holden and I told Emmett, all the while wishing I had more information. When I tell him how Emmett suggested that whoever broke in was here for Holden and not me and Eden, he doesn't agree or disagree. I'm not sure I agree with Holden. It makes much more sense that the people Theo was protecting me from want what is in my diary or that file. If Theo did put something in his record, I need to know.

"I don't want you to worry, Sophie. We have this in hand, and I really think I'll be seeing you in a few days. I may bring Mark or another high-ranking Cole Security team member out there as well. Just know that we aren't taking this lightly."

I sink down on the bed, feeling heavy and sad. "All right. I just can't handle much more."

"You won't have to. We're all doing what we need to keep you and Eden safe."

He disconnects the call, and I start to pace the room. If Holden is right and there's something in the file, maybe he isn't finding it because it wasn't meant for him to find. Maybe Theo put something in there that only I would know. I may not have known Theo as well as I thought I did, but I still knew him better than Holden does. I can go through the record and see if there is something out of place. All of his hospital stays, doctor visits, and surgeries I was there for. His medical history was a huge part of my life.

As gutted as I was that Holden didn't tell me, I'm more angry than anything. I could help.

The doorbell rings, and my phone shows me a photo of Spencer at the door. I open it, letting him in the house before locking it behind him.

"Thank you for doing this."

"There's not much I won't do for Holden or you, Sophie. You guys needed me, and I'm here."

"Well, I appreciate it. I'm sure you have much better things to do with your time than babysit me and Eden."

Spencer shrugs. "Not really. I'm just working on a manuscript, and it's not like I can't do that here."

"Oh, what are you writing?"

"A story of a girl who is a hot mess."

"So, my life story?" I ask with a laugh.

"Close, she does reside in Rose Canyon."

I grin. "I see. You're writing a love story then."

Spencer laughs once. "It's more of the suspense side of it, but I guess, in the end, it's a love story."

"You know, I think that every story around a person involves love."

"Really? Even in thrillers?"

I used to argue with Theo all the time about how, at the heart of whatever movie he was watching, it was really a love story.

"All of them. Take a superhero movie, for instance. On the surface, it appears to be about the hero and his quest to save the world, but what do all good stories have? Love. And it typically comes in the form of a love interest, not just a romantic one, either. It could be parental love or the love of friendship. Lois Lane, Jane, Pepper Potts, Peggy Carter . . . I can go on and on. Even the female superhero has a man we love and root for. I believe it's because, at the core of human nature, there is this desire to belong and to love."

Spencer purses his lips and then grins. "You're freaking brilliant."

"It could also be because they know the women have to endure these films, and we're all a bit softhearted in a way." I shrug.

"Could be, but I like your eloquent answer much more. Brielle, however, isn't softhearted that way, but . . . I think it's probably a mix of both."

I laugh softly at that. "Well, either way, you're welcome to work while having to stay here."

"What are your plans?" he asks.

I am going to go through that damn file. "Nothing, maybe I'll paint a little."

"You know I can read a bullshitter."

"What?"

"I know something is going on. I can see it in your eyes. I was trained to read people and know when they're lying. The fact that you looked to the left is a telltale sign, plus you shifted your weight back."

Great, I am hanging out with Sherlock Holmes. "It's nothing."

"It's something, Sophie. If you're worried I'll tell Holden, I won't. Not unless it's a risk to you."

That leaves me a little perplexed. "Why would you keep things from him?"

"Because what you do today isn't what he asked me to watch. He wants to keep you and Eden safe, not police your activities and tattle."

"That's . . . well, unexpected, I suppose."

Spencer shrugs. "I could use a distraction. The writing is slow, and Brie is testifying today, so I really need to keep my mind busy."

I know the trial began, but I didn't realize Brielle was involved. "Why aren't you there?"

"I'm also a witness, so I can't hear her testimony. We really want this asshole to go to jail, so I'm here, and you're my entertainment."

I ponder if I should really trust Spencer with this. But, again, no one knows Theo's life the way I do, and if I can help, isn't that something?

"Holden got a copy of my husband's medical record. He thought there may be a clue in it, and I was planning to go through it to see if I could find something."

Spencer's grin is wide. "And I am assuming you and Holden didn't discuss this?"

"You're correct."

"Good. I like mischief and mysteries. Let's see what we can find."

I walk into the dining room where the file is sitting and open it. Spencer follows me, and Eden is watching her show and playing with dolls. I check my phone to see if there are any changes in her sugar, she went a little high a few minutes ago, but she's back in the normal range. So, I take the seat in front of the file. Spencer sits beside me, his eyes shifting between me and the stack of paperwork.

"Let's start at the beginning," I say, flipping open the front cover of the file.

Spencer laughs. "It's the best place to start."

We go over things for hours. Spencer and I only get about a quarter of the way through the file because all of it was medical jargon that gave me a headache and we had to take a lot of breaks. Spencer asked a lot of questions, probing into what I remember of each incident. It was hard reliving it. None of the times he was sick are particularly good memories. It was a lot of us trying to make the best of a horrible situation. It's now past dinner, and Eden has long since lost interest in her toys and shows.

"Mummy, do I need more needles?" she asks. Her hair is still damp from the bath, and she's snuggled in her favorite pajamas, ready to settle down and get the rest she needs, so I give her a reassuring smile as I grab the handheld tester.

"We do. Remember Holden said we have to do it three times a day to check it against your machine in your little bag here." I point to the pack that is around her waist.

"I love Holden."

The declaration stuns me. "You do?"

She nods. "Do you love Holden?"

I . . . I don't know how to answer that. I know that I haven't ever felt this way about another man. I know that I want to be with him, to be near him always. The way he cared for me and Eden without hesitation made me respect him deeply. More than anything, it was how he never questioned his paternity that made my feelings for him grow.

Then we had last night, and it was nothing about the past or the things we share. It was about us, and it was beautiful.

"I think I might, love. I think I might."

Eden's smile grows bigger. "We should stay here."

The future I didn't know was possible becomes clearer. The two of us loving each other beyond measure, raising Eden, and setting roots down in this town is a picture I want to hold on to. I see us growing old together, living a full life of love, passion, and devotion. It's all right there—with him.

I tuck Eden's hair behind her ear and smile. "I do too. Now, let's play click, click, boom."

We check her sugar, and she's a little low, so I give her a small cup of juice to bring it up. Once she's level, I put her to bed and find Spencer, back with the file.

"How you're not completely bored is beyond me," I say as I sit next to him. "We've been reading this file all day and have found nothing."

"I'm going cross-eyed, but I can't help thinking Holden was right about this. There are weird things mixed in the notes from this one cardiologist toward the middle. Dates that aren't the same as the appointment, which wouldn't typically be alarming, but it almost seems as if he's talking about another patient." Spencer pushes the file toward me. "Look at this one."

I read the doctor's assessment, explaining his heart has deteriorated more and his need for a transplant is now imminent. He notes the results of the EKG as well as the ultrasound. Then there's one random sentence that states: "The patient should look in Georgia or Texas."

"Is he talking about finding a donor, and do you look by states here?" I ask with confusion.

"No, and I'm not sure what he's talking about."

"Surely, he wasn't advising Theo to get a heart from the black market, right?"

Spencer shrugs. "I can't imagine that's ethical, but I've seen people with money do some crazy shit. Go to the next visit, there's another mention three paragraphs in."

I flip the page and scan to the section he's referring to. There it discusses going overseas to make a withdrawal. A withdrawal of what, though? I keep reading, but it doesn't specify. What does catch my eye is the mention of the medication.

"Well, the medication is incorrect." I point to where it's listed so Spencer knows what I'm talking about. "Theo wasn't on Zebeta at that point. He didn't take that until the last six months. This report is two years before that."

"So, do you think it's an error?"

It could be, but that's a major error to make. To have the wrong medications listed would've caused major issues if he had to be hospitalized. "I'm not sure . . ."

The rest of the page looks fine, so I find his next visit with this doctor. That one starts off reading exactly like a normal cardiology appointment, only this time, there's a random number that could never be a blood pressure reading. He would be dead if that was the case.

"Look at this." I show Spencer. "He would be dead if his blood pressure was 86/753."

"Jesus. And look at the temperature. He was 183?"

"This doesn't make sense. Dr. Frasher is one of the best cardiologists in London. There is no way he or his staff are this incompetent. Either this was done on purpose, or his records were tampered with."

"Look at the next. Let's see if there's a pattern."

Sure enough, the same readings are listed under that appointment too. There's no way this is a coincidence. "How did Holden miss this?"

"He may not have gotten this far into it. I don't think he got it until last week, or maybe he's just scanning the notes and not looking at the vitals, I don't know. Have no fear, Sophie, I will give him ample shit for it."

We both laugh and then I keep going through all his vitals on each sheet, and the numbers flex in those spots. Sometimes the temperature is listed as 86 and then his blood pressure is 75/318, which also don't make any sense.

"I don't understand what any of that means."

Spencer runs his hands through his hair. "I'll be right back."

He heads to Holden's room. I follow, unsure of what he's doing. "Spencer?"

"Did Holden talk to you about the postcards he got from Theo?"

"Yes, but there wasn't anything strange on them."

His chuckle says otherwise. "The fact that he got them is strange enough, but I agree with Holden. There was something about using his license number that was odd. It's why we thought maybe his file would contain the answers."

"All right . . ."

"I'm going off a hunch that they're related in these possible typos."

After rummaging through a few of Holden's drawers, he lets out a triumphant, "Ha!" Then he's holding a postcard, brandishing it in the air. "Found it."

We walk back to the dining room, and Spencer sets the postcard on top of the notes so that the strange readings are right below where Theo had written Holden's medical license number.

"I don't understand," I say, more to myself than anything.

"It could mean many things, but we were all confused as to why Holden's medical license number was on the cards. If I'm right, it means there really is something hidden in the file that he wanted Holden to find."

The second the last word leaves his lips, the power goes out in the house, and Spencer stands, pushing me behind him just as there's a deafening explosion.

CHAPTER
Twenty~Nine
HOLDEN

"Anything else, Cora?" I ask the prosecutor after the third run-through of the questions and documents. "I need to get home."

"I understand, but we want to make sure you're prepared."

"I am."

"Today went well with Brielle, but we need to show the pattern with the drugs used and . . ."

"I know. I really do." I get to my feet. Between my shift and then this, I am freaking done. I want to go home, shower, get naked with Sophie, and sleep.

"I heard about what happened at your house," she says while gathering up papers. "Do you think it's Wilkinson's guys?"

"Could be. I don't know."

"We hoped he would flip and give us who he worked for, but so far, he's tight-lipped."

That's her problem. "Sorry to hear that."

She pulls everything into her arms, and we make our way out of the courthouse. "I want to put this guy away for the horrible crimes he's committed and then shut down the entire operation."

"That's all any of us want."

I can hear the burden weighing on her as she releases a heavy sigh. "I worry. He has a lawyer he definitely can't afford, and while we have plenty of evidence to get a conviction on the abduction of Blakely and the attempt to commit murder regarding Emmett, we don't have anything that completely links him to the missing girls."

I would be stressed about it if I were her as well. We all know he's involved—hell, he literally confessed it to Blakely, but they haven't found anything concrete. He was very good about covering his tracks.

"Won't that be enough for now?"

"Yes, it will, but I want to get justice for the countless girls he's harmed. I need that smoking gun."

"I wish I could give it to you, Cora. All I have to offer is what I saw when I treated Blakely after her abduction and the medical information you're asking about."

A hint of a smile appears. "I think your testimony will go a long way. It'll create the pattern that I'm hoping to show over time."

"Thanks, Cora. I'll see you tomorrow."

She grips my arm as I walk out. "Listen, I don't know if what happened at your house was because of the trial, but I had a few things happen in the last week that weren't normal."

"Did you report them to Emmett?" I ask.

"No, they seemed . . . like maybe I had forgotten to put something away, but after hearing what went down with you, I'm starting to wonder if maybe they weren't just coincidences. But then, yesterday, the ME from Portland was found in her apartment, she's in critical condition and hospitalized after what looks to be a break-in. She clearly can't testify now. It's just . . . too many things tied to this case to be a coincidence."

I swallow deeply as dread fills my veins. Yes, Spencer is with Sophie and Eden, but if this is because of me and the trial, I'll never forgive myself if Sophie or Eden are hurt. After talking with Emmett earlier, he really believed it wasn't the trial. He said the three things that were touched all had to do with Sophie. Her diary, Eden's duck, and then Theo's file. Now, hearing that Cora had something similar leaves me to wonder if we weren't wrong.

"I have to go," I say abruptly.

Cora doesn't say anything else, and I head to my car, once there, I grab my phone and call Sophie.

She doesn't answer, and anxiety fills me.

I throw the car in reverse and peel out, calling Spencer as I move down Main Street at a speed I definitely shouldn't be going.

I can't explain it, but I just feel like something is wrong.

Spencer's phone goes to voice mail as well.

I slam my hand on the steering wheel, hating that I am at least fifteen minutes out. My mind is going in a million directions as I race to get to Sophie and Eden. Rationally, I know that they are probably just away from their phones, and I have no real reason for my heart to be beating as frantically as it is, but fear is a tricky emotion. It doesn't care about logic or reason. There is just this pounding urgency to get home and make sure they are safe because I can't handle anything happening to them. I love Eden with everything I am, and I am falling so hard for Sophie. I want to spend every damn day with her and build a life with our daughter.

If that is taken from me because of this fucking asshole, I'll kill him myself.

My phone rings, and for a second I think it could be Sophie, but it's Emmett.

"Emmett! I can't reach Sophie or Spencer!"

"Where are you?"

"I'm turning on State Street, where are you?"

"I'm at your house now."

"Are Sophie and Eden okay?" The panic is starting to take over, and I fist my hands around the steering wheel to keep them from shaking.

"Just get here safe, and we'll figure everything out."

My heart is pounding in my chest. "Fuck!" I yell, slamming my hand on the wheel. "Just tell me! Tell me if they're okay!"

Emmett is quiet for a second and then sighs. "Holden, calm the fuck down. You're not going to be of any use if you're a maniac. Look, no one handles situations like this better than you, so put your damn doctor hat on when you approach this house."

"I'm two minutes away."

I don't know how I'm going to hold on and do as he says, but I am going to try. I pull down my driveway, and there are police cars, an ambulance, and three men with rifles out front talking.

Throwing the car in park, I rush out, desperate to see my girls. When I get through the door, Sophie is there, her head in her hands as Blakely rubs her back.

"Sophie!" I yell, and her head snaps up.

Then she's rushing toward me. My arms wrap around her, and she clings to me. "They took her! Oh, God, they took our baby."

For the first time in my life, I know what true terror feels like.

"We have search teams out in the area, and Cole Security guys are already running the camera feeds through facial recognition, as well as any tracking options they have."

Sophie and I are on the couch, holding each other's hands as everyone moves around us. Sophie cries off and on as I try to come to terms with what happened.

Spencer described it as a full-scale military attack. The lights went out, and then two flash-bangs were deployed in the room, disabling him and Sophie. Within fifteen seconds, they'd breached the door and had taken Eden. He said it happened so fast it was impossible for him to react before the flash-bangs went off.

I want to scream, to rail at the world and everyone in it. "I should've been here," I say to no one.

"It wouldn't have mattered if you were here," Spencer says.

"I should've . . . I should've hired Jackson's company. I was going to call him today, but now it's too fucking late."

Emmett squeezes my shoulder. "Jackson's company *was* here, Holden. Unbeknownst to us, they've been watching Sophie since she arrived."

"His team was here, and they did nothing?"

"They were incapacitated before the attack but were in the house within three minutes of Eden being taken. The guys who took her weren't amateurs. They were well trained and executed their mission in under five minutes, start to finish."

The two guys from Cole Security walk over. "I'm Miles Kent, and this is Makenna Dixon, both of us were here when it happened. One of our team members in San Diego is coming up with his K-9, Jackson is on the way, and so is Zach Barrett, who was previously on Sophie and Eden's detail." The guy looks to Sophie. "We were both knocked unconscious, so it's clear they knew who we were. As soon as I came to, I saw Makenna already moving to the house. It was as though they were the equivalent of us."

"Your last name is Dixon?"

"Yes, sir. My parents are Mark and Charlie, whom you've met, and

I assure you, there will be serious repercussions for allowing this on my watch. I take full responsibility."

Miles steps up. "I'm the lead guard, this is on me. We already have the tech teams working on things, and thanks to your cameras, we should have something soon."

"How long have you been watching the house?" I ask him.

He looks to Sophie, and she answers. "Theo hired them to protect us. Zach, one of Jackson's team members, brought me to Rose Canyon, and they've been watching out for us this whole time."

"A lot of good it did."

Makenna looks as though she's going to speak, but Miles beats her to it. "It didn't, and for that, we are sorry. After the breach on your home, we should've stayed a little closer than we were, but we were trying to keep eyes on you at a distance so as not to alert anyone of our location."

Sophie wipes the tears that keep falling. God, she's breaking, and I can't handle it. I pull her into my arms, needing to hold her. "They'll find her," I whisper against the crown of her head. They have to.

"We're doing all we can."

"She must be so scared," Sophie cries. "Who did this? Who took my baby?"

Emmett's lips form a tight line. "I don't know, Sophie, but we aren't going to stop until we find her."

She cries harder, and I wrap her tighter to my chest.

I feel sick, my heart is in my stomach, and I can't think. In my life, I have been in horrific situations and have always been able to keep my composure, but right now, I can't. Tears fall as I keep Sophie against me. I just got them both, and now I could lose them. All because of me. All because of this fucking case.

"I'm sorry, my love. God, I'm so sorry."

Sophie shifts, looking up at me. "You didn't do this."

"I promised I'd protect you."

She shakes her head. "I was here, and you need to believe me when I say, there was no protecting us from what happened. Holden, it happened so fast that it was over before I even really figured out what was happening. Before Spencer could react. The only people we should blame are the people who took her, so let's stop trying and just . . . and just focus on getting her back. I need our little girl back." The last few words are choked with tears that threaten to shatter my heart.

I have lived the last three years without Eden, and the last few months have changed everything. My daughter, the very reason I breathe, is missing, and I have no control over getting her back.

"I do too, sweetheart."

People move around the room, taking photos, talking to each other, and dusting knobs and other items, but in this moment, it all fades away. My world narrows to Sophie, the tears streaming down her beautiful face, and the heartbreak filling in her eyes. I feel helpless. We just had a scare with her, almost lost her because I missed the signs of diabetes, and we lost her in another way.

Sophie stiffens, pulling out of my embrace. "What about her medication?"

I've already run through this in my head. "We changed the insulin yesterday. She has enough for another two days—maybe. I don't know. If she drops low, then . . . I . . . fuck!"

Spencer's the first to speak. "Stay calm, Holden."

"She could die. Do you understand that? The pump can help if her blood sugar goes too high, but if her sugar drops, I can't . . . I can't fucking do anything from here."

Sophie breaks down, crumpling to the floor with heartbreaking sobs. I land on my knees next to her, pulling her into my arms as my own tears fall. Eden could die, and I am helpless to save her. I will never recover if I lose her too.

Please God, help us.

CHAPTER
Thirty
SOPHIE

Holden tries to convince me to take a sedative, but I refuse. I don't want to sleep, I want to find my daughter. That is all that matters.

Right now, she's alone and afraid. She could be crying for us or hurt or . . . or . . .

I cut the thought off because it's too terrifying to be allowed to form.

Holden and I sit on the sofa, a blanket draped around us as we stare at our phones and watch her blood sugar levels. She's needed insulin twice, and each time the machine dispenses, I feel sick. Still, so long as the pump is still updating, so long as she still needs it to regulate her blood sugar? There is a fraction of solace in that, even if it also means there's less medication available to her.

Jackson sits on the table in front of us. "We have people everywhere looking, my team in San Diego is checking any traffic cameras, and the police are doing their part from here. Charlie is working with some of her contacts to do things we can't as well. The US Marshals just deputized my team so we can be involved in the investigation."

Holden looks up at him. "If you knew Sophie was in danger, why didn't you have more men here?"

Jackson doesn't flinch. "I had what we thought was necessary. There were two men here and, after what happened two nights ago, a third was on his way at my company's expense. I assure you, no one thought this was going to happen."

"Why didn't they take Eden the night they were here?" I ask. "Why wait?"

He shakes his head. "I don't know. If we consider that there could be someone trying to find out what Holden knows ahead of his testimony, as well as someone connected to Theo who might be looking for you, we could be looking at two separate perpetrators. Eden was taken when Holden was with Cora, which leads me to think her abduction is connected to the Wilkinson case."

Blakely walks over and hands me a cup of tea. "I thought the same. Have we considered that the people looking for Sophie and Eden could be the same people trying to prevent people from testifying in the case?"

Jackson replies, "I have. My team is looking for any connection to Wilkinson or Bill Waugh. I asked Theo point blank what exactly he uncovered, but he wouldn't tell me. He said if the information was ever needed, it would present itself."

Holden gets to his feet. "Well, we need it now!"

Blake rests her hand on his shoulder. "If the people who took Eden are the people Theo wanted you to hide from, then yes, we need it. If it's about the trial, then it won't help us. Listen, if the goal is to keep you from testifying, then this was the way to do it. If it's about Sophie, then I don't see what they gain by taking Eden. Has there been any ransom demand?"

"Not yet," Jackson says.

"Okay. And what about the file, Spencer?"

He glances up and shakes his head. "I've been searching for more references to Holden's license number or why it's on there. So far, nothing really makes sense, but I sent scans of the file to Cole's analysts, so they're working on it too."

All of this happens around me, but I can't really process it. Two competing horrible people after us? I just can't handle it.

So, I look down at my tea and continue to monitor the only link we have to Eden.

They continue to talk and then leave the room as someone calls them out. I am lost, watching the numbers move up and down, but so far, she isn't dropping too low. I pray whoever took her at least sees she's sick.

Holden wraps his arm around my shoulder. "You have to eat."

"I can't. What if she's hungry? What if she is thirsty? I can't if she can't . . ."

Resting my head on him, I cry again, feeling so lost and angry. All night, we wait for a call, for someone to demand something so we can give it to them, but it hasn't come. I let the tears come, my eyes feeling heavy and my body not wanting to cooperate with staying awake.

"You're exhausted, Sophie. Just rest here, you don't have to sleep, but just rest."

"I don't want to rest. I want to go and find her. I want to do some-thing—anything other than sitting here and doing nothing. We can go look for her. We can go to the hospitals, right? I can't just sit here!"

Holden takes my face in his hands. "We are doing everything we can."

It doesn't feel like it. "I should never have come here. After the other night, we should've packed our bags and left. I did this."

This is my fault.

I am going to be the reason we lose her. I knew we were in danger, and I didn't run. Instead of demanding Jackson get us to a safe loca-tion, I trusted everyone around me to protect us. There was a pit in my stomach, telling me to go, and I ignored it.

"None of this is your fault, Sophie! Love, you didn't do anything wrong. You aren't involved in any of what's going on. If it's anyone's fault, it's mine! Again, you did nothing. I'm the one who fucked this up. I'm the one who made you stay because I was so fucking afraid of losing you. I'm the one who failed you both." Holden rubs his face, his eyes red rimmed and full of pain. "I will never forgive myself for this."

Neither of us will. There seems to be enough guilt to go around for us both to drown in it.

I reach for him. "We can't do this. It won't bring her back, and this isn't your fault. Hell, if it's anyone's, it's the people Theo was involved with. But you and I? We didn't do this to her. We didn't make her sick or ask anyone to take her from us. We love her, and while we may be breaking right now, it's because we just want her back."

Holden takes two steps and tenderly cups my face between his palms. "It's all I want."

"Me too."

"I would trade anything for her."

"I keep asking myself, why didn't they take me?" I say. "If this is because of Theo, why not take me? Eden doesn't know anything."

"You don't either," he points out. "What better motivator for either of us is there than her?"

"I wish they took me. I wish . . . I hope they come back and kill me if anything happens to her because I will never survive this, Holden."

He leans in, kissing me softly. "Neither will I. We have to be strong and keep faith in the people around us."

How can he not know that I lost my faith the minute I realized my daughter was gone?

It's been twenty-four hours.

It's as though I'm living in a snow globe where I'm the statue and things are in constant motion around me.

We've heard nothing from anyone. No news. No sightings. It's as though she vanished. The last camera footage shows a black van driving past the coffee shop. After that—nothing.

I can't sleep, eat, or even talk much. Brielle and Blakely have been at my side, unwavering. Holden goes from pacing, to sitting, to yelling at everyone, to crying, and then back to pacing, trying to be strong.

Neither of us are able to keep it together for a long period of time. We're both breaking with each second that passes. After watching me cry for the last hour, Brielle forces me to lie down, and I'm feigning sleep because it's easier than being told what to do or being talked to like she's already dead.

I'd rather just be numb.

Holden is taking a shower, and there are several people in the dining room, trying to be quiet, but I hear each word.

Emmett's unmistakable voice is heard first. "We thought they'd make their demands known. If it's about Holden, then someone should've said something about testifying. If it's about Sophie, then we should've heard what they want that she has."

"If she even has anything, but we've been digging into his financial records," Jackson offers.

"And?"

"So far, it looks like the company he was working for was a shell for either a cartel or some kind of mafia syndicate. We just don't know which one yet," Jackson says.

"Do you think he found out who he was really working for and that's why he made Sophie run?"

"I do. It's why he was so afraid, and it'll take me days to try to stitch together who the shell company could be tied to, but that will depend on whether they made an error in the paper trail somewhere," Jackson says, frustration in his tone. "We are focusing most of our energy on getting a lead to find Eden, that's the most important thing."

"Especially with her medication running low." Emmett's fear is evident. "Hopefully, they are aware of it and doing the right thing."

Jackson sighs. "If she's dead, then they can't use her against them."

"Exactly."

I roll over, covering my head with the pillow. I don't want to hear this. I don't want to think about any of it.

I close my eyes, and that numbness I prayed for comes, sinking me into darkness.

"Sophie! Sophie, wake up." Holden is shaking me, and my eyes fly open in a panic.

"What? Did they find her?" I ask, sitting up and looking around.

He shakes his head. "You're getting a call."

"Everyone silent!" Jackson yells. "Sophie, you need to answer the phone."

I nod, forcing down the bile that threatens to come up. My hands are shaking as I reach for the phone, and Jackson reminds me of what I'm supposed to do if it's the person who took Eden.

"Keep them talking for as long as you can. Ask questions. If they don't answer, ask it again until they answer, okay?"

"Okay." I touch the green button and force myself to say, "Hello?"

The voice on the other line is garbled, disguising who it could be. "We have your daughter."

"Is she alive?"

"You have something we want, and if you return it, we will return her."

My hands are shaking, and I want to scream, but I remain calm—for Eden. "Is my daughter alive?"

There's a pause. "She is alive."

Oh, thank God. "I want . . . to hear her voice."

"You have something that belongs to me, and I want it back."

The fear that I have tried to control rushes forward. "Please, I don't have anything but Eden. Please, she's sick, and she needs to come home. She has diabetes and could die. God, please just tell me what you think I have, and I'll give it to you if I have it! I swear it. I just want my daughter home. Please."

Holden wraps his arm around me, keeping me still. "No need to get hysterical. Your husband took what was mine, and I want it back."

God, it's because of me. My breath comes in short bursts and then Holden turns me to look at him. He mouths the word *breathe*.

We inhale and exhale together, and I nod. "Tell me what it is. I don't know how to look for something if I don't know what it is."

The voice laughs quietly. "Find my money, and you get your daughter."

Then the line goes dead.

CHAPTER
Thirty-One
HOLDEN

"She's asleep. I gave her a sedative," I explain to the group in the house.

After the phone call, she was hysterical. She kept screaming for Eden and begging for us to call them back, give them every penny we all have. Kate showed up shortly after the phone call, and she was a huge help. Even then, it took us fifteen minutes to get Sophie calm enough to listen to us, and then it was another ten minutes to convince her to take the medication to help her sleep. She is no good to any of us in that state.

"She just needs to rest," Kate says, gently squeezing my arm. "She's been through a lot in a very short time."

I nod. "I know. It's a lot for all of us."

"How are you holding up?"

"I don't know how to answer that."

She nods in understanding. "Honesty would be a good start."

I inhale slowly, trying to settle my rioting thoughts. "I'm not okay."

"I didn't think you were."

"This whole thing, I just don't know what to make of it. Why take an innocent little girl? Why put her life in danger for money? And . . . Sophie has nothing."

"People do horrible things when they're desperate. Do you know anything about who her husband was involved with?"

I shake my head. "We know nothing, Kate. Just that Eden is missing, and we have a clock we're racing to get her before she could die. I will never be able to live through it."

She sighs deeply. "I've been where you are. The fear of not knowing but still having to be strong no matter the outcome. Be there for each other and lean on your friends because they'll help you through. When I—" She forces a smile. "It's hard, no matter what the outcome is, but being optimistic is best here."

I watch her, trying to read between the lines. "You speak as though you have experience with this."

Kate gives me a sad smile. "I lost my daughter about five years ago. She was . . . well, she was sixteen, and it was the worst thing I have ever experienced. I didn't think I would live through it either. I wanted to crawl into that casket and be buried with her. I lost my marriage because of it. It's why I came to Oregon, to leave all of that behind. Each day, you find a way to wake up and make a difference in the world. It's a pain that never goes away, you just learn to endure it. I hope you don't go through the same thing and find Eden."

"Thank you, and . . . I'm sorry. I can't imagine this is easy for you, being here."

Kate comes closer and then pulls me in for a hug. "This is what gets me through my pain—helping others."

"You're better than I am."

"No, I'm not, I've just found ways to cope."

And I hope I never have to. We walk into the dining room area where everyone is standing. The discussions are all theories, and my head is swimming.

"Hey," Jackson says as I enter. "Is Sophie sleeping?"

"She is."

"Did she say anything before she fell asleep?" Blake asks.

I shake my head. "She just kept repeating that she didn't have any money. She came here with nothing and has never once mentioned having anything more than the envelope she was handed when she was driven here."

"I can attest to that," Jackson says. "When Sophie arrived in the US, I picked her up and gave her three thousand dollars. That was it, and Theo covered her protection prior to his death and had most of his financial assets put away offshore that he didn't want anyone touching. It was imperative that we never let Sophie have access."

"How much is in there?"

I'll cash out every stock, bond, and bank account I have if that's what it takes. They just need to say the word.

"It's about two hundred thousand dollars, which isn't enough to kidnap a kid over. Not that it's pocket money, but a cartel or mafia syndicate would be after millions."

I sink into one of the dining chairs, angry and frustrated and impatient. We need to find her because each tick of the clock is like a bomb ready to explode.

Spencer starts to pace. "Why not drain it then? We could pull all that money and see if that's what they want."

"We can, but my gut says it's not the money they want. I could be wrong. Did Theo's letter to Sophie give her any instructions or information?" Jackson asks.

"I have no fucking idea," I answer, frustrated and over all of this. "I'm so tired of this! The games and the bullshit. First with Brielle, then Blakely, and now they took my fucking daughter. I am tired of having to unravel clues and search for missing links. Nothing ever adds up, and I am over it. I'm done."

"I know you're frustrated, but to get Eden back, we need to figure out what Theo did with that money," Jackson says, calm and collected. "I'm a father, and I can only imagine how I'd feel if one of my girls was taken. I'd probably be homicidal, but I would hope that there were people with cool heads who could remember what we're doing, and that's to find what these people want."

"They want money. What money? Sophie doesn't *have* any goddamn money."

"She does. She just can't touch it," Blakely adds in. "If she did, people could trace where she was. I agree with Jackson that it's not what they want. I think there's another account that she doesn't know about. Her husband was far from honest with her, and she knows almost nothing about what he was doing other than he worked in finance. So, let's say he stumbled on something in the books that he shouldn't have, which seems reasonable when you remember he was working for a shell company with links to organized crime. What's the easiest thing to use as an insurance policy to keep someone from killing you to ensure you don't spill that secret?"

Jackson is quick to say, "Information or—"

"Money," I finish.

Blakely taps her nose and points at me. "Exactly. If that's the scenario we're looking at here, then her not knowing she has the money doesn't mean she doesn't have it."

The room is quiet as that information settles around us.

"So, you think there's an account with money that Sophie doesn't know about?" Kate asks.

Spencer answers. "I think it's possible. Right now, we're running on possibilities and theories while we wait for a legitimate clue to come up. I agree with Jackson that it's going to be more than a few hundred grand if they're willing to abduct a child to get it back. They're desperate and need it."

The air falls from my mouth and defeat fills my lungs. How the hell do we fix this? How can we find money that no one knows of? If her husband were still alive, I'd kill him myself.

Spencer lifts the file. "It has to be in here. This is the only link we have to Theo, and he wanted you to know it, Holden."

"Give me the file," I say, reaching my hand out. "I'll go over every fucking line of it." He hands it to me, and I turn to walk back into my room where it's quiet but stop to face them first. "Act as though this contains nothing because, for all I know, it's worthless. Find my daughter. Please."

"We're working on it," Jackson promises. "We won't give up."

With that, I head into the bedroom and shut the door firmly behind me.

Hours pass, and I have read almost everything. So far, there is nothing other than one doctor using my license number in his notes. I'm spinning in circles, feeling as if I'm going insane, and finally reach a breaking point. I grab my phone and call the doctor's office. After my insistence that I speak to the doctor immediately, they reluctantly put me through.

"Hello, Dr. Frasher, this is Dr. Holden James, I'm calling in regards to a patient of yours, Theodore Pearson."

"Yes, Mr. Pearson was a patient of mine, but I'm not sure I can help as he's passed away."

"You were his primary doctor, were you not?"

"I'm sorry, but I'm not sure I can answer any questions."

"Dr. Frasher, I am aware that Theo is dead, and I am also going to be frank and explain as quickly as I can. I am Eden's biological father. His wife, Sophie, was sent away because their lives were in danger.

Now, I am asking why, on all your records, my medical license number was used in various ways like as replacements for his temperature, blood pressure, or pulse rates. All things that, to the normal person, may seem off, but to me, say there's more."

He doesn't speak for a minute, but I wait, hoping he'll give me an answer.

"I'm sorry, Dr. James, I don't know what you're talking about. Theo was my patient, but there is nothing I can tell you that might help."

"Please, I'm not asking for me. I'm asking because someone's life is in danger."

Dr. Frasher clears his throat. "Give me a date, and I'll look at the chart to see where a mistake might be."

I flip to the first time my number was used and tell him.

"What seems odd to you, Dr. James?"

"The blood pressure is listed as 86/753."

"You must be mistaken. My records show his numbers were 123/77, which is a bit hypertensive but not enough to cause alarm."

No, that's not what my file says. "I'm reading it now. The printed chart says 86/753."

There is a heavy sigh. "Must've been done afterward because that's not what my records reflect."

I pinch the bridge of my nose and fight back the urge to throw the phone across the room. "Check another date." He does, and once again, the information isn't the same. "How are your files different from the one I have in my hand?"

"I'm not sure, but I'd be most interested to know how you acquired my confidential patient records."

I had the hospital record, his cardiologist, and his primary all pulled and sent to me on the premise I was doing a postmortem investigation on his death.

"It's of no consequence. I'm most interested in why the records have been altered."

"Doctor, I am looking at my original hard copy and telling you exactly what I see."

"Thank you, I won't waste any more of your time."

"Good day."

I hang up and lie back on the bed, saying a prayer to my sister to watch over Eden because I have clearly failed.

I must've fallen asleep because when I open my eyes, Sophie is in bed with me, curled up against my side. I wrap my arm around her and kiss her forehead. I promised her I'd protect her, and even though I didn't, she is here.

My phone shows it's only been an hour since I spoke with the doctor, but it's the most sleep I've gotten since Eden was taken.

Sophie stirs, her eyes fluttering a few times before opening. "Still nothing?"

I shake my head. "No. I tried . . ."

A tear falls down her beautiful face. "I just want her home. I would do anything. I would give anything. I'd trade my life for hers, but they just took her without giving me a chance to give them what they wanted. They took our little girl, and she could die." Her voice cracks.

"We're going to find her. We have to find her."

She nods but more tears fall. "I keep waiting to wake up and find her laying in her bed, sleeping peacefully."

"I wish that were true," I tell her as my own voice shakes. "I would sell everything I own if it would help."

"All the years I spent thinking Theo was an amazing man have all disappeared. He knew we were in danger, and he gave me no way to protect myself. I . . . I hate him, and I never thought I would. I hate that he did this to Eden."

I brush her hair back, wiping her tears with my thumbs. "The answers are here, Sophie. I don't know where, but I think Theo did leave you the way to find them. We just need to make the pieces fit."

"It's been thirty-nine hours. We don't have much more time before her pump runs out."

"I know." That is what scares me the most. "Come on, let's go see if there are any updates."

My phone has a voice mail from an unknown number. I look at Sophie as she's climbing out of bed and tell her.

"Listen to it."

I play it.

"Dr. James, this is Dr. Frasher. My office isn't a safe location to talk. I am sending you an encrypted email that will help answer your questions. I want to say that I am incredibly sorry, and I hope this helps."

"What is he talking about?" Sophie asks.

As I pull up my email, I explain how I'd called him earlier and that he basically said the file I had was wrong.

I scroll through, not seeing anything, so I flip to my work email, and it's there and marked as urgent.

When I open the email, there's a short note and an attachment.

Holden & Sophie,

I cared for Theo over the last two years. During that time, we grew very close, and we also became entangled in something we never should've. My wife and son were killed three days ago, and I'm afraid what happened to your daughter is my fault. I triggered the failsafe, and I am incredibly sorry for that. This is the last you'll hear of me. Good luck, and I hope you find your daughter.

I open the attachment to find that it's a scan of a handwritten note.

If you're reading this, then the worst has happened and Sophie or Eden are in danger after my death. I warned them what would happen if they went after my family, but it's clear that it didn't matter. This was my insurance policy.

I am aware that you probably think I am worthless, and you would be correct at this point. I failed to protect my best friend and the little girl who called me Daddy. Therefore, I hope this will help you not only save them but also destroy those behind it.

The only way I could do this was to place clues, ones that would lead you here. I worked for the worst people known to man. They are delusional in their beliefs of building a greater world and will stop at nothing to achieve it.

When I started working for Havened, it was built up to be a program that would help others, give children a family life that otherwise would be lost to them. And in the beginning, it was just that. I found ways to help the company save more money and shelter funds to help more children.

In my ambition to help the company help more families, I took advantage of a loophole, finding out after the fact that what I had done wasn't legal. When I attempted to correct my error, to own up to what I'd inadvertently done, the owner of Havened used it as leverage to force me to continue processing the finances the same way. My options were limited, and I couldn't bring myself to let them destroy my family for a mistake I'd made.

I fucked up, and my wife and daughter were at risk. So, I did what I thought was right and gathered as much information as I could on each person who ran the organization, desperate to find out who the head of the snake was.

I am writing this letter in the ICU, dying, and I haven't found that information. However, in a safety deposit box located at the main bank in Rose Canyon, you will find everything I have on them. The key is inside the pyramid trinket I sent to you. There is a second copy in Big Ben. If they have killed either Sophie or Eden, give them nothing. If they have been taken and this will help get them back, use it, but know they will never be satisfied if they're let go. You will all need to run. I don't know who he is, but he is ruthless. Read everything in a secure location and don't share what you learn. Trust me.

I am sorry, but I tried my hardest to make it right.

Theo

Sophie's lips tremble as she shakes her head. "We have to find that box."

I nod. "Let's go, I'll wake the world up to get into that bank."

CHAPTER
Thirty-Two
SOPHIE

The bank was closed, but Emmett was able to talk the manager into coming in for us. Then all we had to do was show our IDs and produce one of the two identical keys we'd found, which then allows us access to it. Box number 223, Eden's birthday.

"Take as much time as you need."

Holden reaches his hand out. "Thank you, Ellis. I know it's a Sunday at ten o'clock."

He grips his hand with both of his. "I'm a father. No thanks necessary."

Once the manager has stepped out of the room, I pull the box free and set it on the table.

Holden is the one who lifts the lid, and then we both just stare at the contents. Inside there must be hundreds of pages of bank statements, notes, names of people and places, and dozens and dozens of printouts. "This will take days to go through," I say with an ache in my voice. "We don't have days!"

"Just, we have to be calm. We have to look at this strategically."

Eden is running out of time. We both got an alert on our way here that the pump was low, and we needed to refill it soon. Her insulin is dispensing more today than the others, and I am panicking.

Holden starts to sort the papers. "Here, look at these. See if any of the names or notes he wrote make sense."

He takes one pile while I take the other, and for long moments, the only sound in this vault is the shifting of papers.

The first ten or so pages of Theo's notes are not much. Names of some people we met at galas and some charity donations that he made to a heart center in London. "This name," I say, holding out a piece of paper. "It's familiar."

He takes it and quickly reads the letterhead at the top. "That's the doctor who sent us the email."

"We donated quite a sum in his name."

I pull the bank ledger from my and Theo's joint account and find a line already highlighted. "Thirty thousand pounds."

"Is that the only time he donated money in Dr. Frasher's name?"

I look farther down and shake my head. "No, nothing in that amount or to that doctor again."

"Could that have been the payout for altering the records?"

"Possibly," I reply.

"Okay, put that to the side. Keep looking."

Holden makes a low sound in his throat, pulling my attention to him. "What is it?"

"That doctor's name is here too. He . . . I don't understand. Theo lists him as a man involved in Havened. He wrote that he was in attendance at one of these meetings in Texas?"

"Texas?"

I know that Theo traveled a lot, but I don't recall a trip to Texas. "He always went to Georgia when he came to America."

"It was in the beginning of his notes. He states that Dr. Frasher prescribed medications to help during withdrawals of some kind of drug use. I would never give anyone this, it's not something I handle often, but still, it doesn't make sense. Dr. Frasher is in the UK and couldn't administer medication in Texas anyway."

I shake my head. "I don't know what the drug part means."

"Neither do I, but if Dr. Frasher was involved with these same people, maybe he wanted out and decided to help Theo? They obviously had a plan if something happened, and Dr. Frasher said his wife and son were killed and he was sorry he initiated the failsafe."

"Okay, but what do you think the failsafe was?"

He sighs. "I don't know." For another minute or two, we sift through papers, and then Holden hands me something else. "Look, here he shows his name again, but in the UK."

"Theo was his patient," I remind him. "Having a meeting in London isn't so strange."

"We don't know for certain he was truly treating him. It wouldn't look strange if Theo was seeing a doctor for his heart that worked with his company, would it?"

I shake my head. "No, he was absolutely his doctor. I went to his appointments with him."

"Let's go on the assumption then that Dr. Frasher wasn't actually Theo's doctor. You went to his appointments to make it all look real. All the falsified records are Dr. Frasher's. He had the letter from Theo. What if he and Theo were giving that illusion in order to protect their families?" Holden questions.

All of this is so crazy to me. If Theo or Dr. Frasher would just tell us the truth, we could've gone to the police or gotten help. None of this would've happened. Now we're in a vault, trying to put the pieces together with bombs strapped to our chests.

"We need to find the money."

"I agree. So, let's keep digging."

I start piling through and find a transfer from our personal account. "Holden, look at this."

"That's a nice size transfer."

"It's made every three days for two weeks. I don't know of any account in Belize." I groan. "He went through all of this trouble and didn't think to leave a nice note with the directions of whatever the bloody failsafe was! Fuck! I need our daughter. I came here for what? To lose her because of sodding money?"

He gets to his feet and holds both of my arms. "You came for a life. For a family, and while I don't know that Theo ever thought we'd be together, you came for me. I love you, Sophie. I love you and Eden. I will not give up. You and I are strong together, goddamn it. We will find Eden because we won't quit. I am scared and angry, and all I want is that little girl in our arms, so don't you dare give up on us."

Taking his face in my hands, I lean in and kiss him. "I love you too. I hate that this is how we just said it, but . . ."

"But it's the truth."

"And how do we live through this?" I ask. "I don't know how this ends, and I just want her back."

"I do too, baby. I do too. Let's keep looking and see if we find anything else we can use."

Once again, I spend time combing through Theo's random thoughts and nothingness. Each page we read leaves us closer to nothing. It's incredibly frustrating. As I'm about to give up, I find a note that causes me to pause.

In his thick, scribbling handwriting, it says: "Paramedics take runaways."

"Holden?"

"Yeah?"

"The case that you're involved in, the one you're testifying in . . . what did he do?"

Holden puts the paper down. "We can talk about that later."

"No, please answer me," I push.

He tilts his head to both sides and then begins. "His name is Ryan Wilkinson. He's from Rose Canyon, and he was involved with trafficking runaways and the death of three girls that we know of, but we haven't been able to prove it. He was arrested after having abducted Blakely, and he has been sitting in jail since, waiting for his trial."

"And how was he trafficking girls?"

Blakely told me bits and pieces of this story, but I need to know the whole of it.

"He was a paramedic. They were luring these girls, who were hooked on drugs and desperate, and offering them help, only his version of help was worse than the girls staying on the street."

I push the note to him.

He reads it, eyes widening. "No, that would be impossible."

"Was Ryan the head of the snake?" I ask.

"No, he warned us that some guy would be upset and this wasn't over."

I tap the paper as my thoughts swirl. "But the two things could be connected, right? Otherwise, why would Theo have this in here?"

"I agree that there's something there." He thumbs through a pile and then pulls out a photo. "Something is in Texas. He went there a lot. Maybe someone was working with Ryan, and they're a part of the same group."

Holden gets up and moves to the door so he can press the button to let Ellis know he's ready to go. "Where are you going?"

"I need to go to the courthouse. I'm going to get answers before . . ."

Before it's too late.

CHAPTER
Thirty-Three
HOLDEN

"This is a mistake," Emmett says for the tenth time. "We have people looking everywhere for her. You know that this is wrong."

I don't give a fuck.

"I know my daughter has been missing for almost forty-eight hours. I know her medication is low. I know that there is a possibility that Ryan knows who may have taken her and why. So, don't tell me this is wrong. Don't tell me that you wouldn't have done this if it were Blakely. In fact, I know you would. You'd do anything. So, unlock the cell and let me talk to him."

There is no more time left to wait. No more searching to do. I am desperate and will do anything if it means we get Eden back.

And I do mean anything.

Emmett shakes his head, and I know he's trying to come up with something to stop me. There is nothing else. This is my only hope. "I can't let you do this. You'll destroy the entire case. What about the girls who are missing? What about the parents who have already buried their child?"

I grab him by the shirt, pushing him against the wall. Anger like I've never known fills me, and I am at the end of my rope. "What about my child? Do you think I care about anything else right now? Let me in the fucking cell so I can get the information I need!"

"I love Eden. You are my best friend, and I would trade my

fucking life if it meant bringing your daughter home, but not like this. Not doing something you'll never forgive yourself for. This isn't you, Holden. Going in there to try to make some insane deal that you're not even authorized to make or threaten him? What are you going to do, break him out? Offer him money? Promise to recount your testimony?"

I release him, stepping back. "I was going to beg."

Ryan isn't a bad guy. He is just greedy and desperate. I understand that last part. I'm desperate myself.

"I feel like you're going to leave here more disappointed than you are now."

"I have to try. It's the only possibility I have."

"Then I'm going in with you."

"No," I tell him. Not a chance he's going in. Ryan will never talk then.

Emmett stands firm. "That's the deal. You want to talk to him? Fine, but you'll do it the right way."

I close my eyes because I can do nothing else.

"Come on, Holden, you decide."

"I just need answers."

"I understand that, but I won't let you destroy the case we've built against the man who kidnapped and would have killed *my wife*. I love Eden, I would do anything to help you, but we're going one of two ways. Either I walk in there with you, and we do it by the book, or you're going in the back of my car until you can think straight."

"What would you do?"

He shrugs. "I know when it was Blake, I was a mess. I understand the desperation you're feeling, which is why I'm even entertaining this. If Ryan is involved, then maybe we can appeal to his human side. I don't know. We have nothing tying him to the trafficking ring other than Blakely's testimony. He has no reason to give up anything. Just know that."

I do. I know this is a long shot that will probably lead to nothing, but I have nothing. "Let's try."

"All right."

I follow Emmett into the cell where Ryan spends his days and nights. He looks up, eyes narrowing when Emmett closes the door.

"What do you two want?" Ryan asks with disgust in every syllable.

I don't waste time. "Where is my daughter?"

I watch as his eyes widen for a second. "What?"

"My daughter. Where is she?"

"How the hell would I know? I didn't even know you had a daughter."

I grab my phone and pull up the picture of her smiling with her doll. I took it last week after she had gotten done spinning and laughing as she sang a song. "This is Eden. She's three, and she has diabetes. She was taken from my house."

Ryan looks at the screen and then shakes his head. "I don't know what the hell you're here for. I have an alibi for that."

"My daughter had ties to someone I think you know. There was a note that stated a paramedic took the girls. Well, you're a paramedic, and you took girls."

"I didn't take kids."

Emmett huffs. "I beg to differ, but we're not here to debate semantics with you. We have reason to believe there may be a connection to the people who took Eden and the people you worked for."

He laughs once. "I've been in jail for the last how many months? I don't know who your daughter is or what connections anyone has. Now, if you'll excuse me, I have some reading to do." Ryan grabs his book and tosses his leg over the other.

Emmett was right. This was a mistake. "She's the sweetest little thing. Her smile can make even the hardest man fall to his knees. Last week, she almost went into a diabetic coma, and that's what'll happen in about three hours when her medication runs out. Her blood sugar will rise, and her organs will malfunction. Her body can't regulate itself, and you know this. You're a paramedic. You know what that'll look like, and you know she'll die. I'm not asking you because I give a fuck if the person you work for goes to jail. I just want my daughter back. I am asking you to save a patient who is in desperate need. Please. Please help me. Just tell me where we should look or . . . a name. Something."

Ryan closes the book and slowly places it on the bed. "Why should I believe any of this?"

"Because I shouldn't be here. I never should have come into this room, and Emmett sure as fuck wouldn't have let me if it weren't a matter of life or death. I am asking you as a father, please give me something . . . unless you are a monster who wants a child to die."

That causes him to jerk his head up. "I am not a monster."

Emmett steps a little closer. "No one said you were."

Although, we definitely think it. "If you're not, this is your chance to prove it. Who would do this? Where would they take her? Why would they abduct a little girl? They said they want money, we don't have money, but . . ."

Ryan lifts his hand. "I don't know what is going on. I've been stuck in this place with only a few visitors. However, when I joined the organization, our goal *was* to help others. To make a better world and offer an alternative to the drugs on the streets. I lost count of how many times I had to use Narcan to save a girl who ran away, thinking she could escape whatever issues she had, only to watch her end up with more. I don't know when things changed," he muses. "It's funny how it happens. One day, you're doing good, and the next, the money is coming in like you can't fathom. It changes you. It changed me. I'm not a monster, Holden, but I worked for one."

"Who is he?" Emmett asks carefully.

"There is no *he*. But if that person took your daughter, it means the money ran out. There is nothing they care about more than that."

This conversation is going nowhere. I need to go back to that safety deposit box and find something that tells us where the money is or who is pulling the strings because Ryan Wilkinson isn't going to give us the answers. "Let's go," I say to Emmett. "I have to go back to Sophie."

"I'm assuming you searched the house in Portland after I was arrested?" Ryan asks as Emmett is unlocking the door.

Emmett's hand pauses. "Of course we did. It was empty."

Ryan clears his throat. "Might be worth checking the cellar in the garage. I'm sure you never looked there, but that's just a hunch."

"You both stay here," Jackson commands when we're half a block away from the house where Eden might be.

While I was at the courthouse, Sophie got another call, explaining where to put the money, and if we didn't get it to them in the next two hours, we'd never see Eden again.

After Emmett relayed the information Ryan gave us, Jackson and his team headed to the Portland house and have been doing reconnaissance for the last hour and a half, watching to see any movement. About fifteen minutes after we arrived, they got confirmation of people inside the home that should be vacant, and a two-man team has eyes on the garage, which they believe sits over the back basement Ryan pointed us to. A heat signature showed someone enter and then disappear.

"I'm going with you," I reply. Not a chance in hell I'm leaving her. "If you find her, we have no idea the condition she'll be in. I have everything she'll need if . . . if I have to."

If I have to save her life.

If I even can.

Her monitor went off an hour ago, letting us know that her insulin pump is empty. Her sugar is moving higher, and the stress and God only knows what, if any, food they're giving her are not doing her any favors.

"You are close enough to reach us if we need you to, but you are a father first, Holden. You could get us all killed."

Spencer places his hand on my shoulder. "I get why you want to go in there, I am not saying you're wrong, but you're not trained for combat. You aren't going to know what we're doing, and it will not only put Eden at risk but also us and yourself. You wouldn't help Eden, you might be what hurts her."

I start to pace, knowing they are right but still wanting to fight them on it.

"Holden," Blakely says softly. "I am trained to do everything you need me to do. I will fight, I will search, and I will medically treat your daughter if we find her. I have spent a good part of my life doing exactly what is required right now." She turns to Sophie. "I know you're scared, but I'm not. I am trained, and I am smart, and I know what I'm doing. I'll be in the thick of it, and my entire part of this mission is Eden. Okay?"

A sob tries to escape Sophie's lips, but she covers her mouth to muffle it.

"Do you have the insulin?" I ask Blakely.

"I have it. Show me her latest level." I open the app, my heart falling to the floor when I see how high it is. "Okay. If she's here, I'll be ready."

If she's here.

Those three words that will determine everything. If she's not here, then we have nothing. No hope. No other leads. No options, and the reality of Eden being gone forever will no longer be a possibility, but a reality.

"Here." Emmett hands me an earpiece. "You can listen in, but only if you both promise not to leave this area. If we need to find you, then we have to know where to look."

I look to Sophie, whose hands are clenched together, body trembling slightly. I lace my fingers with hers, lending her the very limited strength I have left. "Okay, we'll stay here, but the minute—"

"You'll hear everything this way, Holden," Emmett promises. "Trust us, we will do everything we can."

These two are my best friends, brothers more like it, and if there are two people in this world I can trust—it's them.

I nod, and then Sophie wraps her arms around me, holding on as they walk away. We can do nothing but stand here and wait.

"Do you want to listen?" I ask, not wanting to be an asshole.

"No, I can't."

"Okay." I slip the radio into my ear and listen.

"I want you two up on the high side of the property. Blakely, Spencer, Emmett, and Zach, we go low and toward the garage. I need everyone to be tuned in and on alert. We have reason to believe she's being held in the cellar that's beneath the garage. Intel is scarce, but Barrett will handle the brief."

"Heat signal shows three inside the house," Zach Barrett says. "There are at least two cars in the garage, one engine was warm. I couldn't see any latches or openings, but I'm going to assume they concealed the basement entrance well. The basement itself is a blind spot, so be on alert for tunnels, hiding spots, false doors, or other exits or entrances that we haven't anticipated. We are assuming the occupants are armed and dangerous."

"Local law enforcement is stationed around the perimeter and throughout the woods to intercept anyone who attempts to run. Everyone is in place and ready to move on our command," Emmett says this time.

My heart is pounding as they sound off that they're ready.

Jackson's voice is strong and steady as he speaks to them once more. "All right. We move silent, boys."

"And girl," Blakely pipes in.

He huffs but chuckles a little. "And girl. No noise unless necessary for my team. Do we have snipers in place?"

"Here," one answers.

"Here and eyes on. I'll keep you informed of what I see."

"All right, teams. Stay safe and alert, let's make this clean and quick. On my count. Everyone locked and loaded. We go in three, two, one." Then everyone falls silent.

What happens next leaves my stomach falling. There's nothing. No noise. No talking. Just steady breathing.

I wait, straining to hear something, anything, but there is nothing to distinguish where anyone is.

"Did they find her?" Sophie asks.

I shake my head. "They're moving in now."

She buries her head in my chest. "I can't handle this. I feel as though I might pass out."

"I'm right here with you. I won't let you fall, just hold on to me."

All the fear that's choking me, I shove down. If she's in there, I'll need to keep a cool head and treat her immediately, so I focus on different treatment strategies.

"One on the left," someone whispers.

I keep my breathing steady so as not to alert Sophie.

I hear a door creak and then there's a scuffle. "One down."

"Two down."

The voices are muddled, so I can't tell who's saying what.

"Third down."

"House clear. Checking for Eden."

After who knows how long, I hear the same voice. "House is empty. No signs of Eden," the voice says. "I'll need the K-9 in here to do a further search."

No one from Emmett's group responds, which tells me Jackson's team hasn't found anything yet, good or bad.

"Jackson, on your right," a deep voice whispers, and it sounds like the sniper from earlier. "I'll take the shot."

"I need something, Holden," Sophie says, her teeth chattering as she moves around a little.

"She's not in the house," I tell Sophie. "Here, sit and just breathe, love." She sits in the back of the ambulance, struggling to stay calm. I squat in front of her, holding her hands in mine as I listen for anything else.

"Beneath car." It was Spencer's voice that time. I would know it anywhere.

What's beneath the car? Is it Eden? Did they find her?

"On two," Jackson instructs, but I have no idea what they're doing.

"I have eyes on two circling the garage. Find shelter." The sniper speaks again.

It's still silent on Jackson's team, and then I hear a car starting.

"Garage door opening," the sniper says. "One man approaching. The other is still on the backside." It's quiet again. "He's twenty feet from the car. Fifteen. Ten. Approaching it now. He's looking around. Stay silent." My heart is pounding so fast I swear it'll bruise my chest. "Perimeter guy just said something."

The other sniper speaks now. "I have a shot."

"Hold your fire," the first sniper orders. "Something has him spooked. He's on his phone. Something was just tossed in the garage. Everyone! MOVE!"

Then all hell breaks loose, and the silence I hated becomes deafening.

CHAPTER
Thirty-Four
SOPHIE

"Holden! Talk to me!" I am beside myself. Everything is happening so fast. People are running around, there was a loud bang in the distance, and Holden is moving.

"I have to go!"

"Go where? They told us to stay here!" I yell back.

"To them! Fuck! No one is responding!"

I reach for his arm as he's grabbing something from the ambulance. "Stop! You have to tell me what's happening!"

He runs his hand through his hair. "I don't know, Sophie. They are trying to get anyone to talk, but after the explosion, there is nothing. Emmett, Spencer, Zach, Blake, Jackson . . . none of them are responding! I have to go there."

"You can't! You don't have a gun or anything! There are cops everywhere who can go in. We can't go in there and make things worse."

"They could be hurt!"

"And I don't want you to be either!"

No. No, no, no! We can't lose all of them. My whole body is shaking, and Holden takes my face in his hands. "I have to go."

I nod because I can't speak. I can't breathe.

"I have to find them . . . and search for Eden."

I want to beg him to stay, but he's not listening, and that little shred of hope at hearing her name holds me back from arguing more. So, I say the only thing that matters in this moment. "I love you."

"I love you."

He kisses me quickly and then grabs the bag before he rushes toward the smoke in the distance.

I stand here, alone and terrified, watching the world around me move. It's like a dream as the outside edges of my awareness blur and fray.

My mind is being pulled, stretched to its limits. My daughter could be dead. My friends, the people who lifted me up, cared for us without hesitation, and ran into the fire to try to save Eden, could be dead as well.

I have no idea what's happening, which I think is the worst part of all of this.

Someone bumps into me from the back, but I don't go anywhere, I just stand there, staring at the last spot I saw Holden.

Time moves, I have no idea how long I'm here, but finally, I see Spencer running toward me. "Sophie!"

I blink, but I can't seem to get my limbs to cooperate.

He comes to a stop in front of me, shaking my arms. "Sophie, we found her!"

That unlocks me, and I take his hand, moving through the throngs of people, desperate to get to her. We approach the garage, people are in handcuffs, and over to the right, Blake is putting pressure on Jackson's arm.

"Fuck, that hurts!"

"Well, you got shot, it usually hurts, idiot. Now, hold still," she says.

Jackson winks at me as I walk by. "Don't worry, it's a scratch."

I keep walking, my throat tight and heart heavy. That's when I see them. Holden is walking toward me, carrying Eden in his arms.

"Eden!" I run, not caring about anything else. "Is she okay?"

"She's alive. We need to get her to the hospital."

I touch her face, she's cold, and I have to hold back my tears as we rush her back the way I came. When we get to the ambulance, Holden starts barking orders while I climb in.

"Get the IV going. She needs potassium. I administered three units of insulin. She's non-responsive." He bangs on the roof. "Go!"

The vehicle takes off, and I stare at my little girl, cradling her tiny hand in mine. She looks so frail and still. Her hair is pushed back, and even though I'd imagined she'd be covered in dirt, she's not. My mind races as I wonder the horrors she endured these last two days, and I pray she'll pull through.

"Pulse looks steady," the paramedic says. "O2 is low."

"Start the oxygen."

When he doesn't move fast enough, Holden grabs the mask, places it over her face, and adjusts a knob. His voice is hoarse as he talks to her. "Come on, Eden. Come on, sweet girl. Mummy and Daddy need to see those eyes."

"Six minutes out," the driver yells back to us.

I kiss her knuckles, tears falling. "I love you, Eden. Please wake up."

Holden turns to me. "She's not in as bad of shape as she could've been. She'll survive this. Even if I have to go to Heaven and drag her back, she'll survive."

The steel in his words almost makes me believe it.

"Pulse ox is back up in the 90s," the paramedic says.

Holden pushes Eden's blonde hair back. "That's my good girl. Breathe." Then he turns to the driver. "I need the trauma team ready when we arrive. Call ahead and let them know we have a three-year-old diabetic in possible ketoacidosis with internal injuries unknown. She inhaled smoke from an explosion and has a minor head injury. She was non-responsive upon arrival."

Eden's leg moves, and a second later, the other leg does as well. "Holden!"

He shines a light in her eyes. "Pupils are responding."

"Were they before?" I ask.

"No."

I watch, waiting and willing her to move again, but she doesn't.

"Two minutes out."

Holden turns to me. "When we get there, the team will take over, and we have to let them take her."

"I'm not leaving her," I say adamantly.

"I understand you not wanting to, but we need the team to focus on her, not us."

He's right. I know he is, but I am just so afraid to let her out of my sight. Then a tiny hand moves. I look over, her eyes are still closed, but she's reaching for me with her other arm. "Holden, look."

"Eden, my darling, it's okay," I say as I grab for her other hand.

"Mummy?" Eden's soft voice croaks, and relief crashes through me.

"Eden. I'm right here."

She looks at Holden, her lip wobbling. "Hi, Daddy."

His voice breaks. "Hi, bug."

She called him Daddy.

"I was scared."

He lets out a shaky sob, leaning down to kiss her forehead. "You don't have to be afraid anymore. You're safe now. You're safe with us."

Eden is stable. They gave her fluids, and she's curled in my arms, fast asleep.

There is a steady stream of people in and out of the hospital room. There are police officers posted outside our door, and Jackson's team is spread throughout the floor while Jackson gets treated for the bullet wound to his arm. No one from the kidnapping will give any information as to who they worked for, so until they find that person, no one is taking chances.

Zach has the watch inside our room, and it's sort of funny seeing his big frame sprawled out in the small chair.

"You can't be comfortable," I say softly as he shifts again.

"Comfort isn't exactly part of my job perks."

I smile and brush Eden's hair back, happy I can do this because she's alive. "No, and neither is having to come back out here after you were supposed to be done babysitting me."

"It was worth it. I missed having fun."

"Fun?" I ask.

"Yeah, getting to go tactical, shooting at people. It's like the good old days. Don't tell Millie I said that," Zach says with a grin.

"So, you and Millie are still together?"

"We are. We are actually engaged."

I smile at that. "Congratulations. That's lovely."

"It is. Everything has sort of fallen into place, even though the road to get here was not easy."

"Nothing seems easy," I muse, kissing the top of Eden's head.

"No, but if it were, nothing would be worth fighting for. We'd just go on with life as it was, never knowing what we were missing. It's why I came as soon as I heard something was wrong with you and Eden. When I met you both, something in my life changed. Things I didn't think mattered, suddenly did."

That makes me smile. "You have been a wonderful friend to us. I'm happy you're here, Zach. And I'm glad you got to have fun as well."

"I'm glad we got the desired outcome. She's safe and will recover."

"I worry that whoever wants their money won't feel the same."

Zach leans forward, resting his arms on his knees. "They won't get through us this time, Sophie. Jackson has personally assigned more guys from Cole Security in addition to the two who were already attached to your detail. Plus, I'm here and so is he."

I figured he would. After we got Eden stable, he went on a warpath to secure our safety. Holden called in every favor he had, and I'm pretty sure he even tried to get the hospital to close down the floor we are on.

"If only I knew what money they were talking about, I would give it to them just so they'd leave us alone. I feel like the link we need is gone."

"Who?"

"Dr. Frasher."

He's not replied to emails, and his office phone is now disconnected.

"Can you share what information you have on him?"

I run through what we uncovered, how he was falsifying Theo's records, and I recall the times I met him and went to Theo's appointments. Then I explain how he mentioned what happened to Eden was his fault and his family was killed.

Zach rubs his scruffy chin. "So, they had something in place if anything happened to their families . . ." He gets up, moving around the room. "It's smart. It's what I would've done."

"But none of us know what the failsafe was, and he's not responded to any emails we've sent."

"You said he triggered it after his family was killed?"

"That's what he said, yes."

"Did he tell you how long ago that was?"

I'm not sure where he's going with this, but he looks as if he's leading up to something, so I try to remember everything Dr. Frasher said. "Three days ago . . ."

"So, the same night someone was in Holden's house and a day before Eden was taken. What if the failsafe being triggered was what caused these people to come looking for you and Eden? They tried to ransom her for money, not information, maybe you guys have been looking at this from the wrong angle this whole time. What if your husband and the doctor didn't take money from them, but instead set up some kind of failsafe to take the money should anything happen to either of their families? It would explain why no one came after you until now."

Bloody hell.

"I have no idea where the money is, so it doesn't help. All it's done is set these people after me for something I don't have and can't give them. It's the opposite of keeping me safe."

"And had they not murdered the doctor's family, then this might not have ever happened. But they did, and if your husband was smart enough to set up all of this so far, then he was smart enough to leave you a way to find that money. You just need to find it, and I'm going to do what I can to help, starting with having my team run all of your and your husband's financials again."

"But you guys have already combed through them, and there wasn't anything there to find. Did you check Belize?"

Zach's eyes meet mine. "You know about Belize?"

"We found a paper in the box with a deposit into an account in Belize."

He nods slowly as he paces from one end of the room to the other.

"We know of that one, we're searching deeper now. If there was a large transaction after hours, it might not have had a chance to process through the system yet. If I'm wrong, I'm wrong, but it doesn't hurt to check."

CHAPTER
Thirty~Five
HOLDEN

"You should be at the hospital," Emmett says as I walk toward him.

"I am driving Sophie nuts. She told me to take a walk."

His brows lower. "So, you walked to the crime scene?"

"I took a cab."

"Okay. Well, you can't be here."

"Did you find who did this to my daughter?" I ask, looking around him.

"Dude, this is an active crime scene."

"I know that, but I am losing my mind, so please, give me something."

Emmett sighs, frustration in his voice. "We're processing everything, working with the FBI and Homeland Security. There is a lot to sift through, but we need to make sure it's done correctly, not just quickly. Jackson is working with the Marshals, but I haven't gotten any updates from them."

Jackson was released from the hospital three hours ago, and he left without a word. Zach, at least, told us that they are working down a lead. We also handed over the contents of Theo's box for them to investigate.

"I know all this."

"Then go back and be with your daughter." I look at my best friend and clench my jaw to stop the emotions. "Hey, she's safe."

"Is she? For how long? We can't stay in Rose Canyon if this is going to be our lives."

"It's way too soon to be making plans to leave. Let us do our jobs and see what we turn up. There are so many people involved that it's inevitable that one of them will screw up, and that will be the break we've been looking for."

Maybe, but all I see is Eden lying in that dirty blanket. The way she wasn't moving, how wide her pupils were, and the dangerously big bump on her head. When I lifted her, she seemed almost weightless, so still. I thought I had lost her.

"I'll never get that image out of my head."

"I wish I could tell you it gets better, but I still see shit I wish I could forget," Emmett admits. "What you have to hold on to is the fact that she was alive when we found her. That Blakely was able to get to her and give her insulin so you had time to get her to the hospital. I know it's hard, believe me, but if you keep your mind on the right path, it gets a little easier."

All of that sounds great, but it's not that easy. "I just want to focus on finding this asshole."

"Which is what *we're* doing," Jackson says, appearing out of nowhere and slapping his hand on my back. "You should be with Eden."

I turn to him. "I want to hire an entire army to protect her and prevent her from ever living through this again."

"And you basically have. Let us all do our jobs and work through the evidence. Come on, I'll give you a ride back to the hospital."

The ten-minute ride is silent, and I'm honestly thankful. So many conflicting thoughts are rattling around my head, and none of them are lining up to any conclusion. I want to run, take the two of them where no one knows us, and figure it out from there. I have enough money saved that we could last about six months, but I wouldn't be able to work as a doctor again. We would have to become new people, which Sophie has already done once.

Still, even if she agreed to it, who's to say they wouldn't find us again anyway? Then, if they did, we'd be completely without aid.

The car stops, and Jackson sighs. "I can only imagine what you're thinking, but I can promise none of it is a good idea."

"Which is why I haven't acted on it."

"Good. I got a call from my guys in Virginia Beach, and after Zach asked them to run Theo and Sophie's bank records again, they found a bank account number that matches your medical license. It wasn't in the records we initially pulled, but it seems as if only you or Sophie can access it. I'd like to talk to you both and get your permission to see what exactly is there. Come on, let's head inside."

The two of us head inside and walk down the hall where security is standing along with Jackson's guys. "Any issues?" he asks.

"None. The psychiatrist and a nurse came to talk to Sophie and Eden. They're still in there evaluating them now."

That would be normal protocol. They want to have someone make sure Eden is okay mentally, and a guard in the room would make things uncomfortable.

"I'm going in," I tell them. I'm her father and am allowed there, and besides, I miss them.

When I enter the room, my blood runs cold. Sophie is sprawled out on the floor unconscious, and Kate is standing by Eden's bedside, needle in hand, about to inject something into her IV.

"What are you doing?" I demand, taking a step forward and then freezing again as the cold barrel of a gun presses against my neck. "Kate? What the hell is going on?"

"I'm so sorry to do this, Holden," Kate says, glancing back toward Eden. "If you had just given me back the money, it wouldn't have gone this way. I never would have to do this to the people you love. Believe it or not, I actually like you, Holden."

"Stop!" I say quickly. "Jesus, Kate! What are you doing?"

"I'm doing what I have to."

"Have to what? What the fuck is going on?"

She shakes her head. "I will not let you people destroy everything. I heard all about the files and the box you have. No, I'm sorry, but I won't leave any more loose ends."

"You already have. What, are you going to kill everyone in Rose Canyon? Everyone you've ever met?"

Kate huffs. "No need. I'll be long gone by then. But first, I'm going to get the money, and you're going to help me."

I shake my head. "You're out of your fucking mind if you think I'll help you."

"That's where you're wrong."

My heart is pounding, and I want to glance to Sophie to make sure she's still breathing, but I can't tear my eyes away from the needle in

Kate's hand. "She's alive—for now. I've given her just enough to make you help. So, are you going to get the money her husband stole from me, or do I dose her up with more?"

Sophie isn't moving, her breathing is shallow, and this woman is a goddamn maniac. "Don't do this, Kate. You're not this villain. You're a doctor, and you even told me how you lost your daughter and husband." She moves the needle closer to Eden, and my panic spikes. "Stop! Kate, just stop. Sophie and Eden have done nothing to you."

"Nothing? I came to this town to keep an eye on things after Ryan was arrested. I had no idea that Theo's widow would find her way here. Maybe I would have let her be, she was so naïve, after all. But then all my money went missing, and I know she has it."

"So, you took a kid? And now you're going to kill her? Think about this, Kate. I don't have your money. If anyone can find it, it's Sophie, and she can't do that if she's dead, and she won't do it if you kill our daughter."

Kate is beyond listening to reason as she taps the tip of the needle against the clear tube of Eden's IV.

"It's hard, isn't it? To watch the people we love die? As I told you before, I know the pain of losing a child. It's like nothing else in the world. One day, you're imagining a life for them that is filled with happiness and possibilities, and the next, you're lowering a casket into the ground." Her eyes fill with unshed tears, but then they retreat. "I know it seems like you'll never recover, but with therapy, you'll find a way through losing them. The good thing is, you didn't even know Sophie and Eden existed a few months ago, so it shouldn't take long for you to return to life as normal."

"If you take them from me, I'll never be normal, and I'll never stop hunting you. If you take them from me, Kate, I swear to God, you'll regret it." The gunman pushes forward, forcing me to move deeper into the room.

"Don't threaten me."

"Well, it seems you need something from me, so if I were you, I wouldn't piss me off."

She looks down at the floor where Sophie lies listless. I move toward her, but the man behind me presses the gun deeper into my skull.

"You want to help her? Then find the money her husband took. I had everything, including millions of dollars set aside that would allow me to become a ghost, but then Ryan got arrested, and he knows way too much. So, I got rid of the rest of the people I needed to ensure my safety."

"You mean Dr. Frasher?"

"He's one. I guess that's where I fucked up. I didn't know that as soon as I made the first move, I'd lose it all. That my money would drain from my account without any way to stop it."

Now I see what she did wrong. She didn't know about a failsafe. "You killed Dr. Frasher's family because you thought Ryan would talk, but you didn't know they would take it all . . ."

"They?" she asks with a shake of her head. "I knew Theo had something. It's why I stayed away from Sophie and Eden, but I didn't know Theo and Frasher were in on it together."

"So . . . now you have nothing to lose, and why not destroy them all?"

She puts the needle down. "Of course you blame me for this and not Theo. You fail to blame the doctor who put this into motion. He is who did this to you."

"They didn't do this. You did. You lost your money, which you never should've had anyway, and then abducted my daughter and drugged Sophie to get it back."

"Abducted is such an ugly word. I like to think of it as acquiring my collateral, but yes. Then, when I realized you two didn't actually know where it was? Well, then I decided I'd make sure she was taken care of while you worked on finding it."

"Kate, we don't know where it is. We've been frantically trying to find it, but so far we've come up with nothing."

"That's where you're wrong. There's an account in Eden's name, and you and Sophie are her parents, therefore, you can access it. All my accountants have been able to tell me is that it's in Singapore."

Fuck. The account Jackson mentioned. I refuse to tell her, though. Not when so many have died because of it. If she thinks I will help her, maybe she won't make this worse, and I can save Sophie.

"How? We don't have an account number or a bank or anything. I don't understand how you can do this? How the fuck you can be such a . . ." The person behind me shoves the gun harder against my skull, and the force of it causes me to stumble forward a step.

"Watch what you say. It's not like I enjoy this," Kate says with her brows raised. "I didn't want it to go this far. I was hoping you'd find the damn money, wire it like we asked, and get your daughter back. Instead, I had to get involved, have people killed, move bodies all over the place, and now I have to kill you."

I keep waiting for Jackson to enter, but he doesn't, so I just keep her talking for as long as I possibly can. "Killing us for what? Haven't you lost enough people in your life? Is this what your daughter would want?"

She rolls her eyes. "I know exactly what you're doing, but for one more second, I'll play along. My daughter ran away, just like those girls, and they sold themselves for drugs and sex and food, just as she did. When we found her, she had tracks up and down her arms. She was nothing but skin and bones, and do you know what she said when I found her?"

"No." I keep my voice even.

"She said, 'Please get me more drugs.' Not, Mommy, I need help. Not, I'm sorry I ran away because you wouldn't let my loser boyfriend take me to Cancun. No. She wanted drugs."

"And what happened then?" I ask, hoping her need to tell this story is enough to keep her from trying to kill my daughter.

"She died. She overdosed, and her heart gave out. After I found her, I died with her. All the hopes I had were gone with her. My husband left. He found a new girlfriend who didn't cry every night or spend hours trying to retrace her daughter's footsteps. I lost everything, and I never wanted another parent to go through the same thing. We started small, helping locally, and . . . it grew."

"So, you're *him*? The guy Ryan warned us about?"

"Yes, I am . . . *him*. So ridiculous that I had to use my husband's name when I was dealing with people, but alas, women and men have gender bias issues."

What I don't understand still is how she went from helping runaways to this. When did it become about more? "Kate, all of this is horrible, but what you did isn't better than letting them die on the streets. You were selling these girls."

She shakes her head. "No, we were giving them a roof over their heads and letting them do what they were doing before. Our organization offers options. They can get clean and work hard at a new life, or keep taking the drugs. Guess what they always choose . . ."

Of all the people in the world, she should be more aware of why that is their choice. She knows what happens when someone is addicted to drugs. It's not a choice. It feels like a life sentence to them, and it's our job to help them see otherwise. Still, right now, debating that won't change anything, and I just need to help Sophie.

Sophie twitches, and I move toward her, but the gun moves to my back. "What did you give her?" I ask, looking at the woman I love.

"You want to save her, get me my money. I don't give a shit about helping people anymore. I just want to disappear."

"I don't know what bank," I explain again.

"So, you want to give up?"

"No, I don't. All you said is there is an account number, so I'm . . . I'll give you anything, but if you hurt Eden, or you don't let me save Sophie, you get nothing, and you'll just have to kill all of us and never see a penny. I'll find that account, Kate, just don't do this. Don't hurt them."

Kate's eyes narrow, and she jerks her chin, which is when I feel the gun come away from my back. "If you call out, yell, or tell a soul, I'll kill you. I'll kill everyone you love. You have one hour to get the money into this account, Holden." She hands me a slip of paper with a number on it. "I'll text you what to give Sophie once I'm free of this building."

She straightens herself and walks out. I rush to Sophie and gently roll her onto her back. Her lips are blue, her pupils are small, and her pulse is slow, she's not breathing. I immediately start CPR and then wait to the count of fifteen, giving Kate time to escape before I yell for help.

"What happened?" Jackson is in the room in a heartbeat.

I don't know what to say, so I just shake my head. "I need a crash cart! Hit the blue button there!"

He does, and the blue sirens blare, letting the hospital team know someone isn't breathing. I keep doing chest compressions and breathe into her mouth. One, two, three, four, five. I count as I press the heel of my hand down.

Nurses flood into the room with the crash kit, and a second or two later, a bed is wheeled in. We lift her onto it, and then I straddle her hips, continuing CPR. "Do you know what happened?" asks a doctor I've never seen before as we roll Sophie out and then into another room.

"She was injected with something. There's a puncture wound in her shoulder, and there is a second needle on the tray table next to

Eden's bed. I'm assuming whatever Sophie was injected with is the same as that."

Jackson immediately turns and runs back out into the hallway shouting, "Guard Eden!"

"And you don't have any idea what it is?"

I shake my head. "No! I went into Eden's room, and Sophie was on the floor." What would Kate use? Think, Holden. What were the toxicology reports on those girls? I go through the list of drugs. Some weren't fatal, but they were always some form of an opioid. "Someone get Narcan!" I yell.

Within a few seconds, they are opening the tube and spraying it up her nose.

I keep pushing on her chest, forcing her heart to beat, focused only on saving her.

The nurse looks at the clock. "Dr. James, I can take over."

Sweat is pouring down my forehead and burning my eyes, but I don't stop. I don't care that my breathing is labored. I need her. I love her. This is too fucking much.

"No, I have it," I say, continuing to push against her heart.

"Two minutes," she says.

"Be ready to dose her with Narcan again," I instruct. "Wake up, Sophie. We didn't find Eden only to lose you."

"Are you sure it's an opioid?" Dr. Gage, the ER doctor, asks.

"It has to be."

It has to be. I need it to be because, if I'm wrong, she's going to die.

One of Jackson's guys runs in the room yelling, "Fentanyl! She gave her Fentanyl!"

"Get that other dose ready!" My voice is ruder than I've ever spoken to a nurse, but not a single person berates me for it.

They prepare the second dose, and then Sophie's eyes open. I leap off her so I can turn her onto her side in case she vomits. She gasps, and everyone moves, attaching her to machines that we didn't have time to connect while I was doing CPR. Sophie's gaze is glassy, but I stay in her view. "Sophie?"

She breathes heavily and then croaks out, "Kate . . . she . . . Eden?"

"I know. I found . . . just breathe, baby. Eden is okay, they didn't get to her."

"Dr. James, we need you to step back." Before I can move, Dr. Gage is shouldering me out of the way. I feel as though I'm going to pass out as I watch the nurses and doctor work on Sophie.

Jackson's employee comes to me, helping me as I start to sink. "Come on, let's get air." I don't want air. I don't want to leave Sophie. "We're just going out to the hallway so I can keep an eye on both Sophie and Eden's rooms."

I nod and allow him to help me into the hall. As soon as he releases me, I sink to the floor and close my eyes, holding my face in my hands. Relief, fear, anger, and despair crash through me at once. In the wake of the crisis, I am stripped bare, and it isn't until I feel the warmth of the tears that I realize I'm crying.

I could've lost her. She could've died, and I don't know how I would've survived. If I had been just two seconds later or hadn't gone into Eden's room, this would've ended differently. Instead of sitting in this hallway, drained and emotionally shattered, I'd be planning a funeral.

Then I think of Eden. My sweet baby girl never would've survived that injection. God, this is too fucking much.

My chest heaves with the force of the emotions battling within.

"Holden?" Spencer's voice breaks through, and I feel his hand on my shoulder. "Did she make it?"

Forcing myself to look at him, I lift my head. "Barely, but yes. She'll need constant monitoring for the next few hours. Kate fucking injected her with Fentanyl." The words come out with so much hatred and disbelief. "She was going to do it to Eden too."

"But she didn't. Thank fucking God she didn't. I don't know how any of us would've survived losing them, let alone you. I'm so damn sorry you've had to go through this, Holden."

I wipe my cheeks and then ask the next most important question. "Did Kate get away?"

"No, we have her. They had to pry me off her when I grabbed her. It's over."

And then I drop my head back down and cry in earnest. It's fucking over.

CHAPTER
Thirty-Six
HOLDEN

"I don't want to hear another complaint. You will do exactly as the doctor ordered, and since I am the doctor, you will do what I say," I tell Sophie as I tuck her into bed.

She rolls her eyes. "You're being ridiculous."

"You almost died. You have two cracked ribs, so . . . be a good patient and stop bitching."

"This is bollocks." She smirks and adjusts a pillow.

"This is the way it is," I reply.

The five days they spent in the hospital as they recovered was incredibly difficult for everyone. Physically, Eden bounced back incredibly fast, but nightmares wake her each night. Sophie had a harder time. We had to give her another dose of Narcan when the first two wore off and she started showing signs of overdosing again, but after that, she stabilized and stayed that way. More than anything, it's been emotionally draining.

The disbelief that someone we trusted did this was hard to work through. I let Kate into our lives. I trusted her, and behind that sweet disposition and friendship was a monster.

"You'd make a very good nurse, if you ever consider a change in profession," Sophie says, bringing her hand to my cheek.

I force a smile, pushing down the rising guilt that comes each time I think about why she's in this bed. "If I do anything else, it'll be handing out beach balls in the Caribbean."

"I could go for that."

I laugh and bring her palm to my lips. "I could go for a lot of nothing."

"Have you heard from Emmett?" Sophie asks. "Anything more about Kate's arraignment?"

"He called this morning to tell me she is being held without bond. The other guy they arrested with Kate sang like a canary. They have been able to connect her to the missing girls, the deaths in Portland, and Wilkinson. I don't have the full list of charges, but it's long and she will be facing a lifetime in prison."

"Good. Wretched woman."

I agree. Cora even managed to talk Ryan into turning against Kate for a slightly lesser charge since we had him now too.

"Know what else is good?" I ask, leaning in, wanting to put Kate out of our lives for now.

"What?"

"You in my bed."

Her lips lift as her eyes brighten. "I guess we're going to be a real couple now and sleep in the same bed from now on?"

"Oh, I'm not letting you out of this bed for a long time. In fact, I may order you to be on permanent bed rest."

She rolls her eyes. "Can I at least use the loo?"

"If you must."

I bring my lips to hers, giving her a gentle and loving kiss. The pressure in my chest lifts slightly, but it's nowhere near enough to relieve the constant anxiety. Sophie's thumb brushes the almost fully grown beard I'm now sporting.

"Holden?" Mama James calls.

Mama James has, for all intents and purposes, moved in, and she's informed me that she doesn't want to hear a single word about it. Of course, she brought the damn cat.

"I'll be right there!" I call out to her.

Sophie grins. "It's nice having her here."

"Is it? Because I didn't ask for her to do this. In fact, she didn't give me a choice. She just showed up with bags and that horrible animal."

"It's what we do for the ones we love. I know it wasn't easy for her after Eden was diagnosed with diabetes, and it was even harder after Eden got taken. She needs to be useful."

I know she's right, but she's driving me insane. First, she

rearranged my kitchen because the flow was not correct for optimal time management. Then she went into the bathroom, again moving things around, and now she won't stop cleaning. No matter how many times I have told her to stop—she refuses.

"Holden James! I need you to come in this living room, it's a mess."

I groan, and Sophie giggles. "You laugh because you're sequestered in bed for the next week. I'm the one dealing with this loony person."

"Just think, in the matter of a few hours, you'll be in bed with me, and I'll give you a proper kiss."

That could be enough to sway me. I lean in, but before I can give her my own version of a real kiss, the door flies open and Eden rushes in.

"Daddy, Mama James is quite upset."

Each time she calls me Daddy, my heart swells larger. "She's always upset."

"No she's not." She smiles and then moves toward the bed.

"Hello, darling."

"Hello, Mummy. Did you eat all your food?"

I grin because she's been enjoying Sophie's bed rest more than anyone. She brings her food, makes sure she eats every bite, helps us keep track of Sophie's medication schedule, and if her mother tries to leave the bed—God help Sophie.

"I did, thank you very much."

Eden is her normal, bubbly self, and as much as I hate to admit it, the satanic cat has helped. Pickles snuggles her and allows her to carry him around like a shawl. I'm pretty sure she was trying to paint his nails, but the beast drew the line there.

"Eden, how about we let your mum get some rest and go see what Mama James needs?"

She is out of the room before I can get up, calling for Mama James.

"She loves you," Sophie says, staring at the open doorway.

"I love her, and I love you."

"That's smashing since we both love you as well."

Sophie yawns, and I smile, leaning down again to give her that kiss. "Rest, my love, I'll be back soon."

Her eyes droop closed as she snuggles deeper into the pillow, and I leave the room. When I get to the living room, I stop. What in the ever-loving hell is my aunt doing? This isn't a mess. This is a disaster.

"Mama James? What the . . .?"

She sighs heavily. "Did you even know you had all these files here?"

I blink because all of my patient files, which were in boxes, are now on the table in piles.

"I . . . did. But . . . they weren't like this."

"They were in boxes in that corner. Why?"

"Because they were just shipped here two days ago," I explain. "Why are you touching them?"

"I'm cleaning this mess of a house so that your daughter and her mother have a fresh start."

I stare at my normally stoic and strong aunt, who has tears in her eyes. So that is why she's been borderline manically cleaning my house. Sympathy fills me, and I move toward her. "I don't know what I would do without you."

She shakes her head. "Stop it. Don't patronize me."

"I'm not. You know this."

"No, you are. I'm just emotional, that's all." She sniffles, and I pull her into my arms.

"Don't cry."

She pushes out of my embrace. "I was so scared. I love your little girl, and I almost lost my mind when she was taken. Then we almost lost Sophie because of that crazy lady. I thought there was something off about her . . . dating George. He's not the smartest man in this world, you know?"

I laugh. "No, he's not, but she was using him to keep up on the case against Wilkinson. They would talk, like most couples do, and then she was able to move her pieces where she needed. What she didn't anticipate was Theo and Dr. Frasher."

"Well, she's a horrible woman, and I hope she can never come near this family again."

"She won't," I promise. Not that it's one I can really make, but I will do whatever I can to ensure she is never near us again.

"Have they caught the rest of the people involved?" Mama James asks.

So much has happened in the last five days that it's hard to keep up. One piece of information leads to another, which leads to yet another, and at each turn, the authorities seem to be making arrests.

"They got a lot of them. Emmett is confident that we aren't in imminent danger, so that's what we're going with."

She lets out a huge sigh. "Oh, good. I didn't think you were, but still. It's been exhausting for everyone."

I guide my aunt over to the chair that isn't filled with files. "Why don't you relax? You don't have to clean and rearrange my house."

"I need to help."

"And you are. You've been with Eden each night and helped with Sophie when I have to run out. Your cleaning, though, isn't helping, it's making me insane."

She laughs and pats my cheek. "All right then. You clean it up, and I won't start a new project."

Of course, I have to fix the mess. Still, I won't argue because I love her beyond words and know this is all from a place of love and heartache.

I turn to get to it and find Pickles sitting on top of the stack, staring at me.

"Can you get the cat?"

Eden pops up from behind the chair. "Pickles loves you, Daddy."

"Pickles loves you. Can you get him and move him so I don't get clawed to death?"

"He won't claw you, right, Pickles?" she coos to the feline.

He doesn't move, just stares at me. "Go on then," I tell it.

Standoff it is.

Pickles licks his paw, places it down, and then starts on the next. Really?

"Eden, can you get the monster to go with you?"

She laughs and hoists the cat away. "Come on, Pickles! Let's go watch the telly!"

I spend the next hour working on putting back the files the way they were. My previous office in L.A. sent this because I have a new patient with a similar issue as two of my old patients, but it's a bit trickier, so I wanted to go over anyone with this diagnosis in case I can find a link. I treated a lot of patients with this bone deficiency.

I figured they'd send the file I requested electronically, instead I got hard copies of almost everyone I treated via courier. Well played.

Somewhere between O and S, I give up, no longer caring if anything makes sense because I just want it put away.

"Is everything all right, darling?" Sophie asks from behind me. I feel her gentle touch on my neck.

I look over with a smile. "Why are you up?"

"You said I could use the loo."

"Which is in our room," I remind her.

Sophie smiles warmly. "I missed you."

"I always miss you."

"What are you doing?"

I put the file in the box. "Recleaning what wasn't a mess." I glance at the clock before adding, "Jackson should be here soon, so why don't you hang out in here—"

My phone pings with a camera notification. I pull it up just in time for the video footage to show Jackson knocking on the front door. Sophie jumps at the sound but then forces a smile.

"It's Jackson," I tell her before I pull the door open.

"Hey."

"Hey," he says as he walks in. "Hello, beautiful." Jackson kisses Sophie's cheek. "You look much better than the last time I saw you."

"The last time you saw me, I was almost dead."

"This is true. Let's go somewhere we can talk and you can sit," I suggest.

Mama James and Eden are in the living room, and as soon as my daughter sees Jackson, she rushes forward, wrapping her arms around him.

Afterward, she shows him the cat, her new doll house, the teepee that has lights all around it and a stack of pillows inside where she can color or do whatever, and the tea set her uncle Spencer bought her. I look at Sophie, who is starting to fade a bit.

"Mama James, can you take Eden somewhere so that we can talk?"

"Of course, dear. Come on, Eden, let's get your clothes out for tomorrow and find something that might fit Pickles."

Once they leave, I get Sophie comfortable on the couch and sit beside her, taking her hand in mine. "You said you found information?"

"We did, but I have to say that Theo was extremely good at his job. It took my guys a lot of hours and hoops to finally find the account that Theo had set up. The money was laundered so many times, we lost track and had to start again, but we finally found it." Jackson passes us a folder. "This is the bank in Singapore that holds the account in Eden's name. I can't access it, but if I'm right, there's a substantial amount of money in there."

"How substantial?" I ask.

He looks to Sophie. "Over five million dollars."

CHAPTER
Thirty-Seven
SOPHIE

"I don't want it," I tell Holden again. "I don't want any money that's connected to whatever that woman was doing."

I'm back in my prison, also known as my bed. We contacted the bank in Singapore with the account number, which is Holden's medical license number, and got confirmation that our account does have five million three hundred thousand seventy-six dollars in it.

"I don't either, but we could do a lot of good with it."

"I don't even want to touch it. She made all that money exploiting children. So, let it sit in that account."

I hate all of it. It makes me sick to my stomach that Kate was this horrible, but knowing my husband was involved as well has me completely wrecked. He was a good man, one who loved us, and while I understand he did this to protect us, in the end, it didn't. It almost killed all of us. I believe in karma, and I would like to have more pluses than minuses in that department.

"What I'm saying is that we could give that money to the families, like Keeley's, or to programs like Run to Me and others like it. We can do good with it instead of letting it sit in a bank account."

All of those are good ideas, it's just too soon to really think about it. "For now, can we focus on ourselves and this family? Kate is in prison, you have to testify in two days against the man who almost killed Blakely, and we are all healing."

He slides in beside me, pulls the covers up, and then opens his strong arms for me to cuddle into. I don't hesitate, this is my favorite part of us sharing a bed. We fall asleep wrapped around one another, and even though we wake up on opposite sides of the bed, I love this part.

My head lies right where his heart is, listening to its steady beat. "When are you returning to work?"

"Soon."

"I want to as well," I inform him.

Holden moves his head, trying to look at me. "What?"

"I miss the children. I miss painting. It would be good for me to do something that makes me happy. Not that you and Eden don't, but the youth center gives me a purpose outside of being a mum."

"Why don't you paint for real again? Go back to selling your art."

I've thought about that, and I might, but I have found a true love in working with children who haven't yet found their inner painter. One of the girls, Mable, has really come into her own. It's been lovely to see.

"I guess I can really do anything now."

"I have tons of ideas of things you could do."

I smile up at him, and he kisses my forehead. "Like what?"

"You could . . . open an art gallery here. You could form a book club. You could learn how to fly."

I laugh at that one. "Not likely."

"Yeah, no danger, I agree. You could kiss me."

"I like that one," I tell him as I move a bit higher to do as he suggested.

"You could marry me."

I stop breathing for a second, staring at him. "What?"

"Marry me? I have lived in a world without you before, and I didn't have happiness. I survived, not thrived. Then you came here, and everything changed." Holden sits up, moving over to his bedside table and extracting a box.

Oh Lord. Oh Lord. My lungs hurt for a completely different reason as I stare at the box that I *think* contains a ring.

Holden opens it, and tucked in the maroon velvet is a stunning round diamond, throwing rainbows around the room.

"Holden . . ." I can't say anything as my hand covers my lips.

"I changed for the better, Sophie. Our relationship changed into

KEEP THIS PROMISE - SPECIAL EDITION 303

something I never knew was possible. We've both been married before, but it was to the wrong people, at the wrong time. You are my right time. You're my right person. You're my world, and I want to walk beside you every day for the rest of my life. I want to raise Eden with you, and maybe we'll have more, but as long as I have you, none of that matters."

"It's so soon," I say, looking at him through watery eyes.

"No, love, it's been too long that we've lived without each other. I'm asking you, Sophie Elizabeth Armstrong, will you be my wife?"

Tears fall, and emotions overwhelm me. "Yes," I manage to get out the only word that matters. He cups my face, kissing me so lovingly it makes more tears fall. "I love you."

"I promise that I am going to make you so happy."

He takes the ring from the box and slips it onto my finger.

"You already do."

"Oh my God! You're engaged!" Brielle squeals as she takes my hand in hers.

"I am! I can't believe it."

It's been two weeks since he asked me to marry him, and I still can't quite believe it's real. When we told Eden, she screamed in delight and asked if she could wear a dress, which of course, we said she absolutely could.

Mama James cried and hugged us both before launching into her demands for a proper wedding.

Blakely laughs. "Holden fell in love with you the moment he saw you, it doesn't surprise me at all. Congratulations, my friend."

"Thank you. How long do you think we'll have to wait before he's out of court?"

Blakely checks her phone, and Brie huffs. "You're not going to know anything for a while. Holden is most likely still testifying."

"He's the last witness before they rest. The prosecution had an amazing case, not sure why the defense recalled Holden."

Brie raises her hand. "They must've thought they could show something medically that will undermine his previous testimony. Either way, checking your phone won't make a difference."

"You say that, but that man wanted to kill me. He put a hit on my husband, held me captive, and worked for a sociopath! I need this to be over, Brie. I need to move the hell on with life and not have this dangling over my head."

I take Blakely's hand and squeeze. "I'm sure we'll hear something soon."

She nods and then turns to Brie. "I'm sorry."

"No, I'm sorry. I think it's a lot of me telling myself the same thing. I think about it and worry, but I . . . can't. It'll drive me nuts."

I know that feeling. "Then let's focus on anything else."

"Yes, like your wedding!" Brie says. "We need a dress, a date, a venue, food plans. Do you guys want a DJ? I loved the guy we had for our wedding."

"We haven't gotten that far," I stop her, feeling a bit overwhelmed.

Blakely laughs. "She's the worst with this. I'm warning you now, if you've heard of Bridezilla, you haven't met Bridesmaidzilla. That's Brielle."

Brielle slaps Blakely's arm. "Hey, that's not nice. Your vow renewal celebration was perfect. You're welcome very much."

Blakely looks to me with wide eyes. "It was torture," she whispers.

"Torture, my ass! If it weren't for me, you would've gone in your old army fatigues with your hair in a tight bun."

"Which I would've been comfortable in!"

Brielle's gaze is incredulous. "Do you see what I had to deal with?"

I grin, loving my friendship with these two incredible women. "Holden and I haven't talked about any of that yet, but I would love it if you both would be my bridesmaids."

"Of course we will!" Brie answers before Blakely can open her mouth.

I look to Blake, waiting to allow her to answer. "I'd love to."

"Oh, really? I'm chuffed to pieces!"

They both look at each other and then to me. "You're what?" Brie asks.

"Sorry," I say on a laugh. "I'm so happy. Thank you both. You're truly perfect friends."

Blakely's phone rings, and she grabs for it immediately. "It's Emmett. Hello?"

There's a pause, and Brielle and I wait to hear what he says. Blakely's eyes fill with tears, and I want to wrap her in a hug because they could be tears of happiness or disappointment.

"Okay," she says. "I'll see you soon then? I love you too."

"Well?" Brielle says as soon as the phone is away from her ear.

"He was found guilty." Then Blakely lets out a sob, and we hold our friend as she unloads her pain.

CHAPTER
Thirty-Eight
HOLDEN

~ONE MONTH LATER~

"You know our family and friends are going to fucking kill us, right?" I say to Sophie when we come to a stop outside of the little white chapel in Vegas.

"They'll have to find a way to forgive us. Besides, we'll still have our proper wedding when we get back, but this is where and how we should be married," she says with all seriousness. "It's where we started."

Last night, we asked Mama James if she could watch Eden and told her we needed to go away for the weekend. We didn't tell her that our goal was to get married.

So, here we are, in Las Vegas, the place we met and made a baby, ready to complete the circle of our relationship.

"I agree, but you and Brielle have been working so hard at planning our wedding."

"She should talk! She ran off with Spencer and did this very thing."

I bring my hand to her cheek, holding it tenderly. "Yes, but you deserve to have everything you want, love."

"You're what I want. This marriage is what I want. The wedding is just that, the wedding, it's not the definition of our life . . ."

"You're perfect."

"You're stalling. Do you have cold feet or second thoughts?" she asks.

"Not at all."

"Then let's go in there and get hitched."

I kiss her deeply, loving the slide of her tongue against mine. I love this woman more than I ever knew was possible. She's my everything, and I want nothing more than to be her husband.

"And then we'll have our wedding night."

She smiles, leaning against me. "But not in the loo this time."

"I think we did all right."

"I'd rather not."

"Fine. No bathroom sex," I agree.

We go into the chapel, pay them one hundred and nineteen dollars, and get married. Sophie and I take a ridiculous photo for the mantle because I want to remember this always, and then we take a few selfies.

We head back to the suite we booked, and I carry her over the threshold into the room. The colorful lights of the strip dance across the walls, but all I see is the woman in front of me.

"I love you, Sophie James."

She smiles. "I love you too, and I like this new name."

"I do too."

"I like that it's us."

"I like that you're mine."

Her blue eyes twinkle as she walks toward me in the simple pink dress she brought to get married in.

"I've always been yours, Holden. In a way, you've been with me since the day we met. I carried a part of you with me for nine months, and I've seen you, even though I didn't really know you, for three years. We will always belong to each other."

My hands grab her waist, and I pull her against my chest. "I want to make love to you, wife. I want to strip you down, kiss every inch of your perfect skin, and love you until you beg me to stop." I slide my fingers against the satin of her dress and then up to her neck. "Tonight, in this city, I'm going to undo our first time and give you a new memory to hold on to."

The flutter of her pulse beneath my fingers speeds up. "I can't wait."

I walk over toward the wall, turning the lights off and moving to see the view. "Come here," I summon her. "Years ago, we came here, unaware of what we'd find."

She smiles. "In the darkness again?"

"No, baby, look at all the lights."

I shift so her back is against my chest as we look out over the city.

My fingers move the strap of her dress, sliding it down, and then I push her hair to one side so I can kiss her soft skin. Sophie moans softly, head falling to my shoulder.

Skimming my lips up her neck to her ear, I run my tongue along her lobe and whisper, "I want you naked in the lights. I want to watch them dance across your skin while I pleasure you."

Her breathing sputters, and I guide her hands up so they are pressed against the cold glass. "What if someone can see?" Sophie asks.

"No one can see, my love." The hotel has a gold film on the windows, so when there is no backlight, it's impossible to see anything. "Not to mention we're on the top floor." I remove the dress completely, leaving her in only her heels.

She pants slightly when I move my hands to her breasts, kneading them gently before pulling the fabric down. "Holden . . ."

"Yes, love?" I ask as I cover her with my hands, pinching her taut nipples. When she moves her hand, I stop. "Keep your hands on the glass, Sophie. I want you to watch the world move around us while I focus only on you. My wife. My love. My heart."

She moves her head to the side, and my hand slides to her throat as I take her mouth, moving my tongue with hers, kissing her while she stands like a fucking goddess.

I step back, wanting to taste every part of her. Moving around, I pull my tie off and toss it to the floor before unbuttoning the top two spots on my shirt. "You're so beautiful. So perfect."

It's been over a month since we've been able to do this, to kiss or make love. Her ribs were much too sore, and she needed to heal. Each night, I held her, wishing I could make love to her, but she'd only just gotten the all clear to resume light activity, which includes careful sex.

I asked, and I don't even feel bad about that.

Tonight, I want every part of her to come alive again.

I'm standing behind her, looking at her naked body with the lights of the city where I found her in the background.

"Holden?"

"You're so beautiful."

"I'm naked in front of Las Vegas."

"No, baby, you're naked in front of me." I step closer, still not touching her. "You're mine."

"I am."

"What should I do with you?"

She shivers. "What do you want to do with me?"

I smirk. "First, I'm going to kiss you, wife."

And I do.

My mouth is on hers, drinking every drop of love she gives me. Then I move around so her back is against my chest as she arches into my touch. I want to stoke her flame even higher. Slowly, my hands slide down her stomach to her clit, circling my finger around her wet heat.

She moves her lips from mine, gasping. "Oh, God."

"Remember what I said about a new memory, love?"

"Yes," she pants, her breath making the window fog a little.

"Look out there, baby. Look at the world going by, unaware that I'm going to make you scream my name as I lick you until your legs give out." I lower to my knees, pulling her panties down with me as I go. I have her lift one foot and then the other before I push her legs apart. "Stay like that."

Her eyes flash with confusion. "What?"

"Hands on the window." I move her chest, so her tits are against the cold glass. "Perfect. You're fucking perfect," I say, tripping my fingertips down her spine. "Keep your legs apart and ass out."

"Wh—"

I cut her off when I spread her thighs and run my tongue against her seam. Her legs buckle, but I hold her up, licking again.

"Oh, oh," Sophie mumbles as I work my mouth harder.

"Tell me what you see." I lick again.

"I . . . I can't."

I run my hand along her perfect ass and then bite her playfully. "I want to worship you while you look at the people below, walking around." I kiss the spot and then move my finger to her clit. "But I can't see what you do, baby. Paint me a picture while I look at what I want most."

Her. She's what I want.

"I . . . I see the billboard across the street."

I reward her by swirling my tongue at her entrance.

Her balance wavers, but she stays up. "I see people walking, moving down the street, stopping to take a photo."

I moan against her, pushing my tongue into her.

"Oh," she cries out.

"What else, Sophie?"

"I see the water show starting, the lights and the fountains spraying. It's beautiful, and the Eiffel Tower is sparkl—oh, God!"

My tongue runs up and down her center, licking and swirling, making her writhe against my mouth. I adjust so I can see her better— hands on the glass, ass out—while I eat her pussy. She's fucking glorious. A goddamn angel sent to me, and I will never forget this picture.

Sophie's hand slips, and I stop for a second, which causes her to whine. "Open your eyes, baby. I want you to see it all. Can you see me behind you? Are you watching me devour you? My wife."

I go back in, licking and tonguing her, pushing inside, drinking every drop she gives me. Her hand falls to tangle her fingers in her hair. "Holden, don't stop."

"I see us. God, I see us and you and . . . I can't hold back."

I want to make her come as she watches the city and then on the bed and the shower and any other place I can.

She groans, and I would laugh, but my mouth has other plans. I pull away, and she cries out. "No!"

I lick softly, giving her much less pressure than I know she needs, and wait for her to talk.

"I see . . . I see lights."

I slide my finger inside, her muscles contracting as I fuck her with my hand. "Good. Keep talking so I can make you come."

"Cars are stopped at a light, and people are laughing . . . there is a couple . . . dancing . . . Oh, God." Sophie moans as I move my finger to her ass, playing with her there. "There are people everywhere, moving around, not aware that my husband is licking my fanny."

I want to draw this out, but I am losing my control. My tongue thrusts into her while I push my finger in her ass.

"Holden!"

I can feel her clenching around me, her hand fisting in my hair, and then she releases me, slamming her hands on the glass as she falls apart. I hold her up as much as I can, working to keep my mouth where she needs me.

After a few seconds, her moaning stops, and she sinks to the ground, and I catch her, shifting so she's on my lap, her head resting on my shoulder as she pants.

"You're glorious," I tell her.

Sophie chuckles softly. "I beg to differ. I think it's you who is glorious."

I move us so that, as I stand, I still have her in my arms and then I set her onto the bed. Sophie naked in the window was gorgeous, but her on the bed in those heels is stunning. God, I might blow my load right here.

With a crooked finger, she motions me to her. "There are things a wife should do for her husband."

"Oh?" I ask, standing in front of her naked body.

She shifts onto her knees, her smile playful. "Most definitely."

"And what might those things be?"

She runs her finger down my chest, unbuttoning my shirt as she goes. "Well, if we think about my vows, the first was to have and hold you through sickness and health."

"I'm pretty healthy."

She nods. "Yes, and when I was sick, you were there."

I push her hair back. "Always."

"Then there was richer or poorer."

That's a very complicated one. We are incredibly rich with money neither of us wants to touch.

She moves to the next button. "No matter what, that's not an issue for either of us."

"No, it's not."

"Then there's the love part, which I have quite in hand."

I smile. "That's a good thing. Honor was another," I remind her.

"Yes, I recall. And obey was one, which I just did."

My shirt falls open, and I nod. "Yes, you did very good with that."

Sophie's eyes find mine. "The better or worse part we brushed past."

Because it's too hard to think about. Almost losing Eden and then her isn't something I ever want to think about again. I want to move forward, forget all the bad things that happened, and rejoice in what's to come.

"I think we endured the worst."

"I agree, husband. Now, I'd like us to have the good. Is there something I can do to make that possible?"

"Come stand here," I tell her.

She does. Sophie is always incredibly sexy, but when she lets me take control like this, I want to fall to her feet and pay homage to her.

"Take my clothes off."

She pulls my pants off, grinning at me as her hand wraps around my cock. She pumps a few times, and her name falls from my lips as she releases her hold.

"Now what?" she asks.

"Get on your knees, baby."

She drops down, giving me a coy smile as she looks up at me from under lust-heavy lashes. I take my cock in my hand, jerking it a few times as she watches. "I want to touch you," she confesses.

"Then touch."

Her hand replaces mine, stroking with perfect pressure. "I love you."

I rub my thumb against her cheek. "I love you."

"I want to show you."

"You do every day," I tell her.

Sophie shakes her head. "Not this way." Her hand falls away, and her lips wrap around me. I moan as she takes me deep, the heat of her mouth moving through my veins like liquid fire.

"That's it, baby, suck my cock." I rest my hand on the top of her head, forcing myself not to push her down harder.

Then she moves her other hand to my wrist, doing exactly that.

"Fuck!" I groan and grip her hair. I set the pace but manage to use a bit of restraint, savoring every second. She takes me deep, moving up and down in a steady pace that has my head spinning.

I'm so fucking close. I want to come so badly but know I need to stop.

"Sophie, stop. Please, baby, I need to make love to you. I want to be inside you when I come."

She lifts her head, wiping her mouth, and she presses her hand against my chest. I lie back, she follows, and then sinks down onto me. Her heat envelopes me in the best way. My God, this is Heaven.

"You feel so good," Sophie says, her hips rocking in perfect time. "I don't deserve you."

My hands tangle in her hair, adjusting her so she's forced to look in my eyes. "No, baby, we deserve each other. We were made for each other."

"Holden," Sophie's voice trembles. "I love you."

"I love you more than I knew was possible," I tell her, rubbing her cheek. "I will love you for the rest of my life. I will love you beyond that."

I will love her until the end of time.

I roll over and am met with cool sheets. Sitting up, wondering where Sophie—my wife—has gone. She's wrapped in a robe, staring out at the Vegas strip.

I get out of bed and wrap myself in the matching robe and then pull her to my chest. "What are you looking at?"

"The sun."

"It's been known to show its face in the morning."

"I know. It just means we head home today."

"I wish we could stay another day."

She turns to face me, hands resting on my chest. "Me too, but I miss Eden, and I'm sure Mama James is exhausted after caring for her."

"It keeps her young."

Sophie smiles. "We're going to have to get a cat once she returns home."

My aunt is moving back home when we get back, thank the fucking gods for that. Her help has been immeasurable, but Sophie is healed, Eden is doing much better, and we need time and privacy to become a family again.

However, what we are not doing is getting a cat.

"No."

"Holden," she chides.

"No. We're not getting a cat. I have yet to meet a cat that likes me."

Sophie snickers. "Maybe it's you then."

"Or maybe they're all insane."

"Yes, all the cats in the world are crazy."

It's possible. "We'll get a fish or something low maintenance."

"You're quite ridiculous."

I shrug. "You married me, babe."

"That I did." She lifts onto her toes and presses a kiss to my lips. "But your daughter wants a cat, and I can't imagine you will deny her."

"Imagine it."

This is all false bravado because I am really fucking bad at telling that kid no. I have a feeling that, in a few days, I'll be going to the shelter and getting a freaking cat. I really need to work on my issues here.

"If you say so." Even Sophie doesn't believe me.

"Am I that predictable?"

"Maybe a little."

I kiss her nose and release her when I hear her stomach growl. "Why don't you hop in the shower, and I'll get us breakfast?"

"Sounds lovely. Make sure you get me a cuppa."

I nod. "Yes, yes, I'll get you tea."

"Not that it's adequate, but I'll make do."

She saunters off, and I smile. I place the order on the television for our meals, getting a variety of things, and then check my phone.

I have a few emails from the hospital, giving me updates on my patients, and then I see a text from Emmett, asking if I'm coming to dinner tomorrow since we couldn't do poker last week.

Might as well get this over with.

So, I send the selfie from last night to him as well as Spencer.

Me: Sorry you fuckers missed it, but we got married yesterday.

Emmett: I guess you needed to have a secret that matched ours? Congrats, asshole.

Spencer: You and Vegas. Glad you finally did something good in that city. I'm happy for you guys, and when you get back, I'll be laughing at the hell that Brielle will give you.

Me: Tell her we did what we felt was right. Wish you guys had been here with me, especially Isaac.

Isaac was my best man when I married Jenna, and while at the time, I thought I was making the right choice, getting married this time was so different. Sophie is who I am meant to be with, and I should've waited until I found her.

. . .

Emmett: He's always with us.

Spencer: And he's looking down on us all now, probably thinking we're nuts.

Emmett: Especially you since you married his sister.

I laugh because it's true. His death changed us all in ways that I don't know anyone could've predicted. Spencer married Brielle, Emmett and Blakely reconciled because that case brought them back together, and I found Sophie again. It's not to say that those things might not have happened had he still been with us, but we'll never know.

Sophie emerges from the bathroom in that robe again, her hair up in a towel. "Everything all right, love?"

I've never been one that put a lot of myself in faith or destiny, but looking at her right here, convinces me I'd be a fool not to. Call it whatever you want, but I was meant to be here—with her.

"Everything is perfect."

And it is.

Epilogue
SOPHIE

~ONE YEAR AND THREE MONTHS LATER~

"I'm so glad you came," I say as I wrap my arms around one of my protectors.

Jackson smiles. "I wouldn't miss it for the world. Congratulations to you both."

Holden shakes his hand. "Thank you."

"This is my wife, Catherine."

Beside him is a lovely woman with long brown hair and a smile that could disarm anyone. "Thank you for coming and for sharing your husband with all of us who need him."

Catherine grins, her eyes turning soft when she looks up at Jackson. "You're welcome. I like when he takes jobs like yours where he can protect people who genuinely need it. I am so happy your story ended this way."

"Me too."

Jackson gets moved to the side, and a familiar face comes into view. "Enough hogging the bride."

"Zach." I smile as soon as I see him.

"Hey, Sophie. Look at you, happy and glowing."

I give him a hug, and then he introduces me to the most stunningly beautiful woman I've ever seen. She has blonde hair falling in waves down her back in the loveliest black dress. "You must be Millie," I say before Zach can finish.

Millie is who saved my life with this wedding dress. I panicked and remembered what Zach said about her store. It was a long shot, but she was able to get in touch with one of the designers she works with, and they had a maternity dress in stock.

"I am, and can I say, as a former wedding planner, this is absolutely stunning, and you are radiant."

"Well, if it weren't for you, I'd be an absolute wreck right now. Thank you for working your magic."

She waves her hand dismissively. "You would've been beautiful in anything, and I was happy to help."

Zach wraps his arm around her from behind before kissing her temple. "She's a miracle."

My heart melts at seeing him with her. It's clear they're perfect for each other. "She sure is."

"We won't hold you up any longer," Zach says, looking back at the line forming. "Congrats, Holden. May you have all the happiness in the world."

Holden pats Zach on the back. "Thanks, man."

It's so strange since we've been married over a year, but today made it feel brand new. We recited our vows again, renewing our love and devotion, and Eden was a part of our ceremony, which was perfect.

The line isn't all that long, we kept our ceremony small and filled with the people we love most.

When the last person in line walks toward us, Holden's entire face lights up. There is a beautiful woman, tall, shorter blonde hair, and she clearly adores my husband. They embrace and then he steps back, moving his hand to the small of my back.

"Addy, I'd like you to meet my wife, Sophie."

A perfectly lovely woman gives me the warmest smile and pulls me into her arms. "It's so wonderful to meet you. I've heard so much about you from the guys."

"You as well! I feel as though we're already friends." She and I have spoken a few times, and Holden raves about her. Addison was a big part of their lives, and I know they all miss her desperately. It's clear that she was more than just Isaac's wife to them. She was their friend as well.

"And this little squirt is Elodie," Holden explains, lifting her up in his arms and kissing her cheek before placing her back on the floor.

I get down low so we're eye-to-eye. "Hello, Elodie, it's lovely to meet you."

She ducks behind her mother's legs, and Holden laughs. "I can't believe she's almost three. It feels like just yesterday we came to the hospital when she was born."

"Tell me about it," Addy says with a bit of exhaustion, which I know all too well. "I can't believe it's been that long since Isaac was killed. Just . . . time moves on, I guess."

"How are you doing in Sugarloaf?" Holden asks.

"Good. I love it there. Being around the Arrowood family has been good for me. They're like their own little compound there."

"I heard you're buying a place there?" I ask.

"Yes! I found this little farm that needs some work, but I'm excited." She loops her arm in mine and starts to walk. "Are you ready for your wedding celebration? I heard it's going to be small, but Brielle said it will be perfect."

I'm not sure about all that. In fact, it's rather not perfect as four months ago we found out that I am pregnant. Holden and I wanted to wait until after the wedding celebration, but . . . best laid plans and all that. My hand moves to my belly, which is no longer flat and concealable.

"As you can see, I'm increasing—again—so we didn't want much of a spectacle. Plus, we're already married."

"No matter what, weddings are always special, even if you're already married. The ceremony today was really beautiful."

"Thank you."

"I'm happy for you both. I worried Holden would stay married to his job, but it seems he just needed to find the right woman he knocked up on that damn trip to Vegas."

"Hey!" he says quickly. "I didn't plan that trip. That was Isaac."

She rolls her eyes. "I'm sure Isaac was totally the one who planned it. Let's be real, it was you three."

"I plead the fifth."

They both chuckle. "I'm glad he came to Vegas. If not, we wouldn't have Eden or be here today."

Holden kisses my temple. "I'm glad too."

Addison smiles warmly. "I'm happy it all worked out. You both deserve a lifetime of happiness. Listen, I wanted to thank you in person for the donation you made."

I look away, feeling uncomfortable. After I insisted we go to the authorities to report the account, Holden had agreed, only to have them tell us that it was, in fact, ours. It turned out that they were not able to trace the money at all, thanks to my brilliant former husband.

"Please don't thank me, I'm happy to ensure it goes to the charities best suited to helping girls in horrible positions."

Holden grips my hand, squeezing it in support. That money has been one of the bigger fights we've had. He wanted us to keep some—for Eden. I wanted to drain the account and burn it.

We compromised, agreeing to help people and families that Kate hurt first, and if there's any left, we'll discuss it then.

"I know the last two months haven't been easy," Addison says with compassion in her eyes.

No, it hasn't. The trial was exhausting. Not just because I'm pregnant but also because we had to relive it all and look into Kate's eyes as she tried to defend herself. The evidence was overwhelmingly against her, and she was found guilty and is now awaiting sentencing in a federal court.

"It's over now," I say, feeling a new lightness since it was over.

Holden clears his throat. "Enough about the drama."

"I think we've all had enough of it," Addy agrees. "So, how have you found it here in Rose Canyon? The town is small, but the people are amazing." She turns to the group of our friends and laughs. "Most of them. That lot is a mess."

"Don't listen to anything this woman says," Spencer says as we approach the group. "She is not to be trusted."

Addison laughs. "Yes, because you are?"

"I'm absolutely not to be trusted! Who said otherwise?"

Emmett laughs. "I sure as fuck didn't."

"Exactly." Addison laughs. "You are all a bunch of jackasses who need to be smacked around, which is why I came here to whip you all into shape."

They chuckle, and Spencer nudges Addison. "You lost that chance, sweetheart. You could've been mine or that fool's, but you chose Isaac when you were too young to see us as the winners we are."

"Please, I chose right. You were the last one I would've dated."

Emmett raises one brow. "Oh? So, who would've won if it weren't for Isaac?"

Addy shrugs. "Probably you. If I could have gotten over your facial hair at thirteen."

Spencer bursts out laughing. "Only kid in eighth grade with a full beard!"

Holden tosses his arm over my shoulders, kissing my temple. "They're all a bunch of dumbasses."

Addison turns to him. "Oh, don't get me started on you."

"Me?"

I laugh. "I happen to agree, you are a bit of a knob."

"Even better!" Addison says, beaming at me. "He's an idiot in England as well."

"To be fair, which this is not, Emmett is the biggest idiot," Holden tries to deflect the conversation.

"I would like to nominate Spencer for that role!" Brielle says with her hand raised.

"Oh, no you don't. It's Emmett, I concur. Wife agrees that he's the biggest," Blake chimes in.

"That's rather unfair," I enter the fray. "Why isn't it my husband? He's quite daft. He also can't hold his booze. Let us recall the bathroom incident of five years past . . ."

The three women nod, Brielle narrowing her eyes at Holden. "We do have to take that into account."

"Also, he is hated by all felines," I remind them of another point.

Holden huffs. "You want me to be the biggest jackass?"

"If the shoe fits . . ."

He pulls me into his arms, kissing my neck with a growl. "You're going to pay for that."

"She already is," Emmett says with a chuckle. "She's knocked up— again—because you're the *one* doctor in America who doesn't understand how condoms work."

Not that I can say much as I happened to miss a pill—twice. I was focused on the trial and really just being so bloody happy. Happy to be married to the most wonderful man I've ever known, who adores me and our daughter.

"Did you find out what you're having?" Addison asks, looking at my belly.

"It's a boy," I tell her and then grin at all our friends. We hadn't mentioned it after our appointment the other day.

"A boy!" Brielle yells.

I nod. "We are going back and forth on names, which is why we didn't tell you."

"I think we need a community vote," Spencer suggests.

"Not a chance," my husband says without any room for debate.

Of course, his friends don't care. "I like the name Emmett," Emmett says.

"No." Holden rolls his eyes. "No Emmett, no Spencer, no other suggestions—"

"Blake?" Blakely offers up.

"No."

I grin, loving the dynamic of this group. They're more of a family than friends, and they've welcomed me in like a sister.

"We haven't settled on it, but once we do, we'll share," I explain.

Eden comes running over, her hand going to her little brother in my belly. This is her only concern in life at the moment. All she wants is for him to come out so she can take care of him and be the best sister ever.

I worried that this was yet another big change in her life, but she has been chuffed about the idea of a baby.

"Mummy, is my baby all right?"

I laugh. "Doing just fine."

She nods once and then turns to her new uncles, who all spoil her rotten. "Uncle Emmett?" She picks the weakest link.

"Yes?" Good, at least his voice has a hint of wariness.

"Can you take me to get something?"

Holden moves to her. "What do you need, bug?"

"Nothing. Uncle Emmett can get it for me."

He purses his lips. "If you want Uncle Emmett to get it, you probably aren't allowed to have it."

"No, Daddy, I'm allowed."

"Okay, then what is it?" he asks.

"Cake . . ."

I pull my phone out, checking her sugar levels, which are in normal range. Holden looks up at me and extends his hand. We've been working on teaching her to read her numbers. I know she can't possibly understand it at this point, and we don't expect her to regulate it on her own, but if she can start to build the habit of watching it, that's all we can hope for.

He shows her the phone, and they talk about what it shows.

"So, I can have it?" Her little voice lifts with joy.

"You can have a small piece," I say, and she wraps her arms around her father's neck. I see where I rank.

She adores Holden. It's as though he's always been a part of her life, and they've never known any different. When he comes home, she runs to the door, tells him all about her day, and he loves on her. It's sweet and more than I ever would've dreamt of. Our lives have taken paths I never expected, but I'm forever grateful that they led me to Holden.

Addison moves beside me as we watch the two of them walk away. "He is a good man."

"Yes, I'm very lucky."

"I had the great love of my life, and even though our story was cut short, I don't regret any moment of it. Having Isaac was the greatest gift I ever had." She looks at her daughter as she's passed around by her uncles as well.

"May I ask you something that's a bit out of turn?"

"Of course."

"Do you believe that, after everything you went through, you'll be happy again or ever love another?"

She shrugs. "Be happy, yes. I am happy. I have Elodie, and we have a great life in Sugarloaf. I miss my friends here, but that's truly where I belong. It's different and not filled with memories of a life I no longer get to live. As for loving again . . . I don't know. I don't know that I could ever find someone like Isaac. I know you were married before, did you think of it?"

I fill her in on my previous marriage and the circumstances—the abridged version.

"Oh! Wow."

"However, I didn't look for love. I came here without even really knowing why I came here, which is ironic as I was sent to the place I should've run from."

"But then you wouldn't have found Holden."

I nod, finding him at the table with Eden. "Yes, and that would've been the biggest misfortune I'd ever had."

"See, things work out. That's what I tell myself, at least."

Holden turns, finds me watching him, and winks. I really love that man. He starts to walk back to me, and I turn to Addison. "I think they do, if not, I wouldn't be married, expecting our second baby, and filled with so much love I feel I could burst."

"Mommy!" Elodie yells. "I hungry!"

She squeezes my arm. "That's my cue."

Addison dashes off, and then arms wrap around me from behind, hands resting on my belly, and I rest my head back on Holden's shoulder. "Everyone is having fun and seems happy."

"None more than me."

"I can think of one more person," Holden says.

I twist my head to look at him. "Who?"

"Me."

I grin and let him have it, knowing that it can't possibly be true because, at this moment, not even he can be as happy as I am because knowing we have a lifetime ahead means this feeling will never end.

Thank you so much for reading the Rose Canyon series. This book meant the world to me. I actually had the idea for Sophie and Holden before any of the other books, so here we are!

However, I wasn't done with Holden & Sophie yet!

There is an epic bonus scene on the next page. I hope you enjoy!

HOLDEN

"Love, did you finish putting the cot together yet?" Sophie calls out from the living room.

"I'm working on it!"

I'm about to pour myself a shot and just wrap it in duct tape. Seriously, I can put together a shattered femur, but a damn crib from Sweden? Nope.

Also, would it be that hard to include directions that aren't images that all look alike, and you can't tell what is right side up? I don't feel like I'm asking for too much.

I grab the stupid directions and turn them again, hoping to make sense of this weird plate thing that attaches to a gate looking thing, and I pick up some 200 cm screws. You know, because I can eyeball that shit.

"Need help?" Sophie is leaning against the doorframe, her belly swollen.

"I am doing just fine."

"When your friends asked me to video this, I wasn't quite sure why, but now I see it."

If she weren't my very pregnant, very beautiful wife—I'd flip her off.

Instead, I smile as nicely as I can. "Do you want to help?"

"No. I'm quite all right."

Of course she is. "I should be done before the baby comes."

Sophie grins. "I should hope so!" Her hand moves to her stomach, and she groans. "Our son is unhappy today."

"Oh?" I get up and place my hands on her belly. Just then, he kicks her hard. "All right, little man, easy in there."

"He has been at it all day."

"You're nearing your due date."

She looks at the unfinished nursery. "He can't come yet, we aren't ready."

"We're ready, Sophie. He'll be in our room the first few months anyway. You got that thing to attach to our bed." Much to my dismay.

"Yes, but I wanted his room done. I wanted him to have his place in our home."

"He does," I assure her. "His place is with us."

"I know. I know." She winces again. "Lord, that was uncomfortable."

Okay, that's two times where it seems to be more than just a kick. "Sophie, how often are you having these?"

"I'm not in labor, if that's where you're going. If anything, it's false because the timing is all over the place."

Well, that would've been one way to get out of this crib thing. "Just keep an eye on it."

"I will, and you get the cot done."

"You want the crib, but we have yet to agree on a name to hang above it. I think that's more important."

Sophie's eyes fill with tears. "I know! I'm sorry."

Oh Lord. These hormones are super fun. "Baby, don't cry. I was kidding. I was just trying to build—or not build—the crib. It's okay."

"We need a name!" Sophie wails. "He's going to come home as baby boy. That's not even a name . . ."

I'm walking into this very carefully. We already decided we didn't want his first name to be after someone else. So, no Isaac or Theo and definitely not after our parents. It's been hard to find something that feels right and slips off the tongue.

"What's your top choice?" I ask, wiping her tears.

"I still like Brody."

I still don't, but I like my life . . . and my wife . . . so I keep that part to myself. "Okay, Brody stays at the top."

She sniffs. "And yours?"

"Archie." I don't know why, it's just sort of regal, and it's English. I want it to be a good mix of us both.

"I don't hate Archie. Archie James."

Wow, last time I said it she made a face and told me that I lost all naming privileges. Of course she told me she was sorry two seconds later and said I could pick any name I liked, but she might veto it.

Which she has.

"What if we did Archie Theodore James?" I suggest.

Her eyes widen. "You want Theo's name in there?"

"He brought you to me after I lost you."

"Holden . . ."

Here come the tears again. "Sophie." I laugh a little. "Sweetheart, you don't need to cry."

"I hate this part of pregnancy. I am a bit too close to my feelings. I just . . . I didn't think you'd want to put his name in our child's."

I lean in, kissing her nose. "If it weren't for your best friend, my daughter wouldn't have had a father for the first three years of her life, and we wouldn't be here now. He was your best friend, Sophie, and regardless of the things we endured, he loved you. I think Theo did his best to protect you, and our son will be honored to know where his middle name comes from."

She practically throws herself in my arms and peppers me with kisses. "I love you so much. I love you so, so, so, very much."

"I love you most, sweetheart. Now, let's get you back on the couch and relaxing."

She laughs once. "Only because you said so."

Sophie takes a step and then stops. "Uhh, darling?"

"Yes?"

She looks down at the floor where there's a puddle. "I think my water just broke."

Looks like we're having this baby, and I don't have to build the crib.

***

"He's darling!" Mama James coos over Archie.

"He is."

"He looks just like you as a baby."

I stare at my son, who is really adorable, but I don't see any resemblance. He's got a thick head of light hair, which he gets from his mother, and his face is a bit squished.

"I think you're nuts," I tell her.

She slaps my arm. "You're ridiculous. Look at him, that face is all yours."

"If you say so."

"Sophie did well?" she asks, concern in her voice.

Sophie had a moment where we were all extremely concerned. The baby's heart rate had dropped, but so had hers. Thankfully the medical staff was already prepared, and they quickly rushed her to the OR before it became serious.

"She did. She's resting now, and after her twelve hours of labor ending in the c-section, she's exhausted."

"Is Eden with the boys?"

"Yeah, Spencer and Brielle are bringing her over now. It worked out that she was spending the day with them, so Sophie could relax before the baby came."

She smiles. "She loves her uncles."

"They spoil the hell out of her, so of course she does."

"Let them. There is nothing more precious in the world than being the aunt or uncle. You get to be part parent without the discipline . . ."

I raise a brow at that. "I would beg to differ."

Mama James scowls at me. "I only did it because your own parents wouldn't. My point is, it's the best part of parenting. You get the love, the friendship, and the fun."

I kiss her cheek. "I love that you were my aunt."

"I loved it too."

"And I know I was your favorite."

"You were something," she jokes.

We talk a bit about the birth and how hard it was for me to not be in charge. She laughs when I explain that I had to be informed four times to go back to my spot. It's like telling a mechanic they can't look under the hood when another person is trying to adjust something. I know what the right tools are, and she's my wife.

"So the nurse threatened to make you wait outside?" Mama James is laughing uncontrollably.

"I would've never left Sophie."

"I believe that, but you really need to trust other doctors."

I don't think so. Not when it comes to my family. However, before I can argue my point, Eden comes running down the hall.

"Daddy!"

Instantly I smile, love filling my chest to the brim. I scoop her up, hugging her tight. "Did you have fun, bug?"

"I did. Uncle Spencer took me to the park!"

"Good. I'm glad he did."

"Some kids were making fun of him, though."

Spencer grimaces. "I hate those kids."

"Still being trolled by them, huh?"

When Spencer and Brielle went on a date, they ended up at a park where they met these kids, and since then, it's been comedy. They make fun of Spencer all the time, and it eats at him.

"Fuck off."

"Uncle Spencer, that's a bad word!" Eden scolds him.

"You're right, munchkin. I'm sorry."

She smiles. "It's okay. Daddy says them all the time."

Kids, man, they dime you out without trying.

"Anyway," I break in. "Want to see your brother?"

Eden's eyes brighten. "He's really here?"

"He's really here."

"Can I see Mummy too?"

Not a chance Sophie would want to miss this. "Of course. I'll bring you to her first and then bring Archie in."

We walk to Sophie's room, where she's resting, and Eden tiptoes in. She reaches the bed and takes Sophie's hand.

My wife wakes, and it's like the sun has just risen. "Eden! My darling."

"Careful with your mum, she had surgery."

"To get Archie out?"

Sophie smiles. "Yes, love. Where is he?"

"The nurse is bringing him now."

A few seconds later, the nurse rolls the bassinet in with our son swaddled and sleeping.

Eden, forgetting her mother exists, runs over, fingers gripping the side, and her nose just reaching the top as she's on her toes. She gasps. "He's so beautiful!"

I laugh. "He is."

"Can we keep him forever?"

I lift her up so she can get a better view and kiss her cheek. "Forever. All four of us."

Exactly as it should be.

Thank you again and I hope you're ready for the next series where we head to Sugarloaf and meet a new family and Addison finally gets her story!

Books by Corinne Michaels

Want a downloadable reading order?
https://geni.us/CM_ReadingGuide

The Salvation Series

Beloved

Beholden

Consolation

Conviction

Defenseless

Evermore: A 1001 Dark Night Novella

Indefinite

Infinite

The Hennington Brothers

Say You'll Stay

Say You Want Me

Say I'm Yours

Say You Won't Let Go: A Return to Me/Masters and Mercenaries Novella

Second Time Around Series

We Own Tonight

One Last Time

Not Until You

If I Only Knew

The Arrowood Brothers

Come Back for Me

Fight for Me

The One for Me

Stay for Me

Willow Creek Valley Series

Return to Us

Could Have Been Us

A Moment for Us

A Chance for Us

Rose Canyon Series

Help Me Remember

Give Me Love

Keep This Promise

Sugarloaf Series (Coming 2023-2024)

Forbidden Hearts

Broken Dreams

Tempting Promises

Forgotten Desires

Co-Written with Melanie Harlow

Hold You Close

Imperfect Match

Standalone Novels

All I Ask

You Loved Me Once

About the Author

Corinne Michaels is a *New York Times, USA Today, and Wall Street Journal* bestselling author of romance novels. Her stories are chock full of emotion, humor, and unrelenting love, and she enjoys putting her characters through intense heartbreak before finding a way to heal them through their struggles.

Corinne is a former Navy wife and happily married to the man of her dreams. She began her writing career after spending months away from her husband while he was deployed—reading and writing were her escape from the loneliness. Corinne now lives in Virginia with her husband and is the emotional, witty, sarcastic, and fun-loving mom of two beautiful children.

Made in the USA
Monee, IL
03 July 2023

38579261R10201